TIME IS A WHEEL

DIANA KNIGHTLEY

For the admins of the Kaitlyn and the Highlander Facebook group, Jackie and Angelique, thank you for helping me keep it all straight...

PART I
DESCEND

DOWN THE WHEEL

CHAPTER 1 - KAITLYN

1709 - BALLOCH

I was standing out on a long, wide, dew-covered meadow, a mist in the air, it was cool — I instantly knew it was Scotland, the smell of the breeze, the damp, the chilly blast, the shades of green disappearing to gray in the foggy distance. I was frozen, scanning the distance, my heart racing, but stilled in fear, one hand clutching Jack who was cradled in a sling against my chest. Isla was grabbing my skirt. I held my other hand out, my palm against Archie's chest, stop — he was motionless.

I heard the long, low, whispered, "Wheeeeeshhhhhht" of my husband from beside me. I didn't dare look, we were deer in headlights, staring into the distance where there was a low rumbling.

Like thunder, coming closer.

My brain said, *Run.*

But the calculation made no sense.

Too far to the trees.

My children.

If I turned my back on what was coming…

What should I do?

· · ·

Then through the mist a line, perhaps fifty wide, of horses, carrying big barbarian-looking men. The horse hooves were thundering. Their leader, looking even more ferocious up on his mount, held a thing at his side, a long stick with the ball at the end with the spikes, what was that... ? He was gaining on us, my heart racing in time to the thunder of his horse, the weapon, that I should have known the name of, about to swing down. He was going to trample us, catch us, murder us with his medieval weapon.

Magnus's voice, "Run!"

I woke up.

I sat up in bed, my breath gasping for air, noooooooooo! No no no.

"Mo reul-iuil, are ye alright?"

He was up beside me, his arm around my shoulders.

"Where's Jack?!" I patted beside me, finding his wee self, lying, sleeping soundly. Content. Not realizing his mother's heart was racing from a nightmare.

It had seemed so real.

I looked around. We were in our room at Balloch, I should have known, but the dream had been so real, that I had to remind myself where I was. I had gone to bed in the Balloch bedroom, of course, I remembered now.

It was too dark to see, but I could tell by the coolness of the air, the scent of must and dust and smoke, that we were there, where we were supposed to be.

"Are ye alright?"

I nodded. "Where are Isla and Archie?"

"They're in their beds, ye ken, in the outer room."

"Right..." I ran a hand through my hair. "I just had a bad dream, it was... scary."

My husband whispered in the darkness, "Tell me."

I said, "We were standing on the um... like a moor, and

there was a fog, we were scared, and these men rode out of the fog toward us, and I needed to run, but I couldn't. Jack and Isla and Archie were—"

"We dinna hae horses? Ye ken tis a nightmare if we dinna hae a horse."

"We were on foot. There was no way I was getting away from them."

"Aye, there is nae way I would allow it." He wrapped my hand in his. It was big, strong, and warm.

I said, "The main guy had one of those weapons, the ball on a stick? He was winding up to hit me with it."

"The mace? Twas a star of blades at the end?"

I nodded.

"Och nae, that must hae been frightenin'." He rubbed a finger on the back of my hand.

"It was, but it wasn't just frightening, as a dream, it was so real, it felt like—"

A scream went up through the darkness.

Magnus jumped from bed. Men were yelling on the walls. Someone was screaming from down the passage. "The children!"

Magnus pulled on his shoes, "Dress yerself, I will get the bairns."

He grabbed his sword and a gun and ran out the door.

Screams echoed through the halls, I heard Quentin yell, "We are under attack!"

I woke with a gasp.

Straight up in bed. Oh no! I clutched my shirt at my heart. Oh, that had sucked.

That had been a dream inside a dream.

Magnus held me, while I trembled in his arms. "Another nightmare, mo reul-iuil?"

I nodded. "It feels so real, it's hard to tell what is happening and what isn't. I was in the moor, you yelled run—"

"The army was the same one? From the past?"

"Yeah, a bit like Domnall and Ormr, but I don't recognize them. Then I woke from the dream, here in the bedroom, and you were consoling me, I was calming down and then there was an attack, you jumped from bed and… then I woke up again."

He lay quiet for a moment. "It sounds verra unsettling, but tis a dream, mo reul-iuil, yer mind is imaginin' it."

"But it feels so real. Like I can't be sure you're real right now."

He sighed. "What dost ye—"

The door creaked open, Haggis pushing it with his nose. He padded to the bed and put his nose on Magnus's foot, his tail wagging. Magnus patted the bed and Haggis jumped up, circled, then lay down with his head on Magnus's chest.

Magnus continued, "What dost ye think is happenin'?"

"I don't know… but…" I looked at him through the early morning light of dawn beginning to spread over our room from the small window. "I think it's something that already happened and it hasn't happened yet, you know… like a time loop."

"Ye've had the dream now three times. If ye think I am goin' tae ever let our family be in a moor with nae horse in the fog with barbarians bearin' down upon us, ye are mistaken, Kaitlyn. I hae heard ye recount the dream. I believe it is an imaginin' but I am forewarned. It winna happen because I winna allow it tae happen."

I knew he was being light about it, I also knew he took it very seriously. He was walking the line he so often had to travel — protecting the family, while retaining a bit of humor or else I would start freaking out.

I picked up his hand and kissed his knuckle. "Consider yourself forewarned then, I must always have a horse, no foggy moors, no barbarians."

He chuckled. "This has been m'rule tae live by since I met ye."

"You met me and said, 'No foggy moors'?"

"Aye, somethin' like that, closer tae, 'ye must keep her safe.' Ye ken, I mean tae."

"Yeah, I know." I lay back down, curled around Jack, holding Magnus's hand. "I really know, it's just…"

"What?"

"I'm worried it's real. Like when you remembered the battles to become the King of Scotland before you actually fought the battles, like that, what if it's a premonition? Ugh."

He said, "We used the Bridge tae fix it. If something breaks again, we will use the Bridge again. Daena worry on it, mo reul-iuil, tis likely yer mind playing tricks."

"Or… and I hate to speak it out loud."

His body tensed. "What?"

"What if something has happened, and you, or someone else, are looping, trying to cover it over? To fix it."

"Loopin' is a mistake, we all ken tis true. It causes chaos. I daena think we would risk it."

"Unless it's the only recourse." I gripped his hand. "I don't know… that's my worry, that's what scares me. Someone might be looping to—"

"Tae save yer life? If I am layin' beside ye, Kaitlyn, and ye are beside me, and we are whisperin' our worries tae each other, then our lives are saved. We canna look for trouble. Lord in Heaven kens we hae enough trouble findin' us. If we are alive, taegether, then we are safe enough. See the light from the window? There is another dawn upon us, we ought tae be grateful for it."

Jack rustled and began rooting for my breast. A second later his face screwed up as if he were famished and about to wail.

Magnus chuckled. "Thank God for hungry bairns keepin' ye up at night, aye, mo reul-iuil?"

I pulled my shirt up and got Jack latched.

Magnus said, "How are ye feelin' now?"

"Better, my heart isn't racing."

"In a few hours we are goin' tae go home, we hae a Florida house tae live in, are ye pleased?"

"I literally can't wait to go to Publix."

"Aye, me as well. I am goin' tae buy so many gallons of ice cream ye are goin' tae be worried upon m'safety. They winna fit in the freezer. I will hae tae eat it all or twill be a waste."

"In one sitting?"

"Aye, like a madman. I will eat ice cream until I am sick from it."

"And then you'll have to work out with a personal trainer to keep it from settling around your waist."

He patted his stomach, he was thin, his stomach taut — it sounded hollow like a drum. He said, "I think that is a chance I am willing tae take. Twould be worth it for the pleasure of the feast. What is yer favorite kind, the first ye will eat, mo reul-iuil?"

"Ice cream? I think vanilla with chocolate chip cookie dough. But actually what I *want* is chocolate chip cookies hot out of the oven with gooey middles. I will use them as spoons for the ice cream."

He jokingly frowned and sighed, looking up at the ceiling. "Tis a fantasy, Kaitlyn, they will never work as spoons, they will fall apart. This is an impossible dream."

"Okay, scratch that, I will have cold crisp cookies for spoons, I will have hot and gooey cookies for draping across the top. And the ice cream that has cookie dough inside it."

"What about the bowl?"

I grinned. "That bowl is a giant cookie, one with M&Ms."

"I see ye are desperately wantin' cookies."

"How about you?"

"I had an idea, but now I want what ye are havin' except I want the sauce beside me, ye ken, the caramel that Chef Zach makes sometimes? I want it right beside me in a whole separate bowl so that I can take a spoon, a real spoon, mo reul-iuil, because yer idea of a cookie spoon is ridiculous, the whole point of the spoon is the lever—"

"Hey, there are no bad ideas in cookies and ice cream!"

"What of sardine ice cream? That would be verra bad, also liver cookies? Ye haena thought this through."

"True, and yes, I agree, real spoons. Cookie spoons would be frustrating, I see that now."

"I will take a spoonful of the ice cream and cookies and then mop it through the caramel. This is how it will be done. Och, now I am thinking on it, I hope Chef Zach will hae it ready for us."

"Maybe he read your mind."

"He often does."

He sat up on the edge of the bed, and patted my ankle. "I am going tae the walls if ye are recovered from yer nightmare, mo reul-iuil. I will check in with Lochinvar for our trip."

"It's been a good visit with your family, but I am really looking forward to going home."

"Aye, me as well."

He stood and began to dress, pulling on his shirt, then arranging the fabric on the floor, pulling it into pleats, wrapping it around himself, and tightening a belt around. He tucked in his shirt and arranged the ends of the great kilt around. Then, finally, he strapped on his sword, holstered his gun at his hip, and pulled a coat over it all. I watched, nursing Jack in the bed, feeling peacefulness in the warmth of an oxytocin rush wash over me.

Then Magnus leaned over the bed and kissed me on the cheek. "I am goin' tae check the walls."

I heard him say good morning and goodbye to the kids in the outer room where their beds were in front of the fire. Then he left.

CHAPTER 2 - KAITLYN

UNLESS IT HASN'T HAPPENED, YET

*I*sla came to the bed, sleepy-headed, and climbed into the spot vacated by her da. Archie, already dressed, because he'd fallen asleep in his clothes, wandered in. "Going to find Jamie and Gavin."

I said, "Coolio, it's our last morning for a while, have fun. Oh and… not to be dark, remember when you leave on the last morning — it's nice to say something good, something about how you feel, about how you will miss them. When you travel you never know when you will see someone again. It's nice to make it meaningful."

He screwed his face up. "Ye want me tae say something nice tae the *Campbell* cousins?" His voice had grown a bit of a Scottish twang while we were here.

I chuckled. "Now that I've said it out loud it *is* kinda ridiculous, but you know, it is still good advice. You don't want to regret things unsaid."

Isla said, "I will tell Mary that I love her."

"Good, and when we get to Florida, Ben and Zoe will be waiting for us."

Isla twisted a lock of my hair around her finger. She said, with a sigh, "You know how I feel about Zoe, Mammy."

"I do, but seriously, she will be your bestie someday, give her time."

Archie said, "Da said he will be ready tae go after lunch?"

"Yep, go have fun."

~

I met Lizbeth in the Great Hall and she dictated while I made a list. "When next ye come, I need a new pair of scissors…"

I wrote two.

Her eyes went wide. "Two! They must be verra precious, two would be too many!"

"You'd be surprised, they can be very inexpensive, but I will get you a good pair that can be sharpened. The reason I wrote two, is because I want you to keep a pair in the store room and have a small pair to carry with you. That way you will always have a pair nearby."

"I would like that verra much."

"What else…?"

She wanted soaps and lotions and small kitchen tools. She asked for some new hand tools for Liam, and we put hand tools for Sean on the list as well.

We sat together in companionable quiet while I nursed Jack until she said, "It has been lovely tae hae ye returned, Kaitlyn. I did miss ye and the bairns missed their cousins, and Sean has been verra pleased tae hae Magnus returned. Magnus seems tae be in a fine spirit. He has won a war and we are verra proud of him. Even mother has seemed tae be subdued, and I mean it in the best of ways. She is proud and victorious, but also a wee bit humbled by the loss of her advisor and lover, General Hammond. It has changed her demeanor a bit."

"I agree, for a few short days there she was almost pleasant. Like a friendly snake in the grass."

Lizbeth laughed. "Aye, ye canna trust it, sunnin' itself by the path, but it might leave ye be, if ye daena startle it."

"I was on my best behavior."

"She likes ye though, I can see it."

"What in the world are you talking about, Lizbeth! I have known you for years and I have *never* heard you say something that ludicrous!"

"Tis true! She is fond of ye, I could see the way she talked tae ye. She thinks ye hae helped Magnus become a king and now ye hae born him a son. She is verra pleased."

I exhaled. "Had I known it would be that easy. Here I thought battling enemies, doing my best to keep her son and her grandchildren alive, and helping her whenever asked was what would please her, but all it took was birthing a boy?"

Lizbeth said, "For queens, this is all that is ever expected of them."

"Remind me to stop finding myself in the middle of death-defying battles then."

"Och, ye will also hae tae keep yer sons alive."

"Yeah, now that's doubly difficult... Thankfully this little guy is not next in line for the throne. Archie is who we have to worry about." I sighed. "He is so adventurous, he wants to be off, out of my sight, and... wait," I looked around, standing up, "Do you know where they are? The boys?"

She stood. "Aye, they are in the fields, battling as they love tae do—"

I headed for the door. "I'm nervous, I need to lay eyes on him."

She followed me from the sitting room and up the stairs to the walls, where we found Magnus leaning on the parapet beside Sean.

"Have you seen Archie?"

"Aye," he jerked his head toward the trees.

I followed his eyes across the field and into the treeline where three boys were wrestling. Another boy was hanging by one arm from a tree limb, then dropped to the ground, joined the wrestle, then they all jumped up and raced off together across the field.

Phew.

"Ye need him? I can hae someone sent down?"

"No, I just got nervous, I… the dream has unsettled me."

"He is in the Scottish air, running across a field. Ye daena need tae be unsettled about him, does she, Sean?"

"Nae, he is a proper Scottish lad, ye see, strong and fearless. Ye canna worry on him, Kaitlyn, ye will make him soft."

"A mother's worry makes boys soft?" I scoffed. "Maybe if I had run out there and stopped him, but I just came up to the wall to check on him."

Sean said, "Ye over-worry like a broodin' hen."

"You are both standing up here watching over him, but *I'm* an over-worrying brood hen? Then you're an over-guarding cock-man."

Sean laughed and put an arm around me. "I am goin' tae miss ye, Madame Kaitlyn, and wee Jack-the-bairn."

I hugged him back. "I will miss you too, Sean. It's been a great visit."

He said, "I think it has been the first visit in a verra long time that ye were nae bedeviled by a monster of some kind. It has been good tae see ye when it inna mid-chase."

Magnus said, "We hae had a lot of trouble, tis fine tae be on the other side of it."

Sean asked, "And ye hae had a nightmare, Madame Kaitlyn — ye ought tae ken, tis probably because ye are so unused tae being safe from trouble. Yer mind is runnin' from danger out of habit."

"Yes, that's probably it. The dreams feel real though, it's difficult to convince myself that I'm safe even when they're over."

He nodded. "I had the same experience after the Battle of Talsworth. Many a night I found m'self seeing a vision of it in my mind. It took a long year tae get past the fight — the sight of

Uncle Baldie down on the ground." Both he and Magnus scowled.

He looked out over the fields in the direction of Talsworth castle. "I thought I was warrior enough tae not be affected, but I felt it all the same. I think we all get battle-dreams, ye hae tae ken they will pass. Perhaps a prayer for respite, Madame Kaitlyn. That is what helped me."

"That is good advice, Sean, thank you."

Magnus's attention had gone down to the courtyard. "Lochinvar is at it again."

Sean went over to look. "Och nae, he is goin' tae cause trouble."

I looked down, a bird's eye view of Lochie, talking very privately with two of the young lasses. They were half-hidden within a dark, shadowy alcove.

Lizbeth tsked. "He canna be left alone with either of them. Sara's father will hae him in front of the Earl, young Mary's father will hae him strung up."

Sean yelled down, "Young Lochinvar, ye ken, ye are tae leave in a few hours. Ye need tae say yer proper farewells and leave the lasses tae their day. Mistress Sarah and Mistress Mary, ye need tae run tae yer mothers."

The young women curtsied up at Sean, blushing.

Lochinvar called up, "M'apologies, Sean."

He bowed and even from up on the walls I could see him smirk and wink at the lasses.

He sauntered away while they rushed to the door, giggling.

Lizbeth said, "Och nae, he is always a trouble."

I said, "That's why we're taking him to Florida, see how much trouble he gets in there."

Lizbeth and I returned downstairs to say our goodbyes.

∽

Soon enough we were all gathered in the clearing, our family, with Lochinvar. Everyone else had headed home already, in teams, so there would be someone to greet the arrivals: Quentin and James, first, then Zach and Beaty and Emma and their children. Then Fraoch and Hayley. We stayed behind to visit longer, waiting for Jack to get a bit older.

Jack was asleep in the sling. He and Isla and Archie had the gold threads on the back of their heads. Sean and some other men dropped us off in the clearing and left with the cart and horses, leaving us alone to jump.

Magnus watched them go and then looked at my face. "I see, Kaitlyn, that I hae arranged for us tae be without horses, though I promised not six hours ago that it would never happen. I regret havin' sent Sunny and the others ahead with Fraoch a few days ago. It made sense at the time, yet here we are without horses, but also, mo reul-iuil, tis a fine day, there is no fog and this is not a moor, but a clearing within a forest."

"True."

Lochinvar said, "What's this ye are talkin' on?"

Magnus said, "I was explainin' tae Madame Kaitlyn that this is unlike her dream, we are without horses, aye, but there is not a—"

Lochinvar nodded. "There is not a fog and this is not a moor, aye, and also, the army of horses comes from the east," he pointed toward the woods, "but as ye can see here there inna a good eastern direction for that many horses, twas a verra large army..."

He saw my eyes widen.

"What are you...? Lochie, are you having the same dream?"

"I daena ken, but I am havin' a dream where I am in a field and there are men comin' through the fog, a large army—"

"Yes! And are we there?"

His face screwed up, as if he were thinking. "I daena remember seeing ye. But tis my dream, I daena ken why ye would be there."

Magnus huffed. "I daena like this one bit. We need tae get out of here, place yer things in this pile."

"I knew it, I knew there was something going on with it. Lochie and I are having the same dream, it's something that is going to happen."

Lochie shrugged. "Or it has already happened."

"Well then, Lochie, how come we don't remember it happening?"

"Tis likely that we hae written over it, whatever went wrong, and likely if an army is coming, something has gone wrong — we fixed it. This is why ye remember it in yer dreams differently." He dropped one of our crates, stood straight, and straightened his coat. "Ye ran intae trouble and I fixed it — that is why ye arna in my dream."

I said, "So you're in a field about to fight fifty men in the fog and you're the hero?"

"Och aye, because I must hae survived it. I am standing in front of ye, flesh and blood."

"I suppose that is true, unless it hasn't happened yet."

Archie looked from my face to Lochie's face, his expression worried.

Our stuff ready to go, Magnus picked up Isla.

I took Archie's hand. "Don't worry, honey, this is all not going to happen. It's literally just a dream. We're just talking."

Lochie put his hand on Magnus's elbow. "Aye, unless it hasn't happened *yet*."

"We ought tae go with haste, we can think on it at home, over our dessert." Magnus's eyes scanned the clearing.

CHAPTER 3- KAITLYN

2024 - FLORIDA

*T*ime travel sucks. We were smarter. We knew how to do it safely and we had a way for the kids to travel without pain, but still, twisting the machine, holding onto each other, knowing that we would have ourselves torn apart and put back together again, or whatever the heck the science was — it was a lot to deal with. It was terrifying to embark. But as I looked down at my kids, sitting beside me, my husband's arm around us, I thought about all the mothers throughout history who had stepped from a dock onto a ship for an uncertain voyage, trying to get their children to a safer, better world.

And those trips had lasted for a long long time.

This would only be minutes, or so, but it was the step that was so gosh darn hard to take, a step from the dock onto the ship.

I clutched my hands around my children and tucked my head to Magnus's shoulder as he twisted the vessel.

A while later, the storm subsided and we were up, in the truck, and then walking up to our Florida house.

Lochinvar looking all around. A high blue sky.

A hot sun.

Sweltering heat. It was early September but felt like high summer.

I said, "Lochie, goes without saying—"

"I ken, I must slather on the lotion or I will be blistered again."

Fraoch laughed, "Like a pink pig, roastin' in the sun!"

The truck pulled up in front of the house and we walked up the steps, surrounded by all our family, kids rushed around hugging and high-fiving, and because it was mid afternoon, the scent of dinner cooking. Zach called from the kitchen, where the music was blaring, and he was dancing in an apron with a spatula in hand. "Early dinner! I was too excited to wait, a feast!"

Magnus put an arm around me and kissed my forehead.

He called in, "What kind of feast?"

Zach juked around the kitchen, opening the oven, pulling out a pan, bringing it toward us and waving a hot-mitt so that the scent wafted around us. "Roasted potatoes and so much steak, just steak and more cuts of steak. Smells good?"

"It smells verra good."

Zach danced back into the kitchen like he was the lead of a mamba train.

Archie and Ben and Isla ran by, headed out to the beach. Zoe toddling after them. Beaty, carrying Noah in a sling, followed them out.

Emma said, "We had to clean sooo much, it was a dirty, dusty wreck in here."

I said, "Well, it looks great, clean and inviting, and smells delicious."

Magnus peeled aside the sling and looked down on Jack,

then reached in and pulled Jack out and held him in the crook of his arm, "Wee bairn, this is yer home!"

He spun, showing Jack the whole room. "Over there are the toys, that whole pile, ye will be able tae play with them soon enough, there is the television, tis magical, and through here is yer brother and sister's rooms." He carried Jack down the hall giving him a tour.

I plopped down on a barstool. "Coca-Cola please, barkeep."

"Coming right up." Zach popped the top off a bottle and passed it to me.

I drank the dazzling sparkling wondrous drink, sizzling on the back of my throat. "Dear God, that is delicious. Seriously, anything better in the world after a medieval castle?"

James said, "You weren't in medieval times, that there is the cusp of the enlightenment."

"Whatever, you get me, it was a castle. Long long weeks in the dark ages." I drank some more.

～

We stood around on the back deck, drinking beer as the kids ran up and down the walkway to the sand.

Emma said, "Well, it seems like Zoe is feeling better, she was feverish earlier, there is a wicked stomach-bug going around at the—" Then she said, "Isla, where did you get that lollipop?"

"From Zoe!"

I said, "Zoe, did Isla take your lollipop?"

Zoe nodded, grabbed the lollipop from Isla, licked it, then shoved it back in Isla's mouth.

Emma said, "Uh oh."

I sighed. "Well at least if they come down with a bug we know it's not a medieval period plague."

"Yep, this is straight up playground plague coming."

I joked, "It's good to be home."

. . .

I walked Jack out to the beach and wandered around the tide pools for a bit, looking for shark teeth.

When I glanced up at the house, Magnus held up his beer — a cheer, an 'I'm pleased tae see ye on the beach' salute.

I watched him, standing in the waning light of sunset, a bit of breeze pushing his hair, his smile wide as he laughed about something said, while Zach pulled steaks off the grill and James looked like he was advising him. Lochinvar sat on the rail laughing too. Fraoch and Hayley played ping-pong, kids were begging to go for a swim in the pool.

What a glorious evening and the feast was epic! There were steaks, grilled to perfection. Oh man, they were delicious. The basics, meat and potatoes, with a salad, but everything extra special, in true Chef Zach style. The steak dripped with flavor. The baked potatoes, crispy skinned, billowed steam when opened. Trays of toppings. A big salad, with oranges in it, for the Vitamin C.

Isla, from the kids table, said, "Mommy, this so much better than food at the castle." She spooned a big dollop of sour cream beside her potatoes and mixed it with ketchup.

"I absolutely agree, Isla, this is fabulous."

Zach said, "Nothing like months of medieval Scottish food to make ketchup taste like heaven."

Isla said, "Uncle Zachary, ketchup *is* heaven." She turned the ketchup bottle upside down and a massive blob of it plopped on top of her potato — way too much ketchup.

She looked at it for a minute, then said, "I meant to do it."

CHAPTER 4 - KAITLYN

A BIT OF A TWIST

Then Fraoch leaned back in the chair and patted his stomach.

James joked, "You building a food baby there?"

"I ken ye are kiddin' James, I am too thin, but aye, I am planning tae eat so much in the comin' month that I will look tae be pregnant."

Hayley said, "This is your goal?"

"Aye, ye will be proud of me, I will be round as a king, and ye will say, Och aye, he is even more pleasin' tae my eyes than afore, because there is so much more tae see, so much more pleasin' tae my hands because there is so *much* tae hold ontae." He winked at her and they clinked their glasses together.

James said, "Here we call that, building a tool shed over the tools."

Fraoch and Magnus howled with laughter.

Fraoch said, "That is exactly what I am going tae do, I am goin' tae build a roof above m'tools."

Magnus said, "I am going tae build a big wide castle tae protect m'jewels." They laughed again.

Archie looked scandalized. "Da, are ye talking on yer," he whispered, "*you* know?"

We all laughed. Magnus said, "Tis impolite at the dinner table, Archie, but aye, sometimes ye must jest upon yer jewels, or the ladies winna remember how tae blush. A blush is important, it helps with digestin'."

He added, "Speaking of digestion, are we tae hae dessert?"

I groaned, "Already?"

Zach said, "Let's clear these plates — I'm looking at you, Archie and Ben and Isla, and then yes, we'll have an ice cream bedazzle."

We watched as Zach and the kids ran back and forth to the kitchen, Isla carrying a tray of sauces, Ben carrying out the chocolate chip cookie dough ice cream.

Magnus grinned, rubbing his hands together. "I am full past bein' able tae think on food, ten minutes ago, and now I am famished again."

Lochinvar said, "I hae a void here in m'middle that I daena think there is enough food in the world tae fill."

Archie brought out a tray of warm cookies.

Lochinvar said, "Och, I believe that might get close." He called into the house, "Chef Zach will there be more? Because I am in nae mood tae share!"

Fraoch growled, took a cookie, and ate it even though it was too hot. He fanned his mouth. "Now ye hae done it, Lochie, ye threatened not tae share and now I hae eaten a cookie and burnt m'mouth."

Lochie grinned. "I think that's on ye, auld man."

Fraoch stood up from the table. "Ye want tae say it again, wee bairn? In this family we share the cookies, ye canna threaten tae eat them all."

Isla said, "Right, Uncle Lochie, ye hae tae share." She picked up a cookie and it fell apart in her fingers, dripping drizzling chocolate down her hands. "Hot hot hot!" She dropped it on the deck

Magnus groaned, "Och nae, the cookies are bein' wasted!"

Quentin, leaned back in the chair with Noah asleep on his stomach, said, "Not this again, boys, I swear, no more arguing between you three. Isla, you too."

She grinned. "I am the best arguer, Mammy says so."

Chef Zach finished piling ice cream on our table, and blew his hair off his forehead. "Dessert is served. And I'm wiped out!" He sat down as someone took the last cookie from the tray. He groaned.

We served massive bowls of ice cream for ourselves, way more than we could eat.

And I did try to use cookies to pick up ice cream, but ultimately settled for cookies crumbled on ice cream, but then, because the warm gooey cookies were so good, I just ate them.

The timer rang, Chef Zach raced back to the kitchen returning with a new tray of warm cookies. "It goes without saying, people, some of you are old enough to know better — these are going to be hot."

Lochie snatched one off the tray and dropped it from hand to hand saying, "Hot hot hot!" Then popped it all into his mouth and chewed it while blowing out steam. "Ouch ouch, hot hot hot." He swallowed, winced, and said, "Totally worth it."

The kids laughed hysterically.

Then we were done.

The kids went inside and parked in front of the TV watching Ant-Man. We adults were sitting around the table, spent from the feast.

James said, "To break the quiet, not to bring down the conversation, or the mood, but Sophie and I were talking about the next step."

Magnus said, "What next step, we hae accomplished all we need tae accomplish."

Quentin said, "You serious, Boss?"

Magnus chuckled. "Nae, I ken there is always something tae do next. Tell me yer thoughts, Master James and Madame Sophie."

James said, "We need to gather all the vessels."

Magnus said "Madame Sophie, ye agree?"

"Aye, I feel it is left undone. We hae these dangerous machines lying about, unaccounted for, we desperately need tae locate them."

Magnus said, "I agree, we will do it first thing."

James said, "What, no arguing? Want me to make my case?"

"Och nae, nae cases, I am sated from a feast, enjoyin' a fine Florida night, a cold beer in m'hand, nae, I daena need tae hear it. I only need tae ken one thing — what is standin' between me and havin' this contentment every night for the rest of m'life?"

Fraoch said, "The vessels, havin' rogue vessels out there that anyone can pick up."

"Aye, tis the only thing."

Lochinvar said, "Good, because I was goin' tae say we need tae go get them."

Fraoch narrowed his eyes. "Ye were goin' tae say the same thing, Lochie? Just like that? Ye are just arrived — we hae been guardin' the vessels for centuries. We almost lost our lives guardin' them at Ben Cruachan. Tis nae as easy as 'we need tae go get them.'"

Quentin said, "How many do we have?"

Magnus said, "There ought tae be twenty-six."

Lochinvar said, "What if we went back in time tae the beginning of the vessels and just gather them all there?"

Magnus said, "Tis too great a risk, for most of us twould be loopin'. And in gaining access tae the scene we might change time. Nae, we arna going tae do it."

Lochie said, "But I am a good fighter. I can battle, I can pick up vessels easily."

Magnus exhaled. "Dost ye believe, Lochie, that I am not goin' because I am not a good enough fighter? Nae, tae go there is tae possibly cause chaos on the timeline."

Lochie said, "Maybe we ought tae vote."

Fraoch said, "Ye think this is a democracy, boy? Ye think ye get tae decide? Och nae, I hae had enough of it. We ought tae vote on whether Lochie is allowed tae speak on important issues or nae."

Lochie huffed.

I said, "Lochie, what you have to remember is that throughout our history we have used vessels, left them places, picked them up, jumped back and forth. To mess with the vessels in the very beginning might disrupt the whole timeline."

I said, "Here's an example: One night, long ago, Archie and Isla and I needed a vessel, and luckily Magnus had planted one under a tree for us. If we hadn't known where it was we would have been captured — if someone had earlier gathered them up, that one might have been in a vault instead of under that tree."

Hayley said, "The key part of that sentence is 'if we hadn't known where it was.' We don't know where *most* of them are."

Fraoch said, "*Exactly,* we ought tae find them, but I daena agree with Lochie. We daena need tae go back in time, only forward."

Hayley said, "Yes, onward to find the vessels!"

Magnus said, "I agree, we hae too many new lives here. We must do our best not tae disrupt the timeline. This is my final decision, Lochie. Do ye understand?"

Lochie said, "Aye, Yer Majesty."

Magnus said, "I need ye tae tell me ye understand."

"I do, if we got the vessels from the beginning, and we would because ye are saying that I am an amazing warrior and I would gain them all, but if we hid them away, our paths, the paths of Og Maggy and Og Lochie, might never hae crossed. I might hae died fightin' for Ormr, so aye, Yer Majesty, I understand."

Magnus nodded. "'Tis a bit of a twist there, but I am glad our paths crossed as well, Lochinvar."

Quentin said, "So we need to begin hunting for the vessels."

Magnus said, "Aye, first thing, but also after I relax for a bit.

And the conversation changed to fun different things.

Hours later we went to bed.

CHAPTER 5 - KAITLYN

IN VOMITING THERE IS NO TRY

*A*t two in the morning, or thereabouts, I heard Isla moan on the monitor. Jack was nursing so I pushed the button, turning it into a two-way radio. "What's up doodle-butt?"

"Mommy, my tummy hurts."

"Come on down to our room."

It took a while before she padded in, Magnus, woke and shifted so she could lie between us. She crawled up onto our bed, right up to me, and vomited in my face.

Magnus exclaimed, "Och nae!"

Isla burst into tears.

I lay there for a second completely dazed — she had vomited on me.

But also, underneath, now that I thought about it, I was feeling feverish, too. And a little queasy.

Magnus lumbered out of bed, headed to the towel closet and brought me a towel. I climbed out of bed, wiping off my chest, pulling off my shirt. "It's okay, Isla, you just threw up, it's fine..."

She scowled, "The bed is wet."

Magnus said, "I ken, bairn, tis yer dinner upon m'bed." He

unfurled a towel and began patting the bed to dry it, but then Isla clutched her mouth.

Magnus grabbed her unceremoniously around the waist, carted her to the toilet, and dropped her down in front of it. Then he retched into the sink.

I said, "Uh oh."

I stripped the bed and put on another sheet. Everyone came back to the bed and climbed in. Magnus moaned with his arm flung across his face.

I asked, "How you feeling?"

"As if there are dark fae dancin' in m'middle."

From the monitor I heard Zoe crying and Emma shushing.

Then our door opened. Archie came in, followed by Haggis. He said, "Ma, Da, I don't feel good."

I said, "I don't think there's room but..."

I climbed from bed, grabbed blankets from the closet, and spread one on the ground between the bed and the bathroom. I tossed a pillow at the head, and a blanket to cover him. Haggis lay at his feet.

I tucked Archie in and then my stomach lurched. I sat on the edge of the bed, trying to decide if I was going to throw up or not.

But finally I lay down and pulled the covers over me.

There was a soft knock on the door. Sophie stuck her head in. "Are ye ill, Kaitlyn?"

I said, "I think all of us. Except Jack, he's sleeping."

She said, "Almost everyone in the house has it now. I am well so far. I will be in the kitchen, call me on the intercom if ye need anything."

"Thank you, Sophie. How is Beaty? Is Noah okay?"

"Beaty and Quentin are ill, Noah seems tae be in good health."

Magnus said, "Is this some kind of plague we brought from the 1700s?"

Sophie said, "Nae, the mums at the park said a stomach bug was goin' around."

I said, "Well, isn't this fun, a whole-house flu, welcome to the modern world."

Magnus moaned. "We canna hae the plague in the modern world, tis nae fair." He clambered from the bed and rushed into the bathroom to throw up.

In the morning, some of us piled on blanket pallets all over the living room. We had bowls in front of the kids because, as Zach said, "You little monsters cannot be trusted, you will throw up wherever the hell you want and I am not standing for it." His hair stuck up crazily. He was wearing his version of pajamas, red plaid bottoms with a black t-shirt that said: Old Punks Never Die They Just Stand in the Back.

He clasped a hand over his mouth and rushed into the downstairs bathroom off the kitchen.

I groaned. I was curled up on the end of the couch, Jack on my chest, a blanket wrapped around me, barely aware of what was going on. The only thing that was okay about this was that Jack wasn't sick, *yet*. Isla groaned, sat up, and weakly threw up in the bowl. Then she pushed the bowl away and it dumped over on the blanket.

I burst into tears.

Emma raised an arm above her blanket-covered lump of a self and said, weakly, "What can I do to help?"

I wiped my tears. "I don't know… What's your fever right now?"

She pointed the thermometer at her forehead. "101." She tossed it to me.

I zapped my own forehead. "99. Fine, I'm pulling up my big-girl underpants. Fine. I will be a grownup, I am doing this." I stood up, carrying Jack, dragging the blanket off us and down the hall to the laundry room. I dropped the bowl in the sink. I got another blanket from the closet. I dragged it to the couch, lay down, and pulled the blanket over me. "Whoa, I can't believe I just accomplished that. Holy shit."

Isla said, "Mommy, I gonna throw up again."

I said, "Zach was right, you are a monster." I climbed from our couch-nest, went to the kitchen, grabbed another bowl, and was bringing it when Isla threw up again. On the new blanket.

"Who's going to do laundry?" I dragged the blanket off the couch and down to the laundry room and got out the last of the blankets in the downstairs closet. I carried it to the couch and put the bowl in front of Isla. " I love you so much, my sweet angel, but if you throw up on the blanket again, we will have nothing, you have to go to the toilet, or direct it into a bowl — in vomiting there is no try."

"Yes, Mammy."

We moaned and threw up the whole damn day.

James shuffled out of his room later on. He looked like hell. "Damn, y'all, there's a regular puke-nado happening. Who needs water?"

"All of us."

He made a ruckus in the kitchen filling up water glasses and pitchers and carrying them to all the rooms. He passed me a pitcher with three glasses.

I said, "You feel better?"

"Hell no, Sophie is sick now too, she made me get up and get water for everyone."

Beaty was in the chair across from me, Mookie at her feet,

Noah on her lap. She said, "Thank ye James, I was so thirsty I couldna think."

"Where's Quentin?"

"He's here under the covers." Quentin's arm rose from under a blanket and then tunneled back into the pile.

James looked around. "We might need to call in a nurse."

I groaned. "How? I can't even get up to use the phone! Do we have phones? What is happening?"

He waved his hand. "I'm goin' back to bed now, too." He padded back down the hall to his room.

I weakly said, "First one to feel well enough, call a nurse."

Emma groaned, then scrambled up. "Oh no!" She raced to the bathroom, yelling, "It's coming out the other end!"

Zach was in the chair on the other side of the living room. Disheveled in his pajamas, socks falling down, holes at the toes, no blanket, just blown back in the chair, sort of watching it all, falling asleep, watching some more. He groaned. "No, no no, *no* 'other end' — that's awful."

I said, "Have you thrown up yet?"

"Yes, once, but no, not again, I am powering through."

Emma returned a bit later. "The good news, when it moves to the, um, lower part, it means you're on the other side of it."

Zach said, dazedly, "Now you just gotta shit it out."

Zoe giggled. "Daddy say 'shit.'"

Zach said, "Where's Mags?"

"He's in bed." I grasped for the bowl, pulled it over, and threw up in it. Isla said, "Mammy that's disgusting." Then she threw up on the other side, splashing against my cheek.

I frowned deeply. "I couldn't make it to the bathroom — this is a horror show."

I got up, padded into the kitchen, and poured the throw-up down the sink. "I regret all these decisions, this is… someone's going to have to clean all this up."

Zach, staring into space said, "I'm on it, soon as I'm done with this."

I rinsed out the bowl, carried it back to the couch, and put it in Isla's lap. I said, "That's good, I feel better, when was the last time everyone threw up?"

Everyone muttered an answer for a different length of time. I said, "Maybe we're at the end of it."

CHAPTER 6 - KAITLYN

NIGHTMARE SCENARIO

A few hours later, "Are we at the end of it yet?"

Hayley flicked the channel to a baking show that even the kids enjoyed as they drifted in and out of sleep. She paused the show. "*This* one is my favorite episode. No barfing during it, everyone, no barfing."

Archie said, "I can't stop barfing Aunt Hayley, just because I say I am not going to."

Ben said, "Yeah, my stomach is not listening to me." He looked down at his stomach and said, "Stop it, stop it!"

The good news, it was our first sign of humor. A good sign *maybe* that we were getting well.

A few hours later, Magnus lumbered down the stairs, with Haggis behind him. I called weakly, "Bring blankets if you're coming to nest!"

He turned around, climbed back up the stairs, disappeared down the hall, and then reemerged coming down the stairs, dragging our bed comforter behind him. As he arrived in the living room, he said, "Och, I wondered where ye all were."

He dropped to his knees beside the couch, kissed my cheek,

and Jack's forehead, then said to Isla, "Ye are too stinky for kisses."

She pouted, and said, "I don't have throw-up here," pointing at the back of her left hand. Magnus picked it up, kissed it, then rolled away, diving into the middle of the boys' floor nest, wriggling until they parted to make way, giggling. He stole all their pillows and got comfortable with their heads on his chest. "We are watching the bakie show? Good, tis m'favorite."

He looked across the room at Zach, still sitting, staring into space. "Ye well, Chef Zach? Ye look as if ye are about tae collapse."

"Nope, just dandy, as long as I don't move a muscle."

"Ye ought tae do as I did and just sit in the bathroom until tis done."

"You rode the porcelain throne, did ya? Yeah, well, I'm not actually sick, it's mind over matter. I am not weak, I refuse to succumb."

Fraoch walked in, went into the kitchen, groaning, leaned over the sink, turned the faucet on, stuck his mouth under the running water, drank, splashed water all over his face, gulped from his cupped hand, and wet his hair.

Zach called weakly, "Glasses!"

"I ken. I canna be bothered, I am turned intae a beast with this plague." He dropped down on his hands and knees and crawled into the living room and leaned against Hayley's chair. "Ye well, m'bean ghlan?"

"No, but I haven't raced to the bathroom for a while."

Lochinvar stumbled into the room, dropped to the floor beside the couch, swayed, then slumped over to the side. Haggis licked his face.

Archie said, "Uncle Lochie, you need a pillow?"

Lochie mumbled. "I will never be comfortable again, tis a dis-ease of the highest order and I canna expel it from m'body."

Magnus whispered, "It daena sound like he wants a pillow."

Archie and Ben giggled.

Quentin, who had been sleeping, said, "First sign that you're on the mend, belly-aching about it."

"Ugh, daena say belly-aching, m'stomach is crampin' up."

I said, "You need water."

We all looked at the pitcher beside me. With a weak, shaking hand I poured some into a glass and slid it toward him.

Magnus said, "Where are James and Sophie?"

"They're in their room."

"The bairns are unscathed?"

Beaty said, "Aye, they seem tae be well."

"Good." A new episode of the baking show started and we all went quiet, weak and dazed, just staring at the screen.

Until Zach jumped up, "Oh shit shit shit!"

He leapt, lankily, over Magnus and the boys, and did a funny walk-run down the hall toward the bathroom.

Quentin said, "First you say it, then you do it."

Ben laughed.

Zoe said, "Daddy funny."

Emma said, "Daddy thought he wouldn't succumb to the bug, but the bug comes for all!"

Soon, Sophie and James joined us. Everyone was there, we had pillows and pallets all over the floor, the baking show playing and the night growing dark. James said, "Y'all entered the second phase now, poopnado?"

The kids all giggled.

Ben said, "Poopnado."

Archie said, "Poopquake."

They high-fived over Magnus's chest.

Magnus said, "I am hungry."

Everyone groaned, except Archie. "Me too, Da."

Magnus joked, looking around the room, "Nae one tae cook for the king?"

Noisy retching sounded from the bathroom down the hall; Zach was throwing up loudly.

Magnus shook the boys off his chest and climbed to his feet. "I am making dinner, daena worry on it, Chef Zach!"

Zach groaned, calling out, "Don't — I'm fine!" Then he retched some more.

Magnus looked in the cupboards dazedly.

Then he looked in the fridge. He pulled a couple of Tupperware pieces out, peeled up the lids and sniffed. Then he grimaced

He pulled a dozen eggs from the fridge. He placed the carton on the counter and opened every cabinet looking for a bowl. Then he opened every drawer looking for the skillet.

By this time a lot of us had our attention on Magnus, instead of the show.

Ben called in, "Uncle Magnus, do you know how to cook?"

"I hae been known tae cook an egg when I was out on m'own, on a hunt or..." He opened a few drawers, looking for utensils. By this time most of the cabinets and three of the drawers were open and he was breaking eggs into what was usually Zach's fancy gravy bowl. He threw the shells on the counter, used a table knife to whip them around in the bowl, then poured the scrambled eggs into the skillet. The cold skillet.

"Och nae!" He turned the flame up and stood holding the skillet above the flame, then lowered it carefully onto the stove top. He nodded, pleased with himself.

Using a batter spatula, he scraped as it cooked, muttering, "...tis sticking..."

Isla whispered to me, "Da is cooking."

"Yep, it's marvelous."

A few moments later Magnus called over, "Who wants eggs?"

Fraoch said, "With ketchup!"

Lochie held his stomach. "Nae."

The boys both said, "Me!"

Magnus separated eggs into bowls with spoon handles jutting up. He dolloped ketchup on top and carried them over, delivering an egg bowl to Archie and Ben to share, one to Fraoch, and one for himself. They ate.

A few minutes later Chef Zach came from the bathroom and stood in front of his wrecked kitchen. He incredulously waved his hands at the mess. "What the *hell* happened here?"

Magnus grinned. "I cooked eggs, Chef Zach, dost ye want some?"

Zach's eyes went wide. "This is a fucking nightmare scenario."

"The mess I made? Och, nae, we can leave it, I will clean it when we are well."

"Not the mess, you cooking, this is not—"

"I ought tae ken tae cook an egg, Chef Zach, it daena mean ye arna a good provider."

Zach trudged into the living room, dropped into his chair, and resumed the position, staring into space. "In the future, I will have soups in the freezer for this kind of emergency."

Emma said, "I hope we don't ever have this kind of emergency again, this is not good."

Lochie said, "We are fortunate there inna a bad guy attackin', I would be the only one able tae mount a defense." He weakly mimed swinging a sword.

Fraoch moaned.

Quentin woke with a start, his head came up from his burrow under blankets. "We need to mount a defense? What?"

Beaty said, "Nae, Quennie, go back tae sleep, tis nae somethin' tae worry on."

Magnus climbed back into the floor nest and ate his eggs and then lay with the boys' heads on his chest, but then it was growing dark, a few end table lamps clicked on, little pools of light. Fraoch snored from the nest, until Hayley, giggling, pushed him onto his side.

Quentin joked, "No one better fart — like in the communal sleeping area in the castle."

James said, "Is that a possibility? The stench was horrific. On that note, I'm going to my comfy bed." He put out a hand for Sophie and they padded down the hall to their room. Hayley turned on the twelfth baking show in a row.

Archie said, "This is boring."

I said, "Agreed, and that means we feel better."

Hayley said, "Fine, little tyrant, what do *you* want?"

Ben said, "Let's watch Star Wars."

Hayley said, "We've watched that five times."

Quentin said, "I don't think you can watch Star Wars too many times. And how come you get the remote control?"

Beaty said, "I love Star Wars, R2D2 is so funny."

Magnus said, "Tis the best of all the movies in the world."

Hayley asked, "How many movies have you watched?"

I laughed. "I think he's watched about five. Most of them over and over."

He said, "They are all the best movies in the world, I canna imagine there is anyway tae improve on it."

She switched on Star Wars and jostled Fraoch to wake him up.

I teased, "You relented so easily."

"It's my favorite too, I just wanted to argue."

"You're feeling better."

Everyone adjusted, and changed their positions to get more comfortable for the movie. Magnus dislodged the boys from their comfortable positions using him as a pillow, to up on the couch.

Isla said, "Da! We don't have room!"

"Och nae, ye hae taken the couch, near yer ma, all day, ye hae tae share." He got between us and wriggled funnily forcing her to sit up closer to the end. He pulled my feet into his lap. She curled up against his shoulder.

I grinned at him. "How are you doing, Highlander?"

"The eggs helped, I am done with it, I think." He clasped my hand.

"Me too, just tired now. I'm psyched Jack and Noah slept through the whole thing."

"Aye, tis a blessing that the bairns allowed us tae be the ones lamentin' for once."

CHAPTER 7 - KAITLYN

LISTEN TO WHAT FOLLOWS

*I*t took until the following day before we were all well enough to be up, eating, the kids were fully better. Zach cleaned the kitchen, made chicken soup, and muttered about how he was going to fill the freezer with soup so that, "If we *ever* have a moment like that again we won't have to suffer through Magnus cooking on the stove."

Magnus joked, "I think ye would rather me cook upon the flame than inside the microwave, I daena think I hae grasped the wonder of it well enough."

Zach grumbled, "You don't have to grasp the wonder, you just have to push the on button."

"Are ye tellin' me ye want me tae cook for myself, Chef Zach? Dost ye want me tae learn how?"

Zach stopped in horror. "No, no, this conversation is getting way past us — this is… let's not get crazy, let's go back to *I* cook, you look on adoringly."

"That I can do. I did rescue some verra hungry people in our family just when they needed it most though, ye ought tae be grateful."

Zach slid some food into the fridge, "Sure I'm grateful, it just wasn't necessary. I wasn't sick, I never get sick."

~

Magnus stood, holding his cup of coffee and swept his arm at the glass doors. "Tis a beautiful day, we are goin' tae relax! We are in good health once more, we will rewind our stress levels. Lochinvar, ye ken in Maine we had long days beside the lake? In Florida we will play on the beach, swim in the pool, spend our evenings upon the deck, perhaps challenging each other tae games of chance and skill. Twill be a glorious time. This morn we ought tae all go ride Sunny, Thor, Gatorbelle, and Osna on the—"

Emma walked past him with her laptop and a binder that said 'receipts' on it.

Magnus frowned comically, "What are we…? Tis nae necessary, Emma, I will fix the books on the other side."

"What do you mean? Oh like, in the future? Like *post*-date it?"

"Aye, if ye want tae hae more money in the account, I can hae one of our men add some."

She said, "I don't know exactly how that… are we okay with that? It sounds like cheating."

James said, "It's not cheating, Magnus is a king of *time*, as a king he can add money to his treasury when he needs to, it's just his need is in a different time from the money. It's logical."

She smiled. "Well, I'm still going to look over the books, I don't want to waste money, but I won't sweat it either."

Magnus said, "Good, we are havin' a 'nae sweat' time in Florida—"

Quentin said, "Except…"

Magnus frowned even more. "Och nae, ye are goin' tae hae an exception, Colonel Quentin? Ye are goin' tae ruin m'good time?"

Fraoch said, "This has been a good time tae ye, Og Maggy? It has been a time of things comin' out of both ends of me and

—" He grimaced clutching his stomach. "Why are we talkin' about it?"

Lochie said, "Ye are the one that brought it up."

Magnus said, "None of us are talking about 'both ends' or 'sweat' or *anything* like an 'except,' but the warm air and the blue skies." He added, "We deserve it, what we ought tae do is…"

He looked at Quentin's face and sighed. "Och, Colonel Quentin, ye are goin' tae demand yer 'except' be heard?"

Quentin said, "Only a tyrannical despot wouldn't listen to their oldest, closest, and most important military advisor when he says, 'except'. Are you a tyrannical despot?"

Magnus grunted, "Nae, but I might decide tae become one if I canna enjoy the beach."

"Well, truly, as your friend, one who has barely recovered from the worst stomach flu ever and is still weak, can barely think, but still has a point to make, you ought to listen."

Magnus's eyes went wide. "I daena think ye hae ever spoken to me with such a forceful 'except', Colonel Quentin."

"You usually listen to my thoughts, but this time you're so intent on having your happy time in Florida that you're not being sensible. You won the kingdom, you're king of time again, all is good, except… you ought to listen to what follows."

Magnus sighed and sat down on a stool. Zach poured more coffee into his mug.

All the men gathered around the counter.

I had been about to go out to the beach with the kids, but instead I put Jack in the sling and said, "Sophie, will you take the kids out to the beach? I need to hear this conversation."

"Aye, it sounds important."

She and Beaty followed the kids.

CHAPTER 8 - KAITLYN

SIX VESSELS IN THE VAULT

*H*ayley stood at the bar beside Fraoch.

Magnus folded his arms across his chest and nodded at Quentin. "Go ahead."

"We decided the other night we needed to get control of the timeline, that we need to gather the vessels. And that it was critical, but then we got sick, now it's been *two days*. I think we are crazy to think we get to relax much longer."

Lochie said, "I agree, and I hae been sayin' it all along, tis critical tae collect the vessels, we canna tarry."

James said, "I agree, though it sounds like a lot of hassle. When we did this before it was a huge pain in our ass."

Lochinvar shrugged. "I think we are like the rebels against the Space Empire, all fun adventures are a pain-in-our-arse hassle."

James said, "True, and though I said it sounded like a hassle, I don't mean I don't agree. I agree. We have to gather 'em up."

Magnus asked, "What are yer thoughts, Fraoch? We daena hae time tae relax first?"

"Nae, I agree with the rest. With reservations with what Og Lochie said, of course."

Lochie scoffed. "What reservations?"

"Tis not a rebel versus the Empire situation, tis a Harry findin' the Horcruxes situation, ye ought tae get yer story straight."

"Stop squabblin', *fine*." Magnus reached in the pocket of his shorts and pulled out an oft-folded paper. He spread it flat on the kitchen bar, "We counted when we were last in Riaghalbane. I put m'list in m'pocket this morning."

Quentin laughed. "So you were already in agreement that we needed to get busy?"

Magnus grinned. "Aye, gatherin' the vessels is first on m'list, after the feasts. I am just grumblin' because I haena had enough feasts yet."

Zach pointed finger guns at Magnus. "I got you, Magnus, we are feasting tonight. An 'I just recovered from the stomach bug' feast. I'm thinking… bananas, rice and—"

Magnus, still looking down at the paper, spreading it with his palms, teased, "Whatever ye cook will be wonderful, Chef Zach, I am happy with anything… as long as it has lasagna in it."

Chef Zach put a skillet back in the cupboard and joked, "I think I'm going back to the store."

"Thank ye."

Quentin said, "Now we just need to compare your list to Johnne Cambell's book, where is that?"

Magnus said, "Lady Mairead shared it with us for a time, but she has taken it back for her own, and has it with her journals, hidden somewhere, she winna tell me."

Lochie said, "Ye ought tae demand she divulge it."

Magnus chuckled. "Och, I would like tae see me try. Nae, I am incensed over her secrecy, but this has been a battle between us for a long time. She winna give up the secrets, but she will always be on our side. I hae grown tae accept that tis her way." He sighed. "And she will die eventually and then I will hae all her books."

Fraoch said, "If Lady Mairead were here she would wonder why ye believe she will die first."

Magnus said, "Aye, she would certainly say it. She would also crow that she has the book documentin' how many vessels there are."

While they were conversing I went to the cookbook closet and pulled out the book, *American Cookery*. "We don't have to ask her for it, because *I* have a copy of the pertinent pages of that damn book." *American Cookery* was wrapped in a leather cover because it was the first edition. Between the cover and the book I slid out a bundle of folded papers. I brought them to the bar and spread them out flat beside Magnus's list.

Magnus said, "How did ye…?"

"Johnne Cambell's book was in my possession, I took photos of the pages. I literally don't know why I didn't think to do it before."

Magnus picked up a page, looking it over. "The reason why we dinna copy it is because tis verra dangerous, we ought not allow it in other hands."

"I know, that's why it's hidden. I just… it's something your mother has that we need. She shared it with me for a while, but I don't like being at her mercy. I think we needed to take the risk."

Quentin said, "Is this the only copy?"

"I hid a copy in the safe at the bank. The other is here in the kitchen."

Zach said, "That *American Cookery* first edition is even more rare now."

"Yep, I thought it was fun to hide it there."

We flipped over pages until we got to the densely written lists of vessels, started by Johnne Cambell, added to by some of the Kings of Riaghalbane, then Lady Mairead, and me.

Hayley counted and said out loud, "Twenty-six."

Quentin said, "We had that time slip, the number of known vessels went down, we fixed it and then the numbers went up. We can't honestly know how many we had originally."

I said, "And note: we have been here to this original moment. Magnus has been there. Reyes was there. Lady Mairead was there. There might have been vessels that left the scene before they were recorded."

Magnus said, "Why did it begin with twenty-six? It feels an indifferent number, as if there would be more."

Emma said, "Twenty-six is a religious number. In Sunday school we learned about how the number twenty-six is the number you get when you take the number that means the name Eve from the number that means the name Adam, like taking the rib, you know?"

Zach's face screwed up. "How the hell does that work?"

"I don't know, I learned it when I was like, six, in Sunday School."

Hayley was looking at her phone. "Twenty-six also means the number of spacetime dimensions in bosonic string theory." She waved the phone at Zach.

"Again, I wonder, how the hell does that work?"

Hayley said, "I'm not reading it, too boring, but it also says twenty-six is the Hebrew number for God. I'm not saying anything, I'm just saying — the number twenty-six is no more or less likely to be a number of vessels than anything else."

Fraoch looked down at her phone blankly, then blinked. "But it daena mean that any of this means that vessels dinna get taken. I was there with Magnus, it was verra hectic, tis likely vessels were purloined."

James said, "I was there too, I concur."

Quentin said, "But we have been at this for years, there have always been twenty-six vessels. Have you found any new ones, Katie?"

"Not since the one that Professor Munro had, that was new

to us." I waggled my finger between us. "But it was already on the list."

Quentin said, "See? Donnan had this book, then Lady Mairead, then you, technically us. I think this is the legitimate number."

Magnus nodded. "Aye, and we must go with what we know: Twenty-six. Now we need to gather them all."

Fraoch rubbed his hands together. "So, how many are on yer list, Og Maggy?"

Magnus pointed at his list. "We hae four here. Lady Mairead has two. She daena need them both, but she winna relinquish one."

Lochie said, "So there ought tae be twenty in the vault at yer kingdom."

Magnus said, "This is where I must give ye bad news. We hae six in the vault and two that I hae hidden for emergencies. So all told, we are in possession of fourteen."

I groaned, I wasn't the only one. "I feel like we've gone backwards."

Fraoch said, "We are missin' twelve? Och nae, tis dire."

"Aye, as ye can imagine we were disappointed, that was after we gathered up the vessels that Agnie, Ian, Ormr and Domnall, had in their possession. We conquered them, took back the castle, the kingdom, only tae look in the vault tae see we had so few. They hae absconded with many, perhaps hidden them away."

Fraoch said, "Tis verra disappointin'."

"Aye," Magnus said, "speaking of where they are hidden — we ought tae find the two I hae hidden away."

Lochie's eyes went wide. "Ye daena remember where they are?"

Magnus joked, "I daena remember where *one* of them is, tis nae as dire as ye are thinkin'."

James said, "And what about yer brothers?"

Magnus groaned. "What brothers? *Surely* I hae killed them all by now."

Emma said, "You didn't kill the rock star."

"I like his music, I thought we might want tae keep him around. But then I did kill him three years from now."

Hayley said, "What? You wouldn't!"

Magnus said, "I am teasin' ye. Tis a time travel joke."

I said, "Could there be any brothers, or any cousins, or anyone related through the line of Donnan, who might show up with another vessel?"

He said, "It has been a while since someone came tae challenge me, I daena think there are any left that are unaccounted for."

I said, "What about the kings that came before Donnan? The founding kings?"

Magnus looked down on the papers thoughtfully. "I daena ken what vessels they carried. I suppose I ought tae look for the records."

Quentin said, "Guaranteed Lady Mairead has already looked it up, already knows."

"Aye, and this is the first I hae considered it." He exhaled. "I ought tae ask her more questions, but yet, tae see her, she is sure tae ruin m'vacation."

Quentin said, "I don't know about you but hearing 'we have six in the vault' ruined my vacation pretty hard already."

CHAPTER 9 - KAITLYN

WE WILL GO TAE THE YEAR 1760

*L*ochie said, "So we need tae get the vessels, *this* is what I hae been saying all along."

Fraoch waved a hand at him. "Well, ye just got here, yer 'all along' is just a verra short time. Ye might want tae consider that I once sat with a gunshot through here," he lifted his shirt. "While guardin' the vessels outside of a cave on the side of Ben Cruachan. I hae known that keepin' the vessels safe was worth dyin' for *long* afore ye were born."

"I am aulder than ye, auld man."

James laughed. "First, that is hilarious, Lochie, second, we don't need to argue about this, do we, boys? I mean, I love a good argument, but the case could be made that the vessels exist and they are a pain in the arse, so wanting to find them all is not the positive goal we are making it out to be. Don't get me wrong, we all want them. We have to get them under our control, but the case could be made that we're insane to think of it. We ought to turn them over to InterPol or something, let someone else manage this bullshit. And, also, gotta say, Fraoch, not a fan of saying they're 'worth dying for.'"

Fraoch nodded. "Aye, I meant not that the vessels were

worth dying for, but that I would die tryin' tae keep the family safe."

Quentin said, "On that note, back to business: we need to collect the ones we know about, first. We'll send a group to dig up the one that Magnus has hidden—"

"Nae, tis under a tree on the shore of the Tay river, near the tunnel door. There is a sturdy oak there, I hae buried it under that tree. Tis there in case we need it."

Emma jumped up and left the room and returned with a large rolled up map. She shoved aside some of the things on the dining room table and unrolled it. "Here you go, this is Balloch."

Magnus looked it over for a moment, then said, "Tis there."

James said, "Great, in case of emergencies, look for oak trees. What does an oak tree look like?"

Magnus waved a hand. "Ye ken, everyone kens what an oak tree looks like, they are all around!"

I said, "Note: we all need to carry a shovel, when you leave the house, carry a shovel. Archie had to dig one of those vessels up once and it was heart-rending to watch."

Magnus said, "But he did it — he was able tae. There was an emergency and the vessel was there, we canna regret what we survived. As long as we are in control of the vessels we ought tae hae a few of them out in the world in case we hae a need for them. I want tae keep the one under the oak tree there."

James said, "Carry a shovel, maybe a book about tree identification."

Zach was making a grocery list, but looked up to ask, "So how do we find the missing ones?"

Quentin said, "We use the tech that remote-activates the vessels, turns them on, then we hunt for those storms and locate the vessels. We scoop them up."

James said, "Where is that tech?"

Magnus said, "Tis a part of the Bridge, I hae it in m'bags."

Fraoch said, "You've been planning this all along, Og Maggy, and ye hae been pretending as if ye haena?"

"Aye," Magnus grinned. "I like watchin' ye come up with an idea as if ye are the only one tae think of it, and tae argue with Lochie about who is the most thoughtful on it. Ye see, while ye were tryin' tae win the battle, I hae won the war."

James said, "We need to go to Kilchurn and put a notch in the stone wall for that win."

Magnus said, "We will head tae Kilchurn first, I believe, we are bound tae hae left at least one behind there."

Hayley said, "So remind me, why can't we just turn them all on and go around and pick them all up?"

Magnus said, "When ye turn on a vessel remotely it begins tae storm in every time. Tis as if it becomes a beacon — day after day it turns on, a brutal storm, in every year. If other men are searchin' for the vessels they will see the 'beacon' and might get tae the vessels first."

Zach said, "Not to mention meteorologists might notice the storms."

I said, "Remember the time the storms made the news and we flew to Scotland and I touched the vessel and ended up in…" I gulped.

Hayley frowned. "Yeah, I remember, that sucked."

I nodded.

Quentin said, "So we need to be well armed. We need to use precision, set the vessels to beacon, then swoop in and grab them before anyone else." He tapped his temple. "We gotta be smarter than all the assholes."

I said, "You need to pick a year, one that we haven't gone to before, so there's no looping."

James said, "End of the eighteenth century, most of the nineteenth century, except some of that might be over-civilized and populated."

Zach said, "If we are in parts of Scotland during the 1800s

we might be able to stay hidden. The um… the population was cleared out in the—"

Fraoch's brow drew down. "What dost ye mean, 'cleared out'?"

"It's known as the Highland Clearances, we haven't told you about that yet? Damn, sorry, Fraoch. A lot of highlanders were forced from their land."

Fraoch grimaced. "I ended up in the New World, fightin', but I could see it comin'. They wanted all the young men tae leave home for farther shores, twas a push. I saw it comin' with m'own eyes."

James said, "In order to not get involved in all that, we could go to the late sixteenth century or early seventeenth century."

Magnus said, "We must be cautious in the sixteenth century, tis near the origination date—"

Lochie said, "I was in Ormr's castle around then… when was it?"

Magnus nodded. "Aye, Lochie, we daena ken all the years ye were there, we need tae be verra careful."

James waved his fist around. "You know what year we haven't been to yet? 1776. Come on, y'all, let's *do* it."

I said, "James, you want to go to *Scotland* in 1776? Want to waste your shot at joining in the revolution on the wrong continent?"

"Yeah, I just got excited." He waved fingers at Quentin. "Quennie, put on the itinerary that I want to go to the states in 1776. Delaware or Philadelphia or something."

Quentin used his finger to check the air. "Check. Me too. First on the list after we find all these blasted machines. Speaking of dangerous times to be anywhere, when did Scotland abolish slavery?"

Zach looked down at his phone. "Looks like 1833 in the UK."

Quentin said, "You know my vote."

Everyone was quiet for a moment, thinking. Magnus trailed

a finger along the map but he didn't look like he was considering it, he was just mulling things over. "We need tae be able tae carry weapons, ride horses, travel through the woods. I believe we ought tae start in the eighteenth century. Twill be familiar. I think if Fraoch or I went tae the 1800s, even if it meant safety for our family member, Quentin, we would be at a disadvantage; we daena ken the manners of the time, and Quentin and James would not ken how tae behave—"

James said, "I could figure it out."

"Aye, tae go tae the year 1776, ye will research first, but in this case we will need tae use precision and speed, we winna hae time tae adjust and research."

Emma said, "And we have the issue of your clothes. You don't want to be in the wrong clothes."

"That is always an issue."

Magnus straightened. "We will go tae the year 1760." Then he asked me, "Hae we been tae the year 1760 afore?"

"Nope, don't remember it."

"Good, tis after Fraoch left, and yet still close enough that things would be familiar. Twill be durin' the…" He grimaced. "Horrible soundin' 'clearances,' but we will be careful." He looked around. "And we winna need tae ken about slavery or nae, because ye arna comin' with us, Colonel Quentin, we need ye here."

He scowled. "I *knew* that was how it was going to go. I was sitting here watching this discussion unfold thinking, 'Someone's gotta stay here and watch over Zach, who's it going to be…?'"

Zach said, "Hey! I don't need a guard, but then again, yes, I do, and I will cook for you, so it's a damn good trade-off I think."

Magnus said, "And all the bairns need guardin', the whole household. I would stay, but I am nae comfortable sending others intae an uncertain time on a crucial mission. I will go, Fraoch will go, James, and Lochie. Colonel Quentin, ye will need a security firm tae come and—"

"This time I'm already a step ahead of *you*." Quentin looked at his gold watch. "I already did the walk-through with Ryan Protection Firm, we'll have security on the walls by the end of the day."

Magnus ran his hand through his hair. "We are decided then, men, we are going on an adventure. Chef Zach I canna wait for the lasagna feast ye promised me earlier, I heard it, did everyone hear it? When Chef Zach promised me lasagna?"

Chef Zach grabbed the grocery list and his keys. "I'm headed to the store!"

CHAPTER 10 - KAITLYN

I AM ALREADY YEARS BEYOND YE

I went back to the couch. Jack wanted to nurse and I was exhausted by the conversation. It had been a meeting that didn't involve me, except in every single way — all of this was to keep the children safe. All of this was going to need the might and prowess of the men, yet I felt certain that I would be able to help if I could go, but I was grounded, nursing a baby.

I would never leave him, not after missing out on those crucial months with Isla, but it wasn't easy to sit in a chair nursing while momentous plans were made, while missions were embarked upon. It took a certain patience and strength to watch people I loved go without me.

Especially when I was, come to find out, a control freak.

Who was I kidding, we had known it all along.

Magnus and Quentin continued talking at the table, but it was strategizing over weapons and other tech. I didn't need to know, I could hear the murmur, see the list-making.

And then a while later Magnus came into the room. He sat down beside me and pulled my shirt up a bit to see Jack's face. "He is sleepin'?"

"Yep."

He pulled Jack from my arms, without waking him, and carried him over to the small cradle we had in the corner. He placed him down, whispered, "Fraoch, keep an eye on Jack?"

Fraoch was sorting through his tackle box. "Aye, when he wakes I will shew him how tae bait a hook."

Magnus chuckled, and took me by the hand, drawing me up the stairs to our room. He pulled me to the bed, and climbed in, fully clothed. His shoe-clad feet hung off the end and I climbed in after him, curled up against his side, my head on his chest, my thigh across him.

"Big conversation, huh?"

"Aye, much was decided, I need tae talk tae ye."

"You're leaving again?"

He was quiet.

A tear rolled down my nose. "I'm sorry I'm crying. I know this has to be done, I'm just… I blame the hormones."

"I ken, mo reul-iuil." He wrapped his fingers in the back of my hair and tugged a wee bit to raise my face, he looked down in my eyes. "I ken, I am sorry I will hae tae go again."

I wriggled up, kissed him, then tucked my head on his chest again.

"You promise you'll come back and tell me how it's going, as you find them, you'll keep me updated?"

"Aye, we will go in steps — we hae a plan, and we will follow the three days protocol, and I will come and go so ye ken. I promise Kaitlyn, we winna lose time, we will accomplish this verra quickly and then we will be in control."

"Good."

We watched the lackadaisical spin of the fan. I asked, finally, "Do you think Jack needs me?"

Magnus scoffed. "Fraoch's watchin' him adoringly as he sleeps, and this is after he has been sleepin' upon yer breast for, oh… let us count the hours."

I said, "One hundred and seventy two?"

"Aye, Jack has been sleepin' upon yer breast for one hundred and seventy two hours, I think tis my turn."

He nudged me to my back and climbed on me, then groaned, went heavy on me, and shook his head.

"What?"

"I hae become too civilized. I am wearin' m'shoes on the bed and I feel like a barbarian and…"

I pushed him off and sat up. "Come sit on the edge." I knelt and untied his Nikes and slowly pulled his shoes and socks off while looking up at him seductively.

He was grinning. "Och, I do like this view of ye, Madame Campbell."

"I like this view of you as well, Master Magnus, how about…" I drew him up to stand in front of me and slowly pulled his pants down, exposing his fully erect glorious manhood. "Oh my."

I glanced up and his eyes were closed with pleasure as I brought him to climax standing in the middle of our room.

After, he dropped back on the bed.

He chuckled. "Ye want tae join me, I will repay ye in kind?"

I shook my head. "How about a raincheck, you can owe me one." I sighed. "Preferably before you leave."

"Aye, that sounds good, I would like another go before I leave, a proper beddin' with all our clothes comin' off." He pulled his pants up, tucked in his shirt, and zipped up the front of his pants. "But if I had kent this was goin' tae be all about me, I could hae saved myself the trouble of taking off my shoes."

I laughed. "It might have been more civilized if you received your blowjob while wearing shoes. Funny how that works, in-bed sex while wearing shoes makes you a barbarian, but stand-ing-in-the-middle-of-the-bedroom fully-dressed, getting a blowjob with your shoes off makes you a little barbarian too."

Then I asked, "Now what?"

"Now we join the kids for lunch. We spend the afternoon in the pool. Ye will allow me tae duck out occasionally tae strategize

with Colonel Quentin. Ye winna hold it against me, and we will
do our best tae keep Archie from suspecting too soon. Then we
will feast and enjoy a fine time taegether and as I put Archie tae
bed I will warn him that I will leave in the morn."

"Tomorrow you will go?"

"First thing."

We played in the pool. I sat on the side, with Jack, dangling my
feet in the water, but when he slept, putting him down and
jumping in, and splashing around. We played a game the kids
invented, where Magnus was home base. He threw them as far
as he could, very far, and then they had to race to his shoulder to
go again. For some reason, known only to themselves, whenever
they touched Magnus they yelled, "I won!"

Isla saying it last, "I won!"

Zoe with her arms in floaties, yelling, "I won!"

For no reason whatsoever. Haggis ran back and forth barking
as if he was playing too, jumping in, dog-paddling to the stairs,
climbing out, barking, jumping in again.

I joined in by being the pusher, Magnus would toss the kids
towards me, I would flip them around, acting like it was a huge
deal, and pushed them back. They would swim to Magnus and
yell, "I won!" And do it again.

Fraoch came in. "How dost we play?"

Magnus laughed. "I hae nae idea, we are bairn tossin' so they
win."

"Och, sounds fun!"

So then it was Magnus tossing bairns to Uncle Fraoch and
the kids won whenever they made it to their shoulders. It was
exhausting just watching them.

Then Zoe floated away from the game, tired. Isla burst into
tears because "No fair, Archie won first!" But mostly because she
was tired and needed a nap.

I hoisted her from the pool. "Go take Zoe inside."

"I don't want to!"

"Now."

She climbed out of the pool. "Come on Zoe, I have to take you inside."

Zoe followed her from the poolhouse.

Ben said, "This is boring now, want to go play Fortnite?"

He and Archie jumped out of the pool and Fraoch laughed. "I will try not tae take it personally, bairns."

Magnus rolled his shoulder around. "Och, I will be feelin' it tomorrow, I was tossin' bairns for so long. Daena be offended, Fraoch, twas a wee bit borin' by the end but it wasna yer fault."

We all dried off and Magnus met with Quentin for yet another strategizing session, later Magnus told me, "Quentin will be up all night with the packin', he is takin' this verra seriously."

"Good, I'm glad. It is serious, we need you to be safe."

Then we were all around the dining room table serving food, and before everyone dug in, I looked up and down at the faces gathered. "Before we eat I wanted to say, I love you all."

Hayley said, "We love you too, now send down the salad."

I grabbed the salad bowl but held it before passing. "I mean it, I really love you all, I can't imagine my life without you."

Hayley rolled her hand. "Us too, now pass." She grinned.

"Yeah I know, it's too much, you can't talk about how much you love me, you must make a joke."

I asked, "Isla, you love your mammy?"

"Yes, *and* lasagna."

"I see how it is, everyone is hungry, no one wants to talk about how much they love everyone else."

Hayley said, "You're just fishing for 'love yous' but your family is famished and the lasagna is getting cold."

Magnus scraped his chair back from the table and raised his

glass. "Mo reul-iuil, I love ye, ye are the shinin' light upon my life, and as I look around the table at this family gathered, I think I might be the luckiest man alive, and also this lasagna looks delicious, and tis nae fair that we canna eat yet." He smiled. "Slainte!"

We all said, "Slainte!"

I passed the salad to Hayley, "Now *that* was what I was fishing for — that was perfect. Everyone eat."

Zach raised his glass. "My turn to fish for compliments, what do you think of the meal?"

"Delicious!" There was classic lasagna, a bit of wine, a salad, and then more ice cream for dessert, because as Magnus said, the last time didn't count because he threw it up after.

We stayed at the table long, talking and laughing, but then Quentin stood. "My apologies, we have a lot to organize for tomorrow, new men standing guard. I gotta get up and get moving."

I helped clean the kitchen and we were all busy until late that night. I was already in bed when Magnus met me there. He sat down on the edge and pulled off his shoes, his head down, a long exhale, staring down at his feet. Then he rolled over onto the bed and pulled up behind me. Spooning me, hugging me hard. He pressed his mouth to my shoulder. "Where is the bairn?"

"He's in his crib, sleeping."

His hand roamed down my stomach and dove between my legs. He hitched me closer. His other hand turned my face so that he could kiss that sensual spot right below my ear. It felt so good to be brusquely handled like this, his hands molding and pulling — sometimes his were pleading hands, and I loved that. Sometimes they were confident. Sometimes they commanded, like now. His hands roamed over my body, without hesitation, with surety. I was his. He pulled my hips closer, shoved my panties down my legs and with his foot, yanked them clear. With one move he had my shirt off over my head. His breaths were heavy, bullish in my ear, against my cheek. His hands were everywhere, a pleasing press all over, stroking fingers pressing between my legs, driving me. He pulled me close and entered me from behind, hard and sure, and drove into me again and again, my moans growing as he brought me up and over the peak. Then he continued until he lay spent behind me, his arms tightening around me, stilled. A hand on my breast. The other pressed against my stomach. A long exhale beside my ear.

We relaxed. I turned in his arms and he lay against my side, his head on my breast. "That was lovely," I whispered.

He kissed my skin in answer.

We lay there quietly, me winding one of his curls around my fingers and feeling it slide around my skin and back into place. He said, "Mo reul-iuil, I will be home in three days."

"I know you will. Or you will die trying."

"Aye."

"Please don't die."

"I winna, I hae too much still tae do."

"Like what?"

"Remember I told ye we would be in the kitchen of the house in Maine and ye would be an auld crone? Ye haena done that yet." He put his chin on my chest and looked down on me.

"I haven't become an old crone?"

He shook his head. "Yer hair is nae gray, ye haena gone squat, ye daena hae even one single whisker comin' from yer chin, so I will hae tae wait alongside ye as ye become those things. I daena want tae miss it."

"You don't want to miss my one whisker? Dear me, you are a delightful man."

"Ye daena think of me as an auld man?"

"I don't know, it's not really something I've thought about. I am so hot for you right now, it's hard to imagine you as something else — wait, no, I have it, I look forward to you with a bit of gray here, at your temples, not a lot, but more than me, please, Magnus, promise me, you will always have a bit more gray than me."

"I promise. I am already years beyond ye."

"Are you?"

"Aye, ye canna tell?"

"I met Old Magnus, he was much older. He was hot, maybe that's why I don't have a set dream of you, because I've already seen you."

"Could be."

"But I do want you to wear reading glasses, I look forward to that."

"Good, we hae a great deal tae look forward tae."

"And Magnus, you are wrong about the single whisker, there will be at least five."

He chuckled. "Even more tae look forward tae."

CHAPTER 11 - MAGNUS

1760 - KILCHURN

*T*he next morn we were out on the driveway with our gear packed intae the bed of the truck. We only needed tae grab our horses from the stables.

We had most of the gear we needed, a few things we wished for, Quentin would gather them for the next jump while we were gone. Fraoch, Lochie, James, and I would be in the past for a week. We would return tae the present in three days.

We dinna ken if we would find any vessels, but we were testin'. If we found one we would adjust and plan for the next.

We were well-armed. Haggis was goin' with us.

We stood in a field farther along the road past the stables, and jumped.

～

I was startled awake tae see Fraoch's face above me. "Og Maggy, why ye down in the mud still? We hae a fine Scottish day upon us." Rain splashed my face. I was sopping wet.

"Why does the mission hae tae start with rollin' in a puddle?"

Haggis whimpered.

James said, "What the hell is this misery?"

"Just another dreich day in Scotland."

He groaned as he climbed to his feet, dripping with mud.

I lumbered up, slowly, and stretched m'achin' back and stiff muscles.

Lochinvar had his arms wrapped around him, shivering. "Tis oorlich, och nae, why canna we look at the weather afore we jump tae a place?"

Fraoch moved tae the treeline and huddled under the shelter of a large oak with Haggis. "Hayley tells me the weather daena go back this far. It says whether the whole year is cold or warm compared tae other years, but twill not give us the daily weather. We must prepare for the full range of Scottish elements."

Lochinvar said, "Dreich tae oorlich, tis cold and wet."

James and I dragged our gear under the shelter of the trees. James shook like a dog, then Haggis shook. Fraoch threw a raincoat at James's face.

He pulled it on. "Kinda late for the raincoat."

Sunny looked at me dolefully. I rubbed his nose. "I ken, ye are upset because it inna a fine day in Florida." I pulled two more raincoats from a saddlebag and tossed one tae Lochinvar.

Fraoch pulled his raincoat on. "I feel relieved nae one is here tae greet us, they might hae seen us sopping wet forgettin' tae wear our raincoats when we jumped. They would think we canna possibly be true Scotsmen."

Lochinvar snapped up the front of his coat. "A true Scotsman daena need a raincoat."

James said, "Lochie, I swear you were just shivering."

I said, "A sensible Scotsman would wear a raincoat, as would a sensible Florida Man. I think I forgot after the fine weather this week, how awful it could be."

James said, "A sensible Florida Man, where have you been living?"

Fraoch grinned, "And, Og Maggy, this inna awful, this is beautiful—" The sky dumped a deluge of rain upon us.

We pulled farther in under the trees and decided we would need tae set up camp.

We unpacked our bags and set up one of the tents, making the decision tae keep the others dry. We had some lock boxes with us, with camouflage tarps tae hide them from view, but we were in a place chosen because of its seclusion.

After setting up camp, the rain ceased for a time, so we mounted our horses and with Haggis beside us, rode from the woods tae the edge of the moor at Loch Awe. We stood within the treeline with a view of Kilchurn castle out on the causeway, a few boats out on the loch. A large section of one of the walls had fallen down in the Battle of Kilchurn back in 1707.

Another downpour started. One lone man on horseback headed away from the castle in the miserable rain.

Last I had visited Balloch, in 1709, I had asked Sean about the rebuild, he had said that the castle was mostly deserted after the fire, but that the interior roofs on the internal buildings had been replaced, and it was now used as a barracks, when troops were in need.

As we skirted the wide fields Fraoch said, "Tis disappointin' that they haena rebuilt that outer wall. Twas a fine castle."

"Aye, I hae a great many fond memories of it. I daena understand how it has stood in such misuse." I added, "I daena see guards on the walls though, perhaps it's unoccupied now."

We continued north tae the edge of the Tay river and dismounted. I retrieved the monitor from one of the saddlebags and noted: we had two vessels with us but there was a third nearby.

Fraoch asked, "Dost ye think tis in the castle, or closer tae the ben?"

"I canna tell, and I had thought there would be more than one."

Fraoch said, "When we activate it we will ken, but let's go check the vault first."

We rode up the auld familiar path up the side of Ben Cruachan with Haggis in the lead.

CHAPTER 12 - MAGNUS

THE CAVE ON BEN CRUACHAN

*W*hen we came to the cave, Fraoch said, "Och, tis bringing back memories." He pointed. "Dost ye see the rock there, Lochie? I almost died upon it, m'life drainin' from me as I lay guardin' the vessels within the cave."

"Ye sound like an auld dragon."

"A fierce auld dragon."

"Almost dyin'."

Fraoch ignored him and pointed at the tree. "See how tall it has grown? Tis from m'shite. I fed it, years ago, ye ken."

Lochie said, "I kent ye are full of it."

"Aye boy, I am enough tae build a forest." He clapped Lochie on the shoulder.

We set our shoulders tae the rock, and shoved it from the door of the cave. There was a vault door within. I wiped my hands of mud, entered the code, and shoved it open. "Lochie, ye are goin' tae go intae this cave and tell us what ye find."

"Why me?"

"Because ye are wee and young enough tae coil."

He blinked at the door, rain pouring down. "I hae tae coil?"

"Aye, and then drop tae the ground and lift out the chests."

Fraoch said, "Hayley has done it more than once."

"Fine, I will go."

He crouched down and stuck his foot through.

I shook m'head.

"Then how dost ye think I ought tae go?"

"Head first, use yer arms tae break yer fall. If ye go in with one foot ye might get stuck with yer legs apart. There wouldna be anything we could do, ye would be stuck like that forever."

He pulled his leg back out and got down on his stomach in the mud. Haggis licked his face. "Ye ken so much, Yer Majesty, perhaps ye ought tae be the one tae do it."

"I hae done it, tis why I am warning ye, use yer hands tae block yer fall or ye might break yer face on the ground. And I am also telling ye tae do it without anymore whinin'."

Lochinvar shoved himself forward, grunting as he shifted back and forth, shimmying his shoulders through. He yelled, "Och nae!" as he slipped through, descendin' intae the cave, landin' with a thud.

Haggis barked and barked.

I said, "Haggis, down boy."

He lay down in the mud, facing the cave, his tail swishing back and forth.

Lochie called up, his voice distant, "There is ample allowance tae stand!"

"I told ye, all yer complaining afore was for naught."

"Tis possible tae get back out?"

Fraoch said, "This is an insensible time tae ask it."

There was quiet, then, "I will be able tae get out?"

Fraoch said, "Og Lochie, ye can get out — I told ye, my wife has been down there multiple times, Quentin has been inside the cave."

"Yer lack of answer is concernin'."

I said, "Ye will get out, Lochie, but tae the matter at hand, what dost ye see?"

"A chest."

"Just one?"

"Aye…" I heard movement then he called up, "Tis locked!"

"Dost ye want tools sent down or dost ye want tae send it up?"

"Up! There's a—" He squealed.

James was doubled over laughing.

Fraoch called down, "What has ye squealin' like a mucag?"

"A bat, ialtag! Och nae!"

There was a bang, then a dragging sound, and a moment later a loud grunt. The chest shot from the cave and rolled past us down the incline, landing in a puddle. A moment later Lochie's top half flopped through the cave door. He yelled, "Pull me out! Pull me out!"

Haggis barked wildly.

James, laughing, grabbed his arms, dragging him from the cave, and dropping him unceremoniously in the mud.

Lochie batted at the air. "Och nae, did he follow me?"

Fraoch said, "Nae, he is a cave dweller. He was chasin' ye out, not followin' ye."

Lochie shivered all over.

I dragged the chest under a tree, crouched beside it, and pressed m'hand to tae the pad. There was a clickin' noise releasing the lock, and the lid sprung open. Inside, nestled in straw were two vessels. I dug through lookin' for more.

James asked, "So beyond what we brought we found two — are there anymore?"

I looked at the monitor. "One more. It must be somewhere at the castle."

Lochinvar said, "We hae tae search the castle?"

Fraoch said, "Nae, pay attention, Og Lochie, we are goin' tae activate, then we can locate it, then retrieve it."

Lochie said, "It sounds simple. Like findin' these two vessels, we are just picking them up."

As Fraoch strapped the chest tae the back of Thor, he said, "Nothin' about time travel is ever simple."

I closed up the cave and James and I shoved the rock in front of the door. I said, "I feel tis the end of an era, we hae finally fully emptied the Cruachan cave."

Fraoch said, "I would agree, Og Maggy, but somehow I feel we might hae done this afore, yet here are vessels again. I daena think we can ever finish with a place."

Lochie said, "Aye, time is a wheel, ye ken."

We rode farther up the mountain, in the drenching downpour, tae hae a view of the castle, the loch, and the forests. Fraoch said, "Visibility is shite."

I wiped rain from my eyes and removed the Bridge from Sunny's saddlebag and placed my hand upon it tae open the lid. There was the obsidian stone, called the drochaid, in the center for bridgin' the timeline. In the left corner were the parts for the remote activatin' of the vessels, a dial tae rotate, a spot tae press. Lady Mairead had shown me how tae use it months before.

Fraoch said, "Daena push the black river rock, ye daena want tae accidentally send the timeline shiftin' and bridging."

"Och, daena worry, I will stay clear." I turned a dial, enterin' the code of the vessel that was showing on the monitor.

I checked the code against the monitor a second time tae make sure.

Fraoch asked, "Why is it takin' ye so long?"

"I hae tae make sure the numbers are correct."

"Och, Og Maggy, I am growin' nervous, we need our vessels far away in case ye accidentally activate them."

"I winna."

He shook his head. "I daena care. I am not goin' tae take yer word for it, tis too dangerous." He unstrapped the chest from Thor and carried it about thirty feet away, Haggis walking alongside as if he were helping.

Fraoch returned and held out his hand for the rest of the vessels, including the one in m'sporran. He carried them all over tae the chest, placin' them in a pile, and jogged back. "Alright, now ye can go."

I turned the activator on.

There was the feeling of electricity through our skin, a headache similar tae the one caused by the Trailblazer, a high pitched scream through our minds, and then a flash of lightning below us, near the castle. Another flash and a loud boom. Storm clouds roiled above the castle down below us.

Because there was already a storm raining down, twas worsening, the downpour cyclin', sucked up, then poured down.

Fraoch said, "Och nae, tis a tempest."

Lightning flashed and lit up the sky, sparking the ground around the castle as if in a dance.

"I wish there had been a way tae evacuate the castle first."

"Ye dinna ken the storm would arise right there, ye thought twould be in the moor."

We stood watching the storm from a safe distance, our rain hoods pulled down tae shield our faces, the rain dripping down the front, obscuring my vision.

Lochie said, "Are we riding down intae it?"

"Nae, we canna go down now, we will hae tae wait—"

Lightning struck the wall, in four different places at once, stone crumbled down the side.

I said, "Och nae, tis difficult tae watch, those were some fine protective walls, they kept m'family safe for a full year. I stood at the top of them, watchful over this land."

The lightning storm lasted for about fifteen minutes then slowly withdrew. The brutal storm clouds rolled away, leaving behind a thick underside of gray rain clouds.

Lochinvar said, "Now what?"

James blew on his cold hands. "So, here's what I think, everyone at the castle looks antsy right now, maybe we ought to go back to camp, spend the night, wait for the crowds to clear before we approach."

I said, "Agreed."

Fraoch said, "Aye, after the lightning crumbled the outer walls, I am sure the guards will be jumpy this evening. We ought tae let them hae a good night's sleep afore we approach.

James said, "Good, and while we wait, I have something to check out. Last night, before we left, I was on a meteorology message board, and a friendly man named at-stormchase said he had been noticing repeated epic storms south of here."

I said, "That could be a vessel."

"Yeah, so I got him to give me the coordinates." He pulled out his phone and showed us a screenshot with coordinates marked. "We haven't seen a storm there today, so I'm not sure it's worth going in this weather."

I said, "How far away?"

"It's a couple miles that way further into the moor, want to check it out?"

I said, "Aye, this is why we are here."

Fraoch carried the vessels back tae the horses and stowed them in bags, passed one tae me for m'sporran, and tied the chest tae Thor once more.

We mounted our horses and rode down the mountain tae the low woods, fording the river at the narrowest point. We watched Kilchurn castle as men and horses streamed from the gates and down the causeway. It had grown too dangerous for even the most rudimentary of shelters. As we waited in the woods surrounding the moor, there was a low rumbling and more of the castle wall crumbled down.

I groaned.

Lochie said, "Ye take yer walls verra seriously."

"Aye, I do."

. . .

We followed a long, worn trail toward the forest's edge and a moor stretching beyond, with a small stream running through the middle of it.

James kept his phone in his hand. "The coordinates would put it out in the middle, there."

Lochie said, "Just laying on the ground?"

I said, "Aye. Or not, we ought tae at least look." We dismounted, and leading our horses, fanned out, walking slowly, kicking rocks aside, looking under bushes, Haggis sniffing everywhere. We met at the stream bank.

"I dinna see anything and there wasna a storm here either."

James looked around. "Perhaps someone picked it up in another time."

Fraoch shifted a rock and looked under it. "Nothin'."

I pulled the monitor from my pocket. "There is still only one extra vessel, I am certain tis inside the castle or near the walls, in the morn we look for it."

CHAPTER 13 - MAGNUS

WE FOUND THREE SO FAR

*W*e put up the second tent in the downpour, splashing puddles and mud. We tied the horses tae the trees, and guarded in shifts, sitting in an open tent door, with Haggis sitting beside us, while the rest slept. While guardin' it was difficult tae stay awake with the rhythmic tappin' of the rain and the comfortin' sounds of sleep in the tents around us.

Sound was dampened and twas impossible tae hear beyond our camp and was doubtful someone would be out in this rain in this century, but we guarded anyway just in case.

Fraoch groaned. "Och nae, tis morn and tis still rainin'?"

I joked, "Everything from Scotland is intractable and determined. If it haena stopped in a full day tis unlikely tae ever stop, this is the rule of Scottish weather."

We ate a meal of rations. I asked, "What do ye think they are eating at home?"

Fraoch said, "Ye must play this game every time, Og Maggy, daena it dismay ye?" He took a scowling bite of his breakfast bar.

"In thinkin' on what they are eatin' I feel connected tae them. I am often far away, centuries away, yet if I consider what food m'travels hae provided for them I feel at peace with it. Tae feed yer sons is the most important part of our journey ye ken."

Fraoch said, "I ken, even when I daena hae a son, as a man I ken tis m'duty tae feed our descendants, I will help feed the sons of m'brother."

"M'uncle Baldie had a similar view, he dinna hae his own son, so he fostered Sean, he protected me, his care and attention made a profound impression on us. He always made sure we were fed. This is why I am always considering what they are eatin' back home."

Lochie said, "The bairns are eatin' from the box of… what dost they call it, the flakes?"

"Cereal."

"Aye, I ken they are eatin' cereal. Chef Zach is grumblin' about it."

Fraoch said, "He has probably made enough pancakes for all of us and yet nae one is eatin' them. He is cursin' everyone."

I said, "Dost ye think he whipped the cream for the top? Has he chopped walnuts tae sprinkle upon the stack?"

James said, "Definitely."

Fraoch and Lochinvar nodded.

I popped the last bit of rations in my mouth and chewed. "Good, tis good tae hae the bairns well-provided for. Are we ready tae ride?"

We mounted our horses and rode them on the trail through the woods, Haggis running alongside us.

We came tae the causeway, just after dawn, in a torrential downpour in time tae see the crumble of more stone and feel the rumble as it slid from the wall.

James said, "Rain isn't usually enough to break stone."

I glowered. "The walls hae lost their strength. The lightnin' strikes broke them, now the rain is erodin' them." I shifted in my saddle to look ahead and behind us. "...much like a river bank erodes, except a river bank is worn naturally, embankments and cliffs formed, there is a positive — nae, this erosion is caused by the unnatural storms of time travel. Tis enough tae wear down stone castles, break down men."

Fraoch said, "Ye are in a dour mood, Og Maggy, tis the rain? Is this why ye are so glum?"

"Aye, I am feeling the downpour heavily upon m'soul, how can ye see this broken castle and not feel a desperate sadness for the loss? There was once a time when it ruled over these lands."

James said, "Remember on my wedding day when we shot off fireworks, sitting out here on the grass?"

I said, "Aye, I remember it well."

James pointed. "I think the wall where we kept track of our arguments is still standing. We have a few notches to add."

Fraoch said, "Heads up, guards comin'."

A train of carts and horses, bundled high with bags and goods rode from the castle gate, past the rubble of a fallen wall tae meet us at the beginning of the causeway.

We slowed tae speak tae the three guards at the head, Haggis barking, our horses stamping impatiently as the men ordered us tae explain ourselves. I made Haggis sit and be quiet.

Fraoch explained. "We are here tae see the laird."

One of the guardsmen answered, "He is gone, as are most of the former inhabitants. Ye daena hae any reason tae continue on."

"The castle is emptied, because of the damage? We thought tae seek shelter."

"Aye, tis empty, turn around and—"

The sky broke open, the rain, problematic before, dumped even harder upon us.

The guardsman waved his arm, gesturing for the train of supplies tae continue on.

I yelled, "We need tae rest our horses! We need shelter afore we can make the journey tae the village!"

He yelled back, "Suit yerself!" and kept going down the causeway.

More of the wall crumbled, stone rolled down the pile, a river of mud and dirt streamed away, rocks and stones rolled down the incline around the base of the castle.

Fraoch led the way tae the gates with Lochie, then James, then myself with Haggis following. We passed a few last men as they carried the final loads from the castle courtyard, and entered the gate that had been left wide open.

We brought our horses tae a standstill in the center of the courtyard.

Fraoch said, "Where dost we begin tae look?"

I said, "I sometimes kept them in the dungeons."

James said, "I'll go!" He dismounted, grabbed his flashlight, unholstered his gun, and hustled away through the rain.

I said tae Fraoch and Lochinvar, "The vessels daena usually activate if they are underground though — twould be unlikely for it tae be in the dungeon."

Fraoch said, as we watched James disappear down the stair. "We ought tae stop him…?"

"Nae, he is too excited, we hae tae allow him tae look."

I looked up at the crumbling wall. "That is where my private office was, and my chamber. Tis now exposed tae the air, dost ye see, Fraoch?"

"Aye."

"Perhaps we hid a vessel there in the walls and now tis activatin'?"

"Dost ye remember hidin' a vessel within the walls?"

"Nae, but one thing I hae learned in time travel, memories can be changin'."

We dismounted our horses.

Lochinvar said, "We are all goin' tae go?"

"Nae, ye wait here, guard the horses, and tell James when he returns we are up on the third floor.

Fraoch and I took the steps at the farthest corner from the crumbling wall. Then we walked warily down the passageways tae my auld chamber. The door was standing wide.

Half the roof was gone. Dust and rock covered the bed. Rain poured down on the furniture. I winced. "Och nae. I daena like tae lose this place."

Fraoch clapped me on the back, entered, and stepped through the door tae the back room that had once been my office.

He called out, "What about this wall here, was there an opening?"

I had been standing, dumbfounded, looking upon the room where wee Isla and young Archie had once lived — their tousled heads at the end of the warm blankets in their beds near the hearth. A vision of Kaitlyn in her chemise, walking barefoot across the room. I shook my head of the memories. "Aye, Fraoch, there was a floorboard loose, we kept some of our keepsakes there, hold on."

I went intae my old office, dragged a chair aside, and using a dirk, pried up a loose board. Underneath was a pile of coins, a stack of cash, some jewelry, and a small velvet sack. I loosened the string at the top tae reveal a vessel. "We found it."

I pulled the monitor from m'pocket and checked. This was the vessel we had been searching for.

James entered the room. "You found it? Another one? We found three so far in one trip?"

"Aye, three vessels tae add tae the collection. With nae drama."

James said, "Great, because I want to get out of this rain, but wait, I want to add to the score on the wall!" He rushed away.

I filled my bag with the things I found in the hole under the floorboards. And Fraoch and I followed him up to the parapet on the walls.

CHAPTER 14 - MAGNUS

THE WALLS FELL

*J*ames had his dirk out and was scraping it up and down against the stone at the spot where we all used tae stand on guard duty.

Fraoch said, "Ye are goin' tae ruin yer blade."

"It will be worth it. We had another argument the other day and Magnus was the winner, we always mark the point on the stone: it's continuity, it's tradition. I'm adding the point."

I stood near him, watching as he etched a groove under the M in our row of initials etched in the stone, lasting for decades.

F, Z, Q, J, M

Right where we had stood and argued and bantered and competed, for long hours every day and night.

Another deluge of rain.

James looked at the work.

Fraoch said, "So count up the points, who is winnin'?"

James said, "It doesn't matter, what matters is that it's up-to-date. I can't stand that it's left without marking the wins and losses." James pulled out his phone and took a photo of the stone.

I said, "We could take the stone with us."

He said, "Holy shit, that's a good idea!"

He used his dirk to try to pry the stone up from the wall, the point of the blade breaking off.

Fraoch said, "Told ye."

"Damn, all the walls over there are crumbling down and this one is too sturdy to let go of one memento stone."

There was a loud low rumble. The walls around us shimmied. The walls on the other side crashed and crumbled, stone spilled down into the courtyard.

"We gotta get off the—"

There was a loud, terribly loud, shrieking, horse scream.

I rushed tae look over the stone down on the courtyard tae see Sunny, covered in rubble except for his head — he was craning his desperate head.

"Och nae!" I ran tae the stairwell and tore down the stair, chargin' intae the courtyard. Sunny was half-covered in stone. "Nae nae nae!" Sunny was struggling to get out, his screams echoing around us, in m'head. I threw hunks of stone aside, attemptin' tae uncover him — a rivulet of blood streamin' near my boot, joining the mud of the courtyard.

Lochinvar, Fraoch, and James were all helping me toss rubble aside. Haggis barked wildly. I was frantic, shovin' stone clear, as more rock slid down — lifting and tossing rubble tae the side — a glimpse of his right front leg, kick, free, then still. I threw two more large stones off and away as he stopped screaming, his eyes wild, he lay down his head. "Nae! Nae!"

I dropped tae my knees beside his head and held on. While the others kept tossin' rubble aside tae clear him, I felt the life drain from him.

Nae.

The rain poured down upon us. Haggis whimpered beside me.

I held Sunny's head, cradlin' him.

Fraoch finally said, "Og Maggy, I am worried on where ye are sittin', if there is another fall the stones will bury ye."

I put Sunny's head down and slowly stood, my chest heaving

with my gaspin' breath. I had lost m'horse. He had been with me for years and I had lost him tae a fallin' castle wall.

I tried tae get on top of my m'pain and fury — this had begun so simple, with such ease, and despite the downpour we had been in good humor. Then it had all gone so wrong. I had sacrificed Sunny while searching for a treasure, while notchin' the wall for past arguments.

I had been thinking on the past without considerin' the dangers of the present

I looked at Lochie, standing with his head down, and a rage built inside. I charged him, pushing his chest. "Ye were supposed tae guard him! Where were ye!"

"I went tae the gate! I was lookin' out!"

"I told ye tae guard the horses!"

"I dinna ken that's what ye meant, I just stepped away tae make sure nae one was coming and—"

I shoved his chest again. He stumbled over a rock and fell back, I stood over him with my arm raised about tae rain blows upon him tae match the rain pouring down from the sky, but then Fraoch's arms locked around me.

"Nae!" I struggled tae free myself.

"I winna let ye go, Og Maggy. Ye canna beat Lochie, he dinna ken, he was guardin'. He dinna ken the wall would come down on Sunny, he dinna ken, ye canna, I winna let ye."

James helped Lochie up tae his feet. My fury was so high that I couldna calm myself.

I struggled tae be freed, but Fraoch wrenched my arms tight behind me, then wrestled me down to one knee, his elbow around my neck. "Og Maggy, ye need tae calm yer arse down."

"He was supposed tae guard the horses!"

"From the walls? The other horses got away, Sunny dinna get away in time — twas an accident. Ye canna blame Lochie. If he had been standing here when the rocks fell, he might hae been buried along with Sunny. Ye canna blame him for somethin' that might hae happened tae any of us."

I stopped struggling and collapsed down tae the mud.

Fraoch stood over me.

"Ye canna blame him, Og Maggy."

I nodded and wiped my face of the rain and tears there. "I ken." I put my arms around my head, pressed tae my knees. "I ken."

After a few moments I put out my hand and Fraoch hoisted me up.

Lochinvar said, "I am sorry I stepped away, Yer Majesty, if I could do it all over I would hae never left yer horse's side."

"I ken," I repeated, glancing over tae the horse, still under the pile.

James lifted a stone and carried it to Sunny's body. "We ought to bury him."

"Aye," I wiped my face again, and we began the heartrendin' work of putting heavy stones upon the lifeless body of my horse, Sunny, a fellow time-traveler, who had once been a steady friend.

I prayed as I worked.

The men went ahead on their horses, and I walked with Haggis at my side, down the causeway tae the shore. The rain dampened all sound except for the rage rolling through my head, presenting like a roar, a thunder rumbling.

There wasna a soul around so we set the vessel there on the shore, without talking, the storm building above us, makin' the sky dark, the land around us drab and gray — my heart worn and sad.

I woke in the sand of Florida and quietly looked up at the bright blue sky. I pulled myself up, slowly, my heart poundin', the roar filling my mind, but then Kaitlyn's voice reached me, "Magnus, where's Sunny?"

I shook my head.

She said, "Oh no!" and dropped tae her knees beside me, her arms around my shoulders.

I clung tae her as tears flowed forth. "Och nae, he is gone."

I was grateful she dinna speak on it. I had nae words, just grief.

Quentin and James led the other horses away, they took the gear and the truck tae the house.

Haggis sat with his head on my lap, as if he understood how m'heart felt, then after a time I stood up. Kaitlyn and I held hands and walked home with Haggis beside us.

On the way she asked, "How did it happen?"

"The walls of Kilchurn fell." I exhaled. "I am without m'horse — och nae, it feels like a bad omen."

CHAPTER 15 - KAITLYN

2024 - FLORIDA, ELEVEN VESSELS

I watched out the glass door. Magnus was sitting on a deck chair, staring out over the beach. Haggis hadn't left his side in hours. They looked stoic. I knew Magnus felt emotional, but I knew that talking about Sunny made him break — he didn't want to break.

Isla padded out down the walkway to sit beside him and hold his hand. Then she came back a while later and Archie went out. First, he ran up and down the boardwalk with Haggis, Magnus laughing at their antics, I knew then that he was feeling a bit better.

I carried Jack down, put him in Magnus's arms so that I could get something done. Magnus knew that excuse was bullshit. But he sat out there having a private discussion with Jack. I assumed he was explaining to him about how the world worked, love and life and growing old, and what it was like to have the strong walls crumble and to lose a friend you had loved…

~

A while later Magnus entered the house. He had a smile plastered on his face, though his eyes belied his grief. He passed Jack to me and sat down at the kitchen bar where everyone was gathered, "I suppose ye heard the tale?"

Everyone said a version of, "Yep."

"We found three lost vessels. We were responsible for the walls of Kilchurn falling. The last final blow." Chef Zach passed him a beer, Magnus held his bottle up.

"Kilchurn's bound to be a ruin now, and there lie the remains of a great and powerful horse on the grounds of the courtyard where he once proudly lived. Twas a majestic castle, strong enough tae protect generations of Campbells from the First Colin tae the last Duke of Awe, from a wonderful Uncle Baldie, tae the laughs of wee Isla as she was swung on a swing in the courtyard, her laughter ringing through the cold crisp air of a long winter — in the year 1760 shite fell apart."

He smiled. "We hae tae remember tae revisit her long afore that year. Slàinte!"

We all said, "Slàinte!"

"Do you want to talk about Sunny?" I asked.

"Nae, I think when we used tae ride twas one of the best things about him, he was quiet. He allowed me tae think. He was a grand horse, and he will be missed, and I winna miss him with words, but with quiet thoughts as he would hae respected. But Isla said something verra grand taeday out on the deck, she looked out on the horizon, looking much like her mother, and she said... what did ye say, Isla?"

Isla said, "I said, 'He was a damn good horse, Da, I'm going to miss riding him.'"

We all said, "Hear hear!" and drank. I kissed his shoulder.

Then Quentin dipped a chip into salsa. "The small, very overshadowed, good news is we got some of the missing vessels back."

"Now we hae eleven for the vault."

James said, "There was one odd thing — a weather guy here told me about a storm out on the moor south of Kilchurn, but when we went to look there was nothing."

"Do you think someone else found it first?"

Magnus said, "Could be, in a different time, the monitor never logged it."

James nodded. "It was probably picked up in another time, or it was not a known vessel. Could the monitor only see *these* twenty-six? Maybe it can't see other ones if they exist."

Quentin said, "How would that work though? If all the vessels came at the same time, the monitor would see all of them right?"

James said, "Cloaking device."

Quentin pointed at him and nodded.

Zach said, "Maybe there are other vessels, maybe they're cloaked, maybe they're part of a search party for the first, this is *all* speculation, but it reminds me of the Dark Forest Hypothesis."

James said, "Remind me?"

"That people living in a dark forest might stay quiet and paranoid of intruders. It's used to explain why we haven't seen space aliens — perhaps other planets remain cloaked and invisible because they don't know what kind of violence an interaction might—"

"How does this apply?"

"Perhaps there are other time travelers on the timeline just in different places, different times, maybe we catch glimpses, but they know it's best not to cross paths."

Fraoch said, "That makes sense, but also means our timeline inna stable."

Magnus said, "Aye, I much prefer bein' alone on the timeline."

Lochie chuckled.

"What?"

"Ye always hae the word 'timeline' in yer mind. Tis a wheel! I say it all the time, but in this case ye ought tae ken, if ye hae a line and they are parallel, ye might never see the other line, but if there are time *wheels*, ye are likely tae loop across and spin around each other."

Magnus said, "I daena like one word of it, Lochie, this is why I am not thinking on it like that. Tis troubling. We ken not tae loop, what if the other group daena ken not tae loop?"

Quentin said, "What if the wheel falls off the truck and goes careening down the ravine, Lochie?"

Lochie put the beer bottle to his lips. "Och nae, that would suck." He drank. "Daena listen tae me on it, just tell me where I ought tae be with m'sword drawn."

Magnus said, "We don't need to fight right now, we just need to pick up the vessels we ken about. Kaitlyn, if yer list shows which vessels are still missing, dost ye hae any ideas where we ought tae look?"

I spread the copied pages from Johnne Cambell's book out on the counter and pointed. "This vessel has the letter J beside it, I think we gave it to James at one time and it's unaccounted for."

James put out his hands. "A preemptive apology for *all* I might have done, though I don't remember exactly what it was."

Magnus nodded. "It does seem likely that there will be some near Dunscaith Castle on the Isle of Skye. We ought tae go there. Ormr and Domnall lived in the area, I am sure we will find at least one."

Quentin said, "Good idea, same plan? Four go, set the remote activator, you casually pick up three vessels, easy peasy?"

Magnus said, "Aye, we hope twill be that easy, but I will need another horse first."

I said, "You could ride Osna?"

"Nae, Osna is yer horse, I will need m'own."

"What about Cynric?"

"Cynric and Hurley are in Riaghalbane and I would prefer a younger horse. Besides I hae promised them a life of leisure after keeping us alive in the sixteenth century. I daena want tae go back on m'word." Magnus looked thoughtful, "I hae a breedin' program at Riaghalbane, I will go and pick out a new horse, a descendant of Sunny might be good… of course it means I will hae tae see m'mother."

I grinned. "Lucky me, I need to stay here with Jack, you'll have to go visit your mommy without me."

He asked, "Who else wants tae go?"

Quentin said, "If you're going on a mission that involves the future, I should go, I'm a Colonel, not that I can do anything more than you can as king, but I can't let those old fart generals forget about me."

Magnus said, "So this time we leave James here at the house, overseein' the guards."

James said, "Yep, I got the homestead."

Lochinvar said, "I will go, I'm always up to go visit the old broad, she's a fine wit."

Zach said, "She's an agent of chaos is what she is."

James said, "An edge lord, always gotta be doing the opposite of what is expected."

Magnus said, "Except when she saves m'life."

"Aye," Fraoch said, "When she swoops in and saves our lives, and dances upon the graves of her enemies — she is a verra interesting character."

Hayley rolled her eyes. "She is the worst."

Fraoch said, "Careful, m'bean ghlan. Ye are liable tae bring the fates down upon ye, or the dark fae wantin' tae cause ye suffering. If ye consider her the worst of everything then the fae are sure tae put her in yer path — what if ye get stuck somewhere with her?"

Hayley shivered. "Ugh, you take that back."

Magnus said, "I am going tae drive the big kids, meanin' all the bairns who can hold a spoon, tae the ice cream shop."

The kids all started cheering. "I can hold one!"

Isla felt it was important to rush to the kitchen, grab a spoon, and say, "See, Da? Me!"

Magnus said, "Looks like I hae four in the car with me."

Zach said, "But what about the meal? I have ice cream here and—"

Magnus grabbed his keys. "I am going tae drive the kids tae get ice cream, anyone want tae come?"

Zach laughed and grabbed a big mixing spoon. "Who can argue against that? I'm bringing my own spoon, Isla!"

The kids got into the truck with Magnus. Zach, Quentin, Beaty, and Lochie followed in another truck. The rest of us stayed home with the babies, relaxing in the quiet house.

CHAPTER 16 - KAITLYN

FRAOCH EXPLAINS THE FISH CONSPIRACY

A little while later the front door opened and Magnus came in, the look on his face, bemused, but pretending to be sad. He was ushering in Isla, who was absolutely sopping wet and frowning, deeply.

I said, "What's up, Isla?"

Isla who had been crying but obviously waiting to get home to really wail, began to really wail.

"Oh my, what happened?"

Magnus said, "We were orderin' the ice cream when there was a splash and a shriek and somehow…" he bit his lips to keep from laughing.

Beaty said, "Wee Isla was swimmin' in the koi pond in front of the shop."

Isla started to really really wail.

I bit my lips too.

Zach held up a bag. "We had to get it all to go."

Fraoch said, "Isla! Ye were fishin' like a bear? Did ye catch any?" He lumbered around pretending to be a bear picking up fish.

She stopped wailing and shook her head.

Magnus said, "The fish were verra large. I daena ken if she could pick them up herself."

Fraoch said, "How large were the fish ye almost caught, Isla-bear?"

She put her hands out.

He said, "So large! I need tae go get m'pole and ye can show me where we can go catch this big—"

Ben said, "Uncle Fraoch, you can't!"

Zoe giggled.

Fraoch said, teasingly, "Why nae? Isla has gone fishin' and come home empty-handed, if we daena catch the fish they will think they hae won, and ye ken what happens then!"

Archie said, "Uncle Fraoch, it's a *pond*, it's not for fishing, the fish are pets."

"Pets! Och nae, they will be lording it over us."

Hayley laughed, "Who, the fish?"

"Aye, the fish!" He tapped his head, conspiratorial at Isla. "Ye ken, Isla, the *fish*."

Hayley said, "What happens if the fish think they won?"

"They want tae rule the world, Isla kens, she was in the water with them, she kens."

She opened her eyes wide. "I think the fish pulled me in."

"See? And they ruined a good ice cream trip. The fish are wantin' tae rule the world, Isla, and they would except for one thing."

She put her hands up so he picked her up though she was sopping wet. "What is that, Uncle Fraoch?"

"They taste good and they are not verra smart."

She giggled.

He said, "We need tae find ye a towel."

And they wandered off. Magnus jokingly said, "Phew, remind me we need Uncle Frookie tae go with us next time, tae guard against the fish."

I said, "How on earth did she fall in?"

Magnus said, "She was just standing there and next thing we ken, phloop! She was in the water."

Lochinvar said, "It was just like the fish pulled her in."

The ice cream group sat at the dining room table and ate their ice cream talking about the excitement of the trip, with Isla, center of attention, wrapped in a towel on Fraoch's lap, shivering from the ice cream, telling the story about how she had valiantly survived.

The next morning I lay, nursing Jack, surrounded by blankets and pillows, watching as Magnus got ready for his trip. He showered, and then wearing his tighty-whities, brushed his teeth, then stood in front of his closet choosing his clothes, giving me a lovely view of his form, mostly undressed. I lay there admiring his epic hotness.

He pulled his clothes out, noticed me watching and grinned as he brought them to the bed. "Ye liked that?"

"Oooo boy do I like that ass."

He chuckled. "Ye are objectifying me."

"True, but I do love you, the whole you, so much, I think you can let me dream about your hotness now and again."

He leaned over and kissed my cheek, then kissed Jack's forehead and then raised up and looked down at his clothes laid out on the bed.

"Ye ken, I could hae dressed in private, I came out here so ye would pay yer compliments, get ye randy afore I go, so ye will miss me while I am gone."

"I will miss you, three days?"

"Aye, three days."

He pulled on his pants, buttoned the top. Then pulled on the white dress shirt, buttoning up the front, smoothly tucking it in. His eyes met mine, and his brow went up, teasingly as he did. His dark hair wet and tousled, his whole manner making me really hot for him. He pulled on his dark uniform coat, the one that fit really well, accenting his wide shoulders. I said, "I am going to miss you so so so much."

He leaned over the bed and kissed me again and said, "See, it worked," and left the room.

After breakfast, he, Fraoch, Lochinvar and Quentin, went to the beach to go to his kingdom.

CHAPTER 17 - MAGNUS

2390 - RIAGHALBANE

*W*e arrived on the rooftop reserved for jumps. I was greeted by one of my commanders, was allowed a good time tae recover, was offered tae go tae the infirmary for care if needed, and then we were all escorted tae m'mother's offices.

She was well dressed, her hair and makeup perfect, though underneath ye could see her age, she had grown even aulder by the looks of it. She greeted us warmly, and asked me tae sit down, providing me with a good chair. Colonel Quentin, Fraoch, and Lochie sat on the couch behind me.

I said, "Ye ought tae be brought tae sit in front of my desk. As the king, this should happen in my offices."

"True." She raised her chin. "But my office is verra nice, newly decorated, and ye ken, Magnus, I am running the kingdom for ye, at great cost tae my own life." She sighed dramatically but then smiled. Her eyes went to a frame standing on the corner of her desk.

I said, "What is with this good humor, ye are practically giddy!" I picked up the frame, and gazed down on a photo of my mother dressed in a gown, appearing verra royal. Beside her stood a man, wearing a tuxedo, and he was, there was nae way tae think it politely, *portly*. "Who's this then?"

She leaned across the desk and pulled the frame from my hand. "This is John Bettelmen. He is a businessman, he sells his own—"

"He has been vetted? Hae there been background checks?"

"Aye, of course, he is from a long line, the Bettelmens, he is verra—"

My eyes went wide. "The *Bettel*mens? Ye mean the family with the orchards? He is a farmer?"

She sighed. "Aye, they make a delicious cider, hae ye tasted it…?"

"Nae, I haena tasted their cider, I daena like it on principle as it inna whisky."

She dusted off the top of the frame. "He is verra kind tae me, he adores me."

"This is how ye are judging a man? He seems young."

"Not so young, he is about forty-two."

"Will he become traitorous? He inna connected tae our family is he? He inna going tae try tae claim the throne?"

"Of course not, he is a man of simple tastes and needs—"

"Yet he has somehow taken up with the mother of a king?"

"He makes me laugh, Magnus, I deserve it! Daena I deserve tae laugh?" She turned tae Fraoch. "Daena I deserve tae laugh, Fraoch?"

He said, "Aye, Lady Mairead, tis long overdue."

"See, Magnus, yer half — I mean yer brother, Fraoch, agrees."

I raised my brow. "Aye, ye deserve tae laugh. I dinna ken ye knew how, but ye deserve tae. What does John Bettelmen ken of time travel?"

"Nothing, as I am grounded here, and expected tae serve yer needs only, and not hae a life of my own—"

I said, "Och, ye are driving this point through m'chest. Dost ye want me tae relieve ye of yer duty?"

"Nae, tis nae necessary, I do rather like being in charge of the kingdom. I am content, so nae, I hae not told him of the time travel. He has heard of it, but he thinks tis a conspiracy theory." She waved her hand. "I will keep it that way. Now why are ye here?"

I opened the sack of vessels and poured them out on the desk. "I found three of the missing vessels, I brought them, along with the Bridge, tae put in the vault."

"Excellent, that makes us all a bit safer."

"We need tae make sure the vault is secure and I need Thomas tae look intae who has access."

"We hae taken all precautions, but will do it again."

"We canna be too cautious." I exhaled. "And... Sunny died."

She said, "Och nae, Magnus, Sunny?"

"Aye."

"I am terribly sorry tae hear it, he was with ye for verra long years."

I nodded, overcome, unable tae speak. "I am here tae pick a horse from the stables."

She nodded. "And are ye well?"

"I am well enough, losin' Sunny weighs heavily upon me."

"I can see."

"I went tae Kilchurn in the year 1760 and the storm caused the walls tae collapse, and..." I looked at the far wall behind her, a painting of a pastoral scene, and blinked. "The walls crushed him."

She winced. "Och, there is a metaphor there I daena like." She cocked her head. "Ye hae witnessed what I try my best tae not see, the passage of time. Tis easy tae protect ourselves from witnessin' it, we jump in and out of days, ignoring what most live through — though if ye think on it, most daena perceive the march of time, it escapes knowing. But for us, we can waltz in and out, and do our best tae miss the idea of age altogether, such as with my Picasso, I kent him when he was young." She tapped her pen on the desk. "I kent he would grow tae be auld, so I chose tae never see him again. I missed it, I dinna see it. I can remember him as I kent him, young and handsome and so verra *capable* with his hands."

I groaned.

"Grow up, Magnus, yer mother took Picasso as a lover. He painted her form in his art, ye ought tae ken, twas my body who inspired his blue period." She raised her chin. "The history of the modern world, Picasso, the greatest artist of the twentieth century, and I was his inspiration. He was sexy, but what does that make me? The *sexiest*."

I said, "Dear God."

Fraoch and Quentin laughed.

Lochinvar said, "I always say ye are verra sexy, Lady Mairead, even at yer age."

She blushed. "Why thank ye, Lochinvar, ye ought tae consider moving here tae the kingdom once ye tire of Florida, I am sure I can put ye tae some important use."

I looked over my shoulder tae see him wink at her.

I said, "Forgettin' this unseemly conversation, we were speaking on something else?"

"Aye, on the passage of time, losing the years, seeing time pass — it can break your heart, I recommend doing your best tae not see the signs of it."

"I will do m'best. This last visit tae Kilchurn greatly unsettled me."

Fraoch said, "Unsettled the walls too."

"Aye."

Lady Mairead said, "Fraoch, ye are well?"

"Aye."

"Colonel Quentin, how is yer bairn?"

"He is very well, Lady Mairead, he and Beaty are happy and healthy."

"And Lochinvar, ye are well?"

"Aye, Lady Mairead, verra well."

"The climate of Florida is treating ye well?"

"Nae, tis overly hot, and I must slather the white paste all over m'body every morn, but tis worth it for the food."

She said, "We hae all the best food here as well."

I said, "Not the way Chef Zach makes it."

Her eyes went far away and wistful. "He does make the best marmalade sandwich I hae ever tasted, he is all ye could want in a chef."

CHAPTER 18 - MAGNUS

TRY TAE BE A GOOD SON

fter our meeting, I stood tae go, and Lady Mairead said, "We will hae a simple meal this evening, just family, and of course Quentin and Lochinvar, and I will invite JB. Please make *sure* ye are all dressed appropriately, well-dressed, bathed, and civilized, especially ye Magnus as ye will be meeting him for the first time."

I chuckled. "I, the king, Magnus the First, will be meeting *him*?"

"Ye ken what I mean, Magnus, this is important to me."

"Aye, ye want tae spend the rest of yer days gigglin' with a gentleman farmer."

She said, "While ruling the kingdom in your absence, aye, I would like tae also hae some pleasantness tae my days."

I held my hands out, "I ken, I am only teasing, I will dress well, and be on m'best behavior like a good son."

"That's all I ask is that ye, for once, try tae be a good son."

Fraoch, Quentin, and Lochinvar followed me to the door, bowing and taking their leave.

. . .

Colonel Quentin left m'side tae go tae the war room tae meet with the generals, while my guardsmen followed us down to the stables. The head horseman there, Sanders, showed me around the corral. Fraoch asked, "How many horses are here?"

Sanders said, "Near a hundred."

Fraoch rubbed his hands together. "This is going to be fun."

I dinna agree, it pulled at m'heart tae replace Sunny, and so soon, but I needed a horse for the coming journeys.

Sanders led us down the stables introducin' horses by name and breed. I met with Cynric and Hurley and was reminded of their age — they had a good life here, I wouldna take either of them from it.

Some of the horses Sanders showed me were verra fine, I considered them, until I was taken down the middle walkway tae see three horses that had been sired by Sunny. One, named Dràgon, I had ridden before. He was tall, broad, strong and fast. Sunny had been chestnut-colored, this horse was a fine deep black. He rippled with energy.

I stepped tae his stall. He put out his muzzle and nudged my shoulder with his nose. "How are ye doin', boy?"

He whinnied, low, and then jerked his head back. "Ye want tae ride?"

His nose brushed my cheek.

I entered the pen and brushed down the side of his head, runnin' my hands along his neck. "I hae two jobs for ye, verra important jobs — ye will need tae attend me on m'work and twill be dangerous, would ye be willin'?"

Dràgon stomped a hoof.

I rubbed a hand down his withers. "Ye are verra tall and strong, on yer days off from the dangerous work, ye will need tae carry bairns, would ye be gentle enough?"

His nose went against my cheek.

"Verra good boy." I pressed m'forehead tae his, his head bowed for a moment. Then I said, "Aye, we are decided."

Fraoch said, "Och nae, Og Maggy, ye are decided after

lookin' at ten horses? We were goin' tae spend the whole afternoon!"

I shrugged, "When ye meet yer horse, tis easy tae decide."

Sanders said, "Sire, I was going to introduce you to the thoroughbreds and the Arabians and—"

"Tis nae necessary, but if Fraoch and Lochie want tae look they may. I am decided."

Fraoch said, "Hae ye ridden him yet?"

"Aye, a few times, but never with the idea that he would be mine. I ought tae ride him now, I think."

Sanders said, "I will have him saddled for you, Your Majesty."

"Nae, I will saddle him while ye continue the tour for Lochinvar and Fraoch."

Sanders continued on the tour of the stables, saying, "Over here we have the Mustangs, these are..." as they walked down the aisle between the stalls and I saddled up Dràgon and went out for a ride.

We rode out upon the grounds of the castle. Dràgon followed my movements well, and seemed eager tae listen. He was bound up energy, explosive power when I urged him tae go, and was difficult tae rein in. We practiced over and over, demanding that he charge, pulling him short, until at my command he would stop, stamping irritatedly, but in one spot, his will deferin' tae mine.

I rode him back toward the stables, where Fraoch and Lochie leaned on the fence. "What dost ye think, Fraoch, did I pick well?"

"Aye, I see why ye like him, he has the look of Sunny, with the power of a young horse. He will be a favorable horse for ye."

"Thank ye, Fraoch, I am glad ye agree. Lochie, did ye pick out a horse?"

"Nae, I get tae pick a horse?"

"Aye, but it must be smaller than mine."

Fraoch said, "And mine."

CHAPTER 19 - MAGNUS

2390 - DINNER

*W*e entered the dining room where Lady Mairead was dressed in a long dress with a formal air about her. I said, "Ye are overly dressed for a 'family' dinner."

She rubbed her hands across my shoulder. "I wanted tae look nice." She glanced at Colonel Quentin, Fraoch, and Lochie. "Ye gentlemen look verra fine, thank ye for heeding my request."

Fraoch smirked.

Lochie looked uncomfortable in his suit. He had complained about wearing it, and I had had tae threaten him. Twas my request, not hers, that had brought them well-dressed.

John Bettelmen was announced and led intae the room by my butler.

Lady Mairead warmly greeted him with a hug. He kissed her on both cheeks. He was short, rounded, winded from the walk tae the dining room, and looked appropriately nervous, and yet, carried a good humor. He looked tae be about ten years aulder than Sean, so twas the first time Lady Mairead was in a relationship that was almost, as Kaitlyn would say, age appropriate.

I was introduced and he bowed very deeply. "Your Majesty." He straightened and patted his forehead with a handkerchief. "I have never met the king before, pardon me if I'm but a lowly farmer. Please call me JB." He passed me a bottle. "From my best crop. Rose apple cider." The label read: 'the Royal Riaghalbane Rose Cider.' The year stamped on it. A plain cork.

"Thank ye kindly, JB."

He stopped short, gawking at Fraoch and Lochinvar. "My apologies for being rendered speechless, I recognize you both from the arena battle!"

Fraoch said, "Aye—"

"My father will never believe this! He was pulling for Lochinvar, but I was pulling for you, not politically of course, your Majesty, but just for the arena. We all, my whole family, our business, everyone, of course wanted Your Majesty to win the war. We are pleased with the outcome. Long live Magnus the First, all hail the power of Riaghalbane, Your Majesty." He bowed awkwardly again.

I placed the bottle of cider on the table and one of the waiters swooped it up to open it, and check it, as was protocol with every gift for the king.

Lady Mairead said, her voice soundin' overly merry, "We should sit, we hae quite a few courses to get through as this is a verra special evening."

JB pulled the chair at the head of the table out for Lady Mairead, who sat haughtily.

I said, "This is fine, Lady Mairead, ye may take the head of the table."

JB blushed. "My apologies, sire, I dinna realize, of course ye would take the head of the table, my sincerest—"

"Nae, JB, tis truly fine, I will sit here at the side, the better tae reach the dinner rolls."

JB laughed hard. "Oh! You are funny! Lady Mairead told me you were!"

He sat across from me. Fraoch, Quentin, and Lochie took their seats.

We were served the first course of cucumber soup.

JB said, "So Fraoch, you were on the side of the king all along?"

"Aye, I was playing on the other side." Fraoch buttered a roll. "I daena like tae think on it much, I was under the command of Ian for a long time, tis distressing—"

Lochinvar said, "Ye think twas distressin' because ye lost tae me."

JB's eyes went wide. "Wow this is amazing."

I said, "Careful, if ye give them attention, their bickerin' grows—"

Fraoch waved his butter knife as he spoke, "Daena mind the boy, he has tae hae his win acknowledged or he weeps like a bairn, daena ye, Og Lochie?"

"I daena weep, but I think I ought tae be given due respect for havin' won."

I said, "Och nae, here we go."

Fraoch said, "Even when I ceded the fight? This is the kind of win ye want tae crow about?"

Lochinvar said, "If twas yer win, ye would never let us think of anything else, but since I won ye are goin' tae act as if I am 'crowing'. I just think we ought tae acknowledge that I bested ye in the arena—"

"I was throwin' a warhammer at the king! How was I fightin' ye, when I was truly riddin' the kingdom of the usurping king?" Fraoch tossed down his napkin, "Och, ye hae turned me off my dinner roll and twas the perfect warmth. The butter was drippin' on it and now I am upset."

JB was open-mouthed watching them argue, his head moving back and forth from face to face.

I said, "Fraoch, ye may hae another roll, they are warm on the platter, and Lochinvar, ye did win, effortlessly, but ye won by watchin' Fraoch for signs, and though ye did technically cede the fight, Fraoch, ye might hae been killed by Lochie if not for him savin' yer life, so we ought not argue on it. Ye are both winners in my heart, now wheesht, so I can enjoy the dinner rolls." A server rushed up with a new tray of warmer rolls and pulled away the one we had been eating from.

Lady Mairead said, "Everyone needs tae hush, this is the kind of talk that will ruin a meal. Nae politics. Ye must ken, a war was fought, the king has won. Whatever the arena battle wrought, it succeeded in restoring the crown, this is the only important thing."

Lochie muttered, "That, and that I won."

Fraoch smeared butter on a new roll. "We ought tae talk of better things. I am wonderin' how did a farmer, such as yerself, meet the mother of the king?"

He blushed again. "As the son of one of the older families of the kingdom, I was invited to the ball. I considered it an honor, I tell you. Sadly, I am widowed, so I went without a dance partner, but I do love to dance. I was on the dance floor, Lady Mairead saw my dance moves, and she joined me."

She batted her eyes. "Ye did hae verra nice form."

Fraoch's eyes went wide, I thought he was going tae choke on his roll.

I poured some cider in my glass and took a sip.

JB asked, "What do you think, Your Majesty?"

I nodded. "Tis verra fine, I do like the taste of rose in it." I looked at the label, emblazoned with the word Royal and Riaghalbane. "So Lady Mairead approached ye?"

"She asked me if I wanted to dance, the floor cleared, I was terribly nervous, but—"

She swayed in her seat. "He put his arm around me. He spun me and dipped me back," she pantomimed dancing in her chair.

Quentin dropped his spoon, then mumbled his apologies.

Lady Mairead put her chin on her hand and looked at JB dreamily though his face was still flushed and there was a bit of sweat on his hairline from the exertion earlier. "He was verra romantic. He is a fine dancer, I enjoyed myself tremendously."

The servers brought out our main course, Beef Wellington,

one of Lady Mairead's favorites, and placed our plates in front of each of us.

Once we all began to eat I asked, "JB, are ye also a collector of art or...?"

"No, I am not much for art, but Mairead has shown me her collection."

I added, "But what dost ye talk about, ye and Lady Mairead?"

They looked at each other. He said, "What do we talk about, Mairead?"

"We talk about the best movies. I tell him about art. He tells me about apples. We converse, Magnus, as *anyone* does."

I glanced at Fraoch.

He shrugged.

I poured a bit more cider intae my glass. "I guess what I am wondering is... did ye seek out m'mother tae enrich yer business? It must bring ye a great deal of prestige tae be in a relationship with the mother of the king."

Lady Mairead said, "Magnus, it is not on ye tae get tae the bottom of anything, this is my relationship, ye are being rude tae my guest."

JB said, "Now, Mairead, it's fine, yer son is being very reasonable."

I said, "His *Majesty*. His Majesty is bein' verra reasonable."

He said, "I apologize, Your Majesty, I never met a royal before. Here is the truth, the most beautiful woman, the most prestigious woman, the mother of the king asked me to dance at a ball. It was... I almost fell on the floor right there, but somehow I managed to get up, started dancing, and so I dipped her, you know, back, over my arm, and she laughed, and I knew then that it would be my aspiration in life to make this beautiful woman laugh."

Lady Mairead patted the back of his hand, adoringly.

He continued, "This was all it was. Now, I understand there would be questions about my motivations, I tell you, I *know* —

when I got home that next morning I thought, oh, I have really stepped knee deep in the applesauce, as we say down at the orchard, with this relationship, the rumors will fly. People will of course suspect that I sought out the relationship with the Queen Mother to enrich my family. But anyone with any sense knows that Lady Mairead is discerning. She is not going to allow herself to be used—"

Lady Mairead said, with her chin up. "I give and I receive, I am never taken advantage of — on principle."

"Exactly!" He added, "The fact that I am eating in your dining room, Your Majesty, will be enough to drive business to my family for the next century, but also, if I end up on the wrong side of Lady Mairead's good graces, it could ruin my business, there is a risk." He shook his head. "But I was so intrigued by her that none of this dawned on me until later."

"But ye did think of it…?"

"Yes, but what kind of business man would I be if I *never* thought of it? Business before all else!" He and Lady Mairead raised their glasses and clinked them together.

Fraoch said, "This is verra true, ye hae tae see that a relationship with Lady Mairead will aggrandize ye."

I joked, "Some might say tis the only reason tae begin one."

She said, "Magnus, ye are teasing me."

I took the last sip of the cider, and said, "I am only teasin', Lady Mairead, and I appreciate yer honesty, JB."

There was music playing in the room, the shifting images on the walls projected natural scenes: shifting and bending, changing the light as they went from forest dark to a light beach scene, but the music had a beat that JB would dance to — shimmying his shoulders, bopping his head.

Lochinvar tilted his head, watchin' with a bemused expression.

Lady Mairead, astonishingly, dinna seem tae mind as he wriggled in his seat.

Fraoch started dancing in his seat as well.

JB nodded approvingly. "I tell you, Fraoch, if there is music, you must dance. That's how I stay fit." He laughed and patted his stomach.

"What else dost ye like tae do, JB, besides growin' apples?"

"I love to journal."

I said, "What is that exactly?"

"To keep a journal of my affairs, the history of the world, things I find interesting — I have a list of questions that I answer every night: What did I see that was interesting? What did I learn that was important? What was the news of the day? That's some of them, but these days it's about my daughter, Samantha, she's about the same age as your son, I think?"

"My son, Archibald? He's seven."

"Yes, Samantha is six years old, it's a wonderful age, they understand a great deal of the world."

I nodded. "Archie is a fine lad, I am verra proud of him. I hae another son, Jack, he is a few months old."

"Wonderful, I don't believe Jack's birth has been announced yet!" He leaned back in his chair, his fingers entwined on his plump stomach. His fingers tapping. "I will note it in my journal, it will be the first mention of it outside of your family."

I said, "I see that ye do hae something in common with Lady Mairead, she keeps her secrets locked in journals as well."

JB said, "Ah, but mine are not secrets, mine are simply the lowly documents of a gentleman farmer."

He danced in his seat some more.

Lady Mairead said, "Sometimes the lowly documents become the most useful. Ye never can tell, and... I have a gift for ye, JB." She slid a small wrapped gift toward him. It was simply wrapped with brown Kraft paper, tied with a red ribbon.

"A gift! Whatever could it be?"

He blushed up tae his damp hair.

Lady Mairead smiled and teased, "I would think the book shape, the size, and the fact that I mentioned it while ye were speaking on your journal might give ye an idea what tis."

He chuckled. "Yes, you got me, Mairead, but that was my exclamation of surprise more for the gift than what it is — it is definitely a book, is it my birthday?"

"Nae, I just wanted tae give ye something fine."

He tore intae the gift and pulled out a leather-bound book.

She said, "I had one of the world's best book-binders create the journal for ye, I hope ye like it. I was thinking ye could begin by recording the details of the evening."

"I love it, Mairead, what a glorious journal, I will—" His face lit up and he patted his pockets. "I happen to have a pen!"

He pulled a pen out of one of his interior pockets, opened the book, and flipped open the first page.

She said, "Ye could begin by recording the guests and perhaps asking them tae tell ye the names of their wives and bairns."

"Great idea, Mairead!" He wrote down the page as if he were writin' a list. "I listed your children, Your Majesty, how auld is Isla?"

I said, "She is three years old, the image of her mother."

"Just wonderful. I described the meal and… Colonel Quentin, do you have children?"

"My wife, Beaty and I have a son, named Noah. He's five months old."

"Wonderful!" He wrote and then turned the page and continued. "What of you, Fraoch?"

"I am married, tae Hayley, nae children."

I said, "He is a fine uncle."

"I dinna realize that Fraoch was yer brother, Your Majesty. That is truly wonderful."

"He is a son of Donnan, and… Lochinvar is as well."

He snapped his finger. "That's right! I remember now! Lochinvar, do you have a wife and children yet?"

Lochinvar groaned. "Nae, I am too busy being a hero."

Fraoch rolled his eyes and grunted.

JB wrote a bit longer, then placed the book back in the

wrapper and tied the bow around it, and tried tae force it intae his pocket, causin' it tae rip. It wouldna fit.

He said, "Well that was embarrassing, I feel as if everyone was watching me." He placed the gift down beside him on the table and tapped his fingers on it. "But there you have it, working the apple orchards and writing in my journals. These are the simple interests of a gentleman farmer."

I leaned forward, "What dost ye do taegether then? What does Lady Mairead *do* with a gentleman farmer who picks apples and writes in a journal?"

Lady Mairead said, "We talk! He tells me about his orchards, I tell him about art. I swear, ye are being insensible, Magnus."

JB said, "Mairead, would you like to dance?"

"At the family dinner?"

He got up and did a hip-shaking dance across the room headed toward the intercom connected tae the sound system. He said intae it, "Play the interludes by the Shakespeares." The projections changed from the soft glow of color and light tae videos of a band on a stage.

JB shook his hips dancing tae the table and put out a hand.

Lady Mairead put down her napkin and did a waltzing walk tae him, and they began tae dance taegether, swayin' and spin-nin' around each other. He would break away tae perform some fancy footwork toe-tapping business, then he would shake his hips and waltz back tae her and spin her again.

She laughed, enjoying it verra much. I, on the other hand, and the other men at the table were bemusedly discomfited.

He announced, "Everyone ought tae dance!"

I bit my tongue tae keep from laughing. "I think not."

We tried tae avert our eyes as Lady Mairead and JB gyrated together tae the modern music.

Finally, the song over, they collapsed intae their chairs in time for the dessert of small cakes.

JB was sweatin' profusely, his face beet red, he mopped at his brow with his dinner napkin, sayin', "I am so relieved ye liked the rose cider, Your Majesty," he breathed heavily, "phew, out of breath, I thought about making it with a bit of orange, but the rose flavor has a long royal history, I knew it might please you."

I said, "Tis verra good. I enjoyed it much more than I expected. Hae ye considered bottlin' some whisky?"

He shook his head. "You have a taste for whisky? I am not a fan of it much. It doesn't compare to cider, I think, which is the best of the drinks, light and crisp as an autumn day..."

Fraoch pulled a flask from the inside pocket of his coat and passed it tae me.

I swigged from it. "Now that is a verra fine whisky, which one...? Wait, daena tell me." I smacked my lips. "Och nae, tis The Macallan 15 from m'bar in Florida?"

Fraoch chuckled and held his finger tae his lips. "Wheesht, daena tell Og Maggy."

"I am Og Maggy." I took another sip. "Och, tis verra good. Ye ought not pour it in a flask for yer private use, but bring the whole bottle with ye tae dinner."

Lady Mairead said, "I agree, I hae whisky, Magnus and Fraoch, ye daena hae tae drink from a flask at the dinner table like barbarians!"

I gestured toward the waiter tae serve a round of whisky.

Lady Mairead continued, "Our finest whisky, perhaps the Highland Park single cask..."

CHAPTER 20 - MAGNUS

A FALSE PEACE SETTLED UPON THE KINGDOM

*A*fter dinner I went tae the rooftop with Fraoch and Lochie and Quentin. The sitting area, destroyed during the war, had once again been set up with lights. A bartender was in attendance tae serve our drinks. I got comfortable in m'seat and asked, "And what did ye think of JB?"

Fraoch sipped from his drink and started tae chuckle. "Och, he was a surprise, not at all what ye would think of for yer mother. He must hae some talents he inna mentionin'."

Lochie said, "He must be *full* of talents. I daena ken how tae say it politely… He must be verra good at playin' at the Hot Cockles."

Quentin laughed. "The Hot Cockles!"

Lochie said, "Aye, ye ken, the Bringin' the Cannon tae her Fortress, the Makin' Butter for her Market… ye ken." He giggled.

I had drunk a few too many, and started tae laugh m'self, but pulled it taegether. "Tis the mother of the king ye are speaking on."

Lochinvar said, "I am nae speaking on yer mother, but on the prowess of our new friend, JB, he must be verra fine at the plucking of apples from the tree."

I bit my lip. "Och nae, ye canna—"

Fraoch said, "He had a funny jig, he must make up for it with a verra large jag."

Quentin laughed so hard I thought he would fall from his chair.

Lochinvar said, "His form at Pully-Haw must be topnotch."

I said, "All of ye best wheesht on it."

Lochie said, "Aye, Yer Majesty, I just will close with sayin' he will bring Lady Mairead a great deal of happiness and comfort with his joustin' in her waning years."

I groaned. "Are ye finished?"

They all nodded. Fraoch raised his glass. "Tae yer mother, and her new friend. If they are havin' fun, let it be quiet enough for us tae not hear it through the walls."

We all raised our glasses and said, "Slainte!"

I shook my head. "After all these years of seeing her with kings and conquerors and world famous artists, he seems *unlikely.*"

Fraoch shrugged. "If ye think on it, he is the most likely — she is exhausted from the effort, so she is relaxing. JB seems harmless, he might be the most favorable thing she has ever done for herself." He added, with a chuckle, "And she has probably done him a lot."

We all laughed again, I finished my drink, and beckoned for another. "Did she seem aulder than ye remember?"

They all shook their heads. Fraoch said, "Ye are rememberin' it wrong. But I will stick up for her as she considers me family now — I finally won her over. Did ye hear it, Og Lochie, Lady Mairead said, 'twill be a family dinner, plus Quentin and Lochie' she included me in the family part."

Lochie scowled. "I heard her."

Quentin said, "Hayley is going to be pissed."

"Aye, but she'll be protected, how cruel can Lady Mairead be tae Hayley if she thinks I am like a son?"

Incredulously, I said, "Fraoch, did ye not see all that Lady Mairead has done tae Kaitlyn?"

He waved his hand and drunkenly laughed. "Och, I forgot. I must hae been lulled by her womanly charms."

I said, "Aye, ye forgot — ye canna lose yer skepticism where Lady Mairead is concerned, ye must always be on guard, and ye are forgetting something crucial about her, she never takes up with anyone without it havin' a reason. JB has a purpose, I just daena understand it yet—"

Quentin said, "She made a big deal about him writing in his journal, listing all of our names."

I nodded. "Aye, ye are right, Colonel Quentin. See Fraoch, ye hae tae be suspicious of all her actions, but especially when she has taken up with a farmer." I sipped from my whisky, "But enough of m'mother and her wiles and her men, we have accomplished what we came here for, a horse for me, tomorrow we will head home."

The men nodded.

Colonel Quentin looked out over the night view. "It's peaceful out here."

"Aye, there is still a great deal of reconstruction being done, but the castle and grounds are finished — and there is a peace settled upon the kingdom."

We sat up for a time watching the night grow long, then went tae our rooms tae sleep.

CHAPTER 21 - MAGNUS

OUR TIMELINE MIGHT HAE SHIFTED

*M*y chamberlain roused me awake in the middle of the night. "Your Majesty! Your mother bids you come to the command tower."

"Och nae, what is…?" I looked blearily around the room.

He switched on the light.

I sat up. "Is this the 'robe over my pajamas' sort of summoning, or the uniform…?"

He laid my uniform out on the bed.

"It is in the command tower, Your Majesty"

I dressed, and left my room, and took my private elevator tae the main floor where I was met with Colonel Quentin, Lochinvar, and Fraoch. There we crossed tae the elevator bank at the base of the command tower and took one of the main elevators tae the top floor.

We entered the main meeting room, the soldiers on night-guard saluting as I passed. This room had large windows and a fine view of the grounds, the river Tay, and the mountains beyond. In the distance we could see lightning, streaking down from a bank of clouds.

A storm.

Fraoch pointed in another direction, more lightning lit up dark storm clouds, it was unmistakable.

Quentin peered out at the night. "I don't like the looks of this. Where's your mother? I thought she was going to join us."

Fraoch said, "Och nae, 'daena like the look' seems a verra casual way of saying, this is a horrible sight. A terrible thing tae wake up tae."

We stood, leanin' against the conference table, except Lochie who sat, his chair tipped back, balanced on two legs, his feet up on the table.

Lady Mairead bustled in and batted Lochinvar on the head. "Shew some respect tae the room, or I will send ye from it."

He pulled his feet off the table, put his chair legs down, and sat up straight.

I asked, "What is happenin'?"

"Magnus! Ye must see what is happening!" She turned the screens on the back wall tae a weather report that showed the clusters of storms. "These storms were unexpected! There are more than one!"

My eyes swept the horizon, there were three disparate locations where storms were roiling, flashes and strikes lighting up the darkened sky. I walked tae the windows on the back wall. "There is another back here, that makes four within our visual area."

She said, "This is why I am in an uproar!" I hae convened the generals, troops are headed tae the locations—"

As she said it helicopters lifted from the rooftop landing pad, flying in formation, then dividing up tae fly away in different directions. "There they go, now we are waiting for word." Lady Mairead huffed. "How much danger can our kingdom face? We need peace and quiet, but here we are with another threat."

"Tis always a trial, thank ye, Lady Mairead, for addressin' it so swiftly."

"Yer welcome, Your Highness, this is why I am yer steward."

She leaned on the table beside me.

Fraoch looked out over the landscape, "What do you think is happening?"

I said, "There are a few possibilities, the most likely is some kind of invasion. There could be multiple landing parties at different locations tae spread out our defenses."

Lady Mairead said, "But who? We have nae credible threats."

Colonel Quentin nodded, "That is our working assumption." Then he asked, "Could we be looking at the remnants of our own jumps?"

I said, "This is unlikely, we haena had anything like this in all the years that we hae been jumping."

Lochinvar said, "What if some person has picked up a vessel and accidentally set it off?"

I said, "It wouldna cause this many storms."

Fraoch said, "So what is most likely?"

"A possibility is someone else is tryin' tae collect vessels afore we get tae them."

Lochinvar said, "Shite."

Lady Mairead said, "Aye, I hae the military going tae the spots tae make sure tis not an invasion, but... I do hope that is all tis, we hae an army, we are ready for them. Also, please watch yer language, Lochinvar."

He said, "My apologies."

Fraoch said, "Which do we prefer, invasion or someone collecting?"

Quentin, Lady Mairead, and I all said, "Invasion."

Lochinvar said, "Shite." Then, "My apologies, Lady Mairead."

Lady Mairead said, "Lochinvar ye must put yer head down on the table and wheesht."

Lochinvar put his head down.

She continued, "If it inna an invasion, if it is someone collecting the vessels—"

I interrupted, "Our vessels, someone gatherin' *our* vessels."

She nodded, "Aye, if this is happening, whoever is doing it, collecting our vessels, is a madman. Only a madman would use the remote-activator and retrieval, as dangerous as it is—"

Fraoch said, "Twas what we used, Og Maggy? I hope this wasna caused by our collectin'."

Lady Mairead turned tae him sharply. "Ye used it?" She turned tae me, "Magnus, ye used it?"

"Aye, we were in the year 1760, we told ye — we used it near Kilchurn—"

Colonel Quentin was speaking tae one of the commanders and he gestured tae the southwest where another storm had started, and another, the whole landscape lit up with lightning-powered storms. Fraoch said, "Och nae, this looks verra bad."

Lady Mairead said, "Aye, tis verra bad, and, Magnus, I canna believe ye used the remote activator in the eighteenth century! Quentin, are there storms around Kilchurn now?"

He looked over the radar. "I don't see storms there right now."

She huffed. "Still, it remains tae be said, I told ye never, *ever* tae use the remote activator!"

I said, "I agree that this is a verra bad situation, Lady Mairead, but ye did not warn me against ever using it. And because I used it in the eighteenth century it has naething tae do with this. How is the one related tae the other?"

"I daena ken! But nae one used the activator, now ye hae used it — though I told ye nae, and now this! I told ye 'nae!' I told ye twas too dangerous tae use!"

I said, "I daena want tae argue on it, Lady Mairead, ye dinna tell me 'nae'."

Lochinvar mumbled from his head down on the table. "This is why ye daena let women decide strategy, they will change their story on ye, and—"

Fraoch said, "What dost ye ken on women, Lochie? Ye ken less on women than Og Maggy kens on these infernal machines. Ye ought tae wheesht and let the adults discuss it with Lady Mairead, who, I will say, kens the *most* about the machines."

She raised her chin. "I do ken a great deal, but Donnan kent much more, and usin' the remote activator and retriever was how he would bring his sons when he was ready tae meet them." Her eyes softened as if she was rememberin' the time of Donnan with fondness.

I humphed. "I hae terrible memories of that time. He was a brutal king, twas dreadful tae be called upon tae war with m'brothers."

She said, "But it was a successful endeavor overall. He had many sons and chose the best of them for his throne. Twas a good strategy. If ye were interested in strength and power, ye would consider having a few more sons for the betterment of the—"

"Ye want tae recommend I take after Donnan? Ye want tae recommend that I take up with other women and leave sons throughout history? Och, ye are a pain in m'arse sometimes, and most of the time ye are a pain in m'arse when we are dealin' with dangerous things."

"Ye hae an heir and ye hae a son who might want the throne, tis likely they will fight for it — ye might want more sons so they can practice the art of waging war, but fine — ye daena hae tae heed my warning. Ye may hae two sons only and hope for the best." She sighed.

I shook my head. "Archie and Jack will grow up tae be fine men. Archie will be a king, and twill be fine, they will be fine." I huffed again.

She asked, "How many vessels are unaccounted for?"

I looked down at the list and counted, but then said, "At least eight."

Quentin counted the storms on the horizon. "Each storm could be one of those vessels."

Lochie raised his head and stretched. "Or one vessel, at different times, like an echo, reverberatin'."

Fraoch said, "If ye daena stay quiet, Lochie, I am goin' tae send ye from the room."

"This is a valid point!"

"I ken, but ye are irritating me by sayin' it!"

I said, "We need less wheeshtin', less sparrin', and only pertinent strategy as I am tryin' tae think."

Lady Mairead said, "All the men around here need tae do far more of it, I lay this at *your* feet."

Lochie muttered, "Women are always blamin' us for everything."

Fraoch shot him an irritated look.

Lochinvar yawned, loudly, and put his head back down on his arms on the table. "Wake me when we ken if we are at war or we are goin' tae go kill the madman."

Fraoch said, "Changin' the subject back, how is this our fault?"

She said, "Because... I daena ken, but ye used the device and now we are either being invaded, best case scenario, or we hae yet another maniacal relative tae deal with."

I said, "Did we put the vessels and the Bridge in the vault?"

"Aye, just after our meeting when ye first arrived."

"Then that is where they are, safe, but... ye ken... time travel." Then I asked, "When will we ken what we are dealin' with?"

Colonel Quentin said, "I will hear from the commanders any minute now."

I said, "Yet we hae our answer, if twas an invasion, we would ken already. This is a madman collecting, my military is taking a long time tae determine the cause of the storms because there inna anything there."

Lady Mairead said, "Shite."

Lochie looked as if he were sleepin' but we could hear him chuckle.

We waited. I said, "I daena like being powerless, watchin' the process."

Lady Mairead looked at her watch. "I hate waitin' for word."

She sighed. "I hate being powerless as well — when I was first given a vessel, there was a ring around it, dost ye remember, Magnus?"

"Aye, we were at Donnan's beck and call, the rings made it so that our course was set, the vessel could only go on one path, from Scotland tae Amelia Island, then here."

Fraoch said, "I wonder who decided for ye tae go tae Amelia Island the first time?"

Lady Mairead said, "I suspect twas a time traveler. One of us likely put Amelia Island in our way tae set this whole thing in motion."

Quentin said, "It's a little like the chicken and the egg. Someone wanted Magnus to meet Kaitlyn?"

Lady Mairead smiled. "How dost ye ken someone dinna want *me* tae go tae Amelia Island? I hae become verra rich and now my bloodline rules over a kingdom. I think *I* might be the one who has won the most — who wanted tae put Amelia Island in my path?"

I chuckled. "One thing is certain, it ought tae always be about ye."

She raised her chin. "Remember that, always." Then she asked, "Magnus, ye daena ever get notes from yer future selves, or yer descendants, hints tae tell ye what ye ought tae do tae make yer travels more successful?"

I shook my head. "Nae, never. I daena interfere with my past. Ye do?"

"I do all the time, I keep notes, I make records, and I will dispatch a messenger if I need tae. I will warn if necessary. And if I get a warning, I will make alliances if I believe it will help our family."

I said, "Speaking of useful alliances, as it could be the only explanation, where is JB now?"

Her brow raised. "I sent him home."

I nodded. "I notice ye daena deny it."

She pursed her lips. "A woman can hae many reasons tae invite a man tae dance, pleasure is but one of them."

Quentin glanced at his watch and around at the satellite storm images projected on the walls around us. Then he received a call. While he spoke Lady Mairead said, "Och nae, a new one has started!" He followed her direction with his eyes and continued talking intae the radio.

Finally he reported, "Troops have gained access to the point of the first storm, there is no army there and they don't detect any vessels."

He returned to the radio, a report was coming in from the second storm, soldiers were headed to the third, fourth, and fifth locations.

We were quiet, listening while he conferred.

Lady Mairead shook her head. "Nae... there is a collector, this is dangerous. If this scoundrel has taken a vessel from where we need it tae be — he could change our timeline, someone might be changing our history."

"I ken, this seems verra dire."

Lady Mairead's hands were shaking. "I truly wish Hammond were here, he always kent what tae do in a situation such as this."

Quentin said, "We've checked every storm, no armies, no vessels were found."

Fraoch said, "Now we know. There is a madman activatin' the vessels, we ought tae go stop him."

Lochinvar stood up and drew his sword. "This is the most sensible thing we hae said all night. Tis time tae fight."

I said, "Nae, Lochie, there inna anyone there tae fight."

Lochinvar exhaled and sheathed his sword. "These storms hae me agitated, I forgot they are echoes. " He sank intae a seat, lookin' disappointed.

Lady Mairead said, "Twill be a miracle if the timeline remains—"

Lochinvar muttered, "Tis not a time*line*, tis a wheel."

Her brow drew down. "What are ye speaking on, Lochinvar?"

I explained, "Lochinvar and I hae a debate about whether time is a line or a wheel."

Lady Mairead said, "Tis a stupid argument, tis both."

"At once?"

"Aye, we are moving forward and going around, tis insensible tae not see it, only a man would think it must be one or the other. But philosophy is a waste of our time, we hae other things tae think about *now*, there is an evil villain collecting vessels."

My eyes swept the landscape, now there were storms in every direction.

Lady Mairead said, "Ye ken what makes me furious? *I* hae kept my vessels safe, but some in this room hae been careless. Magnus, ye hae left vessels throughout history—"

"I hae battled and fought for a kingdom, tis a part of war tae sometimes leave a weapon on the battlefield."

She said, "This is not optimal, others will come across it. *Governments* might become curious."

"What governments?"

"All of them. And ye can imagine the trouble if Switzerland found it! Och nae, they would alter the history of the world tae please their neutrality." She shivered. "Can ye imagine the wars?"

I said, "I will agree with ye, involving other people will always be dangerous, but we need not incriminate, we need tae come up with a plan."

Fraoch said, "The plan is: locate the madman."

Lochie said, "Kill him."

Quentin glanced at his watch. "Almost dawn." He rubbed his hands up and down on his face.

Lochie groaned. "I dinna want tae ken."

Lady Mairead said, "We must look through our records,

look for anomalies, and historical discrepancies, but as soon as possible ye must return home."

Fraoch said, "Why so soon?"

I said, "Because our timeline might hae shifted. We need tae make sure our household is the same as we hae left it."

Quentin said, "Oh shit, Noah."

"Aye."

Quentin began stuffing his tech and paperwork intae a bag.

CHAPTER 22 - MAGNUS

2024 - FLORIDA, VERRA COMPLICATED

*I*t was pouring down rain when we landed in Florida, thick gray clouds, dense, hanging down over us. I stared up at the sky and thought — it looks as if tis brooding.

I looked up at Dràgon from flat on my back in the sand. He looked furious tae hae jumped and tae hae rain pouring down on him, unceremoniously, on a beach.

I rubbed my hands on my face and raised my head, James and Zach were here, armed, tae guard — *good...*

Then Kaitlyn, Archie, and Ben came intae view. They were wearing rain gear. Kaitlyn's hood shielding her face from the downpour. She grinned down. "It's been storming since yesterday."

"Och, I am verra relieved tae see ye both, are ye well, are the bairns well?"

"Yes, yes, we're all fine, did something happen?"

"Aye, we hae had storms, a great deal of storms. They lit up the sky over Riaghalbane, and though we sent soldiers tae the epicenters, we couldna find any vessels. Lochinvar called it an echo. I am sure someone else is collecting the vessels, which means our timeline might be unstable. We were up most of the night."

"You must be tired."

"Aye… and now I am relieved." She passed me a raincoat tae pull on though I was already soppin' wet.

While I pulled it over my drenched clothes, she said, "Two beautiful horses."

"Aye, Lochinvar got a horse, the black and white one, his name is Cookie—"

The boys laughed.

"—and this is *my* new horse, his name is Dràgon."

Archie and Ben said, "*Aaaawe*some."

"Aye, he is awesome, and best part, he is Sunny's son."

Archie said, "Can Ben and I ride to the stable with you, Da?"

Kaitlyn said, "In the rain? You want to ride in the rain?"

I said, "Och aye, he wants tae ride in the rain, that is the best time tae ride a horse, and we must get Dràgon and Cookie tae the stables." I stretched. "This is why they are saddled already, for Archie and Ben's first ride."

I helped Archie up tae Dràgon's saddle, Lochinvar lifted Ben up tae Cookie's saddle.

Kaitlyn said, "Mind if I come? This looks more fun than carrying your luggage to the truck in the rain."

I said, "Aye, ye can come, besides they are almost done."

Zach ran by, a box in his arms jostling up and down, humorously. "We gotta go fast, it's pouring out here."

Ben said, "Daddy, I'm going to ride the horse!"

He said over his shoulder, "That's because you're a lunatic, but have fun."

We waved as Zach pulled the truck from the sand and headed home. Kaitlyn walked beside me holding my hand as the rain dripped down on us and we led Dràgon and Lochinvar led Cookie down the beach headed tae the stables.

I breathed in deep, taking in the scent of rain, the sea, the modern smell of road and civilization, mingling with the scent I remembered from the past, before this civilization was here, of pine and oak, of swamp and moist decay. I exhaled, "I daena ken how tae explain tae ye, Kaitlyn, my concern that things had shifted — I feared ye would hae forgotten me, tis good tae see Florida unchanged."

"I've had that feeling before, it is not fun, but we are good — our days have been normal. Except Zach's cooking is a little lame when you are gone. His heart isn't in it, he lets the kids win and feeds us all chicken nuggets. As you know, even homemade they're not special."

The rain started tae wane and the birds began tae sing. The day seemed like it might grow hot.

I unzipped my raincoat.

She said, "You're so wet you're practically steaming."

I asked, "Did ye hae another nightmare while I was gone?"

She looked up at Archie and lowered her voice, "Yeah, I did."

"Ye look pensive, what happened in it?"

She whispered, "It was the same except... when I looked down Archie wasn't there, or Isla. It was incredibly frightening. Even more so. In the past-dreams, the kids were with me, I was trying to protect them. I guess *that* was more frightening, now that I think of it, but this time I had all the same feelings — I had to get my kids out of there and looked down and they weren't there."

"Och nae. While I was gone the dream shifted?"

"Yep, but on the good side, that idea is irrational, that I *think* they're there but they aren't—"

"How is that a good thing?" We skirted a mud puddle, but Dràgon splashed through.

"Irrational, it's much more like a traditional nightmare, instead of what I was thinking it was... a *memory*, or, you know, a *portent*."

I nodded. "There is some solace in that." I chuckled. "I would hate for our lives tae be irrational."

Kaitlyn said, "The experience in Riaghalbane really got to you, huh?"

"Aye, if ye had seen it, Kaitlyn... the sky above m'kingdom lit up with storms. Twas as if the hand of God were working upon our world. I was chilled through, these werna the storms of the natural world, these were the storms of time travel and there was a clear warning, we are not alone."

She shook her head. "Ugh, that's not good."

"Aye, I am relieved naething changed."

"Nope," she grinned. "Just doing so much laundry, cleaning up from the throw ups, trying to get it all back in order. We noted, more than once, that all of you deserted us without helping."

He joked, "M'choice was 'visit m'mother' or do laundry after our plague? I think I would rather take the chance with m'mother."

She laughed, then sighed. "What are we going to do about the storms?"

"I will need tae return tae the kingdom verra soon. I need tae figure out who it is that is settin' off the storms with my vessels."

She glanced at my face.

I said, "Aye, I am feelin' verra stern on it, these are *my* vessels. I am the king of Riaghalbane and the devices hae come tae me through a long line of kings, I fought hard tae gain the throne and tae secure these vessels and whoever is messin' with them canna hae them. I winna allow it. He needs tae make peace with his maker because he will be meetin' him soon."

Ben, up on Cookie's saddle, whispered, "Cool."

Archie said, "My da is very cool."

Kaitlyn said, "Speaking of your mother, what is she doing about the situation?"

"She is lookin' for anomalies, stepping up security around the vault, and gettin' me a list of names for the reckonin'."

She said, "Those are the things she does well."

"I hae a learned somethin' about Lady Mairead as well."

She said, "You're grinning! What could it be?"

"My mother has taken up with a farmer!"

"No! Really? No, she can't have! A *farmer*?"

"Aye he is an apple farmer, calls himself a gentleman, though I daena think this is a name one can apply tae oneself. He grows apples and makes cider. He positively gloats upon his cider."

"Did you try it? You don't normally like it."

"I had tae, as he had named it, the Royal Riaghalbane Rose cider, or some other slosh. Twas good enough, fine at best." I grimaced. "He is preenin' over landin' the *royal* mother."

"What does he...? I'm speechless, what does he offer?"

"He is apparently a good dancer, he makes her laugh, and from the looks of it, she admires his plumpness."

"Oh my, this is fascinating. He's not an artist or a king? What the hell is going on in your kingdom?"

"I would blame a timeshift, but m'mother took up with him afore the excitement. I daena ken what she sees in him. He is simple, perhaps she wants a simple life with a gentleman farmer, or something... Tis verra difficult tae understand her mind sometimes, but she often has reasons beyond what I can discern."

We entered the stable, and led Dràgon and Cookie tae their new stalls, with Kaitlyn saying, "I can't believe it."

Lochinvar said, "Ye dinna see him dance, twas sight tae behold. He wriggled his way intae her heart, I dinna ken twould be so easy." He started dancin' around in the straw and the boys laughed.

I shook my head watchin' Lochie. "Ye are goin' tae need lessons."

He said, "Hey! This was good enough for Lady Mairead, surely I can get a young lass hooked." He shook his arse and the boys laughed even more.

I said, "I looked over JB's background report, half-hoping there would be a skeleton in his closet, a reason for him tae be interestin', but instead he is simply a man, nothin' special about him."

"Maybe that's a relief for her, maybe she picked him because he is easy and uncomplicated."

"Perhaps, and tis hard tae blame her; the rest of our lives are complicated, verra complicated."

We left the horses there and called for James tae come pick us up in the truck.

CHAPTER 23 - KAITLYN

GATHER THE VESSELS

*W*e returned to the house and the kids were thrilled to have their da back home. Chef Zach had a lot of food prepared and we sat around the table. Magnus had his eye on the back deck, spattered in puddles, but beginning to dry in the fresh sunlight. "Ye haena noticed any time-travel storms?"

I said, "No, I mean, it's been terrible weather, but the first *storm* storm meant you were coming home."

Quentin got out his laptop. "Let's check the international weather."

James opened his own laptop, because they were both so competitive they had to see who could look things up fastest. Quentin clicked, then said, "Check out this radar."

As he turned the screen to us, James said, "I'm already seeing it."

There was a big blob over Europe, and then smaller, dark red loops centered around England, and France. And then a deepest red radar bullseye over Scotland.

Magnus asked, "Do we know if this is a normal storm?"

James said, "I'm not sure, we can ask on the message boards." He scrolled, and typed.

Quentin started typing.

James said, "Posted onto Euro-weather watch."

Quentin said, "I asked on Storm-chasers, UK edition."

He tapped his fingers on the table waiting. The contest now was who would get a response first.

Magnus dipped chips into French Onion flavored dip. Zach put a plate of cheese and fruit in front of us.

Magnus said, "Ye always ken what I need tae eat, Zach, tis verra considerate, thank ye." He began to retell us the story of the cider farmer and the king's mother. He got up and mimicked how the cider farmer danced, painting such a picture that we were all astonished by it.

Emma said, "This would make an excellent children's picture book."

"A cautionary tale."

A few minutes later Quentin said, "I got a response! Okay, he says…" He read. "He's wondering the same thing, says the storms over Scotland seem weird."

James said, "My guy replied with a list of barometer and temp readings. I win."

Quentin said, "My guy said, 'weird', did your guy say 'weird'? Or did he just tell you what the gauges say? I think 'weird' is actually more descriptive than 'there was low pressure.'"

While they discussed the storms, I asked, "So how worried should we be?"

Fraoch said, "The sky was lit with them — in all directions, as if vessels from all our jumps were activated at once."

Lochie scooped a whole bunch of dip into his mouth and with his mouth full, crunching, said, "Like echoes…" He swallowed, "bouncing around on the wheel."

Fraoch said, "Dost ye need a spoon, Og Lochie?"

Isla pointed, "Uncle Fraoch, you have dip in your beard."

"Och nae, one of ye bairns must hae put it there."

She giggled.

I said, "So we are worried. Okay, what do we do?"

We all looked down thinking, then Magnus said, "I think we continue with our plan, gather the vessels."

Fraoch said, "I agree, we go tae Dunscaith castle next?"

Magnus nodded. "Aye."

CHAPTER 24 - MAGNUS

1712 - 1612 - 1595... WEARY

*W*e picked the year 1712, a couple of days in the late spring, and we jumped tae the lands outside of Dunscaith on the Isle of Skye.

It was a cool crisp day with a blustering breeze blowin' off the ocean.

James said, "Why does every day in seventeenth century Scotland seem like a scene from a movie where the point is — cold and dismal, the warring army is about tae attack?"

Fraoch said, "Because twas cold and dismal and an army is bound tae attack."

Lochinvar spun Cookie around tae check behind us.

Fraoch said with a smirk, "Ye afraid, Og Lochie?"

"I am just being cautious."

Our view was of a gray sea, churning against the rocky shore. The castle was gloomy in the distance, ruined by time, approachable only by land-bridge. It had large walls for defense, crumbling under the weight of the years. "Och nae, another castle ruined?"

Lochinvar said, "Tis not yer castle, I lived there for a time, I am glad tae see it destroyed."

"Daena get me wrong, I feel emboldened by its lack of

defenses, but tis still difficult tae see how the centuries plague a place."

Fraoch said, "The centuries plague a man as well."

James looked over at our horses, chewing grass, looking unscathed by the jump. "How do you think they do it so effortlessly?"

I said, "I think they scream durin' the jump but when tis done they forget it much faster than we do."

Fraoch joked, "This is probably true, if ye heard screamin' that was Thor, not me. I am not the screamin' type."

Lochinvar said, "All I did was scream, I scream the whole time, there is nae shame in it. I barely survive, and yet I do. I am proud of the fact."

Fraoch stretched his back by swinging his arms. "If ye had a woman with ye, ye would be ashamed of the belly-achin'. I heard ye, squealing like a bairn."

Lochie scowled, "Daena remind me. I haena had a lass in so long, I hae forgotten what twas like. Ye've ruined me, Fraoch, I canna hae a lass from Balloch because they are too cumbersome, I canna hae a lass from Florida because they daena understand my ways — how am I tae find a lass?"

Fraoch said, "I daena ken, tis going tae be complicated for ye. In the meantime, so we daena hae tae listen tae ye, we might set ye out on a raft tae an island well away from all of us."

"Are there lassies on this island? Because without a lass I am going tae fight ye. Ye winna get me on the raft, I will die first."

Fraoch laughed. "Och nae, we need a woman for the lad, he is a'complainin'."

I checked the monitor for vessels, found none, and decided tae set the remote activator anyway.

Fraoch said, "Are ye sure about it, yer mother—"

"M'mother daena always ken what she is talking on, she seems tae think we can find vessels just from a careful accounting of our past, but I hate tae tell her, we are well beyond that point. We need tae collect the vessels without delay." I pushed the button and a distant storm started on the far other side of the hill. We mounted our horses and rode that direction, and as it took some time the storm was dissipatin' as we neared.

Dràgon did well, listened tae my commands, and wasna skittish around the waning storm, so we charged toward the focal point.

There we found nothing.

The last dying wind gust blew, then the air went still. Fraoch stood with his hands on his hips. "Och nae, tis becomin' clear that someone is grabbin' them afore we get there, right? What are we goin' tae do on it? We canna let this arse, whoever he is, take our vessels — we ought tae hae a plan."

I chewed m'lip, thinkin', then decided, "We will split up. Each of us will go tae the same place in a different time, I will set the remote activator, we will each go tae the middle of the storm. We will meet back here, hopefully one of us will hae found it."

Fraoch said, "There will be a lot of jumping alone, tis a risk."

Lochinvar shrugged. "We can fan out and cover more ground, I am willin'."

I said, "This means setting the remote activator a few more times, daena tell Lady Mairead."

James chuckled. "I can't make any promises on that, she gives me one look and I'm confessing it all."

Fraoch teased, "Og Maggy, did ye hear, James will tell yer Ma what ye hae been up tae."

James said, "Can you blame me?"

I said, "Nae, I canna blame ye, she is well-practiced in gettin' men tae help her in her affairs, but remember this might bring my wrath down upon ye."

James said, "I don't know, I think I fear her wrath more than yours."

I chuckled, "Tis true?"

All of them nodded.

. . .

We determined the years we would each check, and set the plan in motion.

∼

I jumped back, tae the year 1612. A hundred years. I woke up alone, and set the remote. A big storm rose over the woods. Under it there was nae vessel.

I patted Dràgon. "Ye good, boy? Ye want tae do it again?" He and I jumped tae the year 1595. I set the activator once more. This time there was nae storm.

Dràgon and I looked out over the land. I said, "This might mean James, Fraoch, or Lochie has found it already."

Dràgon stamped his foot. I said, "Aye, I agree, I am exhausted from the jumpin'."

I returned tae the meeting place and we discussed our next step, because none of them had found the vessel either. They had each gone tae three different times and come up empty handed, Fraoch had seen two storms. James had only seen one. Lochinvar hadna seen any storms, at all.

We couldna interpret the pattern and we were weary from the jumping, so we returned home.

CHAPTER 25 - KAITLYN

2024 - DISCREPANCIES

*M*agnus was finally home.

It had been storming for days and so we had a wet, gloomy world. And people were cranky. As Hayley said, "Kids are cranking out all over the place."

Isla ran out through the rain, zooming up and down the boardwalk while dinner was being made, then came in screeching like a banshee.

She clutched her knee, scraped, bleeding.

Emma said, "Another one? Man, every knee has got a booboo."

Ben, crouching beside Isla, said, "Wow, Isla, that looks bad, does it hurt?"

I went to the cabinet and pulled out the box of Band-Aids. "This is going to require more than one, thankfully we've got a full box."

"We do? How…? Weird, I thought we were almost out. I had it on my list, I think… didn't I have it on my list?"

Chef Zach pulled a tray from the oven and dropped it onto the stovetop. "Your mind is going, Em, Band-Aids are *the* most important of all the things. Without Band-Aids civilization comes to a stop."

She laughed, reading down her list that was stuck with magnets to the fridge door. "Hmmm, I must have remembered it wrong, weird."

Ben said, "Brainfart, Mom."

"Yep, total brainfart, but I'm going to add them to the list anyway, you can never have too many." She wrote Band-Aids on the list.

We watched movies and put the kids to bed late, and then went to our room.

We were brushing our teeth in the bathroom, grinning at each other. I said, "I think you're a sight for sore eyes or something, you look really hot tonight."

"I do? I hae been gone for three days, tis enough for ye tae think I am 'hot' again?"

"No 'again,' you are always hot, but there's something about you, kind of..." I reached out and ran my fingers through his hair and sprung one of his curls by his ear. "Kind of *really* hot."

He picked me up, and growled, "Wrap yer legs," and dropped his toothbrush on the counter.

I wrapped my legs, mumbling, "Need... spit..." and leaned over his arm to spit out the toothpaste and tossed my toothbrush down.

Laughing, he carried me to our bed and tossed me down.

I said, "Hot and ready without question?"

He dove onto me, "I am always ready, mo reul-iuil, without question, tis the way of it."

"True."

We made love.

When we woke up it dawned on me that I had terrible cramps. I pulled the pillow over my head and curled up in a ball.

"Dost ye need yer wee pill?"

"Yes, and a glass of water…"

He climbed out of bed.

I moaned. "And tell Emma I need *Happy* the water bottle."

He padded down the hall to the bathroom to relieve himself.

I called to him, clutching my stomach, "I can't believe I have cramps. I felt like I had grown out of them."

He stuck his head from the bathroom where he was brushing his teeth. "It has been a long time since ye were belly-achin' about it, I am just glad we had sex already."

"Me too."

He came from the bathroom. "Do I hae time tae dress, or do ye need it fast?"

"Fast."

He left the room wearing his pajamas.

I lay there thinking about the past few days — how Magnus always had to consider the big life or death issues of living, while I dealt with the day-to-day — Band-Aids and washing vomit-covered laundry, and riding the red wave of a visit from—

He padded in, put a glass of water beside my bed and two white pills in my hand.

"Emma said call if ye need anythin'."

"Just gonna lie here, hold down the fort."

When I emerged downstairs, after I felt better, some things had been decided.

Magnus was raring to go again, he had picked a date, and a place — 1741, St Augustine.

Reyes had been there, Magnus felt sure this would help them find a vessel.

The next day we drove James and Fraoch and Magnus to the beach to jump.

I sighed. Another three days without Magnus, totally sucked.

CHAPTER 26 - MAGNUS

1741 - ST AUGUSTINE

The air was balmy and smelled like marsh. "Ye smell it, Fraoch? Dost it smell like ye remember?"

"Aye." He lay there for a moment then scrambled up. "Gators?" He looked wildly left and right. "Och, there arna any gators." He clutched his chest. "I thought there might be gators." He pulled a flask of whisky from his sporran and drank, then passed it tae me.

"Should we nae drink go-go juice after we jump?"

"We hae just jumped intae a marsh in the eighteenth century in a god-forsaken part of the world, in a place that we once barely escaped with our lives. We need whisky tae get through it."

James batted mosquitoes from his face. "This is lame. This is not the kind of historical adventure I like. Why did I let you talk me out of horses?"

I passed him the flask. "I dinna want tae risk them. We are goin' tae go on foot."

Fraoch said, "Twas a mistake. Ye always need a horse, but we brought an inflatable boat. We are goin' tae travel in style if we hae tae run away, on *foot*."

James groaned. "Who are we runnin' away from?"

I counted on m'fingers. "Gators, pirates, Spaniards, evil men, former prisoners, irritated Scotsmen, starvin' soldiers."

Fraoch was unpackin' weapons from the bag. "Daena forget the natives."

We slung rifles across our shoulders and crept through the forest toward the fort.

Within sight of the fort walls we came upon a footpath and peered out. Troops were comin' up.

We ducked behind an embankment.

I mouthed, "How many?"

James peeked up over the rise and counted.

He gestured that there were about thirty men.

We sat and waited, silent, until the sound of the troops had passed. Fraoch let out a low phew. "Glad we dinna bring the horses."

I said, "See, Fraoch, I am right in everythin'."

We peered out tae check that the coast was clear, then I checked the monitor. It shewed an extra vessel, centered near the fort. Using a binoculars we looked out in the direction. "Dost ye hae any idea where it might be?"

James said, looking through binoculars, "Could be anywhere. There are guards all along the walls though, it won't be easy to search for it."

I took out the Bridge.

Fraoch said, "Yer mother told us not tae use it, and here we are, usin' it verra regularly."

"Daena tell her, she inna the king, she daena get a say." Then I joked, as I set up the remote-activator, "But if ye see her comin' let me ken so I can run."

James laughed.

We turned on the remote activator and a majestic and

powerful storm rose in the sand right outside the fort. The guards rushed from the walls tae seek shelter inside.

We watched the center of the storm.

Fraoch said, "There must be a vessel at the base. Look at it, the power!"

I said, "Aye, there must be — cover me!" I ran from our hiding place toward the flurry of circling winds. Towards the center I slowed, ploughing through the squall, and then I heard a gunshot, behind me more shots.

James ran past me, his knees high, hands whipping back and forth. "Cover me! Faster!" He sped past.

As he gained the middle, he put his arms up tae cover his head, slowing his pace, a shoulder forward into the wind — a man raised his head up over the wall and fired down.

I aimed and returned fire.

Fraoch shot at another man.

Then, with one hand down, James took two final steps. He plucked the vessel up, yelled, "Got it—!" as the storm rose, wind gusted, lightning flashed, he disappeared.

The storm immediately began tae dissipate. More heads appeared over the walls, shooting down, Fraoch returned fire as I raced toward him — we raced tae our hiding place in the woods. I made it, and kept going, he turned and fled alongside me, our paths parallel as we raced through the woods, jumping over logs, windin' round trees.

He yelled, "About ten men!"

"Behind us? Sounds about twenty!"

A crashing sound as men neared.

"Grab my arm, I'm twistin' the vessel!" I pulled it from my pocket, as gunshots sounded. Fraoch veered so our paths would merge, five, four steps, three, two, and then without breaking pace, he clamped his hand on my arm. I twisted the vessel.

The force of the wind about knocked us from our feet as we were then ripped through time.

~

We woke up on the beach, with James groaning face down beside us.

I said, "Och ye made it, how did ye make it back?"

He raised up his face, beaten all tae hell. "Wasn't easy."

Fraoch raised his head to look at him. "Och nae, where's our rescue — we need tae get ye tae a hospital."

He said, "No hospital — looks worse than it is."

I said, "It looks as if ye beat a man with yer face."

The truck pulled up at the edge of the sand, Quentin, Kaitlyn, Hayley, and Zach jumped out and rushed up.

Quentin said, "What the hell happened to you, James?"

James said, "I woke up in a forest, beat ten men with my face, then met the man who is doing *all* of this to us — you're welcome. He sent Mags a message."

I sat up and rolled m'hand for him tae continue. My voice wasna much more than a mumble. "Who is the man?"

"His name is Ranulph."

My arms on m'knees, head hangin', I asked, "And he is…?"

"Our worst nightmare."

"Och nae, another one?"

Kaitlyn sat down beside me in the sand and put her head on my shoulder.

James said, "He's a cousin, son of… who was he a son of… that arse, you fought him a long time ago, and his brother is Roderick."

"A son of Samuel?"

He weakly snapped and pointed. "Yep."

Fraoch said, "Bet *he's* got an ax tae grind."

Hayley said, "Mags killed his dad and his brother? He's probably pissed."

James spit sand out of his mouth as he pulled himself up to sitting. "Oh he is, he definitely is."

CHAPTER 27 - KAITLYN

2024 - DAMAGE TAE OUR TIMELINE

Quentin said, "We need to get you to the house, your face looks like hamburger." He plucked a vessel out of the sand beside Magnus, then asked, "Where's your vessel, James?"

"Ugh, I don't... wait, it's not here?" James lumbered to his feet, while Quentin felt around in the sand.

Hayley kicked sand trying to uncover it.

Quentin asked, "Did we see anyone near here? Was there anyone with you?"

James said, "No, they sent me alone. It's gotta be here."

Quentin drew a gun.

Magnus pulled the monitor from his bag and checked it. "There are two vessels, but one is over..."

We looked out over the trees in the middle of the island. Where storm clouds were growing.

Quentin said, "Well, someone was here. Someone took that vessel and now that someone is leaving with it. That's some serious premeditation there. We've *never* been that organized. We're getting our asses kicked."

Magnus said, "For future reference, how about we daena

compare our strategies tae their strategies? Unless tis tae say that ours are better. I daena like tae lose."

Fraoch scoffed. "Yer majesty needs tae win so bad, ye want us tae lie? What are ye talkin' on, Og Maggy?"

"I daena need tae be reminded we are gettin' our arses kicked."

Quentin said, "I thought by pointing it out it might focus us — we need to learn from our mistakes."

"Fine, but how about I get intae the house, with some food in front of me, *before* ye tell me how I am not as good as this bawbag Ranulph."

Quentin said, "Deal."

We helped James up to the house. He was limping a bit and holding his arm around his middle, but wouldn't go to urgent care.

We sat him down on a chair in the dining room and Emma put Zoe down and rushed away for the first aid kit.

I grabbed a stack of hand towels. Zach delivered a pitcher of water to the table with a stack of cups and go-go juice in mugs for the travelers. Emma sat down, opened the kit, and started cleaning James's face, wiping blood away from a cut on his cheek. She put two butterfly-style bandages on it.

Ben pointed at James's hand. "Uncle James is bleeding there too."

Emma rifled through the kit then said to me, "Katie, can you get the Band-Aids from the hall closet?"

I ran to get them, and called back, "Dammit, we're out, someone put the box back empty."

She called, "Add it to my list please, we always need more!"

I went to the list on the fridge and wrote: Band-Aids.

Then I paused.

Something wasn't right.

It wasn't anything I could feel, or see, or... *what was it...?*

I tried to be focused: What was confusing me? I was simply writing Band-Aids on the list.

I turned the paper over.

Then put it back up with the magnets. The list had usual things, it was our usual list. And we always needed Band-Aids.

Beaty asked, "What are ye worryin' on, Madame Kaitlyn?"

I shook my head. "I don't know... it's just... something doesn't feel right."

I walked back to the dining room, trying to think it all through.

Magnus noticed my face drawn. "Did ye hae another dream while we were away?"

"Yeah, last night — that's probably what happened. Archie's screams are rattling through my head still, it's not..."

I dropped down in the chair beside him. He took my hand, then said, "Well, we hae learned who the enemy is: Ranulph, son of Samuel, who died at my feet long years ago. This is useful for understandin' how tae fight."

He asked James, "What does he hae that we need tae hear, what was his message?"

James drank some of the vitamin drink to wash down an aspirin. "Hey kids, how about you run out and play for a minute while we talk."

The kids ran off to play. Once they were gone, James said, "His message was, tell Magnus 'I'm collecting all the vessels and it's too late to stop me.'"

Magnus sat quietly.

Fraoch grunted. "That is an asinine thing tae say. He could hae said *anything* through a messenger and he says, 'I'm collecting all the vessels' which we ken, we already know it. Then he says, 'Tis too late tae stop me'? This is a ridiculous message."

Quentin said, "Good point, Fraoch, he didn't say 'I have

them all', or 'I have ten', or *anything* badass. He must not have many or he would be crowing about them. We think there's twenty-six altogether and we have... like how many... seventeen? Even if he had all the other ones he would still have less than half. How does he think he's winning? How is it too late to stop him? You're right Fraoch, that's asinine, he's just trying to scare us."

Magnus nodded but looked solemn.

Quentin said, "You don't agree, boss?"

"If he had a few crucial vessels, he might do a great deal of damage tae our timeline. Possibly. It might only take one and I'm reminded that when Kaitlyn found Johnne Cambell's book, we kent the original date of the vessels was the most dangerous date. If someone goes there they could change our whole history."

I nodded, gulped, and said, "I hate to think about it."

"I do as well."

He clutched my fingers. "We will carry on though, we dinna gain another vessel but we ken who our enemy is. There is a win there. Dost we continue tae search?"

Chef Zach shook his head. "Not sure, we've lost more than we've found. I wouldn't want to fuck up anything you know?"

James joked, from his battered and bruised face, "Yeah, we wouldn't want for anything to get fucked up."

Magnus said, "Thankfully we are all here, accounted for, but aye, we daena want tae cause any harm. We must carefully consider our next step." Then he smiled. "I think everyone needs tae take a shower, I can smell m'men from here — the past has caused a stench tae settle upon us."

I joined him after he had sudsed up and washed off, because he *had* smelt horrible, and after I climbed into the shower we had a bit of fun kissing, hugging, cuddling, hands stroking down our bodies until he was out of his mind with pent up desire and bent me over, my palms pressed to the wall and took me hard in the shower. It was lovely with the heat and steam rising, the effort, the climax, the scent of shampoo and soap mingling in the air — finished, I turned in his slippery arms, and chest to naked wet chest we kissed long and longer still.

Then I stepped away and lathered up my hair. " I love shower sex."

His muscles bunched, his abs oh so heavenly, I ran my hand up and down, exploring his muscle and form as he lathered his own hair. Then I kissed his neck. "I'm going to step out, let you do some shower thinking."

"This is the best place for it."

CHAPTER 28 - KAITLYN

A COOLER IN SCOTLAND DOES NOT PROVE TIME TRAVEL

*O*ver dinner we discussed our situation, trying to assess all the possibilities.

Quentin said, "I know we're safe, we're accounted for, but I also know that with the picking up, finding of the vessels, the fact that we're in competition apparently against this other guy—"

Magnus grunted, "Ranulph. And he thinks he is winning—"

Hayley said, "Over my dead body, he is not winning, ever."

James said, "We need to beat the hell out of him, is what we need to do." He sneered, winced, and said, "I need painkillers, can someone please bring me more…? How come we're eating steak? My head hurts, my jaw, the whole everything…"

Zach poured a couple of pills in James's palm and shifted his drink closer. He said, "I made steak to replenish the men. You, a bellyaching bairn, need baby food?"

James said, "I don't know, soup?"

"I don't actually have soup, I ought to, that's something I could store in the freezer for when people are sick and wounded. Want something else?"

"How about eggs? Something soft, like an omelet, with cheese all over, maybe salsa on top."

He grinned at Ben. "Or what about, maybe, some soft cookie dough, on a spoon?"

Magnus carved a slice off his steak and popped it in his mouth, chewing, he said, "If ye are goin' tae hae cookie dough, Master Cook, ye ought tae hae the ice cream with it, tis the only way tae eat it."

Zach exhaled a long low defeated kind of exhalation. "Sure, coming right up."

Magnus chuckled and winked at the boys. "What is comin' up, Chef Zach? The omelet for James or the ice cream for the king who has just asked for it?"

Zach ran his hand through his hair. "The omelet, the cookie dough, the spoon, and the ice cream, not in that order — now finish your steak, Your Highness."

Magnus grinned. "I got us ice cream."

James said, "To continue — yeah, I want to go on the record as saying we need to beat the hell out of Ranulph."

Magnus nodded. "I hae been considerin' it, and I think we ought tae check in with the Balloch clan. I am worried they might hae run across him at some point, perhaps they ken where he is, or can help us gather what we need tae fight him. It has been a long time since we were last there."

I narrowed my eyes. "Has it…?"

Magnus said, "Aye, I canna even remember the last time."

Everyone ate quietly, thinking.

Hayley said, "Right? That's right, *right?*"

Magnus said, "That's right."

Beaty tossed a piece of apple to Mookie who was waiting patiently beside the table.

We had to collect things to take with us. And tried not to be bothered by the fact that we grew confused as we packed. Quentin came in from the garage where he had been going through the weapons chest. "Did you know we have this many guns — come look, everyone come look, except the kids of course."

We followed Quentin out to look down in the gun chest.

"Do you remember buying all these? I mean, I'm sure I did, I just... I'm having trouble remembering when."

James said, "That is crazy, but also, I just went with this key," he waved a key on a floatable keychain, "To the other garage to get the quads, and there aren't quads there. Didn't we have them?"

Quentin stood with his hands on his hips. "Who knows, probably, we've had so many adventures. I'm surprised we managed to keep this many guns."

Zach came out of the door and stood with his hands on his hips.

"Anyone seen the coolers? Jeez, we have got to stop leaving stuff behind. With a misplaced Yeti cooler we're going to alter the fate of the world."

I laughed. "By leaving a cooler in the past, the *world* will crumble apart? What do you think is going to happen?"

"I don't know, Katie, maybe someone is doing an archeological dig, they uncover a modern-day cooler in an ancient site, and the veil of secrecy around time-travel is pulled back — world governments discover that time travel exists, there becomes a race to see who can colonize the most historical periods with bigger arms to gain more power, and the past collapses in on itself. Humanity ceases to exist."

I said, "*Or*, the archeologist says, 'Whoowee, what's that there Yeti cooler doing in my dig? Hey everyone stop leaving your shit in our archeological dig,' and everyone says, 'Sorry sir,' and no one thinks about time travel at all because a cooler in Scotland does not prove time travel."

James said, "They could carbon date it, but 'oh wait — this is from this year, never mind, don't know how it got in our dig site, but we should toss it away and move on with uncovering pottery shards.'"

Zach said, "Yeah yeah, you're right."

I said, "It's like with diapers…" I blinked and put my hands on my hips and stared at my feet.

Then I looked at Magnus. "Weird."

"What is weird?"

"I don't know why my mind went to diapers then…"

He put his arm around my shoulders and squeezed and kissed my head.

"Yer dreams hae been givin' ye moments of worry, ye daena need tae worry on it, mo reul-iuil, it is going tae be okay."

We decided we would have to wait at least a day to go, because as Magnus said, "We hae plenty of guns, but without plenty of packed coolers, what is the good of a trip?"

The following day we had the coolers packed with food and a chest full of gifts for Magnus's brother and sister and even something for the Earl though we all scowled while packing it.

We dressed in our eighteenth century garb, taking gold and money and jewels with us.

Hayley and Fraoch would travel with us, James and Quentin would stay and guard the house, get some things done. James needed to check in with his businesses.

Hayley and I linked arms. She held Fraoch's hand. He held the reins of our horses, Dràgon, Thor, Osna, and Gatorbelle.

Magnus said, "Are we ready? We are about tae ride on God's arm."

Fraoch chuckled. "What does that mean?"

"I was watching Ben play with his cars this morn, ye ken how he pushes them around? I was thinkin' we are like that car, and God is like Ben, pushin' us through time. It helps me tae think on God doing it, tis the only way I can convince m'self tae go."

Fraoch said, "Alright then, bring on God's arm."

Magnus twisted the vessel and we went to the past.

We awoke in the clearing, where I had awoken what felt like a million times before.

CHAPTER 29 - MAGNUS

1709 - THE CLEARING IN SCOTLAND

Sean's voice came down tae me from his horse. "Och, Young Magnus, like a pig in swill ye are lying there in the mud, if I had evil in m'heart, ye'd be dead already."

"Ye do hae evil in yer heart, because ye considered it — every time I come tae visit ye mention how ye might kill me if ye could. Tis a sign that ye wish ye might."

"Aye, tis true, we are brothers, are we nae? I would die tae protect ye from harm, but when ye are asleep I think, 'Och, he is verra easy tae kill right now, I might put him from m'misery.'"

Magnus grumbled as he got up. "The desire goes both ways."

Sean dismounted from his horse. "But if ye killed me in my sleep, who would be here tae pick ye up from the muck and mire of the forest floor, Young Magnus? Ye must think verra highly of yer own prowess that ye believe ye are able tae protect yerself from danger, the way ye are sleepin' there on the ground."

I glanced down, Kaitlyn was stirrin' from her sleep. She pushed against the ground and rose with a groan tae sittin'.

Sean said, "Young Magnus, ye look well and healthy, if I dinna ken any better I would say ye are younger."

"Tis the fine food they hae in m'kingdom, I hae brought ye coolers packed with food cooked by Chef Zach!"

"Good, good."

I stood up and brushed off m' kilt and m'back.

Sean said, "And where is Jack?"

"Jack who?"

Sean froze. "*Jack,* yer *son.*"

I felt as if a shockwave had gone through me,

my heart skipped a beat, the auld familiar pain of a weak heart,

I stared at m'brother,

"What?"

"Yer son, Magnus, where is he? Has somethin'…?"

I took a step back and nearly tripped over a cooler. I dropped down tae sit on it.

Sean raised his voice. "Magnus! What has happened tae yer son?"

I looked at Kaitlyn. "Kaitlyn, what has happened…?"

Her eyes wide, she shook her head slowly. "What is he saying… ? Magnus, I don't understand…"

Sean said, "Magnus, stop yer dissemblin', ye were here, visitin', Kaitlyn gave birth tae a bairn… ye were here, ye…"

I shook my head.

Kaitlyn muttered, *nonononnonooo…* "What is going on, Magnus?"

Sean drew his sword. "Young Magnus, ye hae only one moment tae explain this sorcery…"

I put up m'hands. The look in his eyes held fury and fear and I knew twas a dangerous combination, even though twas m'brother holding the hilt of the sword — "I daena understand… I canna explain."

Fraoch rose tae his feet. "Sean, we can explain it, we need tae confer, we must…"

Sean held the sword out menacingly. "Ye look younger as well, Fraoch. How long has it been since yer last visit?"

Fraoch put his hands up, placatingly, "I think it has been a year at least."

Sean said, "Disarm yerself, throw yer sword and yer dirk tae the side."

"Why, what hae I…?"

Sean roared, "Do it!"

Fraoch disarmed himself and tossed his sword away. Fraoch said, "Do Hayley and I hae bairns?"

Sean's brow drew down. "Nae, ye daena hae bairns, but when yer family was here last Quentin had a new son and—"

Hayley said, "Quentin and Beaty have a son?"

"Aye, his name is Noah, and ye daena—?"

She shook her head.

Sean stepped back. "Nae, nae! Och, this is a dangerous evil afoot!"

Then he and Liam spoke tae each other, their words barely comin' tae my ears over the howl of fear. "…how dost Magnus not ken the birth of his son?"

Sean said, "I daena ken, Liam, but tis an evil that has overtaken them, a spell. I daena understand."

Sean aimed his sword at m'heart. "Ye hae one moment tae explain how ye daena ken where Jack is…"

I, with my hands up, said, "I daena ken who ye are speakin' on."

He turned his hands on the sword quickly and thrust the brunt of it at my head, so fast that I dinna hae a moment tae block the move — pain exploded against my head.

Kaitlyn shrieked.

I collapsed from the cooler tae the ground and the light around me went dim.

I returned tae consciousness a time later, lyin' in a cart, being wheeled through the forest. My hands were bound behind me. The cart jostled and bounced me uncomfortably. I raised my head. Hayley and Kaitlyn were walking beside the cart, their arms around each other. Fraoch's wrists were bound, the rope tied tae the cart, leadin' him tae stumble behind us.

Sean, from on his horse, met m'eyes. "Daena try anything, Magnus. I am warnin' ye, I will kill ye."

I glanced up tae see Liam ridin' the horse that was pullin' the cart; he looked back at me, a cold glare in his eyes.

CHAPTER 30 - KAITLYN

1709 - BALLOCH CASTLE

*W*e drew toward the castle gate. I felt like I was in a horror movie — the sky was darkening, the guards all looking over the edge of the wall at my husband tied up in the bottom of the cart. Liam ordered the gate opened and crowds gathered and stared as we entered.

I had a son?

Where was he?

Why couldn't I remember?

A hush fell over the crowd.

The cart jostled, Magnus groaned.

Hayley whispered. "I don't understand, Katie, what is going on?"

"I have forgotten a… oh my god, a—" I couldn't say it, I clutched my stomach and my mouth. *Oh no.*

As we entered the courtyard, Sean whispered, "I want ye tae be silent on the matter, ye canna tell anyone in the castle about this evil."

John, the son of the Earl, rushed up. "Liam, what is the meaning of this…?"

"I will explain it in yer offices, we will need, with yer permission, tae put these men in the dungeon."

"Who, Young Magnus?" His hand went to his throat. "This is unusual. Lady Mairead will throw a fit... and what of Madame Lizbeth?"

Sean dismounted his horse, stalked to the side of the cart, and yanked Magnus up by the arm. "Madame Lizbeth daena get a—"

Madame Lizbeth rushed into the courtyard and then froze in shock. "What has happened, Sean?"

"These men are goin' tae the dungeons."

Her eyes wide she said, "But this is Young Magnus, what did he do?"

"He inna tae be trusted." Sean shoved Magnus forward tae the doors of the dungeon. Liam untied Fraoch from the cart and began shoving him, following Sean.

Lizbeth turned to me. "Madame Kaitlyn! What has happened?"

I shook my head, I barely got out the words, "I don't know. I don't understand."

"It must hae been something! Where are yer bairns?"

I shook my head.

"Jack?"

I sobbed, "I don't know, I don't know who Jack is."

Hayley clutched her arms around my shoulders.

Lizbeth took a step back. "Isla? Where is she?"

Tears streamed down my face.

I shook my head.

She took two steps back. Her hands drawn up, her fingers out, forming a cross. "Kaitlyn, where are Isla and Jack?"

"I don't know who they are."

Lizbeth fainted down into the dirt of the courtyard. Women rushed to her side.

I buried my face in Hayley's arms. "Do you remember?"

She said, "I don't remember anything."

CHAPTER 31 - MAGNUS

1709 - THE DUNGEON

I was unceremoniously tossed tae the ground inside a cell. Fraoch was shoved in, stumbling past me.

He said, "I daena understand what is happening, why are we being held?"

"Because ye are either liars or murderers or thieves, perhaps all of it, and until ye give me a satisfactory explanation I winna listen tae ye on anything else." Sean slammed the door shut, and stood starin' at me through the small window in the thick wooden door.

I lay there, not even wantin' tae rise, feeling as if my heart might break. "Where is Kaitlyn?"

"I am sure Lizbeth is seein' tae her."

"She is probably verra frightened."

"What did ye do tae yer bairns?"

I looked up at the ceilin' of the stone cold cell. "What dost ye mean by bairns?"

Sean's voice was measured, "Ye hae Archie, he is almost eight years auld."

I mumbled, "I ken Archie."

"Ye hae Isla—"

"Och nae." I rolled ontae my side, my temple pressed tae the hard-packed dirt ground, I asked, "How old is she?"

"She is three years auld. She is a pain in yer arse. How can ye not ken of her?"

I shook my head. "And there is another boy?"

"Aye, his name is Jack. He was born in yer room upstairs, not four months ago."

"Och nae, something has gone wrong."

Sean and Liam stood in the door lookin' down on me. "Ye hae had an evil overtake ye."

I said, "Sean, brother, I hae told ye of the time travel?"

"Aye, that is the evil I am speakin' on, ye canna go against God, Young Magnus, tae go against the order of the world. Time is meant tae roll along, ye canna play as a God, tae—"

"How could I forget the bairns?"

Fraoch slumped tae the ground beside me. "I am sorry for it, Og Maggy, it inna fair."

Sean said, "I daena understand how ye could forget them, Magnus."

I said, "There is a man, his name is Ranulph, he has been changin' time, I think."

Sean exhaled. "All I ken is ye told me, once, that if ye ever came and ye dinna understand what had happened in time, that I was tae subdue ye and put ye in a cell. Ye told me not tae listen tae ye, that ye would be changing time, possibly looping upon yerself, ye told me that it would be dangerous."

Fraoch said, "He wasna wrong, this is dangerous."

I nodded.

Liam said, gruffly, "What of my bairns, how many ought I tae hae?"

I said, "Two by Lizbeth. She has a son by her first husband."

He grunted.

I asked, "Tis right?"

"Aye."

Sean said, "And what of me, Young Magnus?"

"Ye hae had yer sixth bairn, and of them there are five sons."

Sean looked down. "This is right. Why daena ye remember yer own?"

I shook my head.

Sean said, "So that is why ye are here, and I am not lettin' ye go until I speak tae Kaitlyn. Ye ought tae figure out what yer plan is and how ye are going tae solve this and I will tell ye, Magnus, if ye do something tae time that causes me tae lose my sons I will kill ye, and I winna consider it for a moment first."

"I understand."

CHAPTER 32 - KAITLYN

LEAVE AFORE THE DAWN BREAKS

*L*izbeth was revived and was sitting on a stool, where she recovered enough to look up at me.

She shook her head. "How could ye?"

Tears streamed down my face. "I don't know!"

Hayley said, "Can we go talk somewhere private, this is all very upsetting, and people are watching."

Lizbeth stood, her hands shaking, and gestured for us to follow her along the familiar passages up to her chambers. She had a sitting area where there was a sofa and two chairs in front of the hearth.

She closed the door, and gestured for us to sit.

She paced in front of me. "I canna understand it, Kaitlyn, ye hae forgotten yer bairns?"

I ran a trembling hand through my hair. "Bairns? More than one?"

Her eyes went very wide. "Aye, Kaitlyn, there is Isla, she is three, and then Jack, who is newly born. I was there, I saw him born!"

I slumped back in the seat.

She said, "Ye remember Archie?"

I nodded.

"Where did the others go?"

Hayley said, "Maybe we're from another time, maybe we're just younger versions of ourselves in the wrong place. That can happen right? How would we know?"

I said, "Lizbeth, do you remember what year it was in our time?"

"Nae, ye never mentioned it, but…" She considered it for a moment. "How old is Archie?"

I said, "He's almost eight years old."

Lizbeth folded her hands as if in prayer. "Och nae, Kaitlyn, that is the age he is supposed tae be — he was just here the other day, and before he left he said some verra kind things tae his cousins. They told me they mocked him for it, but ye could see they think highly of him, they are great friends as well as cousins. Mary said that Isla told her she loved her. Nae, nae, how are ye without yer bairns?"

Hayley squeezed me around my shoulders.

"I don't know, I think I need to see Magnus."

"I need tae ask Sean first."

"Ye need to ask…? I've never known you to defer to Sean before."

"I hae never heard anything as serious as this before, Kaitlyn, this is a horrible thing that has happened tae us, and tis because of yer adventures. Ye hae made the possibility of bairns disappearing… och nae! Tis a terrible thought, it *must* be against God's plan for us!" She paced, "It must be. We hae a life, we are born and we die, how is it possible that we can hae our bairns disappear without knowing them?"

She turned to me. "What does Lady Mairead say on it?"

"She doesn't know."

"She is always the one risking our lives with her adventures. Ye must tell her. She needs tae help ye understand what is happening."

She dropped down into the chair across from us. "We will wait for Sean, he will tell us what tae do. I hae never come across such a tryin', evil, circumstance as this, I hope he has a wisdom I lack."

It was a very uncomfortable wait, there was a fire in the hearth, crackling and popping, but my chair was far away, the room was cold, and I was shaken to my core.

I stared down at my hands.

No one spoke.

～

Sean entered a bit later with Liam following. Sean sat down beside Lizbeth on the sofa. He exhaled, his elbows on his knees.

"Madame Kaitlyn, ye daena ken where yer bairns hae gone?"

I shook my head.

"Ye daena remember them?" He asked very quietly.

"No."

Lizbeth was wringing her hands. Then she sat bolt upright in her seat, her eyes frightened, "How many bairns do I hae?"

I said, "Three."

She sank back into her seat. "Good, aye, that is right, thank God in Heaven for keeping m'bairns safe."

Liam put his hand on her shoulder to calm her. She patted the back of his hand and looked off in the direction of the window.

Sean said, "How will ye proceed? What will ye do?"

"I have no idea, but I need to speak to Magnus."

He said, "I ken, ye must make a plan, ye must... I am telling ye, Kaitlyn, ye canna bring this danger here, ye must solve it but ye canna involve us. I believed it tae be God-less, but I thought ye were keepin' the evil of it from us. I thought ye were traveling tae the 'kingdom' and returning, without causing the evil tae spill out ontae our lives, but here ye are, there is some dark magic afoot, and ye hae brought it tae our doorstep."

He added, "What happens if ye change our time and we lose our bairns? God forbid, what if ye hae already? Kaitlyn, how are we tae live with the knowledge that ye might be bringing this nightmare intae our world?"

I nodded again, tears streaming down my face. Beyond this whole tragedy there was something devastating in Sean's tone. His voice measured and stern, almost cold.

Magnus and I had lost our bairns, but... there was a feeling of detachment. I didn't know I had bairns, it was a horrible thing to not know and to have no feelings about, and now Magnus's brother and sister were telling us to go away. They were repulsed by what had happened to us, and didn't want it to spill onto them. I couldn't blame them, not at all.

Sean said, "Thankfully the minister inna here, or he would ask after the bairns, and as we canna explain it, we must get ye gone afore it happens."

"It feels very confusing, I just don't know what has happened, I don't understand it, at all..."

"I ken, neither can I, but ye... will ye need tae go tae the chapel tae pray?"

I nodded.

"Good, take Magnus, he will need it, but then ye will hae tae gather yer husband and Fraoch and Madame Hayley and ye will leave afore the dawn breaks."

Hayley stood.

I stood.

She nodded and led me to the door.

Sean filed out behind us, then led us silently down the hallway to the stairs.

CHAPTER 33 - MAGNUS

ALL THAT IS WRONG IN THE WORLD

I was sitting on a low bench in the cell, when the door opened and Kaitlyn rushed in and collapsed on me, her face pressed to my neck, she spoke intae my skin, "They say there are bairns. They say they are ours and we have forgotten them!"

"I ken."

I said tae Sean, "Can ye let m'wrists from the bindings?"

Sean said, "Are ye goin' tae try tae fight me? Because, again, I am not enjoyin' yer company and I will kill ye rather than put up with ye."

"Nae, I will be sensible. I just need tae comfort m'wife."

He untied m'wrists. "Fraoch, ye winna fight me?"

"Nae, I want tae go on the record though, twas not me that did any of this, I daena ken why my wrists are bound."

"So ye winna kill me for binding Magnus. I ken how ye will protect him, as a brother."

"Says the brother threatenin' tae kill him."

Sean untied Fraoch's bindings, and asked, "What would ye hae me do?"

Fraoch said, "I daena ken, this is unheard of."

"Aye, these are the singular deeds which might cause a man

tae go out of his mind with rage. It requires a butt tae the head and bound arms tae give him time tae think."

Sean led Fraoch from the cell. "We will give them a moment."

I rubbed my wrists, then put my arms around Kaitlyn.

"You promised me," she said, simply.

"I ken, I promised ye tae keep ye safe and—"

She pushed me away. "You promised me you would keep me safe. You promised me you would give me children." She shoved on my chest. "You promised me, Magnus, you said you would! Not this horror show where the world doesn't make sense and I HAVE HAD BABIES and I don't know them!"

"I am sorry, mo reul-iuil."

"Where did they go? What if *everyone* had forgotten them? What if we didn't know this had happened and we just lived a life without my babies?"

I shook my head, "I meant it, I ken this is dark and dire, but I meant I would keep ye safe, and our bairns safe and…"

"Are they with me, in an alternate universe or something? Or are they alone somewhere? Or have they died? Why haven't I had more and—"

I reached for her.

She shoved my arms away. "And what if that was my only chance and now they are gone! You promised me!"

"I meant it, mo reul-iuil. I meant every word, and I will fix this, I will."

"How? How will you fix this? We are in a dungeon in the eighteenth century."

"The door is open, mo reul-iuil, Sean winna keep me here. He just put me away until I could calm myself down, or rather he could calm himself down."

"He said we have to leave, he said we can't stay. It all feels very frightening, like I'm being accused of something that I didn't do, but it also involves children and…"

I looked off into space. "Is it in the record book in the chapel? Would that list them? Can we go see it?"

"Aye." I stood and dusted off and followed her from the cell.

We passed Sean. "Where are ye goin' Magnus?"

"Tae the chapel, then we will leave for home. I will leave ye the coolers, the food, ye can pass it out tae the family."

"Good, thank ye for understandin', I canna risk that ye might bring harm down on us in some way. I canna lose m'bairns, Magnus, Maggie would die."

"I ken." We hugged.

"Make sure ye pray, Young Magnus."

"I will."

I led Kaitlyn down the passage, with Fraoch and Hayley following us.

At the chapel we went up tae the table near the altar where the book of family records was kept. Kaitlyn dinna speak, she looked over my arm as I flipped the pages tae the records: Magnus Archibald Caelhin Campbell and his wife, Kaitlyn. The date of our marriage, month and day. My finger trailed along the record, it listed Archibald, and then there was a name, written in my hand, Isla Peace Barbara, and then another, Jack.

I said, "Och nae."

I glanced at Kaitlyn's face, tears covered it. She wiped her eyes on her sleeve.

I pulled her into my arms, and held her though she struggled. "Where did they go? I hate you, what did you do to them?"

I held her, until she stopped struggling as she sobbed and then clutched around me and held on, sobbing in my arms.

I said, "I ken, I ken Kaitlyn, yer heart will break from it."

She said, "My heart wants to break because I don't feel anything at all."

~

Fraoch and Hayley sat quietly waiting for us tae recover and then we conferred. We would go home. I said, "I need tae talk tae the group about what tae do."

Sean sent for our horses and they met us at the gate. Twas dark. The guards, m'friends and extended family, watched us as we left, Sean walking alongside us.

"What else do ye ken about m'family, how many bairns do Chef Zach and Emma hae?"

"Two bairns, Quentin has one, James and Sophie daena—"

"Who?"

He glanced at m'face. "Sophie is married tae James Cook, and then there is Lochinvar, ye remember Lochinvar, daena ye?"

I shook my head as we walked. "Nae," I said simply. Then I asked, "What will ye tell the Earl? The other men?"

"I will tell them that ye came home for a short visit, but that ye were drunk and disorderly and that I kept ye until ye felt better and then sent ye away. I will tell them that ye will return."

Kaitlyn mounted her horse.

I mounted mine. I asked, "Will I?"

Sean said, "Ye canna stay away, Magnus, this is yer family, but ye canna return if ye bring this danger tae us — ye will need tae decide. Ye ken, I will fight alongside ye, I will ride intae battle for ye, but this is… I canna help ye battle this."

"Aye, I understand," I said, "give Lizbeth m'love."

"I will."

I turned my horse and we rode through the gate.

On the other side, our horses trudging through the darkness, the only light the moon, we went in the direction of the woods.

Fraoch said, "What he daena ken though, Og Maggy, is if this danger has befallen us, I daena ken how he is safe. If ye arna there, it daena mean that time winna change for him. He might not know, everything might be different."

"I ken, but I winna argue that it is more dangerous than he thinks, he believes it is plenty dangerous, and he believes I am the one causing it."

"Tis like a brother tae blame ye for all that is wrong in the world."

"In this instance he is correct."

I glanced at Kaitlyn, her cheeks wet, her hair mussed, her heart broken, and I wondered how we would fix this problem.

CHAPTER 34 - KAITLYN

2024 - THOUGHT THIS WAS M'HOME

*M*y everything hurt and I felt depressed. I curled up around my knees in the sand, not even caring if people came and rescued us or not. A horse whinnied nearby.

Magnus groaned.

We had had a family. A big full family with children, and now what did we have? A few friends. Nothing more.

Friends were great of course, but knowing that I had lost more, had lost my family, lost all…

I felt numb, unable to imagine how hard it would be to go on.

Magnus raised his head, figured out where I was, then rolled to his stomach, dragged himself closer, and dropped his head on my chest.

"How will we fix it? How will we fight it?"

"I daena ken how ye will fight, but I ken ye will, mo reuliuil."

A gull flew across the sky. "Somehow I'm supposed to be the kind of person who fights for kids she doesn't know, she's never even met? It seems unlikely, and I don't know how."

"We will figure out how, Kaitlyn, I canna bear it, not

knowing how, I canna leave ye without yer bairns, without our family."

My chin trembled as my eyes followed the gull tae the wet sand near the waves.

He watched me for a moment. "Please forgive me."

"You didn't do anything."

"Aye, please forgive me for it."

His voice choked, I looked down on his face and then hugged around his head, holding him to my chest, and there we sobbed in the sand of a Florida day as our friends picked up our gear and carried it tae the truck, waiting for us to rise.

James offered to take Dràgon and Osna to the stables, and so Magnus, Hayley, and I rode in the truck, with a dour mood settled on us, staring out the window. Quentin asked, "So what happened?"

"We will talk about it at the house."

"Does it involve anything that we need to arm ourselves over?"

"Nae more than our usual state of emergency."

"I suppose that's a relief." He parked the truck in front of the door and we climbed out on legs stiff and sore from the jump.

I looked up at the door and Magnus followed my eyes.

Would there be children there — *had* there been children there?

We hadn't wanted to ask Quentin, it was too painful — do we have children?

Far better, less painful to see, with our own eyes.

We slowly trudged up the steps to the door.

And the answer was clear…

. . .

Chef Zach cheerfully said, "Welcome home! Food is on!" Then he saw our faces and said, "Ah man, what the hell happened?"

Hayley said, "It's what didn't happen. They need a stiff drink."

We dropped into chairs and Zach brought over a pitcher of go-go juice with small glasses. He placed it in front of us. "Not until after vitamins, I can't look at the distress in your face and give you a stiff drink, that seems irresponsible."

Emma said, "I don't know if I've ever heard you use the word 'irresponsible' correctly in a sentence."

He laughed. "I'm growing, I'm learning. Now what the fuck happened to you?"

Magnus and I were sitting with our hands clasped together on the table. He said, "Time has changed. I daena ken how exactly, perhaps it happened when we saw the storms, perhaps it has been happening slowly for a time, I daena ken, but none of this is the way tis supposed tae be."

Quentin said, "Hold on, James is coming up the steps."

We waited for James to enter, come to the table, and drop down in a chair. I said, "What did I miss?"

"Magnus says time has changed."

James tipped his chair back and looked around. "How would we know?"

I put my head in my hands.

Magnus said, "We are missing bairns. Lizbeth and Sean said when we were last there we had bairns that arna here now."

Emma's eyes were wide. "When were we last there?"

I dropped my hands down, palms up. "Weeks ago — Emma, do you remember being there weeks ago?"

She shook her head.

Zach said, "Fuck."

Quentin straightened in his seat. "Nah, this shit is... this is not okay, none of us were there — but why did we pick that date? Why did we go there after a time when we were already there, you know? It's like our subconscious did it."

Zach pointed. "Very good point, Quennie, yes, why did we pick that date? If we were there, we must have had a memory of when to go, something that protected us from looping... Anyone remember going to visit?"

Quentin said, "But I do keep having vague ideas that things are missing, or I remember having more of it than we have, or... but those are just misrememberings. Or so I thought."

Emma said, "Yes yes, I'm having misremembers all over the place, but you're saying we're missing people? Actual babies? More than one?"

I nodded.

She stood up. "What about me and Zachary, are we missing babies?"

I said, "No, they said you had two, Ben and Zoe."

She nodded and returned to her seat. Zach said, "Phew, there was a half-moment there where I was going to have a heart attack."

Hayley said, "Shush," she gestured toward me, "They said that Kaitlyn had given birth to a boy named Jack just months ago, and that she also had a little girl named Isla."

I shook my head, sadly. "I don't remember my own children."

Zach said, "Damn, I'm so sorry Katie."

Hayley said, "They also said that Quentin and Beaty have a baby."

Quentin said, "What the hell! No no no no, that is not..."

Beaty was sitting at the end of the table with her feet drawn up in the chair. Mookie beside her, his chin on her thigh. "Quennie, I don't understand what they are sayin'."

He moved to the chair beside her and put his arm around her. "They are saying we had a baby, and that there has been a timeshift."

She shook her head. "Wouldna I ken, how dost I not ken?"

"I don't know, Beaty, I really don't."

James said, "Well this shit sucks."

Hayley said, "Yep."

James said, "Well, what is done can be undone, and guess what, what is undone can be done up again."

Magnus said, "Aye, like laces on a bodice."

"Exactly, we just lace this shit up."

Magnus said, "But how?"

Emma said, "I hate to say it, this is big — you'll need to go ask Lady Mairead for advice."

Magnus said, "I was just there, verra recently…"

I said, "Why did you go without me?"

Magnus looked at me blankly. "I daena ken why — ye werna there."

"That seems odd, why wouldn't I go?"

Quentin said, "So Sean just knew something was amiss?"

"Aye, he asked me where m'new son was, and I had nae recollection. He kicked m'arse and put me in the dungeon."

Zach said, "You couldn't remember your son and you got put in a dungeon? That's medieval."

Magnus said, "I canna blame him, tis a frightening thing tae lose a memory that profound. He was furious and Lizbeth was upset. They were fearful that shifting times might cause them tae lose bairns as well. They forced us away, twas all they could do, I am not allowed tae return until I re-order the world."

Everyone sort of winced.

James said, "Guess that's what we have to do: a man's gotta be able to go home."

Magnus said, "I thought this was m'home, but tis hard tae ken anything anymore."

I put my head down on my arms and began to cry.

CHAPTER 35 - KAITLYN

COFFEE MUGS AND PHOTOS

*T*hat night Magnus and I clung together in bed, talking about how the world was shifting without our knowing it. It was one of our 'frightened' conversations, trembling, sometimes weeping, consoling, but without hope — hope is necessary after all. We had all of our hope tied in the idea of checking in with Lady Mairead, but we couldn't imagine what she would do — what *could* she do?

We made love and it was a wonderful release, building from comfort to caresses and then to a pressing urgency, peeling of clothes, gripping and holding, tight and desperate — perfectly done. Then post-climax we held on, thoughtful and loving until slowly the fear and confusion crept in again, and we slowly let go, moved apart by degrees, by shifts in our breaths, separated. Then slowly we drifted to sleep.

～

My nightmare returned, the fog ahead of us, a brisk night, a distant thunder had my heart racing as I peered into the mist trying to see — *what was coming?* The thunder rumbled like a storm, but approached like an army… *who?*

My arms enclosed my baby… My hand encased a wee hand. I looked down, my bairns were there, looking up at me, a flash of recognition — my bairns!

Then the army bore down through the bracken of the moor, Magnus yelled, "Run!"

And I ran, the barbaric man bearing down on me — I ran, alone.

I woke with a start.

Magnus's voice came through the darkness — "Twas a night-mare, mo reul-iuil. Ye are safe."

"They were there!"

He lay quietly waiting for me to finish.

"They were there, Magnus, there was a…" I thought for a moment trying to get the memory to come back.

I could feel the flash of recognition, the weight in my arms of a baby… the feel of a wee hand in mine but…

I wrapped around my knees and pressed my eyes to my knee caps. "They were there and I recognized them and now I can't think of their faces. I have no idea."

He said, "Twas a dream, perhaps the horror of it came tae ye because ye ken there are supposed tae be bairns—"

"It wasn't my mind playing tricks, Magnus, this is the dream I've been having for weeks, the kids are in it, my kids, but they are just an…" I shook my head, because it felt like I had heard this word before, describing this, but I wasn't sure where or how, "An echo," I finished and lay back, sprawled.

Then we both lay there, my heart racing, my eyes traveling back and forth on the ceiling.

I said, "It's like we're on an alternate timeline, like…" I tried to remember. "Has this happened to us before?"

He exhaled, long and low. "I daena think so."

"I don't think so either, I only know one thing."

"What?"

"We need to kill this dude."

"Aye, Ranulph, consider him already dead."

"Good, and I want to go see Lady Mairead first thing in the morning."

He picked up my hand and kissed my fingers. He was still clasping my hand as we managed to sleep once more.

We got dressed for a day of travel to his kingdom and then went down for breakfast.

Zach said, "You look rested, like you feel better."

I said, "Not well rested, don't feel much better, but yeah, we at least have a decision: we're going to go—" I opened the cabinet to pick a mug for coffee and gaped. "Why we got so many coffee mugs?"

I opened up another cabinet and another. "And plates and wine glasses, holy cannoli, look at all the wine glasses, why?"

Zach shrugged. "For entertaining I think, probably."

I opened another cabinet, "But these are the *fancy* wine glasses, right, this is a set of, how many?"

"I probably got it in a pack of twelve, that's how I usually think…"

I went back to staring into the regular, daily wine glass cabinet. "I mean, I know we're rich, but there are twenty wine glasses in here."

I closed that cabinet and stood in front of the coffee mugs, turning my head on the side, trying to figure out. "I have forty-two mugs to choose from, how many people live here—?" I did a mental headcount. "Ten right? Is that right?"

I counted again, "Eight, wait… am I forgetting someone?"

I glanced around.

My heart was pounding, "Ten? Is that right?"

My breath was coming fast and I grabbed hold of the edge of the counter to keep from falling — Zach rushed behind me. "Shit, you gonna fall down, Katie? Breathe, come on…"

My eyes felt wild, I was trying to see, but my sight had drawn to a pinpoint, there was not enough air and — Emma said, "Are you having a panic attack? *Katie?*"

Magnus's face swam into view. His eyes were worried, but he had a smile plastered on. "Ye hae fainted from countin' the number of coffee mugs, mo reul-iuil. Usually ye are more sensible."

I blinked as the whole episode came back to me. "But there are so many!"

"I ken, there are too many."

"Don't you think that means there are *people* missing? Maybe we're missing even more people than we thought."

Zach said, "Or, not to discount your worries, Katie, *or…* it could be that I hoard dinnerware, perhaps stemming from the past, when I served many-a meal in mismatched dishes with plastic cups."

I looked around at all their faces. "Yeah, that's probably it."

I put out a hand for someone to help me up and dusted off my pants. "Yeah, probably." Then I huffed. "But we wouldn't know, and it seems like a way that we *could* know. We own enough dish ware for a much bigger family and, you know, maybe we don't need to be worried about it, not unnecessarily, but maybe we better get solving this issue, fast."

Zach said, "I agree, either I'm a hoarder, or we lost people and we better find them, whoever they are. But also, this makes me sound high. It's far more likely that I'm just a hoarder."

Hayley dropped down in a chair. Placing a stack of three shoebox-sized boxes beside her and snapped her fingers. "Coffee please, I'm exhausted!"

James said, "Katie was just sprawled out on the ground from a panic attack, but yeah, let's make it all about Hayley, that sounds good."

She said, "Katie, you cool, or was it just one of your drama-queen moments?"

"I'm cool. Why didn't you sleep?"

"Because of all of this — so I sat up with our boxes of photos. Thanks to our resident photographer, Beaty, we have lots."

Beaty dropped a bite of apple at her feet for Mookie.

Hayley opened one of the lids and pulled out photos.

We all sat down around the table.

Zach said, "Swear to god, Hayley, if you have photos of ghosts of people we don't recognize, I'm going to faint clean on the floor, maybe run screaming into the woods."

"Nah, there's no ghosts, nobody here I don't recognize, and... actually let me just say, Katie, there aren't any babies here, no kids... I'm sorry, I think it would have been good to have proof, you know?"

I sighed. "I'm not entirely sure, that might be more horrible, like the photo of someone you're supposed to remember, but you don't? It could send me to the floor again."

"Yeah, it would suck either way... but it's not gonna happen. I looked through it a few times. Some great photos, by the way, Beaty."

"Thank ye kindly, Madame Hayley."

I sipped my coffee. "So what did you find out?"

"Nothing, really. It seems like there's an absence and it isn't something I can easily prove. Like, if someone isn't in the photos, it doesn't prove they're not there, they might be hiding in the corner, you know? That was what I was thinking about in the middle of the night. Then I thought… and it hit me like a hammer to the head: there isn't anyone else with us."

She placed out five photos. Standing in groups, we all looked happy, one big happy family.

James said, "Not sure what that shows."

She tapped on the photo. "Why the hell are you here?"

He shrugged, but looked thoughtful. "I don't know, wanted an adventure?"

She ignored him. "And what about me? Do you know how old I am? I'm almost thirty. I'm in every single photo." She pointed at one and another and another. "Why am I alone hanging out with Katie and Mags and you know," she waved her hand at everyone else.

I said, "Is this a mid-life crisis?"

"No, but kinda. Why are James and I hanging out with you so much? We need lives, we need someone, a relationship, a family of our own."

I squinted. "You don't want kids."

"You know what I mean. Here's my two questions: one, why are James and I, two very eligible people, hanging out with you and your family all the time? And second, why the hell don't we get a life?" She pushed the photos into a tidy pile. "I think we're missing people. I think there is a reason why we are hanging out here, beyond a couple of random babies, I think there are grown ass adults lost in time too." She huffed. "I need a drink."

Zach said, "You don't drink, want a waffle?'"

"Fine."

I said, "I just had a similar epiphany, take a look sometime at how many coffee mugs we own."

Quentin said, "Enough for an AA meeting."

"Yep, and not some small podunk-town AA meeting, a full-on Hollywood AA meeting. So since you're up all night researching and horrified by what's going on, do you want to go with us to talk to Lady Mairead?"

"Heck no, that lady is horrible to me." She stared off in the distance. "And I have no idea why."

CHAPTER 36 - KAITLYN

2390 - A TIME OF INCONSISTENCY

*M*agnus was in king mode, his jaw-clenched, well-armed, wearing his uniform. Quentin had stacked gear around us. I was wearing a power suit, the kind of outfit that one wore to speak to Lady Mairead, a little like an 'I'm in congress but I'm young and hip' kind of outfit. Nice shoes too, but standing in sand in them was a ridiculous thing.

Magnus was hot as all hell. I wrapped my arm around his and pressed my forehead to his shoulder and shut my eyes. I found myself praying. Magnus and Quentin had a final brief consultation about what we were taking with us, and whether they had remembered what we needed. I wasn't doing anything, except *going*.

Magnus twisted the vessel and we were torn from our time.

When I fully came up from unconsciousness, Magnus was standing beside me. I was flat on my back on a stretcher, a blanket over me, a physician nearby. Protocol was funny here, they were concerned about us, as if the trip was dangerous —

most of the time I woke up on a muddy forest floor having been chased there by an evildoer.

Magnus was already in the middle of his duties: organizing men, discussing posts, strategizing. His highest ranking general was there, updating Magnus about recent issues.

I sat up on the edge of the stretcher, gathering my strength, then stood up. Magnus said, "Ye good?"

"Yeah, let's go talk to Lady Mairead."

"I sent word, we are meeting her in her dressing room."

We swept from the landing pad, through the door to the long corridor, toward the royal apartments. There we finally came to Lady Mairead's royal chamber, with two guardsmen posted outside the doors. Magnus knocked. "Lady Mairead, tis us."

Her voice, "Come in! I am sorry I am dressing, I hae a gala tonight. I wasna expecting guests!"

We entered an expansive ornate room, with a round settee in the center, surrounded by closets. One closet was full of hanging clothes; one had shelves of boxes of shoes; drawers for her under-clothes occupied a third; and there was a closet dedicated to eighteenth century garb. There was a very large mirror in the middle, and she leaned in, applying lipstick, her hair swept up in a lovely stylish coif. She wore a dark burgundy long velvet dress, with a deeply plunging back, and had an incredibly expensive-looking pearl necklace at her throat. She looked dignified and timeless, like an incredibly rich benefactor heading to a fundraiser that would include the Getty family, and the Roth-schilds.

She continued in the mirror as we entered. "I was nae expecting ye, Magnus, nae so soon."

Magnus gestured for me to sit on the settee. He continued to stand. "I am relieved ye remember I visited ye recently." He paused, then spoke again. "We are experiencin' discrepancies in time." He stopped and cocked his head. "Are ye younger?"

"What dost ye mean? Nae, I am a few days past when ye last saw me."

His brow drew down.

"Perhaps tis my makeup and dress."

"Perhaps. Ye do look striking."

"Why thank ye, Magnus, what dost ye need?"

He exhaled, then said, "Kaitlyn and I hae discovered that we... we are missing bairns."

Her hand stopped mid-smear of the lipstick across her lips, her face frozen in fear. "What dost ye mean, Magnus? *Bairns?*"

"Aye, I..." He shook his head, looking overcome.

She put the lid on the lipstick and stood it on the glass shelf. She turned and raised her chin, imperiously. "I haena seen *any* discrepancies."

"I believe they are so profound that we arna noticing them — until now."

She said, "What would make ye believe it? We hae never lost a bairn tae a time-shift, *never,* and we arna starting now, ye ought tae..." She let her words trail off, watching Magnus's face. She exhaled. "Explain it tae me."

"How many bairns do we hae?"

She pulled long gloves from a drawer, she gestured with her head toward me. "*She* daena hae any bairns, she winna give me a grandson — ye hae one son from Bella, who understood the importance."

Magnus glared, then his face relaxed, he almost looked humorous about it. "And the great and all-knowing Lady Mairead, who understands all about the world, dost ye see the issue in this scenario?"

She adjusted the fingers of the glove on her hand. "No, enlighten me, I ken the truth of 'this scenario'."

"How auld are we? Auld enough tae hae bairns taegether, right? We've been married for years, we want children, why daena we hae any?"

She blinked looking at the wall. "Ye want children?"

"Aye, desperately, how come ye daena ken it?"

She played with the strand of pearls distractedly. "I'm not sure."

"And if we hae been married this long, for *years*, and we want bairns — why haena we told ye? Why haena ye asked? Suddenly ye are the voice of reason, of *patience*? Dost ye think ye might hae asked us why we dinna hae bairns afore?"

"Ye are correct, I haena mentioned it — I wonder why?"

"Because we hae bairns, two as a matter of record, a girl named Isla and a son named Jack."

Her eyes went wide. "Where are they?"

Magnus said solemnly, "I daena ken. But there hae been shifts, since the storms when we were last here, and we hae lost our bairns tae history."

She sank onto the settee. "But... how do ye *ken*?"

"Kaitlyn and I visited Balloch, Sean and Lizbeth assured us that we hae a daughter and a son."

"I daena ken what tae do, this is verra upsetting!" She stood and strode over to the long wide drawer under her makeup table, whipped off the gloves, pressed her hand tae a keypad tae unlock it, and pulled the drawer out. Inside I could see rows of ancient books, spines up. They were the size and shape of the journals she often carried.

She gazed down in the drawer for a moment, pulled out a book, and flipped through some pages, running her finger down a leaf. Then closed it, put it down on the counter, and pulled out another, farther along the row. She opened it, ran her finger down the page, placed it on the other, and took out a third book. She sped up, a little frantic, running her finger down five or six pages—

Magnus said, "What are ye looking for?"

"Wheesht! I am trying tae think." She placed that book down, and with her palms on the counter, she stared down into the drawer.

Finally she pulled out one more book, flipped through it, then stacked it on the others. "I hae nae record of bairns, Magnus, there arna bairns."

I said, "We are in an alternate history."

She slid the drawer closed. "I find this outrageous, I am not in an alternate history, I am in the *true* history. This is always the way of it."

I said, "If the next generation of our family is somewhere else, who is in the true history, and who isn't?"

She stared off into the distant corner of her enormous closet, then sighed. "This is disastrous. What do we do? Where do we begin?"

Magnus said, "Perhaps we ought tae move tae a conference room tae discuss—"

"Nae, I am dressing, I hae an event, we can remain here, dressing rooms are where some of the most important matters of state are decided, the ones between kings and their queens."

Magnus said, "But we are nae here tae speak tae m'queen — Kaitlyn is the queen, we are here tae speak tae m'mother, the Lady Mairead, daena get above yerself."

"Ye ken what I meant, Magnus, twas a turn of phrase. And I need tae get tae my event, so I daena ken what ye expect of me this evening." Her hand shook as she patted the side of her hair. "We can speak on it in the morn—"

"Nae we canna wait, we must—"

"I hae an event, I canna be late!"

Magnus dropped down to his knees, holding out his arms, imploring. "I daena feel as if it can wait, Lady Mairead. Kaitlyn and I hae found that our timeline has shifted, our bairns are gone — are they gone for good, or are they lost souls? My heart canna bear it, I must find them. I canna wait a second more in case tae wait adds tae the misery of it."

She put her hand on his jaw and lifted his chin. "Ye almost hae the look of the boy ye once were, down beneath me, pleading yer case. This is a verra nice look on ye, the heroic man brought low. I would nae want tae see it often, but now and again ye are verra pleasing, my son, I see why Kaitlyn would love ye, despite all the troubles ye hae brought intae her life." She huffed. "Ye can get up from yer knees though, I will remain for a bit longer tae discuss. How do ye think this has happened? What do ye ken?"

"I believe there is a man, Ranulph—"

"Samuel's son? Nae, he is nothing, he is inconsequential."

"I believe he is attemptin' tae steal all our vessels. — ye and I hae discussed this once before."

"Ranulph the Repulsive is causing this much trouble?" She scowled and opened the drawer again and ran her finger down the spines of the books, looking for one, then plucked out another book, and read through it. "I hae only come across him a couple of times. I found him lacking in any qualities that might interest us. He wasna goin' tae fight ye in the arena, I kent that much. He is verra wee compared tae ye."

"Thorns are wee, they can still topple a great beast."

"This is true, tis why I hae noted him. He might be inconsequential but still noteworthy." She flipped a few pages and then said, "Here's a note: 'Ranulph is collecting the vessels.' Tis odd, I daena remember writing it, and why is it here in the middle of this book? Ye would think I would hae marked it in some way, or remembered it as important."

She skimmed another page. Then closed the book with her finger holding the place. "Ye will need tae kill him."

"How? And would that fix the timeline?"

"The changes he has created are *not* mere ripples, Magnus, they are deep and devastating."

"I ken. Twould hae been nice tae hae some forewarnin'. I believed that was the purpose of yer journals, not tae tell us ye had known after the fact."

"If I canna remember the note, how would I warn ye of it? I am also being shifted, Magnus, I am perhaps suffering most of all."

Magnus growled.

"Fine, we daena ken who is suffering the most."

Magnus straightened his coat. "I will go and kill him. I just need tae find him."

She flipped through a few pages. "I hae nothing more on him as I considered him inconsequential—"

"Ye call him inconsequential, but I tell ye, he appears tae bring a great deal of consequences.

She skimmed down another page. "Ye will need tae be careful — he is altering our timeline from verra deep in the past, when there is a great deal of turmoil. Johnne Cambell and his brothers mess with history — och nae, tis a clan of horrible Campbell men."

She exhaled as she returned the books to the drawer. "I daena ken what tae say on it, Magnus. Ranulph has surprised me, and he has done a great deal of harm. And I want tae say once more, your meddling with the devices, usin' the remote activator, is how we got in this trouble."

"Ye daena hae proof of it."

"Ye used it, and now this, *there* is your proof. And daena get an idea about using the Bridge, promise me."

Magnus huffed. "I canna promise anything, I am tryin' tae survive."

She shook her head. "We must move carefully… please daena run off and use yer devices, ye are goin' tae ruin everything."

"Beyond what is already ruined?"

"I canna speak on this anymore. I am supposed tae go tae this party and…"

Magnus asked, "Is the farmer going with ye?"

She stared at Magnus blankly. "What farmer?"

"The cider farmer, ye ken, JB."

She shook her head. "Nae, I daena ken who ye are speaking about — why would I, the great and powerful Lady Mairead, mother of a king, be accompanied by a cider farmer?"

"Twas my question at the time."

"I would grow bored, surely!"

"Ye said he made ye laugh."

She shook her head. "That sounds unlikely. I would need far more than that from an escort. I will be escorted tonight by Wilfred Weaver."

"The actor from that borin' movie about nothin'?"

"Aye, the famous actor, the acclaimed actor, the award-winning actor, Wilfred Weaver from the movie, the Shadow of Nothingness."

Magnus repeated, "So, the actor from the movie about nothin'?"

"Och nae, Magnus, we daena need tae argue with each other. He is famous, this is all that is important. And handsome. And it pales in comparison tae the issue at hand."

"When I was here last ye were all about the farmer, I am confused by yer inconsistency."

She shrugged. "This is a time of inconsistency, and from the sound of it, not that important compared tae missing bairns." She checked herself in the mirror again. "I must get tae this gala, will ye be in the mood tae come, Magnus? Ye haena been invited, ye werna expected, but if ye want tae…?"

He shook his head. "Nae, Kaitlyn and I will find something else tae do. We hae a great deal tae talk on."

CHAPTER 37 - KAITLYN

AS LONG AS WE STAY TOGETHER

We went to Magnus's apartment, mine too, I supposed, though I had only visited — he had often lived here without us.

Us? I meant, me.

It felt to me like a hotel room. There was nothing in it for me to do. As Grandma Barb used to say, 'A woman doesn't live in a place until she's dusted off all the dust of the women who lived there before.'"

There were many queens who had lived here in the two centuries of the kingdom's existence.

The war had ripped a hole in the side of the building, but it had been fixed, though there was still plastic sheeting up at one end of the room, covering where construction had been recently completed. They hadn't expected us back so soon. The sitting room was unscathed though, and dust-free.

Magnus called for a meal to be brought to us, and his chamberlain served us drinks and left us to discuss alone.

I said, "Shit, I thought your mother might have an answer, or I don't know, a pushy-button to solve this."

Magnus grunted. "We hae the Bridge, that is a pushy-button, tis a verra dangerous button, she daena want us tae use it, but we hae it." He was quiet for a moment then asked, "Dost ye agree with her on it?"

"I don't know. I mean, she often seems to know the most about these infernal machines. We don't know what the Bridge does, really, or how it works, but yes, we have it. It seems like it might fix this, so I kind of agree with you, but we don't know where to use it. I kind of agree with her — what if we damage our whole timeline?"

"More than now?"

I sighed.

Magnus said, "I think it daena change the timeline so much as stabilizes it."

"But… what does that even mean? What if we lost kids and then in trying to fix it, I lost you?"

Magnus said, "I ken, mo reul-iuil."

I drank from my glass of wine. "There are *so* many questions: The timeline would be stabilized but would it be stable in my favor? In yours? What if you're not supposed to be time-traveling around?"

"Aye, I am out of time—perhaps a stable timeline would be one that put us all back in our regular times."

"Quentin might lose Beaty, ugh. We've been worried about this so much and now here it is, but last time we used the Bridge there was no need to worry, it was unnecessary, nothing got overwritten, no one disappeared, the time bridge just shifted everyone back. That's the way it will work, probably. But then again…"

Magnus said, "The Bridge has verra many unknowns, but sometimes ye hae tae fight a war with the weapons ye hae."

"We are at war?"

"Aye, and we dinna ken it, we hae almost lost before we even kent the war was raging. We might need tae use our best weapon."

I said, "Yeah, yeah… when you put it like that, it's a weapon in our arsenal. We need it." I looked down at the plastic sheet hanging at the end of the room, shifting in the light. It was see-through, obscuring, as if I couldn't see what was there, but I could make out the edges.

I gulped. "I feel like there's too much obscured. I agree with Lady Mairead, the Bridge is too dangerous to use."

Magnus nodded looking down at the melting ice in his glass. "I winna use the Bridge, but I am still goin' tae kill Ranulph. I will find him, hold him, torture him, and make him confess tae what he has done. Then I will undo it, after killin' him."

"You make murder sound easy sometimes, not sure we can accomplish that, just because we want to."

Magnus poured some whisky into his glass, then said to the room, "Show me a photo of Ranulph, son of Samuel."

The projection on the wall showed a photo of a big guy. Magnus said, "Och, he looks like he daena hae a brain in his head — this is the man causing all this trouble? He daena look capable of it."

I laughed.

Magnus said, "He daena look like he masterminded it — I wonder if twas his plan, or if he is delighted by the accident of it? He might hae decided tae steal all m'vessels and the changing of time, the destroyin' of lives, might be incidental." He sipped from his whisky. "I might be able tae hang him over a precipice, tell him I want him tae fix what he's broken, and scare him tae death until he does."

I said, "You don't want to scare him to death before he can fix it."

"Aye, not all m'ideas are m'best ideas."

He swished his ice around in his drink and then swallowed the rest of it, finishing it. "Would ye like tae go out for a bit of a walk on the grounds?"

I shook my head, staring at the obscuring, waving, shifting plastic curtain — a bit like fog. "No, I think… it's a little like my dream, no, a little nervous right now."

He said, "How about if I am well armed, my soldiers are

with us, and there are horses? Would ye go then? We could take Cynric and Hurley out for a ride."

"Okay, yes, let's do that."

In the stables Magnus said, "We winna go intae the woods, we will stay in the open, so ye might see the stars, tis hard tae be frightened when ye hae the moon lightin' yer way."

"We will see the stars?"

"Aye, I asked for the lights tae be turned off, aircrafts are downed, we will hae stars as if we are home at Balloch or Kilchurn."

"Oooh, I love when you flex your power. Nicely done, Master Magnus." I mounted Hurley and followed Magnus and Cynric from the stables out into the night. The soldiers remained a considerate distance away.

Magnus bowed a bit with his head and let Hurley and me go in front. I raised my brow, "You want me to ride in front, Master Magnus?"

"Aye, ye ken, tis the view I like."

My horse rode down the path, a gentle jostle up and down, I looked at the reins in my hands, and said, "Thank you for loving me like that, even all these years later."

He said, "Ye're welcome, mo reul-iuil, but how could I not? Ye are as lovely as the day I met ye, and ye cause a stirrin' in me." He grinned.

"A stirring? Oooh, that's lovely to hear."

He pulled up beside my horse, pulled me to a stop, then leaned in and kissed me on the edge of my lips. We pressed our temples together and remained there, paused, our horses side by side, an embrace, much like when we lived back in the early sixteenth century, by ourselves.

I whispered against his cheek, "That was nice."

"Aye, twas," He pulled away and drew his horse in front of mine. "What a beautiful night sky, inna it, mo reul-iuil?"

"It is, it's so beautiful, this is a good idea."

I stroked my hand down Hurley's withers. "I missed you, old girl, did you miss me?"

Magnus said, "She has a grand life here. She and Cynric truly just want tae live taegether in their auld age. They hae plenty of food, tis what's truly important."

"Cynric told you that?"

He chuckled. "Aye, we spoke long on it. He wishes he could be in service tae me but the pull of a good meal is too strong for him."

I said, "He always was a horse after your heart."

"Aye, much like Sunny, he has been one of the greatest horses of m'life. They do hae a way of insertin' themselves intae m'heart."

We rode quietly. The night was beautiful, the grounds were well landscaped, and wide, far flung, and then the outer edges rimmed with forests.

"One question I have, is what details have changed, you know? We were a whole year in the past, when did I have time to have a baby? Was that the old timeline or the new? I feel a little like I've gone crazy."

He turned his horse. "Ye haena gone crazy, we hae caused an issue with the timeline, and we will fix it — we do it all the time."

"Where do you think the babies are though, do you think they are somewhere missing us, longing for us? I can't bear that idea."

He turned his horse around and rode for a bit without talking then said, "One of the theories is that we hae different timelines, alternatives, ye ken? This is the way Chef Zach explains it, the way I take it tae mean is I think there is a Magnus here, and then there is another Magnus there. They are side by side in the same place but with different lines, but, and this is my thought on it, there is only *one* Magnus who has m'soul inside of him, who is conscious, with all the memories that belong tae my consciousness. Somehow we hae our consciousness, or our souls, in the wrong timeline."

I said, "That is a big mistake for God to make."

"God daena make mistakes — whatever is happening has a purpose, tis not on us tae ken what it is."

I said, "Sure, but this does, really, feel like a mistake."

He arched back and looked up at the sky. "Nae, mo reul-iuil, with the stars unfurled overhead, a sky spun with stars, tis impossible tae find any fault with his creation. If m'soul is in an alternate timeline, perhaps tis tae protect the bairns, maybe we hae them in one spot so that we can…" His voice trailed off.

I said, "What? I was liking that idea, maybe that *is* what happened. Maybe we are more in control and this is… why did you stop?"

"I stopped because it daena sound like me. If we had tae keep the bairns safe, certainly I would hae left ye with them — they would want their mother."

"Yes, that's true. But maybe you didn't have that choice, maybe this is us being selfless — we tucked the kids in, we're going to go save the history of the world, we're going to wage war against an evil bad guy, and then we will figure out how to get the kids back."

He smiled. "Ye are being hopeful."

"Full of hope and faith and a terrible-arsery, we are going to try to fix this issue."

"We started with my hope and ended with yers."

"Yep, somehow we reversed. And I know you want to use the Bridge and your mother and I have urged you to be cautious, but I will defer to you, because I don't know — I'm leaving it up to you."

"Aye. Thank ye, I will be cautious, but I haena completely disregarded usin' our whole arsenal, I will consider all sides. The Bridge may yet be the best shot we hae at winnin'." He took a deep breath and looked up at the stars again. "These are the same stars in every time, mo reul-iuil, abundant and guiding. They illuminate our way."

I looked up at the stars, the familiar patterns and shapes, we had ridden under these stars for so many nights in the deep dark past. In my young life I had never spent enough time out in the dark to get to know them, but in the past it was always dark after sundown, and the night had become familiar. The ebb and flow of the stars and the orbits of the moon. The familiar gusts of wind at sunset, the close calm in the middle of the night.

But then I started, I could see, coming from the base of the trees circling the grounds, a fog drifting in.

Just like the fog of my dream.

His eyes followed mine, noted the fog, and said, "We ought tae return."

"We're going to be okay, right Magnus?"

"Aye, as long as we stay together."

"Yeah, that's what I think too."

But as we rode back to the stables to put the horses to bed, I was quiet, thinking about how his voice behind me in the dream had yelled, "Run!" through the fog and how I had run *away*.

CHAPTER 38 - KAITLYN

ONE THING CERTAIN

I woke up early, a slow coming to awake, draped over Magnus's chest that I loved, as he didn't mind. I lay there for a while spinning my fingers on his skin, kissing there occasionally, until I found out he was waking up too, in all his full glory. With his eyes closed he grunted as he pulled me over onto him.

"Are you sleeping?" I whispered.

"Aye," he muttered, "I am nae awake at all."

I giggled. "Oh I think a part of you is *very* awake. It's poking me, insistently."

He smiled, his eyes remained closed. "It took ye forever tae wake up. M'cock has been verra patient, if ye kent how long he has been waitin' ye would hae yer pajamas off aready."

"Oh my, well, if the cock's up we must all be up." I slid my panties off. And then seductively, slowly, with kisses and nibbles on his lips, lowered myself on him. I moaned against his skin.

We began tae rock and shift together, pushing and pulling, teasing, small movements, my forehead pressed against the side of his cheek. We built up to a lovely release and then I collapsed down on him and sighed. "Oh Master Magnus, you do make me so... *pleased.*"

"Do I now? This is a good word. I like it when ye love me, when ye are passionate about me, but I do like the days when we are pleased with each other, there is a good, I think, in that."

I kissed his cheek. "There is a pleasure in that, a friendship, a satiation, yes, I'm glad you liked it, because I meant it with all those good things. At night I want you so badly, I'm hot for you, sometimes in the morning sex feels very regular, but not bad, it's kind of like a helping each other wake up and meet the day. There's something very pleasing about it."

He nodded, then said, "Perhaps we ought tae get up, speak tae Lady Mairead—"

"It would be great if she remembered more than she did last night."

"Aye, but likely she has told us all she kens. She will harangue me about not usin' the devices, and I will give her a list of things tae accomplish here in the kingdom and ask her tae try tae discover anything she can about Ranulph, I will tease her more about the farmer—"

"I can't believe she didn't remember him, did you just make that all up?"

"Nae. Twas true, it happened." He said to the computer, "Show me a bottle of Royal Riaghalbane Rose cider."

The shifting colors of our projection wall shifted tae a bottle.

He chuckled. "That is the cider! JB made that for m'mother! Och, the world has gone verra screwy. We ought tae head home."

I said, "What if…? What if we go back and there was… had been… a time shift? What if we were, I don't know, I feel stupid saying it, what if we found out that it was all better? I can dream, right? What if there are…?"

"Daena get yer hopes up, mo reul-iuil, there is one thing certain, this situation inna going tae fix itself."

CHAPTER 39 - KAITLYN

WHEN I COUNT TAE THREE YE WILL RUN

*W*e arrived on the beach at our usual jump spot, on the agreed upon date, but lay there for a while staring up at the blue sky. I brushed sand off my face, sat up, and looked around. Magnus rose and shook his head, sand sprinkling into his lap.

"Who is coming to get us?"

"I canna remember, I would imagine Colonel Quentin."

"Shit." We lumbered up. I brushed sand off my pants.

We scanned up and down the beach and then started trudging up the boardwalk to the road.

I gulped. "Have we ever not had a welcoming crew?"

"Nae, and I daena like it. Tis worrisome."

I looked around. "So here's a question, what if it's us changing time, by looping?"

He shook his head. "I believe we hae learned our lesson on that by now."

"What if it's something egregious, like the death of one of us — we might forget the lesson… you know?"

"Nae, mo reul-iuil, we canna forget the lesson. If I died, I ken ye would miss me, but tae loop — ye ken it wouldna work, and ye might lose the rest of… exactly *this*. Ye might lose members of our family. Loops cause time shifts and… I daena think ye would risk it, and I believe I hae learned the lesson thoroughly through the years. I canna be sure, grief is a tragic thing, but I think I would ken better."

I stared off at the ocean, churning. "What if it's a child we're trying to save…?"

He nodded. "I hope the one or other of us would reason with us — we canna loop tae save a life. It might work, but there is too big a risk tae all the other lives around us."

We began to walk down the road toward our house.

"Another question I have, could it be someone from our past timeline, like your great-great-great grandfather and just the way he is living his life is changing yours?"

"His life would hae already happened. Whether time is a line or a wheel, we hae already passed the time of my great-great-great grandfather, his life and his adventures are set. I daena believe he can disrupt my life, there must be some order tae it."

"True." My clothes were wet and sandy. I brushed off my sleeves as we walked. It wasn't too hot, but the sun was high, the shadows under the trees darkened. "So a hundred percent, it's this rogue guy collecting all the vessels?"

"Aye, Ranulph, son of Samuel, is stealing all the vessels, he is the one messing up—" He stopped walking, turned, and looked behind us. "Kaitlyn, behind me."

I stepped behind him, grasping his shirt at his waist. "What…?"

His head turned as he scanned the woods. "There is a vehicle following us, dost ye hear it? Tis big."

"I don't, but my senses are still shook from the jump." I kept my head down, eyes clamped shut, afraid what I might see.

He said, measured and slow. "The house is ahead of us, when I count tae three ye will run straight tae it."

He glanced in that direction. "It looks clear. Ye will run. Ye winna look back."

"What are you going to do?"

He pulled his gun. "I will be right behind ye, daena worry."

A moment later, "Ye ready?"

I nodded, my forehead against his back.

"One, two, three… run!"

I turned, in a full blown panic, and *ran*. I kept my feet to the edge of the road, but mindful of the sandy edge, my feet thudding on the ground in a beat, fast fast fast, go!

I heard him behind me, three steps behind, and then farther behind the both of us, a rumble — the sound of something big, bearing down.

We arrived at our gate. I pressed my finger to it, holy shit, holy shit, Magnus arrived, a step behind, the gate slid open a half foot, Magnus yelled, "In in in!"

I squeezed through the opening and raced to the house. Magnus remained at the gate, his hand slammed to the pad, pressing, trying to get the gate to change course — not open, close!

A big armored vehicle surged up to the gate, Magnus jumped to the side as it crashed through. Magnus yelled, "Get Quentin!" as he ran across the yard and around the house.

I yanked the door open and rushed in. "Quentin! Quentin!"

Zach said, "What the hell…?!"

I doubled over, unable to speak, huffing, and out of breath.

Quentin rushed in from the garage where he had been grabbing guns. He had a bag that I knew held a grenade launcher, he tossed a rifle to Zach.

Magnus ran in through the back door. Quentin tossed him a rifle.

He caught it in the air. "Headed tae the roof."

I said, "Where are the… kids?"

"Emma has them at the park." Zach added, "Where do you want me?"

Quentin slammed a helmet on Zach's head. "Up on the roof, go go go."

Zach ran up the stairs with an apron on, a dishtowel hanging from his waist ties.

"Me?"

"In the house, locked down." He pressed his hand to the pad and typed in a code that locked all the doors and pulled armored hurricane screens over the windows.

"No, give me a rifle, I'm up on the roof. My house too, I know how to shoot."

"Fine." He passed me a rifle. "Everyone up then."

Shots were fired outside. Three, loud. I shrieked.

He said, "You got this Katie?"

"Yeah, I got this." I gulped and raced up the stairs.

Quentin's feet thudded up the steps behind me as he pressed a helmet down on my head.

I came out on the roof. Magnus was on the right, the north side, his gun aimed down.

Zach was on the left. I went to stand close to Magnus, where there was a thin barricade, visual protection but it wouldn't stop a bullet. I crouched behind it.

Magnus, his gun aimed down at the ground, asked, "Colonel Quentin, why is Kaitlyn here?"

Quentin tossed me a helmet, "Put that on Boss's head." To Magnus he said, "Boss, I ain't got time for arguing."

Magnus looked through the sight on his gun. "My arguing or hers?"

Quentin said, "Hers, still don't have time — who's shooting?"

Magnus waved his gun. "There's a man behind the wax myrtle, he jumped from the vehicle as I got here, dinna hae time tae shoot him."

Quentin raised the grenade launcher to his shoulder. "How many men are in the car you think?"

"I suspect three, three in other places in the yard."

Zach was on his knees, his gun aimed out on the yard. He

looked like that was what he was supposed to do and no one was bothering him, so I got on my knees and looked through my scope. I couldn't see anyone.

Quentin said, "Say bye bye truck."

He shot the launcher with a p-phoop sound and a second later, an explosion. The armored truck lifted and then crashed over onto its side, becoming a barrier they could hide behind. Guns fired from bushes and trees. Magnus and Zach fired back. It was so freaking loud.

I thought I saw a flash behind a tree, I fired, again and again in that direction. I caught a movement in the armored vehicle, a flash of light. I aimed there, shooting the truck, my heart racing.

One of the shooters was firing at Zach. He ducked. Quentin aimed the launcher at his position. P-phoop. It exploded in front of the armored vehicle, pushing it back, but the barrage of bullets continued shooting at the walls of the house.

A gun was firing directly at me too. I dove down, slamming my knees onto the hard surface. "Is the house going to hold?"

Quentin yelled, "Yes, until it's breached, but it's not breached yet!" He put the grenade launcher down, picked up a rifle, and began returning fire, yelling, "If you shoot, they have to hide, get your ass up."

Fine. Sure. Of course. I pulled myself up, aimed my gun, and began firing.

Magnus said, "Och nae, one is around the corner, I canna get tae him."

I looked. "I could get him from a window."

Magnus said, "Aye, but stay down."

Quentin said, "You'll have to unlock the window, you know the code, and here's a radio!" He tossed it end over end. I missed.

He said, "Katie, you got this?"

I said, "Hell yeah, I got this, you've been training me for years." I crouch-ran across the roof to the stairs and climbed down, to use one of the windows on the second floor — I was going to try and shoot some asshole from the guest room window.

CHAPTER 40 - MAGNUS

FADING AND SHIFTING

"*I*s there a chance Emma rides up with the bairns?"

Zach said, "I told her to stay away until I called." He glanced at his phone. "She's taken them to my mother's house, it looks like." He aimed his rifle. "I can't believe you got here without my noticing. I kept looking, all morning, and then suddenly Katie was running in the house."

Quentin said, "Yep, that was insane, I didn't know you arrived until the gate opened."

I said, "We've had some time-shifts. Caused by this man — I assume this is Ranulph."

Quentin looked through his scope. "I am not a fan." He fired toward a man hidin' on the edge of the yard.

Zach said, "Why the hell aren't the police coming?"

I asked, "Where are the guards, daena we hae guards?"

There was a verra big explosion from the other end of the house, shaking the foundation, debris flyin' — the loud crashin' of yet another of m'walls crumblin' down, and a cloud of dust and smoke risin' overhead.

Quentin looked down over the edge of the roof. "The house is breached!"

Another firefight erupted, shots from downstairs, we rained

bullets down. Then there was a pause, we ducked behind the wall.

A shot fired from the side of the house, and another and another. I called Katie. "Ye good?"

From the radio, "Got him, but…"

I said, "But? What 'but'?"

No answer.

"Och nae, Quentin, why is she sayin' 'but'…?"

The radio squawked and Kaitlyn's voice, quietly, "…someone…in the house…"

Quentin said, "I'm going down." He crouched and ran to the steps and started to climb down. But then a man's voice from the radio. "Magnus?"

I glanced at Quentin, and said into the radio, "Aye, who is this…?"

"My name is Ranulph, I expect ye've heard of me?"

"Why would I hae heard of ye? Ye sound inconsequential."

He chuckled.

"Tell Quentin not tae come down."

"He's already got ye in his sights, tis too late."

The man turned on the radio tae sigh, overly loud. "Mag*nus*, my man is showing me that yer man, Quentin, is headed down here, tell yer man tae turn around and go back tae the roof — we daena want him, we will kill him."

I bellowed, "Quentin!"

His head came back up the steps, "I heard him. Screw that. I'm going around to the side."

A moment later we heard a shriek from the front lawn.

Zach and I looked down over the edge.

Ranulph in a military uniform, wearing a bullet-proof vest, was striding behind the barrier made by the armored car, he held a struggling Kaitlyn.

I yelled, "Let her go!"

Zach and I raised our rifles, aiming at him.

I asked, "Zach, do ye hae a shot?"

Quentin from the deck on the south wing began shooting, exchanging fire with the men. While their attention was diverted I shot, but I had nae clear view — Kaitlyn was their shield. "I need tae get down there."

A squawk on the radio, Ranulph's voice, "Magnus, hold yer fire. We need tae speak."

I said, "Quentin, did ye hear?"

Quentin said, "Yeah, but he's in my sights, the asshole moves the wrong direction and he's dead."

I said, "Ranulph did ye hear m'colonel?"

"Aye, I heard him."

I lowered my weapon.

Then I called down, "Release Kaitlyn, now!"

"We daena want her, we got what we came for—"

"What did ye get…?"

He chuckled.

Zach met my eyes. "You think he got our vessels?"

"I daena ken. I hae one here in my sporran, the rest are locked up in the house."

"Katie might have opened the safe for him."

"Twas verra fast, he was in there but for a moment…"

I returned my attention tae Ranulph. "Ye canna take m'wife, ye hae what ye want, then leave her. We will grant ye passage."

"Bullshit, Magnus, I give her up and I'm a deadman."

I saw the wind pick up in front of the house, from behind the armored truck, a bit of a breeze whipping—"

"Daena go! Daena take her!"

Quentin said, intae the radio, "Damn, he moved, I lost my line of fire."

I said, "Ranulph, I'll trade ye, I will go with ye, give us Kaitlyn."

Through the radio I heard him chuckle again, malevolently. "I have the option tae take a king with me instead of his lowly wife? This day is turning out verra well." He bellowed up at the roof, "Come on down, hands on your head."

Zach asked, "What's the protocol here, what the fuck should I do?"

"I daena think we hae done this afore, tis unprecedented."

Quentin barged up the steps. "What the hell? I can't let you go, we gotta fight these guys."

Zach said, "If they want you they have to fucking go through me."

"Nae, Chef Zach, ye canna lay down yer life for mine, och, what kind of world would it be?"

Tae Quentin I said, "This is somethin' I hae tae do, Colonel Quentin, it canna be Kaitlyn tryin' tae survive it, it must be me." I passed him my gun and we crossed tae the stairs.

As we climbed down tae the ground floor, Quentin asked, "How do you know you'll survive?"

"I haena died yet — we ought tae assume I am immortal."

He chuckled the low chuckle of a commander who was walking alongside his king and friend tae turn him over tae a barbarian as a hostage.

As we came tae the front door, Quentin rifled through the drawer in the hall table. He plucked something up and held it victoriously. "Here's a tile beacon. For your... put it in your sporran or something, no, wait, put it on your belt."

I pulled my belt away from my middle and he pressed the tile to the leather. "Will ye be able tae find me with this wee button?"

Quentin's face screwed up. "I doubt it will work, in all of time and place, but heck, if it does *somehow*, it will be awesome. "

I nodded. "Aye, twould be awesome."

We hugged, clapping each other's back and then he opened the front door. He held his rifle at his shoulder and I put my hands on my head. We stalked across the porch tae be met by four men who shoved a weeping Kaitlyn tae Quentin.

She said, as Quentin pushed her toward the house, "Magnus, don't! Please, please don't go!"

I glanced back at her, cryin', standin' in front of our grand Florida home, and I wasna sure how I would get back here, so I made sure I saw it, the high blue sky, the fresh air, the sand under my feet, and the house, with the windows, shaded, hiding the interior where my family lived… and… it felt as if twas a large family, though I couldna place the full memory of it, and that was the thing, the memories, we couldna trust them, they were fading and shifting and I dinna want tae forget what was important. I dinna want tae lose Kaitlyn and the life we had built together, our long lives together. My heart felt heavy, as she was pulled toward the stairs. The men surrounded me and shoved me toward the armored vehicle. The gusts of wind began tae pick up, someone near us had twisted a vessel.

I looked at the house and twas as if the details were fadin', the house was weathered, Kaitlyn looked alone and frightened, the sky was covered in gray clouds — once more, a brutal storm risin' and then something heavy hit me on the back of the head and my knees buckled.

And twas as if I was nae more.

PART II
ASCEND

UP THE WHEEL

CHAPTER 41 - KAITLYN

2024 - WHAT HAD I BEEN DOING?

I walked into the house, slowly, dazedly. My head hurt. Actually my whole body hurt, almost like I had just jumped, but not. I hadn't jumped. I had just been — what had I been doing...?

The house was quiet. I entered the foyer as I heard the familiar sound of dishes, clanking in the kitchen. I padded toward there, I was wearing a distinguished looking pantsuit and the pantlegs were damp at the bottom, stretched long, dragging on the tile— why was I wearing a a damp pantsuit?

I looked down at the hem, covered in sand, I brushed my hands down it — sand sifted to the floor.

Weirdness.

Why was I wet?

I called out to whoever was listening, "Sand in the foyer, careful, I'm going for a broom!"

No one answered. I went to the kitchen, Zach was wearing an apron, standing at the sink. "Shit, sorry Katie, didn't hear you come home!"

I stared around. "Did I come home? Where was I even?"

I opened the cupboard and got out a bottle of ibuprofen and took two.

"I don't know, out. I don't know half the comings and goings."

He pulled two baking sheets from the cabinet and cranked on the oven.

"Baking cookies?"

"Yep. Em will be back with the kids in a minute."

"Where's Quentin? He usually greets me."

"Can't believe he didn't notice you arrived, but he's been weird today."

His eyes drew out to the back walkway.

I poured water over ice in a glass and went to the doors and looked out. Quentin was standing on the end of the boardwalk, holding a rifle.

Zach whisked eggs in a bowl.

I watched Quentin, he looked fidgety out there, looking north and south, but facing the house, and I felt anxious, but about what? There were cookies baking, Emma and the kids were at the park, the house was… everything seemed fine, nothing worrisome here. Easy. I asked over my shoulder, "Where's Hayley?"

"Work, she'll come by for dinner."

I said, "Good," and slid the door open and went out to talk to Quentin.

CHAPTER 42 - KAITLYN

FOGGY

Quentin raised a hand in hello, but had a look of befuddlement on his face. One arm resting on the firearm strapped across his shoulder, the other hooked on his belt, he stared at the house as I neared.

"Hey Quentin!"

His brow drew down. "Hey! Thought you were out."

"Funny thing about that, I was… but, man, I feel foggy, you feel foggy?"

"Yep. My head is screwed up."

"I took some ibuprofen, hope it'll kick in soon."

"Good…" His voice trailed off as his eyes scanned around, and settled back on the house. "Got things on my mind. Where were you?"

I considered it, my memory felt cloudy, there was the gray sky overhead, my feet trudging on the road, the scent of wildflowers and I remembered now, I had gotten stressed out and had needed a break. "I went for a walk. I needed to clear my head, but come to find out it wasn't a walk I needed, it was the ibuprofen. That's the lesson kids, drugs first." I chuckled.

Quentin nodded looking up at the house.

"Did you hear my joke, Quentin?"

"Yeah, I heard. That's great, so what's the—" He shook his head. "You know what I can't stop thinking about?"

"What?"

"Look at the size of this house. It's got nine bedrooms, seven bathrooms—why the hell is your house so big?"

I laughed, nervously. "Because we're rich."

"Sure, but... *why?* It's the biggest house in the area, there's no need for us to be in this big a house, we need four bedrooms, you, Zach and Emma, their kids, me. Five, if you include a guest room for when Hayley stays over. This seems an odd choice — why go for such a big house?"

I blinked.

He continued, "I don't know... it bothers me — why so many bedrooms if we only have a few people living here?"

I shook my head. "These are all very good points. And is this why you have a rifle out on the back deck? Did something happen?"

"I just... I got nervous... what if people are missing?"

I had my hands on my hips, following his eyes up to the house. "Wow, that's a lot to wrap my head around, *who?*"

Quentin chuckled. "If I knew that I probably wouldn't be standing out here staring at the house." Quentin waved his arm at it. "What am I not remembering? *Who* am I not remembering? And what the hell is going on? That's why I'm uneasy and I feel like we've been waiting for Magnus for a really long time."

"Yeah, I know." I exhaled, long. Then said, "I think I need to get back to the house. I want to meet the kids when they're..." I couldn't really remember what I had been talking about.

I wandered back up to the house.

I heard Emma at the gate and so I went out to the front porch as her car pulled up.

I looked around. It was clean and tidy, some plants, a couple of chairs that no one ever sat in, and in the corner a little pile of sticks. The kind that looked planned, chosen, not firewood, but a curated pile of long sticks with *character*.

Something about it caught my eye. One of the sticks had yarn wrapped around the end of it, like a decorative handle. The bottom of it had been chiseled with a knife.

I sank into one of the chairs, staring down at that stick. A flash in my mind, a glimpse, a wee pale hand, thrusting that stick into the corner, "*I putting it away!*" But who was that, whose hand…?

Was it Ben?

Emma climbed from the car and pulled Zoe from the car seat. "Why are you in a pantsuit? You only wear those when you go to the kingdom."

I looked down at my clothes, the hem of my pants now dry. Why was I in a pantsuit? An uncomfortable, distinguished, pantsuit? It was Florida, modern day, I was hanging around the house, this was a decidedly not-a-pant-suit activity.

"I think I was in a weird mood," I said, then, "Whose stick is this, yours Ben?"

Ben was running past me into the house. He called, "No!" as he passed.

Emma said, "I don't know, I think those sticks were here when we moved in, I ought to clean that up."

I said, "I wouldn't worry about it, it's not… I kind of like them. Like it's someone's collection. I wouldn't want to dislodge it."

"Yeah, I think that's what I thought too."

That night I had a dream.

I had my arms around a young child, not too young, the age where they are gangly, it was a boy, tense, too old to be hugged as hard as I needed to hug him. *How you doing little guy?*

Good. His voice was echoey, and sounded like it came from inside myself instead of through my dreams.

I miss you...

I hugged him again.

The boy jokingly pushed me away. *Now Kaitlyn's just being weird.*

I'm Kaitlyn? I grasped his shirt, a t-shirt with Luke Skywalker holding a lightsaber on the front. I was looking down at it, not at the boy's face, and though I tried I couldn't look up.

Yes.

And who are you?

My hands held nothing.

I looked at the place in front of me, there was nothing there. I said, *Who are you?*

My voice echoed in the space as fog rolled in.

If we are missing people, where would they go?

Where would they go...?

Rumbling horse hooves galloping, gaining on me. The man on the horse, a man I had seen in these dreams so many nights, swinging his mace, covered in furs, barbaric looking — my every sense overloaded, my heart beat fast, my senses heightened, the sound deafening, the scent of the moor filled my nose, the cold air chilled my skin, and from behind me, Magnus's voice, *Run!*

The wind whistled through my hair as I raced as fast as I could.

I sat up, wrapping my arms around my knees.

· · ·

I tried to think about Magnus's voice, so far away, but also the bellow of it, loud enough to reach me, *run!*

Dammit.

I remembered a conversation we had had:

His rumbling voice, *Och nae, another one?*

I nodded, staring down at the sheets of the bed, not looking at him, hearing his voice, *I yelled 'Run', what else did I do?*

I don't know, I didn't see you, I just started to run, I was all alone.

His hand on my back, his voice right behind my ear — *If we are all alone, ever, dost ye remember what ye are supposed tae do?*

I sniffled. *Depends on whether I'm the one who's lost or not.*

I plucked at the sheets, concentrating on his voice. It sounded so close, as if he were right here.

His voice like a whisper, *How about if I ask it this way, if I tell ye tae run, where am I tellin' ye tae run tae?*

If I can, I should go to Maine, my lake house.

Exactly, we will meet up there, and if we miss each other, we will leave a note.

Remember when we did this, way back at the beginning of our marriage, I got you to memorize my grandparents' address?

I do, I still hae it memorized.

His voice whispered, *Daena worry, I winna forget it, mo reul-iuil.*

CHAPTER 43 - KAITLYN

WHY SO MANY CHAIRS?

Zach had made mac and cheese, homemade, with ham and broccoli in it for dinner, one of my favorite comfort foods. It sounded childish, but he added white wine to the cheese, topping it with a panko crust and serving it with crumbled toppings like feta, and with cranberries and almonds to sprinkle on top.

The kids cheered when it came out of the oven and I joined them.

He put the casserole dish in the middle end of the table and we spooned it on our plates. Quentin sat at the head and Emma and Zach and Hayley and I were on the sides. Zoe stood in her chair, yelling, "More! More!" as Emma spooned it in.

Emma said a quick grace over the meal and then we all started to eat. Zach asked, "Why's everyone so quiet?"

I said, "Hungry, eating, too delicious to talk," with my mouth full.

Quentin's brow drew down. "Why so many chairs?"

Hayley said, "This again?"

"Yes, until I come up with a good explanation, yes, this again. Why so many chairs? Why such a long table?"

Emma said, "Potentiality, I think, I always buy the biggest of everything, that's why this huge house. It's also why we're doing so well on the financial markets." She and Zach raised their glasses and clinked.

Quentin's face looked like he wasn't going to let it drop.

"What's really going on in your head, Quentin?"

"I just wonder what we might have forgotten. What if time has been overwritten and we're on a new timeline? Could we be... on a new line, that overwrote actual," he whispered, "people?"

I said, "That's impossible. How could that be a thing? People just disappear? Where do they go?"

Hayley said, "Are they ghosts? I know you don't believe in ghosts. I'm worried about you, you need to touch grass. How about a vacation? Maybe go out and meet someone."

Quentin huffed.

Zach said, "Also, you keep saying the timeline got overwritten, the *line*. I don't know... I'm beginning to believe it's more like a wheel, because..." His face screwed up. "Don't remember where I heard it the first time, but a wheel makes more sense..." He jumped up, grabbed a notebook and pen off the counter, and dropped back into his seat. He drew an unraveling spiral, like a tornado, that moved across the page. "Like this, time is a wheel, rolling."

I chewed some more mac and cheese and pointed at a place on his spiral. "So we are here, is what you're saying. So maybe we aren't rewriting, maybe we're more spiraling down and around, in another place on the wheel. Like we could be here, another person could be there."

Zach said, "Yep, that could be something that happens."

Hayley said, "Make you feel better Quentin — if there are missing people, they don't disappear. They're just there and you're here. That's what I think at least."

"I just get this strange feeling, and like, we should do something, you know? What if we're supposed to be hunting for someone? What if we're supposed to be a search party but because of some… I don't know, brain damage, we're not searching? What if someone is lost and we don't know it?"

Hayley said, "Look, this is how people get in trouble, if you're lost, you stay put. If you don't know who you're searching for, and you don't know if you're the search party, then likely you're the one lost. We stay put."

I said, "Exactly. We stay put, where someone can find us. Whoever 'someone' is." I grinned at Zoe. "Hear that, Zoe? If you're ever lost you stay put."

Zoe said, "Stay put! Mac and cheese! Pway with Eyewa."

I put down my fork.

Hayley said, "What does pway-with-eyewa mean, Zoe? You're silly."

Emma said, "She keeps saying that, I think she just made it up."

I watched Zoe's face. "Who's Eyewa, Zoe?"

She shrugged and shoved some macaroni in her mouth.

I chewed my lip and then looked back at Zach's diagram. "So we might be here and someone might be there? And we're the ones who are lost, they're looking for us on the time wheel? This is true?"

We basically all shrugged.

Zach said, "What you're not really thinking about is all these loops in this spiral, these are all different alternative loops on the time wheel, so you are not here, lost, you're here and here and here and… you get me, you're in all the infinity-lives."

I said, "So this is just one life and we're here all alone, but this is it, this is our reality, and no one is looking for us and we aren't lost, this is just *it*…?"

Hayley sighed. "This is why I don't come to dinner anymore, it's depressing around here."

Quentin said, "And yet we have games, we have a pool table, why do we have a pool table if none of us play?"

Emma said vaguely, "I think it came with the house."

CHAPTER 44 - ARCHIE

2408 - SAMANTHA FINDS JB'S JOURNAL

*S*amantha came into the room.

"Hello, m'lord, how are you doing?"

I patted my chest over my heart. "Good, I guess, melancholy, maybe, it's been a tough week."

She hugged and kissed me on the cheek. A big bear hug, she released. "It's been an anniversary, I thought you were going to be melancholy about it. I also thought you had distractions that were going to help."

I said, "I had meetings all morning, they did distract, a little bit. What were you doing, Lady Sam?"

"Well, as the daughter of a lowly apple farmer—"

"Married to the man who was once king."

"Oh, how I scrambled up that social ladder!"

I looked around. "*Is* an exiled king ranked higher than the daughter of one of the most important brewing families in the kingdom? The jury might be out on that."

"So you married me for the status?"

"No, I married you for your beauty."

"Thank you, that's a high compliment and I know you're downplaying my amazing personality, but anyway, I was looking through the last of dad's things over at the orchard. I've needed to do it for, oh, about ten years, but finally got to it today. I found something." She pulled a small stack of books from inside her bag and passed them to me.

"Your dad's?"

"Yes, from decades ago. He's got a whole stack of journals, it will take me *months* to go through them all, but this one caught my attention, because of the cover, see that? It's different from the rest." She ran her hand over the exquisitely designed cover. "The rest are leather-bound journals, fine, but fairly plain, but this one was red, has gold details and gold edging to the pages. It stood out." She flipped it as she showed the details.

Then she passed it to me. "Now look inside. First page."

I opened it. In a long looping cursive it said:

A gift to you — best regards, Lady Mairead

I said, "My *grandmother* knew your dad?"

"Apparently so, enough to give him a gift. Odd, right? I am glad you agree, I was worried you would say, 'Of course she knew him, we all knew it.'"

"No, I am totally surprised. No one ever mentioned it."

She jokingly wiped her forehead. "I was also worried you would say, 'I told you!' My memory seems to be shot these days."

I said, "We all seem to be having lapses."

"Yes, we do..." She looked down at the book in my hands. "So here is the really shocking part of this, you, m'lord, need to—"

"You know I love it when you call me lord."

She smiled. "That is why I do. Especially when telling you such a big thing, you need to steel yourself. There are things in this journal that are going to confuse you and I don't know... it makes me feel insane."

I said, "Uh oh."

She said, "'Uh oh' is right. My dad came to the palace to have dinner one night. He met your father." She pulled the book from my hands and flipped forward to one of the first pages, bookmarked with a label that read: 'the Royal Riaghalbane Rose Cider.'

"He met Magnus?"

She nodded.

"Your family made a royal cider?"

"If they did, they don't anymore, it must have been discontinued when the throne was passed from you to Ranulph, yet you would think I would have heard of it before. All of this is a mystery. Dad apparently bottled a cider for your grandmother, back when your family were royals. Lady Mairead and JB were *friends.*"

She passed me back the book, tapping a finger on the page. "Read that."

I read:

Things I found interesting—

Magnus I: Archibald, Isla, Jack. Archibald is almost eight. Isla is three. Jack is a newborn. Magnus I says Isla is the image of her mother. (He has a Scottish brogue and is sometimes difficult to understand. I found him charming and a bit frightening. I am thankful Lady Mairead is there to keep him in check.)

Beef Wellington. Carrot cake.

Colonel Quentin: married to Beaty. Noah, just born.

Fraoch: Hayley. No children.

(Brother to Magnus) Also Lochinvar. No children.

Then after the list he had written a long form entry:

What did I see? I rode to the castle in a fine limousine and as I arrived there were marching soldiers on the grounds. A hawk swooping through the air.

The weather was warm, unseasonably so. My suit was a bit too heavy and constricting on my waistline. Note to self: Diet!

I was ushered through from the car to the dining room, the staff walking much faster than necessary, I was breathless by the time I arrived.

There I dined with Lady Mairead and her son Magnus I.

The meal began at 7 pm sharp. I presented His Highness with a bottle of my apple-rosewater cider, labeled as the Royal Riaghalbane Rose cider. The King seemed very pleased with the gift.

Lady Mairead was dressed in a velvet dress with lavender accents and was beautiful. I told her as much and she accepted the compliment graciously.

We were served a meal of cucumber soup, Beef Wellington and a dessert of petite carrot cakes.

We were also accompanied by Colonel Quentin and the two men who had recently battled in the arena during King Ian's reign, Fraoch MacDonald and Lochinvar. I was thrilled to be in their acquaintance. The conversation was wide-ranging.

Things I learned for future reference if I am invited to dine with Lady Mairead and her family again:

Colonel Quentin has a wife, Beaty, and a son, Noah, who had been born about five months earlier.

Fraoch MacDonald was a lively fellow and was married, he had no children of his own, but enjoyed being an uncle.

Lochinvar was young and had not married yet, he was very humorous about his plight, wishing he had a woman to keep him company. He and Fraoch sparred a great deal like my own brothers.

Magnus I and Queen Kaitlyn have three children at this time. Their first, Archibald, is almost eight; Isla, who is three years old; and they welcomed a third child, Jack, just months before.

·   ·   ·

I blinked and reread the list and then the passages. "Wait… what does this mean?" I reread the list and then reread the last line. "Magnus the First and Queen Kaitlyn had three children? This is so confusing."

"I know, for one, I thought your mother was Bella."

He nodded. "Yes, and she died when I was young. I don't have any siblings."

"What about all those other people? Lochinvar and Fraoch and… do you remember any of that?"

"No, that's all… can I keep this?"

"Yes, of course, that's why I brought it. These other books are the ones that were on the right and left of it on the shelf, in case you want to go through them too, but on first glance they are not nearly as interesting — oh, and this."

She pulled a small wooden chest from the bag and passed it to me. "This was also with his journals."

It was a similar color of red lacquer to the book that had been a gift from Lady Mairead, it had gold corners, hinges, and a clasp. It was stamped on the lid with an ornate letter M.

"Where was it, just on the shelf?" I turned it over. "It needs a key."

"Look at the book again."

I opened the book and flipped through, finding, in the back, a ribbon that fastened a small gold key to the binding. I said, "Your day was very eventful. Have you opened it?"

She said, "I think this chest belongs to Lady Mairead, I do not know why my dad had it, but I think you should open it."

I placed the chest on the desk, dropped down into my chair, and inserted the key from the book into the lock. It fit.

Then I turned the key; the latch clicked open.

Samantha leaned in as I lifted the lid.

Inside was what I knew to be a vessel.

My grandmother had spoken of them through the years: she had told me of their use, what they could do, but I had never

seen one before because she didn't have one, she had lost them
all. She told me they were all gone.

Sam whispered reverently, "Do you know what it is?"

"Yes, it's a vessel for traveling through time."

She searched my face. "That's not just a made up story? I
thought it was a conspiracy theory."

"No, it's not, it's true, and now…"

I picked the vessel up and a memory flashed in my mind: I
was holding one, in the dark, under a tree. I turned to look back
at the woods, the sound of a helicopter above us.

"Weird," I said, "I have a memory of using it, of holding it. I
never remembered that before."

I turned it around in my hands and noticed a give in the
middle. I gave it a tiny little twist that caused it to briefly vibrate
— the shock of it like a jolt.

I flung the vessel across the room. "Shit. I did not like that."

I rubbed my palm, it felt like I had been shocked. "I wish
Lady Mairead was still here so I could ask her about this."

Samantha reached out and poked it. "She must have given it
to my dad for safekeeping and then forgotten about it."

"There has been too much forgetting. We should go to the
storage, maybe Lady Mairead left behind something, too."

Lady Mairead's storage warehouse was like a doorway to the
past. She had, once upon a time, before we lost the kingdom, a
huge art collection in a large grand museum. But once the
kingdom was lost, she had bought this big warehouse and stored
the art inside of it. The art pieces had been crated and toward
the end of her life she didn't have much interest in visiting. I had
asked her why and she had answered, 'It feels like a relic,
Archibald, tis from a past I canna recover.'

I thought she had grown bored of collecting, but now, seeing
the vessel, I realized she had been grounded from time-travel. It

was curious how I remembered this suddenly, having forgotten it through the years.

I pushed the door open on her office, unoccupied, except by maintenance men, and went through to Lady Mairead's personal offices and the art library, off limits to everyone. The library was full of first edition books and safes containing precious priceless documents. The maintenance man had told me that he wanted to go through it all, take an inventory, but there was something about that that felt transgressive. Lady Mairead would never forgive us.

She wasn't here, but she had always been private, she never let us rifle through her things.

But since she was gone, I would rifle. I just would do it carefully, out of respect.

Samantha said, "What are we looking for?"

"Anything, maybe a journal or..."

She pulled open the top drawer of Lady Mairead's desk. "Like this?"

There was a notepad with a list of names:

Fraoch MacDonald

Lochinvar

Agnie MacLeod. This one was scratched through.

Colonel Quentin and Beaty

Isla.

Then in script, circled three times:

Who else am I forgetting?

"Yep, this is important. We need to find more like this."

She looked around with her hands on her hips. "She didn't keep journals? She strikes me as the kind of lady who would keep track of things. Where else did she keep locked drawers?"

"Her closets, maybe, her bedroom? I don't go in there on principle."

CHAPTER 45 - ARCHIE

2408 - WE FIND MY GRANDMOTHER'S BOOKS

We drove back over to our manor home and entered Lady Mairead's chambers.

Samantha sighed. "This is reminding me how much we are ignoring. We ought to go through, decide what to do with it all, and…"

I joked, gesturing, lighting a match and catching the whole thing on fire.

"Archie! You wouldn't!"

"It would be a lot easier than going through Grandmother's stuff. She was a hoarder. I do not look forward to it."

Her rooms were crowded with objects. I picked up a frame, a photo of Lady Mairead in a fancy dress, her chin up, regally posed, she looked to be young.

Sam glanced at the photo. "She was a beauty."

"Yes she was." I put the frame back. "This is a lot to go through."

Sam looked around, turning in a circle. Then said, "I remember once, she once told me that the one place a woman can keep her secrets is in her dressing room."

"Then that's where we will look." I crossed the room and opened the door. The lights flickered on overhead.

Samantha inhaled. "Ah, it smells like her perfume." She picked up a bottle, uncapped it, and sniffed, then sprayed the air and stepped into the cloud. "I love this scent."

I went up to the wide drawer under the counter. It was locked. "Great, I will never get into this, see, a presspad with—" I pressed my hand to it and it clicked open. "Lady Mairead gave me access to the locks?"

"Without telling you? That's a classic move."

The drawer was filled side to side with journals, all on their fore edges, spines up toward us. I ran my finger down the row. A few were printed with numbers, some had markings, but not all. A few were pristine, a couple were, well, overly worn. Samantha noticed a book in the back and pulled it from its hiding place.

It was a very old book.

I carefully flipped through.

It was full of diagrams and tiny writing, and looked ancient, as if it was a very rare book that had been much read. On the front page it had the name: Johnne Cambell.

I discovered a drawing that looked much like a vessel. "Oh yes, this is good, this is… wow, this seems to be an instruction book for the vessels."

I placed it on the counter and continued searching down the row of Lady Mairead's journals. I pulled out the last one, the most recent.

It looked new.

When I flipped through, there was only writing in the first third.

On the last page of her notes, she had written:

Fraoch MacDonald is in Scotland, near Loch Lomond, in the year 1744. But how would I get him a message? There was a small piece of a map, folded many ways to be very small. I opened it up and found a loch in the center, with an x marking a spot on the shore.

· · ·

Then she wrote: *Ranulph is here in the kingdom, how can I get a vessel from him?*

And then finally: *Must get to Magnus, I believe he is being held in I..cha…g*

I couldn't make out the final word, and that was the last thing she had ever written.

I asked Samantha, "Do you think my father is still alive?"

She said, "I don't know, how could he be…?"

I tapped the page, "Lady Mairead seemed to think so but she never mentioned it to me."

"Is there a date? Maybe the books are out of order."

I flipped back a few pages. "No, this is an entry about her luncheon with the ladies of Kingsland, that was two days before she died, right?"

Samantha nodded.

"Is my father alive?" I gulped. "I lost his kingdom, if he's still alive, he's going to be pissed."

"You were a little boy, nine years old when your kingdom was stolen. If he's still alive and not here, then he is responsible, right? Where the hell is he?"

"A different time, or at least I think that's how this works."

I reread the latest entries, and flipped through more leaves of the book. "She wrote: *Ranulph.* We all know who that is, he's the king, so of course Lady Mairead would be irritated by him, journaling about him. She woke up every morning of her life in this, as she called it, wee manor house, incensed by Ranulph I."

Sam said, "I really miss her rants."

"I do too. The old lady really knew how to get worked up." I flipped the page. "But wait, look at this, she wrote: Inchadney village, 1499. Followed by the word: Old. That's the same word she wrote on the last page."

I flipped to the last page and tapped. "Inchadney is written here too. She drew arrows to it, as if she was thinking… this seems important."

Samantha leaned over my shoulder as I read. "It does sound as if she thinks your father is there."

I gulped. "If he is alive he is seriously going to kill me."

"I wish we understood any of this. What is she talking about with the 'Old'?"

I flipped back and forth, shaking my head. "I don't know. If he was old in the fifteenth century, then he's long gone, you know?"

She pointed at writing on a page. "What does that say?"

"It's very small." I passed her the book and she held the page close. "She says 'I need a vessel' and then 'find Fraoch' and then 'ask him to get Magnus.'"

"She wants to ask a man named Fray-ooak to find Magnus. Why didn't she remember about the vessel that she stored with your father?"

"She was pretty old before she died, maybe she just forgot."

"Well, I have a vessel, sounds like this is what I need to do. My grandmother would have wanted me—"

Her eyes widened. "Archie! You have never been to… no, you can't! You can't time jump! It's too dangerous!" She made me meet her eyes. "Archie, promise me you won't run off half-cocked, heading out to do some crazy time-traveling, go-save-your-dead-father craziness."

I leaned back in my seat, my mouth on my hand, my elbow resting on the arm of my chair, in thought. "I get you, Sam, I understand, I do — but truly, my father might be lost. There are, according to your dad's journals, a brother and sister who are gone, and I have the journal telling me how to begin to look for my father. I have an instruction booklet, and most impor-tantly, a vessel. If my grandmother wanted to figure out a way to rescue my father and that was what she needed, what kind of a grandson would I be, what kind of son, if I have these things and didn't go do my best to find him?"

She sighed. "I suppose, m'lord, you would be a pretty horrible son."

"Yes, I would, I ought to rescue the former king so he can kill me for losing his kingdom. So what do I do first?"

"Well, you need to learn how to use the vessel. Then I think you need to find this Fray-oak guy."

"Is that how you pronounce it you think?"

"I have no idea, I suppose you have to ask him to find out."

CHAPTER 46 - ARCHIE

2408 - WE MEET A MAN NAMED LOCHINVAR

*T*hat night we were having dinner and the cook entered and whispered, "Your Highness, there is a visitor calling."

"Can it wait until after dinner?"

"He said it is urgent. He asked for your father first, and then for your grandmother."

"What was his name?"

"He said it was Lochinvar."

"Lochinvar?" I glanced at Sam as I put my napkin down beside my plate. "Send him in, set another place."

A tall big man with ginger hair entered, bowed low, and bellowed, "Archibald! Wee-un! I apologize for interrupting your meal!"

I gestured for him to sit. "Lochinvar... how do I know you?"

He narrowed his eyes on me as his food was delivered. He exhaled. "Ye are a sight for sore eyes, ye look just like yer da, and remind me of the little boy I used tae ken."

"I do *not* remember meeting you."

"Nor I ye, wee'un, this is highly irregular." He forked a

mouthful of food in and chewed. "I canna think of a moment when I met ye, and I haena thought on ye once, in the thirty years of m'life, yet yesterday morn I woke up, lyin' in bed, thinkin' on the comin' day, and it came tae me — I thought, 'och aye, I remember where tis!' I climbed from bed, got in m'truck, and rode tae the lands outside of Balloch, near the old yew tree. There, I dug down, in the first place I considered and found a chest. I opened it up and found inside a vessel." He took another big bite of food. "I honestly haena thought of the vessels in a verra long time, I daena ken why I dinna, but there twas. M'second thought was, 'I ought tae go see Magnus, and tell him about it. He was always lookin' for the vessels, I figured he would want this one. I time-jumped tae his castle, I had almost forgotten how to use it, mind ye, but I was able tae work it. There I asked a guard tae speak tae the king. After some misunderstandings that almost got me killed, he said Magnus wasna there — there was a new king, surprise, surprise, and one of the guardsmen told me that Magnus's descendents lived in exile and he let it slip that yer exile was in the town of Middlevale. I took m'leave and traveled here. And here I am."

He smiled. "Where is the old chap?"

"Magnus the First?"

"Aye, Og Maggy as Frookie used tae call him — we need tae get taegether, it has been a long time."

"Magnus I is long gone, he is not... I was the king of Riaghalbane, but we have lost the kingdom, long ago."

"Ye were a king and not anymore? Och nae, yer father would be verra upset." He shook his head. "Ye still hae the look of the boy I once knew, I used tae change yer nappies."

Sam stifled a giggle.

I shifted in my seat. "I do not believe you ever changed my nappies, sir."

He winked. "Well, I might be exaggeratin' on it, the memory fades, ye ken, but ye were running along the shore of the loch in Maine, with a long stick, ye always carried a long stick tae sword fight, and ye were clamorin' tae learn anything ye could about the ways of—"

"I do not understand what you are doing here, not sure what you mean by any of this — these memories that I do not have, how can you have a memory of me that I do not know? I have never set foot in a place called Maine… this is highly unusual."

He plopped his lower arms out across the table. "Och nae! Ye daena remember Maine? What of our time on the shore of the loch in New York? Or at Balloch? Ye were with Ben and…" His face screwed up as he looked at the ceiling. "I'm having a time rememberin' the rest of their names, but sure as I am sittin' here, ye were runnin' in a whole mob of bairns and ye were their leader. None of this is familiar tae ye?"

I shook my head.

He exhaled and leaned back in his chair. "This is verra concerning." He stared up at the ceiling. "When were ye crowned king?"

"I was nine years old."

"Nine! Och nae, this is verra… when did ye lose the kingdom?"

"I was ten. We have been living here in exile ever since."

"Lady Mairead was yer steward while ye were young — can I speak tae her?"

"She is gone too."

"Twas her malicious spirit that finally got tae her? That lady had a fine capacity for revenge and turmoil."

"No, it was old age."

"Och, m'apologies, wee'un, she deserved a warrior's death."

I groaned. "This is very very unacceptable, I might not be a king, but I was at one time, and you are showing me a lack of respect and… to speak of my grandmother that way… how dare you."

His eyes widened. "I once saw the auld broad stick a dirk in her enemy and twist it, but ye…?"

He looked at me for an agreement, then shrugged. "Perhaps

she calmed down in her auld age, though I hate tae think on it. Some birds are meant tae be unfettered and free. Especially the raptors, if ye get m'meanin'. So we are down tae yer Uncle Fraoch. Where's he?"

I said, "I don't know who you are speaking about."

He straightened in his seat. "Och nae! What has happened!"

Then he leaned in. "Seriously, what has happened, wee Archie, tae make this all go amiss? Yer Uncle Fraoch was yer favorite person in the world, even if ye lost him at the fine age of seven ye would still remember him, wouldna ye? He was married tae Hayley, verra close tae yer mother."

"My mother, Bella? Who died when I was very young?"

He fell back in his chair.

I said, "Are you insane?"

"Nae, though I can understand the question. M'memories are verra different from yer own. Tis as if we are speaking on different worlds, and I would almost believe ye tae be a verra different man than the young lad I kent, but ye are the image of him. Ye look like yer father. Ye were once on his throne. Ye wore his crown. Ye must be Archie, but…"

He narrowed his eyes. "Ye ken twas me that fought in the arena that won yer father back his kingdom? Without m'talent with the sword, ye would hae nae throne tae lose in yer youth — ye are verra welcome."

I said, "What do you mean, fighting in the arena?"

"Och nae." He put his palms down on the table, and pushed himself up to standing. "Fine, I will go speak tae yer Uncle Frookie on this." He straightened his coat. "I wonder how I find him?"

"I might know. I was thinking about going to talk to him."

"Finally, the wee'un says somethin' sensible! I will go with ye. This will be an adventure. On our way I can recount the battle in the arena and how yer father and Uncle Frookie, though fine men and warriors, were in agreement that I was the best fighter of them all." He sat back down. "But for now, will there be dessert?"

That night I lay in bed beside Samantha staring up at the fine canopy of our royal bed, moved into our manor house, as if I were a king on vacation and not a former king living in exile in the countryside, basically under house arrest. This bed was appointed as if I were a great king of a bygone era. My eyes traveled up the pattern of the fabric, an embroidered floral that calmed my mind as I was considering what to do next.

I sighed.

Samantha said, "Well, *that* was an interesting dinner."

"That Lochinvar fellow comes in off the street, gets past my guards, demands to be heard, says nothing that is sensible or true, and somehow convinces me to let him accompany me as I travel through time. I am apparently going to travel through time! With a man who urges me to call him Uncle Lochie! He's an absolute stranger, and yet... I am going to run away and go with him to the 'past'. As if we are talking about going to the country for the weekend or something."

Sam said, "I do not understand what has happened, but you and I uncovered a mystery and that *very* night he showed up — repeating the same names, talking about time-travel, all but corroborating what your grandmother wrote in her journal."

"And my dreams."

She said, "Yeah, have you had another?"

"Last night, the same one. I was frozen, watching a field, an army on horses, bearing down on us, terrifying. I can hear yelling and I freeze, I can't move. I don't know what to do. I'm powerless— kind of like in my life."

"In your dreams you're a little boy, of course you are powerless."

"In the dream I can not even turn my head to see who else is there. But last night there was a change, I saw a flash, a little girl beside me. At the time I thought it was you."

"But maybe it was a sister you don't remember."

"Yes, maybe — this return of memories, it seems prescient... I need to act. And Lochinvar is ready to go, so it seems to be the thing to do, but... do you think I am being too trusting?"

"No, I usually don't think you should trust anyone — everyone wants something from you, but I'm glad you're trusting Lochinvar, this seems like a time to trust someone to help."

"He seems authentic right?"

"Yes, I don't understand it, but somehow... he knows you, he knows your father, he wants to help you."

I nodded. "Yes, I agree. It is scary to trust him, I am not sure. I did lose everyone, and now it looks like they might not be lost at all... this is so strange, it feels almost like a dream state — what is real? Am I really going to go find my father, the former king of Riaghalbane, just living in a village in the fifteenth century? And what am I going to say to him? 'Hello father, how are you doing? I was young when you left me to go galavant around, oh by the way, I lost the kingdom, try to forgive me.'"

"Yes, *if* he is alive. I'm not entirely convinced. And he will forgive you, Archie. You were ten, what were you to do? And you've lived in exile, you have had guards stationed around you ever since. You've been all but captive."

"I have been grateful to you that you joined me here in this form of captivity, you could have been free to do whatever you wanted, and instead..."

She looked up at my face. "Archie, I would not trade our life, never! We have a country estate, a manor house, and yes, guards, but they don't bother us, we go about our business, and... nothing bothers us."

"Except we are here at the favor of Ranulph. He could decide we are too much trouble and..."

"He would never. The people hate him — they love you. When he meets with you his approval ratings go up, if he speaks badly of Magnus or you, his approval goes down. He wants you to live on, it makes him look magnanimous."

"I suppose… you are right, and I am usually content, but now I have glimpsed a life, a whole family, that I didn't know I had — that I could have had but missed out on…"

"That's a really hard thing to learn. It's been a tough day. I don't think it is going to get easier."

I exhaled long. "You know, you have to come with us. I can't go and leave you here, how would you explain my disappearance? I am not allowed to leave. Ranulph would hold you responsible. I can't allow that."

Her finger trailed in circles on my chest.

Finally she said, "If I need to go, then I will go with you."

"Good, I will take my wife Sam with me on this insane adventure into the dark ages with a dude off the street named Lochinvar."

"…that you met mere hours ago."

I chuckled. "Yep."

"I hope that we find what you're searching for, m'lord. But whatever happens, I would not trade a minute of my life with you."

"Nor I you."

"We leave at dawn?"

"Yes. Get some sleep, we'll need it."

And I felt her fall asleep, slowly, while I continued considering the canopy overhead.

I had been told of a great many things that I had no memory of… but now I had some images in my mind, things I could not place — I was young, running down a white-sand beach, warm sun on my skin, my hair flowing back, a stick dragged behind me leaving a rut as I ran in a weaving route, enjoying my speed and my mastery, and I yelled, "Mammy, look! I am making a design for the birds!"

And behind me, a woman's voice, a somehow familiar voice, the kind that filled me with warmth, said, "I see it, Archie! That's beautiful!"

I could not place the beach, the time, or the woman's voice, and it gave me pause — this whole day had been marked by the confusion of memory lapses, a learning of forgotten things. Surely, I had only remembered running down the beach because Lochinvar had mentioned my youthful love of sticks. He had somehow dislodged a memory, brought it to mind. Adults forget things from their childhood all the time.

And because I had been orphaned, and imprisoned, maybe I just didn't have someone around to tell me stories from my childhood.

It was not my fault I forgot the little things.

But how had I forgotten the big things?

This echoed in my mind: *Mammy, look!*

I wondered what big things might be forgotten.

CHAPTER 47 - ARCHIE

2408 - WE FLEE

I was not allowed to leave, ever, without my arrangements being planned and approved first, so Sam and I would sneak out just before dawn with Uncle Lochie. He promised that our time travel would involve a massive storm that would keep guards from impeding us. He also said that we could return, probably the following day, but I would need to decide.

Sam thought we were coming back.

But I knew we were leaving for good. This had been my home. I had lived here on this large estate, running the lands, my whole life, and it had been a good life, but though Sam said she did not mind, we *were* under an arrest of a kind, kept quiet and content out here in the middle of nowhere.

But I kept this decision hidden, because I didn't want to frighten her: I knew that if I stepped out of line I would lose my life.

That had always been at the back of my mind.

I was fleeing my imprisonment.

It was an easy decision for me. I wouldn't come back.

But to keep Sam from being too frightened, I acted as if we would return. We gathered what we thought we would need from the storerooms, and I had gone to the garage for a vehicle, one that I used to carry loads around the estate. We met in the middle of the west field at dawn. Lochinvar said, "Ye brought this vehicle? How does it run? Daena ye hae a horse?"

"Did you bring a horse? I don't have horses, I have vehicles. I have lots of vehicles."

He said, "Och, of all the troublin' things ye hae said, yer lack of horses might be the worst of them. Yer father loved horses almost more than he loved his family. Almost." He tossed his bag into the back of the open vehicle. "It daena hae a roof, what will we do about the rain?"

I placed my pack in the back and Sam's beside it, grumbling, "A horse doesn't have a roof either."

It was discomfiting to hear what my father would and wouldn't like from this stranger.

"But tis a horse! Ye canna compare the two, if ye are wet inside a vehicle, ye are drenched, on a horse ye are enjoyin' a fine ride in the elements!"

I said, "This will be better than a horse, there are all-terrain tires, four-wheel drive, it's all but silent, and compact for the smallest of roads—"

Lochinvar grinned, holding a vessel. "There arna roads where we're goin' wee'un, so hold on tae m'arm."

I held on around Sam and gripped his elbow. He said, "Sam, please hold onto the vehicle for us."

Sam said, "Oh, of course." She put a hand on the door as he twisted the vessel. She said, "Is that all there is to it, this is ea—"

CHAPTER 48 - ARCHIE

1744- WE ARE IN A LONG AGO FOREST

I woke in the mire of a Scottish forest.

Sam said, "Ugh. What was that? Is that... is that what's supposed to happen?"

I said, "I am glad you're complaining, I thought you might be dead."

"Are you sure we aren't dead? This feels like I died, maybe we're all dead."

Lochinvar's voice came from behind the vehicle. "This is the way tis supposed tae feel, this explains why when I hadna seen the vessels in a long time. I wasna lookin' for them because they are evil."

I said, "I agree. The pain, and it's dark as hell, the sound, is your sound muffled, Sam?"

She said, "Yes, m'lord."

Lochinvar said, "Och aye, ye hae a good proper wife, wee'un, ye hae her trained verra well."

Sam and I both groaned.

We slowly got up. I asked, "So the pain, the torturous pain is normal — what year is this?"

"This ought tae be the year 1744. If we had gone further back, twould hae hurt even more."

Sam said, "Why, but why would it need to hurt?"

Lochinvar said, "Because ye hae tae ken, tis from the devil, this inna God's work — he is furious on it."

We stood looking around the clearing, we were surrounded by thick woods.

I said, "Do you see a path? Which way are we going?"

Lochinvar pulled on a cloak. "I told ye the vehicle wouldna help, there inna roads."

"I see that, *now*, it seemed like a good idea at the time."

He opened one of our sacks and pulled out some wrapped sweet cakes I had asked the cook to pack for us.

He stuffed a bit in his mouth and with crumbs flying, said, "If ye listen tae me in everything I will lead ye the proper way."

I said, "Lesson learned, we can hide the vehicle in the woods, cover it with limbs, but then where will we find Fraoch?"

"I am not sure, but I feel certain he is as close tae the water's edge as he can get."

CHAPTER 49 - ARCHIE

WE FIND FRAOCH MACDONALD, NEAR LOCH LOMOND, 1744

*T*he walk took hours.

Sam and I were nervous, I jumped at a sound and Uncle Lochie laughed and laughed. "Ye daena get outside much, wee'un? I canna wait tae see the look on yer Uncle Frookie's face when he sees what a cautious boy, soft and pasty as a wee bairn, ye are."

"I am not soft and pasty, I am not a wee bairn, but I am cautious. I'm definitely not used to a medieval forest. You can't blame me for not liking the deep dark woods with no castle guard."

"Ye are right, I canna blame ye, but tis still a hard turn of events — ye ought not be so sheltered. I am surprised yer grand-mother put up with it."

"She didn't have much choice, she lived a quiet life, without much to do but scour the records for her ancestors and family. Ultimately there wasn't anything she could do about our exile."

Uncle Lochie swung his dirk at a thin limb so we could pass, but the rest of the limb rebounded and whipped across my hip. I yelped, then coughed, trying to cover up the sound.

He smirked. "Pull yer dirk, lad, help me carve the path."

I patted my hip. "I don't carry a—"

He put his hands on his hips. "This is outrageous! The son of Magnus daena carry a dirk? I saw yer father fell a man with a sword so long he had tae carry it between the shoulders and it almost dragged in the dirt, he could pull it from its sheath with one hand though it was as heavy as three men, twas made from the steel of a rare ore, cut from the middle of ben Cruachan — och, he was a mountain of a man, all who met him bowed tae the ground before him."

I gulped.

He continued leading the way, hacking at the path until we came to a sparser part of the woods. He added, though it had been so long since he had been talking that I had almost forgotten the point, concerned as I was with my mental health, *where the hell were my memories,* "Except for me."

Sam said, "Except for you, what?"

Uncle Lochie said, "Except for me, I dinna bow down in front of him, as I told ye, the only man who could best yer father in the arena was me."

I said, "These 'arena battles', what do you mean?"

"In yer kingdom, if ye had a blood-claim tae the throne ye could challenge the king in the arena. But if ye died, twas yer loss. Most men wouldna be brave enough, or dumb enough tae try — yet ye are livin'. How did Ranulph win the kingdom from ye when ye were ten?"

"He strolled into the castle, a conqueror. Lady Mairead tried to block his access, but he came on in, declaring himself king. Her vessels were all gone."

"All of them?"

"Except for the one with Sam's father, but somehow it was forgotten."

"Much like how I hae forgotten things, and how ye act as if ye never kent them tae begin with." He shook his head.

Sam said, "I don't think I can walk another foot, we have been going for hours."

Lochinvar pushed aside a branch, "Ye are in luck, we are almost there."

We came out on a moor beside a long loch. I pulled a monocular from my pack and trained it on the shore. "I don't see anyone."

Lochinvar squinted at the shore on the east. "Ye daena see the buildin' there?"

"Oh, what — that hovel, a person might live there?"

"Aye, that is the kind of shelter a man would build who just wants tae be alone tae fish. If I remember him well, this is the kind of building our Frookie would live in."

He shielded his eyes from the sun and peered. "We ought tae go near, but we need tae be sure not tae spook him. He's likely armed."

I glanced at Sam and she muttered, "What in the world are we doing, creeping up on an armed hermit that we might spook?"

I joked, "We are following a man named Uncle Lochie to go surprise a man named Uncle Frookie in the middle of the wilderness in the eighteenth century."

She said, "Just another day in the life of an exiled king."

The sky was gray and misting as we crossed the moor. The trail was wet and mucky and hard to traverse. I used my monocular but Lochie pointed and exclaimed, "Och, he has taken off, he is tryin' tae elude us!" A man was lumbering away up the hillside in the distance.

Lochinvar put his hands around his mouth and bellowed, "Frookie!"

The man turned, briefly, and looked down at us, then continued on. Lochinvar said, "Och aye, that is him! I am goin' tae hae tae catch him." He took off running with us splashing behind him through the wet expanse of land.

We passed the hovel and Sam was doubled over, out of breath, I said, "Should we wait for him to come back?"

He was up on the ridge now.

Lochinvar yelled, "Frookie! Frookie!"

I joined in and then Sam, all yelling, "Frookie!!"

He turned and looked down at us.

Lochinvar said, "I told ye twas him."

The man paused there for a long time, and we waved. Then finally he began lumbering down the path to the base of the mountain, heading toward us.

We waited in the doorway of his hovel, Sam looking around with disgust. Inside the small room, there was a mattress lying on the ground, a pile of wool blankets on it. A cup and a plate, a small stool. Outside there was a boat pulled up on the shore, a small bench in front of the house.

He neared and looked wild, hair sticking out everywhere, a long full beard. He was shaped like a big bear, wearing a long coat over a kilt. He wore leather boots that looked very old.

He bellowed, "Who are ye, what the hell are ye doin' on m'land?"

Lochinvar bellowed to match, "I am Lochinvar! Ye used tae call me 'Og Lochie' in years past. I am here tae see m'auld friend, auld man Frookie."

Froach stopped still, his face stern, frozen.

Lochie continued, "It must be ye, I can see it in yer eyes, but what has happened tae ye? Ye used tae not be much for bathin' but twas more regular than this."

There was a passing recognition in Fraoch's eyes. "Og Lochie? *The* Og Lochie, ye…?"

Then he waved his hand. "I daena ken ye," and tried tae brush past, but Lochinvar stepped in his way.

"Ye ken me, I am a brother tae ye, our father is Donnan Campbell—"

Fraoch pushed past Sam and I to enter his hovel. "Ye hae me confused with someone else, m'father was a man in the clan MacDonald and—"

Lochinvar grasped his sleeve. "Nae, ye were fostered by MacDonalds, but ye are a Campbell, same as I, and ye are married tae a lovely lass by the name of Hayley and ye are the brother of Magnus." Fraoch put his hand on the door frame.

"Who?"

"Magnus, Og Maggy, ye ken — daena ye ken, Fraoch?"

He turned and looked me in the eyes. "And ye are Archie, grown?"

I nodded, looking him in the eyes, "But how do I know you?" His eyes were at once familiar, and in my head the sound of a big booming laugh, I couldn't place hearing it, yet, here it was, remembered from somewhere, years ago.

His eyes grew misty. "Och nae, ye are grown!"

He threw his arms around me and hugged me tight. "Archie!" He put me out at arm's length. "Och where hae ye been? How come… we daena… where is yer da?"

I shrugged, too overcome to speak.

Lochinvar said, "This is why we are here, because we are looking for Magnus."

Fraoch clutched his chest. "Och nae, what has become of us?"

He built a fire in the hearth at the end of his hovel, sayin', "Madame Samantha daena look like she can withstand a proper Scottish summer."

Lochinvar said, "Auld man, ye choose tae live here on the edge of the loch like a fish?"

"Aye, and I am not so auld tae ye, Lochie, ye are how many years auld now?"

"Auld enough tae ken better, as James used tae say."

Fraoch and Lochie both stood stock still.

Fraoch said, "Och I haena thought on him in a verra long time."

Lochie patted him on the back. "Me neither, Fraoch. We ought tae come up with a plan tae solve this problem."

Fraoch sat on the ground in front of the hearth and put his feet out, almost taking up the whole floor, physically and with his stench. Sam and I sat cross-legged around him. Lochie sat on the stool.

Fraoch took out a flask, swigged from it, and passed it tae Lochie. "By 'come up with a plan' it seems as if ye are talking about doin' somethin'. I haena agreed tae doin' anythin' or tae goin' anywhere."

Lochie looked incensed. "What ye got tae do around here?"

Fraoch waved a big arm, a waft of odor filling the room. "I got things tae do, fishin'."

Lochie took a swig from the flask. "Fishin' is the dumbest of the things tae do, I canna believe ye hae been lost tae yer family and the whole time ye were here fishin'." He scowled. "I might cry just thinkin' on it."

"Ye always were a big bairn."

"Kicked yer arse in the arena though, ye ken?"

Fraoch put his head back. "Did ye now? Och, that seems unlikely, maybe I let ye win."

Lochie grinned. "Maybe, I canna remember." He pulled his own flask from his pocket, and took a swig and smacked his lips and looked at the flask, admiringly. "Tis royal whisky, aged, civilized, the long tradition of whisky from a civilized world…" He put the flask in his pocket. "I see ye are verra busy, Frookie, but I need ye tae help me rescue Magnus, the boy needs his da."

Fraoch said, "Ye arna goin' tae share yer whisky?"

"Nae, tis for heroes."

Fraoch huffed, then asked me, "When did ye see yer da last?"

"I was just about eight years old, I think."

"Och, I lost m'own da, tis a travesty, a heartbreak." He looked at Lochie. "So ye believe his da is alive?"

"Aye, I believe he is alive, I believe he is in the year 1499."

"The year 1499! Och, how are we going tae—?"

"We will time-travel there, usin' one of these."

Lochinvar pulled the vessel from his coat pocket.

Fraoch took it from him and looked down on it. "Tis a shock tae m'system tae see it, all the memories that come rushing in return."

Lochie said, "Aye, tis a clarity, as if we are comin' out of the fog."

CHAPTER 50 - KAITLYN

2025 - I LEAVE FLORIDA

*T*ossed my purse in the passenger seat and slammed the van door shut. I brushed off my hands. "Done! Ready to go." I passed the keys from one hand to the other and looked around at them all. "I miss you already."

Zoe put her hands up.

I lifted her to my hip. "I will miss you desperately, Zoe, but I will come visit."

She said, "Pwomise?"

"I promise."

I kissed her and put her down. I hugged Ben, and then Emma, Zach, then Quentin and Hayley, then Emma again. James had said goodbye the night before. I made a speech. "This is just for a little while, I just think it'll be good for me, I've been kind of struggling, you know, and so I ought to go do something new, and fresh."

Zach said, "I don't know if Maine is 'New and Fresh'."

I grinned. "Yeah, that might be overstating it, but it's a house just sitting there, waiting. I ought to go haunt it a little. Speaking of, you have your plane tickets?"

Emma said, "Yep, we'll be there for a month this summer, wouldn't miss it."

"Okay." I put my hands on my hips and exhaled. "Okay, I will miss you, but hey, if this sucks, I'll come back. You've got my keys, all my passwords."

Emma said, "Yep."

"Okay," I said again like a moron.

Hayley said, "Call on the road, and I'll get tickets, I'll be there next month. I'm just slammed at work."

"Yeah, I get it, economy, turmoil in the world, I know, I'll be up there, we can Skype, no worries. Have I told you all how much I love you?"

Hayley said, "Every day, all the time, we know."

"Good." I gave Zoe another kiss on the cheek, then went around to the driver's side of the van, climbed in, and started it, waving goodbye to my friends.

I pulled away from our house, our neighborhood, our town, leaving for the bridge off the island to the highway that led to Maine. It felt like a relief. Like starting anew. But also a part of it was leaving stuff behind, and it wasn't all bad.

Our house in Florida had grown weird over time, full of odd items and strange memories and a sort of fogginess that had Emma googling 'Black mold symptoms' because of something she saw on a morning show. But nothing she found truly explained what was happening to us, a listless melancholy. A forgetting. We all felt as if we had stopped living, stunted in the prime of our lives. As Hayley had said, "Aren't we fabulous? How come we're all a bunch of spinsters?"

Quentin had said, "Speak for yourself," but we all knew what she meant.

Why were we basically alone, clinging to each other as if we were on a life raft in the middle of a storm?

And that had been the thing, one night, a few months ago, there had been a big long storm. The kind I used to watch because they had meant 'change is coming'. I had always felt kind of breathless, but this night I had thought, watching the storm cross over the ocean and head south down the beach, *I'm not in the right place, I promised I would be in Maine, I PROMISED.*

I had woken up and began planning the move.

I had the empty house in Maine, I would just open it up and live there, I had things to work on, and... I wasn't sure 'what' next. I didn't know what I was waiting for. I just knew I was supposed to be there.

Because of a promise. That pulled me to Maine.

CHAPTER 51 - MAGNUS

1499 - LEFT IN A DUNGEON

*T*was the dream that I kept havin'.

I had been in a field, and around me the sound of thunderous hooves coming through the bracken of the Scottish woods, I wanted tae yell 'Run!' tae warn those around me, but the frightenin' aspect of being outnumbered, overpowered, and somehow, all alone, made it impossible tae speak.

As the ax swung down on me — I awoke in a cell with a start.

In a quiet castle, I listened, m'ear pressed tae the door. I sensed that I was alone, and that meant unguarded, but also I had m'dirk at my hip, which meant that whoever had left me here had not cared that I was armed. He had not worried about me at all. I grabbed the handle on the door, and tried tae budge it. He hadna worried that I would get free, because I was alone. I sat back on the small bench for a moment tae gather m'wits. How had I come tae be here?

I considered, I had been walking along, half carried, half forced tae move — a state I had been in often, surrounded by soldiers, a knife at m'back, m'feet stumbling on the terrain.

I remembered once down a long hallway, a carpet under m'foot, a stark white wall on both sides of me, plain doors, soldiers forcin' me down the passage, the thought in m'mind, fear — *would I be able tae win the battle?*

Another memory, soldiers forcing me tripping along a marshland, *where had that been?* There had been the shriek of locusts, and the buzzin' of mosquitoes, a hum of the air, a stifling heat and sopping wet feet. Soldiers flanked me.

And yesterday, that feelin' once more, soldiers flanking me, pain ripping through me as I forced my feet tae move, one after another, stumbling across a moor, tae here, this castle prison.

I was thrown intae a cell, the door had clanked shut. The night had been stormy, dark, and I had gone unconscious.

But who had it been and why?

I felt mad from tryin' tae remember.

With caution I used m'dirk tae carve at the wood around the door hinge. I dinna want tae break m'blade, I would need it tae cut the throat of the men who put me here.

It took a day tae get free. My hands were bloodied, but my thirst drove me. I burst from the cell tae a tunnel and snuck out, emerging at a riverbank. I stumbled tae the river's edge, pooled water in my cupped hands, and drank deeply, m'parched throat causin' me tae cough. I splashed water on my hair and all over m'beard, then turned ontae my back and stared up at the tree limbs overhead, the blue sky beyond, a rare warm day. I lay, half in, half out of the water for a long time. The water rushing around my head. The water cool and bringin' a sense tae my mind.

I would need tae hunt for food. I would need tae find shelter. I would need tae survive this — I rolled tae my front again, for another drink, my hand just above the water, ready tae cup another drink, but I was paused at m'reflection — there was an auld man peerin' back at me. He was gnarled and grayed, and looked hungry and small and weak.

It wasna the lack of food, or the being held captive, both had lasted a day. I looked as if I had gained the age of seventy, perhaps more, and yet I couldna remember the last forty years. I dropped back on the heels of m'hands, and scrambled up the bank tae get away from it.

I was frightened of m'visage, because it exposed m'loss of memories.

I dinna ken where I was and long years had passed.

And now that I was back, present within my body, I realized that my knees were pained. I turned my shoulder in it's socket. Och nae, I had a pain in m'shoulder. I stood stiffly, feelin' hobbled by it. *How would I hunt?*

I held a tree tae steady m'self, then lumbered up the bank tae the woods where I climbed tae the top of a hill. There I looked around. I could see a ben in the distance that I recognized, and remembered with clarity my home.

I walked a long ways, m'goin' was slow, but finally I arrived at the village. My memory was restored, this was the path, beside my small house, there was m'horse standin' beside the wall. I lumbered up, and said, "Och, Dràgon, tis a relief tae see ye here, I had... I daena ken... I feel as if I were misplaced. Did ye feel it as well?"

He whinnied.

I rubbed and stroked his withers. "Ye hae been with me a long time, Dràgon. I swear I kent ye when I was young and now here I am, apparently withered and auld, and ye hae barely aged."

He whinnied again.

I said, "I am famished," and turned tae go intae m'house,

unsure what I might hae tae eat. A voice called out from the path at the end of the garden, "Mag, ye are returned?"

I nodded. "Aye, how long was I away?"

"This time for a few days."

I put m'hands on m'hips. "A few days, and what did ye mean by 'this time'?"

"I daena ken, every now and again ye go away and return aulder, ye hae the weight of the years upon ye, where do ye go, Mag?"

I shook my head. "I daena ken, I suppose I need tae wander away, but I always come home." I put my hand out tae steady myself at the words, it seemed to echo inside me.

I always come home

Reverberating as if twas somethin' I was used tae sayin', but tae whom? And why? "Thank ye for watchin' over Dràgon while I was away."

"Nae problem, Mag, he is a good horse. See ye at the sermon tomorrow?"

"Aye, see ye then." I remembered fully then, this was the year 1499.

CHAPTER 52 - ARCHIE

1499 - TO FIND MY FATHER

*W*e looked over the book Sam and I had brought and considered what to do. We needed to find my father, and I had one hint: the name of a village and the year 1499.

Sam said, "You know what? I do not want to do that jumping thing again. Not at all. Maybe we can just live here, right?"

Lochie said, "In the hovel with Frookie?"

"Maybe, yes, it would be better than time jumping. Standing here watching you twist that vessel, knowing that the pain is coming, it's too hard." She shook her head. "Nope, don't want to."

Lochie said, "It has tae be hard, if twas easy we would do it all the time and as Magnus used tae say we would destroy the history of the world."

Fraoch pointed up at the trees. "Och, Madame Samantha, dost ye see the shiny thing up there?"

Sam said, "Where, the—?"

Lochie grabbed our arms while Fraoch twisted the vessel.

· · ·

We woke up, my head on Sam's stomach, in the dirt in a really really old part of time.

Lochie said, "Och nae, this keeps gettin' worse."

Fraoch said, "I think it canna be as bad as I remember, but now I remember it has always been terrible, it daena improve."

We got up, stretching, grumbling, and bickering. I said, "How far do we have to walk?"

"Too far."

"I can't believe I have a vehicle in the woods back there. I have deserted it, and now we have to walk."

Fraoch said, "How come ye thought twas a good idea tae bring a vehicle? Daena ye ken there are nae roads?"

I said, "I have no idea what is going on! Until yesterday, I had no idea time travel existed."

Fraoch stopped and narrowed his eyes. "Truly?"

"Truly, I couldn't remember any of it—"

"Ye canna remember Kaitlyn? Yer da?"

"No, I have no idea who Kaitlyn is, I can barely remember da, it's all..."

Fraoch shook his head. "I hope we find yer da, but I wish I dinna hae tae be around when ye tell him—"

"When I tell him I lost the kingdom?"

"Nae, that winna bother him as much. He only ever wanted the kingdom tae keep ye safe. He will be far more upset that ye daena remember yer life when ye were young. He tried verra hard tae give ye a good life."

I said, "Maybe in an alternate universe he did."

We walked a full day and neared the village at dusk. Fraoch said, "We ought tae sleep, we daena want tae surprise the village in the night."

Sam said, "Sleep where — here, out in the open?"

Fraoch said, "We are under a tree!"

Sam's eyes went wide. "What about, I don't know, a hotel?" At Fraoch's further eye-narrowing, she said, "You know, an inn?"

He said, "But tis a fine night!"

Sam said, "What about... I don't know, *monsters?*"

I said, "Monsters don't really exist, Sam." I gulped. "Of course a few days ago I didn't really believe in time travel either."

Fraoch said, "Monsters hae better things tae do besides botherin' with us. Tis a bother tae attack and eat a person, we like tae put up a fight and we are likely tae give them indigestion with all our belly aching. Nae, I think a monster would want tae eat a coo, that would be their favorite meal."

Sam put her hands on her hips and blew the hair off her forehead. "So there *probably* aren't monsters, and we will sleep outside because though it's a risk it's not *that* big a risk because we would give a monster indigestion? This all seems unwise."

Fraoch said, "I hae thought it through from all directions, Madame Samantha, we will be unharmed, I promise ye." He dropped his sack, and uncinched the top. "I will take the first watch, Og Lochie, ye can take the second."

I looked from Fraoch to Lochie. "What are we on watch for?"

Fraoch grinned. "Monsters."

Samantha groaned.

~

We slept in a circle with our backs against trees.

I put my arm around Sam, she whispered, "This will probably be fine, as long as it doesn't get dark."

A little while later she said, "Oh, it's so dark."

~

Sam's voice entered my consciousness. "Archie, Archie, wake up — you're having a nightmare."

I was groggy and confused. I looked around at a cold, foggy, landscape that felt much like my dream. "Am I still in it? It happens in the woods, just like this."

Fraoch said, "What kind of nightmares are ye havin', wee'un?"

"I am in a woods like this, there are men on horseback, charging toward us, I'm frozen in place."

Sam said, "But you're a little boy in it, it's just a dream."

Fraoch nodded. "I hae a similar one, I am kneelin', I look up and daena hae time tae react. I am a spectator, ahead of me is a battle I canna join."

"Do you hear someone yell, 'Run'?"

"Aye."

I had woken up numerous times, listening to the shifting and murmuring of Fraoch and Lochie as they kept watch and then traded off sleeping. I had been guarded my whole life, but the guards back at Riaghalbane had been there to keep me from leaving, imprisoning me. It was a relief to be out on my own, not having to answer to anyone, to be guarded and protected by men who called themselves my 'Uncles'. I was unaccustomed to this thoughtful protection.

Lochie stretched. "That was a good night's sleep."

I chuckled. "You were both up most of the night!"

Lochinvar shrugged. "A night up guardin' is a good night, I hae always liked guard duty."

Fraoch said, "Aye, me as well. Tis in the night when ye understand the meanin' of the world."

I asked, "And what is the meaning of the world?"

He gestured toward Sam in my arms. "Tae hae someone ye want tae keep safe."

I kissed Sam's forehead.

She stretched, fully waking up. "And who do you want to keep safe, Fraoch?"

"First, ye ought tae call me Uncle Fraoch, and," he pointed at me, "I want tae keep this wee'un safe, for his da."

I said, "Thank you."

Sam said, "Anyone bring coffee?"

I said, "I didn't even think of it, what a mistake."

Lochie teased, "Almost as big as bringing the vehicle but nae horses."

Fraoch said, "This is how it goes, Og Lochie, whining as soon as ye awaken?"

Lochie said, "I hae been up for hours, plenty of time for thinkin' on how useless that vehicle was."

Sam stretched. "I have been up for hours, questioning why I ever showed my husband the book and started this whole thing."

I said, "But here we are. Let's go see if we find my father, I mean, he's probably not there, you know, how could he be? For my whole life? That is such a tragedy."

Fraoch slung a pack to his shoulder. "If he is here he needs tae be rescued."

CHAPTER 53 - ARCHIE

1499 - INCHADNEY

*W*e followed along a path, passing a couple of small crofts and a man met us tae ask what business we had enterin' the village.

Fraoch spoke tae him while we tried to blend into the landscape. Fraoch leaned on a stone wall, and they discussed the weather and a few other things that took a long time, pointing at the horizon, discussing the church, asking about the bridge, and then some things that were difficult to understand, then *finally*, Fraoch asked about Magnus.

The man asked who he meant and there was some disagreement and misunderstandings and then the man pointed up the road.

Fraoch said, "We hae found him, he is in the third house."

I said, "He's here? *Here* in this village? He's been gone since I was eight and he's *here*?"

Fraoch said, "Aye." He adjusted the pack on his shoulder and began to walk up the road with us following behind.

~

We came to the third house and it was small. Not much bigger than Fraoch's hovel had been. There was a horse tied to the wall, it stamped as we neared. The interior of the house was very dark.

A shadow passed within the window.

Fraoch waved his arm telling us get back. Lochinvar and I crouched behind a low stone wall. Fraoch called in, "Magnus!"

A gnarled voice called out, "Get off m'lands."

Fraoch said, "I canna, I hae come tae speak tae Magnus, are ye he?"

"I hae a gun trained on ye, dost ye want tae live or die?"

"Och nae, this is an irritatin' question, I want tae live like all the men of the world, but I also want tae ask if the auld arse in the wee house is the Magnus I kent of auld and if he is, why the hell has he got a gun trained on his brother?"

There was a long pause.

Then the voice said, "I daena hae a brother. I will give ye one moment tae turn around and leave m'land and—"

"This is yer land? This patch of dirt in the village of Inchadney in the fifteenth century? Och nae, Og Maggy, ye are fallen far from the man I—"

The gun fired.

Shot hit the ground near Fraoch's foot.

He yelled, "Och!" then said, "Auld man, I will kill ye for it — ye shoot at me? I hae saved yer life, yer kingdom, I even remember once holding yer hair while ye retched in the forest after eatin' a witch's brew —"

The voice inside said, "Ye are insufferable. I will shoot ye just tae keep ye from continuing on with yer raving."

Fraoch shook his head.

Sam nudged me, villagers were gathering, more coming from down the road, the men held tools, the women approached out of curiosity.

Fraoch put up his hands and took a tentative step forward. "Og Maggy, ye daena want tae shoot me, ye will regret it. I am tryin' tae save yer life."

The gun fired again. The shot forced Fraoch to scramble back a step. He said, "Ye winna shoot me."

"What about the fact that I hae shot at ye twice already do ye not understand?"

"I understand m'brother, Og Maggy, and if he wants tae shoot someone he winna miss." He took another step forward.

"Those were warning shots, I winna miss again."

"Och, ye are like an auld dog growling in the fields. Dost ye remember yer auld dog, Og Maggy? Haggis?"

There was a long pause again. "Haggis? M'dog Haggis, how dost ye ken him? He was…" His voice trailed off.

Another tentative step. "Aye, I was there when ye got him. Haggis was a cù math."

The voice said, "How did ye…? What did ye say was yer name?"

"I am Fraoch, I found ye in a swamp in Florida, and we sailed across an ocean together. I am yer brother and fought alongside ye in many battles."

Another long tense pause.

"Ye are the arse that was bellyachin' in the ship's hold?"

"Aye, I am that arse! Yer memories are coming back!"

"Why did I… what dost ye mean, m'memories?"

"I daena ken, Og Maggy, we are… can I come speak tae ye inside? This is for private ears and we hae a crowd gathered."

Another long pause and then an auld man hobbled out from the front door.

He yelled out to the neighbors, wavin' an arm, "Get gone! Ye daena need tae be here, this is m'brother, come tae visit!"

As a man turned to go he said to another, "Tis just auld Mag ravin' again."

The other man said, "How come he has grown so auld?"

"Must be a trick of our mind."

They wandered down the path.

Magnus had gray hair and a long beard and he hobbled as he

walked. He held the door with one hand as he unsteadily stepped into the yard, his other hand held his rifle.

Fraoch said, "Och nae, look at ye, Og Maggy, ye are auld as the mountain ye are livin' under."

Magnus said, "The years go by… tis a thing time does, it marches by in a—"

Lochinvar stood up. "Auld man, daena be finishin' that sentence, tis not a line, ye canna believe it, tis a wheel — och ye are as senseless as ye were long ago."

Magnus tilted his head back, "Who are ye… are ye Lochie?"

"Aye, Lochie, ye remember me?"

"Ye are m'brother, but… ye are wearin' the years as well — how come…? What has happened…? Where hae ye been?"

Lochie said, "The question, auld man, is where hae *ye* been?"

Magnus looked confusedly around at his house and then at his horse. He blinked. "I canna tell ye. I think I hae been here, but tis a mystery, as I hae grown auld, but m'horse… M'horse is young, ye see, he has never aged and I daena understand the meanin' of it."

Fraoch said, "Yer rifle is a modern rifle."

Magnus looked down on it as if seeing it for the first time. "How did I…?"

Fraoch said, "Yesterday I was in the same situation, Og Maggy. I was living on the shore of a loch and Lochinvar and Archie and his wife, Samantha, came and—"

Magnus looked over at me and blinked. "Archie?"

I raised a hand, "Hi da."

He strode straight toward me, "Archie!" he threw his arms around me, rocking me a bit. He was delighted to see me, as if he knew me, whereas I barely remembered him and my memory wasn't of this aged man — my memory was of a much different father.

He pushed me out at arm's length. "Ye look just as I remember ye." His eyes were misty. "And this is Samantha!" He hugged her as well, then wiped his eyes. "Och, tis verra good tae see ye, but I daena understand."

Fraoch said, "What I daena understand is how I hae talked ye down from shootin' me by tellin' ye that I saved yer life, more than once, and I haena gotten a hug yet."

Magnus hugged Fraoch and then hugged Lochinvar. He said, "I would ask ye tae come inside, but tis cold and damp, and as tis a fine day we ought tae go tae the back and talk in the sun.

We went around to the back of the house. He dragged out a stool for himself, and the rest of us sat around him or leaned against the wall. None of us would take the stool as he looked as if he desperately needed it.

With one hand on his knee, the other on his rifle still, he said, "Explain it tae me."

Fraoch gestured to Lochinvar, who gestured to me. I said, "My wife, Samantha, came to me the other day, having found a journal with memories in it that I didn't recognize and..."

His brow drew down.

How to make it clear? "We basically found a time travel device."

Sam said, "We accidentally activated it for a moment, which somehow kicked some things in motion—"

Lochie said, "I suddenly remembered where a time travel vessel was. I went to your castle in your kingdom to give it to you. You were always collecting them, trying to protect them, and—"

"My kingdom? My castle?"

"But you were not there."

I said, "My apologies, Da, I lost our kingdom."

Magnus said, "Ye lost our kingdom?"

Lochie said, "In his defense, he was just a lad. If ye were going tae hold it against someone it ought tae be yer mother."

"Lady Mairead."

Fraoch and Lochinvar said, "Aye."

Magnus breathed in and out.

He looked around at all of our faces as if considering. "There is time travel involved in this?"

Fraoch nodded.

Magnus looked over at the horse.

He shook his head and looked down at his hands.

Then stated as if a fact. "I had a kingdom. I had a throne and a son and brothers and…" His hands between his knees he rubbed his knuckles. "The vessels are used tae travel from one place tae another. We are jumping back and forth along the line —" He waved a hand at Lochinvar. "I ken, Lochie, ye are adamant tis a wheel, I remember the arguments now."

We watched him as he mulled. "How did this happen, was it Ranulph?"

Fraoch nodded. "Aye."

Magnus raised his head, staring off at the horizon. "What did he do?"

Lochinvar said, "I daena ken, I think he took all the vessels and it shifted us off our wheel."

Magnus looked down at the dirt. Then he asked, "Where is Kaitlyn?"

We were all quiet.

Magnus looked down at his hands, shaking his head, then he peeled back his belt and showed us a round disk on the end. "Can ye explain this?"

Fraoch said, "I think twas one of the trackin' discs Quentin would put on us when he worried we were goin' tae be lost."

Magnus nodded, "Colonel Quentin… I remember. But his tracker dinna work." He put his belt back and said, "I need tae pray."

He hobbled to the stone wall, through the opening, and began heading up the road.

We all looked at each other. Fraoch dusted off his clothes. "It has been a bit of time since I graced a church. I ought tae join him."

Lochinvar stood and followed them both.

Sam and I looked at each other. "Want to go to a church with my aged father in the medieval times?"

She nodded. "Apparently this is happening." We followed them down the path as a procession with Magnus in the lead: he never looked back.

CHAPTER 54 - MAGNUS

BEGGIN' YER FORGIVENESS

I passed the auld well in the churchyard and climbed tae the church built on the slope, nestled in the trees. I entered the chapel, knelt at the altar, and prayed. I kent these new unfamiliar people were behind me, also kneelin', also prayin' for guidance, and I was unsettled because they were becomin' familiar. The more I thought, the more memories returned, a flood of them. My mind was like a weaving, grown sparse over time — I couldna remember anything clearly, just threads, some taut, some unraveled. I wondered if twas m'age. I had grown tae be forgetful, my neighbor reminding me that I hadna gone tae market on the day. Many times I had stood staring around at my house, wondering what I had been doing afore.

Then of course I awoke in a cell just yesterday.

I dinna remember how I got there.

What I did remember was that Archie was m'son. I remembered Fraoch and I remembered Lochinvar. They were brothers. When I thought verra hard I had brief glimpses of a past with them.

This was how I remembered them:

Fraoch's shoulder beside mine as we sat in the woods.

Lookin' down and seeing Lochinvar's footsteps alongside mine as we stalked down a passage tae a... *where were we headed?*

I remembered an arena battle where I was surrounded by a cheering crowd, projected on the walls, videos, and I remembered yelling above the clamor, "I am Magnus the First!"

I shook m'head and began tae pray.

I begged God for forgiveness and for guidance. I grew distressed with the words, as pain crept up m'thighs from m'knees, as I was swept along in a barrage of questions. Prayer usually calmed m'mind, but this one brought more questions, and I pled for help makin' sense of it all.

Was this God's plan, tae hae me live a life in which I couldna remember?

Tae hae been a king, tae hae lost m'throne?

And tae hae lived a life as the auld man at the edge of the village of Inchadney? With a horse that never aged? *It canna be the plan.* This canna be what God meant for me — tae hae lost the years of my life?

And Kaitlyn.

I had nae memory of her, but just that she 'had been.'

It had come tae me at once — like a breath intae gasping lungs and now I was left unable tae exhale.

Kaitlyn.

How had I lost her and when?

How would I find her?

I prayed longer and heard an answer, *ye must look.*

But how? I dinna remember where she might be.

My prayers were answered finally, I had clarity on it.

Kaitlyn was m'wife and I needed tae find her.

I was not lost, I had been found. Now she was lost — I hoped she would stay put, until I could find her.

Ready tae rise, I waved an arm and Fraoch rushed up tae heft me from m'sore knees. I had tae lean on him tae the door, but then I quickened, the blood pumping had me movin' on m'own, as we came out tae the churchyard, I said, "I hae decided tae go tae get Kaitlyn."

Archie said, "Good, we'll go there next."

I looked out over the graveyard. "Nae, ye canna come, Archibald. There is a risk that ye might loop upon yerself, I am out of time, ye are out of time…" I said, "I hae prayed that I might fix what has happened, daena ask me how, but I want tae, and I hope I will be able tae meet ye again, that our paths will cross when we are both younger. We daena want tae risk being stuck in this time. I am too auld."

Archie nodded. "I understand. And my time, our time, is in the future."

"Dost ye hae any bairns?"

He shook his head. "We haven't felt like we can, given our situation."

"And what is it like, yer situation in the kingdom?"

Archie looked uncomfortable. "I don't want to piss you off."

I put a hand on his shoulder. "Tell me."

"I am under house arrest, living in exile."

"Och nae, since ye were… how auld were ye when it happened?"

"You have been gone since I was about nine years old, I lost the kingdom when I was ten."

"Och nae, Archie, ye canna go back. Ye canna."

"It wasn't that terrible, it was a big manor house with lots of land, but it doesn't matter, you are right, I can't go back, he would have me executed." I glanced at Samantha, she was chewing her lip worriedly.

I scanned the horizon, then shook my head. "I raised ye tae be a king, I might not ken much, but I ken that. My son should nae live as a jailed man, even if tis a large estate—"

Lochinvar said, "I hae a house, they can live there, in the twenty-fifth century. We hae two vessels, I will take one and leave the other with ye and Fraoch. I will meet ye, where should I meet ye?"

I looked at Fraoch, "Ye in for a tough road? We hae tae fix this mess while I am as auld as a mountain."

"I had tae lift ye up off the floor and ye weigh as much as a mountain as well."

"'Tis nae true, I am hungry, near all the time."

"'Tis less that ye are heavy, more that ye are weak."

"I will agree with ye there — which leads us back tae the question, are ye willin' tae follow a weak man on a mission tae find his long lost wife?"

"The question for ye is, Og Maggy, do ye think ye ought tae find yer wife in yer current state? I could try tae rescue ye when ye're younger. Ye are likely tae frighten her in yer current state."

"Nae, the world is shifting — ye found me, I canna risk becomin' lost again."

"Then ye ought tae go when she is yer same age."

I nodded.

Lochie said, "I agree, then if you're mistaken, if you're confused on how this works, you won't loop on yourself, likely. Go when she is…" He waved his hand around me.

"Auld?"

"Aye. Where will ye look?"

"I winna hae tae look far, she is likely in Maine."

"Then I will take Archie and Sam tae my house, get them settled, and meet ye in Maine."

"That is a lot of time-travelin'."

"Aye," he grinned, "but as Frookie used tae say, I am 'young and stupid,' I daena care about it."

Fraoch said, "That does sound like somethin' I would say," and clapped him on the shoulder.

∾

Archie said, "Can I speak to you alone for a moment?"

"Aye." We walked off a bit, then he grew quiet, and looked uncomfortable.

Then began, "I have a policy, to always say something nice before I go, in case I don't get a chance to again." He shifted. "I am sorry I didn't come earlier, I wish I had known, it feels like lost time, you know?"

"Aye, I ken, but I am verra glad ye are here, that I hae a chance tae meet ye, ye seem a fine man. I am proud of ye."

"Thank you, Da, I appreciate that."

"Ye ken, ye learned that, tae say somethin' nice before ye go, from yer mother."

"Bella?"

I breathed deep. "Nae, Kaitlyn, ye truly daena remember her?"

"No, never met her."

"I will kill Ranulph for this. I regret that I am so auld that I canna do it at the end of a sword."

Archie said, "I think Lochie and Fraoch would fight for you."

"Aye, yer uncles are good men."

He exhaled. "Da, there's something else I need to tell you. Something I read about in Sam's father's journal."

"What was it?"

"He said you had two other children, that I had a sister and a brother."

I shook my head, looking down at the dirt. "Nae, that canna be true. Nae. Twould be a horrible thing tae hae happened." I looked out over the landscape. "Now I want tae kill him even more, but I daena ken how tae fix it."

"Me neither. And Da, you aren't pissed — that we lost your kingdom? I am so sorry we lost our kingdom."

I clapped my hands on his shoulders. "Son, ye did yer best, dinna ye do yer best?"

He chuckled. "I was a boy."

"Aye, just a boy, my boy, and yer grandmother did her best, I ken because she always wanted the kingdom more than any of us, if she lost it she had nae choice in the matter. Ye forgive yerself on it, Archibald, I daena hold it against ye. And besides, until a moment ago, I had nae memory of the kingdom. Ye hae lived it, I hae forgotten it. I ought tae be beggin' yer forgiveness for deserting ye when ye were just a lad. Dost ye forgive me?"

"Aye, it's not like you went off to have a good time, this croft looks like a depressing place to live."

"Especially alone."

"Sorry about that, Da."

"All I ever wanted was a big family and a castle with strong walls tae keep them safe. I am sorry, Archie, that I dinna provide it for ye."

He nodded. "It was really good meeting you again, Da."

"It was good meetin' ye again, Archie, I love ye, I wish the best for ye."

We hugged and said goodbye. And then they left.

CHAPTER 55 - MAGNUS

2068 - MAINE

I watched the storm taking Archie, Samantha, and Lochinvar away. Twas a familiar storm, bringin' with it many memories. Fraoch and I were sittin' on the ground within the woods. I said, "How many times hae we seen those storms?

"I dinna believe I had ever seen them, but here we are watchin' one, and I realize I hae seen them many times afore. Hundreds. I think."

"I think so too."

We stood and dusted off our clothes tae do our own time-jump tae Maine. "I am worried though, Fraoch. What if Ranulph, the man who did this, who disordered our world so completely, what if he does it once again?"

"He canna do it again, Og Maggy, we arna tae be defeated. He has done it once because he was lucky, he winna get lucky again."

He pulled the vessel from his pocket and I put out m'hand for him tae place it in my palm. "Och, it feels comfortable, as if

I had been used tae it." I bounced it in my hand, feeling the weight, noticin' it felt alive.

"Dost ye need me tae help ye put the numbers in?"

"Nae, I remember the numbers now, this is all comin' back tae me."

~

Fraoch and I woke up in a clearing in Maine, in the year 2068.

I groaned. "Except that."

He said, "Except what? Ye are auld as the hills and after a jump ye are goin' tae wake up talkin' as if ye were speakin' on something? Are ye losin' yer faculties, Magnus?"

I chuckled. "Nae, I meant that the time-jumping was comin' back tae me but the pain part wasna expected, except twas. I was tryin' tae be humorous."

"It inna funny." He groaned as he sat up, then held ontae a tree trunk tae stand. He exhaled.

I put up a hand. "Heft me up, Fraoch."

"Tis m'job now?"

"Aye, ye are thirty years m'junior." He pulled me up tae my feet, and everything hurt. "Och, ye ken, Fraoch, tis unsettlin' tae be so close tae the end of m'life, and find so much of it has been forgotten."

He said, "Well we are in for a long stroll, we can talk about our memories as we go. What dost ye think we are forgettin'?"

We began tae pass down the lane. I had thought it would be foreign tae be here, havin' all my life, or so I thought, lived in the fifteenth century. I had had some vague dreams, discrepancies that had seemed tae mean I had seen other lives, other places, but I had thought they were m'imaginings. I had grown used tae the idea that I was a man overcome with strange imaginings. But here I was and twas all familiar, as if I had had my thoughts adjusted. Not much had changed from the decades before when we had come here, because as soon as I had awakened in the glen I had remembered it: the wildflowers, the barn, the brisk air, the sound of the loons, the lapping of the lake. It had flooded back tae me, living here, at one time with her grandparents, at another time I felt sure I had lived here with her and… many more people.

I remembered fragments. "Do ye remember when Lochinvar was here and he went tae the pub down the street and got intae a great deal of trouble?"

He nodded. "But I am havin' trouble placin' who else was there."

"Aye, me as well."

He asked, "Do ye remember I had a fine boat?"

I thought on it as we walked. "I daena remember yer boat. Tis another gap."

Fraoch said, "I daena like the gaps, how can we hae gaps? Tis likely tae hae a person lost in the shadows of a gap."

"Aye."

We were quiet then and slowed as we neared the house. "What if she inna there?"

"Then we will come up with another idea."

"What if she daena remember me?"

"Like when ye dinna remember me? Ye will just put yer hands up and tread slowly, tis all there is tae do, ask her tae remember ye, tell her somethin' about herself, but… she will remember ye, Og Maggy."

"She might not recognize me though."

"Aye, ye are verra auld, she might think, 'Who is this stranger?' but she might see it in yer eyes and yer smile that ye are Magnus and all this worry will be for naught. She might be waitin' for ye."

"After all this time?"

"After all of it. Tis a wheel as our friend Og Lochie tells us, it might hae been nae time at all in her heart."

"Funny that ye think of him as a friend, I think at one time he was yer adversary."

"He is a good lad, ye ken why?"

"Why?"

"He rescued me first."

"Aye, he did, I haena thought of it."

"He's practically a son tae me now."

I chuckled.

"Alright, I am goin' in."

"God be with ye, Og Maggy."

CHAPTER 56 - MAGNUS

THE OLD CRONE

I walked down the slopin' driveway tae the back door and knocked.

A young woman came tae the door. "Yes?"

"Aye, Madame, I am lookin' tae speak tae Madame Kaitlyn Campbell."

"She's… we weren't expecting any visitors today." The door tightened.

"And who are ye?"

"I am her nurse."

I shook my head. "I dinna ken I was comin', could ye tell her that Magnus is here tae see her?"

She stepped out of the door and closed it behind her, her brow drawn down. "Her husband?"

"Aye."

"I don't know what they've told you, she's…"

I said, "Who?"

"Who… what?"

"Who would tell me… what?"

"She is suffering from memory loss, it's… profound. I'm not sure she would want to see you."

"She will definitely want tae see me, I hae been away and…"

"I don't think she'll remember you."

"Och nae." I looked back up the hill at Fraoch.

He jogged down tae meet me at the door. "Tis a trouble, Og Maggy?" He put his hand out tae shake the woman's. "I am Fraoch, brother tae Magnus, is Madame Kaitlyn here?"

"Katie, I mean, Mrs Campbell, is here, she's just... I don't think she will remember him, that's what I was explaining."

Twas Fraoch's turn tae say, "Och nae."

Finally he said, "It winna cause *harm* though, tae see?"

The nurse said, "It might agitate her, she's easily agitated. She has nightmares, she's often talking to people that don't exist. I don't know if we should... you could contact the estate, they could arrange a visit with a doctor present and..."

Fraoch scowled and said tae me, "We could come back another time."

"I daena want tae come back another time, I need tae see Kaitlyn."

The woman said, "But you might frighten her."

"I daena want tae frighten her," I said, "What if I promise I will leave if she grows agitated? I just need tae speak tae her — if I frighten her in any way I will go, I promise. I will leave and I winna return."

She huffed. "Fine, but not him, he's too big."

Fraoch put his hands up. "I was goin' tae hang out up at the road, it daena involve me." He strode away.

The woman opened the door tae the house.

I stepped in. It smelled wonderful, like the house in the past, memories flooding back. My eyes drifted tae the sofa, a newer one, and I gazed around at the closed bedroom doors, the art, all much the same, except... My eyes settled on an embroidery that I had last seen on the wall in Florida. And then I had flashes of our house in Florida, something I haena considered before, hadna remembered.

I mumbled, "Fraoch *did* hae a boat."

The nurse said, "Excuse me?"

"Nothing, I was remindin' myself tae tell Fraoch somethin' later."

She led me through the door tae the porch, though I could hae found it on my own, the house being full of memories and there on the porch, in a rockin' chair, sat m'wife. Her hair gray, her aged and weathered hands idle on a blanket spread across her lap.

She said, her voice tremulous, "Jenny, who was it?"

"You have a visitor, Katie, someone here to see you."

My wife turned her head to mine and her brow drew down. She looked confused.

I said, "Mo reul-iuil, I hae traveled a long way tae find ye."

Her brow lifted. "Magnus?"

"Aye." I pulled a chair to her knee and sat down close. "Aye, tis me…" My voice broke as I was overcome. I took her hand in mine, the two of them aged with spots, sharply defined tendons and veins, thin skin. I stroked the back of her hand. "Aye." I kept my eyes down, her face was difficult tae look at, twas unfamiliar, the lines there surprisin', the paleness and the colors of blue from within. Twas a face I had always loved, but the shock of the age upon it kept me lookin' away until I could grow comfortable.

I raised her hand tae my lips and kissed the back of it. "How are ye, m'love, ye are good?"

She said, "I have been better, but this is amazing. You're really Magnus? Truly? Where have you been?"

Her eyes were also focused on our hands. We were waiting tae grow accustomed tae the years that had settled upon our bodies.

"I hae been livin' in a village called Inchadnay. Tis a stone's throw from where Balloch was, ye remember when ye were in Balloch as it was bein' built?"

She nodded. "I do, I don't remember much, but I

remember the cold stone, the snow. I remember the tent stakes in the snow… And you would fish. It seems a very long time ago."

"Twas, centuries ago, ye were there, ye breastfed a bairn there."

"How?"

I smiled, "I daena ken the mechanics of it, I—"

She leaned forward and looked at me earnestly. "No, I mean, how did I breastfeed? I must have had milk, did I have a baby, Magnus?" She sank back in the chair, "I can't remember!" A tear slid down her cheek.

The nurse said, "Sir, she is agitated."

I said, "Kaitlyn, I promised if ye grew overcome I would leave, please daena make me go, I beg of ye."

She recovered. She took a tissue from the box and blew her nose and wiped her tears, and said tae the nurse, "Jenny, I want him to stay, can you please give us some time alone?"

"Yes, sure, Katie." She left for the other room.

Kaitlyn sighed. "I have to do my best not to grow agitated, apparently everyone thinks *agitation* is the worst thing for me. I hate to tell Jenny, but in my earlier years it was my common state."

She clutched the tissue and then asked, "Was it? I mean, I think it was, I think there was danger and adventure, but…" She dropped her head back. "I don't know."

"Ye deserve a rest."

"Screw that, no I don't. What is this, sitting in a chair to the end of my days? No, I don't know much, but this is not what I wanted at all."

I said, "I was livin' at Inchadney, in a wee house, with a horse, his name is Dràgon."

Her face lit up. "Oh, I remember him!"

"Ye do? Ye remember m'horse?" I chuckled. "Ye remember m'*horse, Dràgon,* who lives with me in the fifteenth century?"

She nodded. "And I don't remember what I was doing pretty

much from the age of 25 to 55. Do you remember when you left?"

I shook my head. "Nae, but it must hae been long ago."

"It seemed like it happened all at once, you were gone, and you had always been gone, and I didn't know how to miss you, because I didn't know why you weren't there. Did you miss me?"

I stroked the back of her hand. "Tae be truthful, mo reul-iuil, I had forgotten our life. Twas horrible tae think, but perhaps twas a mercy, as I couldna get home even if I had wanted tae."

Her head sank back to the pillow on the chair. "You forgot me?"

"Aye," I took a deep staggerin' breath, "and until the other day when Fraoch found me, I might hae died not knowin' ye existed." I pressed her hand tae my cheek. "I need ye tae understand, mo reul-iuil, I dinna stay away on purpose, look at me, I am a man of auld age, my shoulders are hunched, m'knees ache, I stare intae space, and the worst of it, my life has been not more than the life of an animal with nae sense of the past, just a present where I wonder how tae gain m'next meal. Please understand—"

She turned in her chair and put a hand on my cheek. "I do understand. I really do — and I'm sorry you lived like an animal, but good."

"What dost ye mean by 'good'?"

"It would have been heartbreaking if you had remembered me and couldn't get to me. I don't think I could bear you being that lost, and I forgot you too, mostly, except in my dreams."

I kissed the back of her hand again. "Thank ye for yer forgiveness, Kaitlyn, it means a great deal tae me."

She said, "Tell me about your memories."

"I daena hae many, until now, now I feel as if I hae them all. It has seemed as if my life was a threadbare rug, great holes that I would push furniture over, much as the Earl used tae do in his dinin' room, ye remember?"

She shook her head. "Who is the Earl?"

"He is m'uncle. Dost ye remember m'brother, Sean, or m'sister, Lizbeth?"

She shook her head. "Lizbeth? I remember... but it's dim, as if she's shrouded in fog, but I hear her voice sometimes... she was wise, I think."

I hung my head. "My memory is a threadbare rug, yers is a fog — we are a fine sight, arna we, mo reul-iuil?"

She said, "I am so damn old. Everyone walks around me as if I'm on the edge of freaking out, but I can't keep myself in control, things will set me off, like, I will put the milk away and the next day there will be more milk in the jug and no one will admit to having gone to the store. It all feels maddening."

I nodded. "I am the dodderin' auld fool that tried tae shoot at Fraoch when he came on m'land. I missed. He thinks twas on purpose, but I missed because I couldna hold the rifle straight and m'eyes arna verra good."

"Has he been to see Hayley?"

I looked at her blankly.

"His wife, Hayley. It just came to me, just now, he's married to Hayley."

"Och, I daena think he remembers her, not yet."

She smiled. "See? As worried as you were about forgetting me, you remembered me before Fraoch remembered his wife, so you win. I forgive you for not coming sooner."

"I dinna hae a vessel. I came the moment I had one."

Our hands wrapped around each other's. We both leaned back in our chairs and looked out on the loch. She pointed. "See the loon?"

"Aye, this is a magical place, tis just as I remembered it."

We watched the lapping water for a time and I asked, "Ye never remarried?"

She shook her head. "No, how about you?"

I shook my head.

Then we grew quiet again, until she asked, "And this... this memory loss, this confusion, this is all because of time travel?"

I leaned forward in my chair. "Aye, we are time travelers, at one time we were the most powerful people in the world. We could go from time tae time and I was a king, a great and powerful king, and ye were my queen."

She dolefully chuckled. "Och, we have been brought low, Master Magnus."

I patted my heart. "I love it when ye say it, and aye, though I hate tae admit it, we hae been brought *verra* low."

"Neither of us remembered each other, who was going to save us?"

"Apparently Archie and Fr—"

Her eyes went wide. "Archie?" She clutched my hand to her chest. "Our Archie! How is he?"

"Ye would hae been proud of him, mo reul-iuil, he is strong and capable. He has a lovely wife, but our kingdom was lost and he has been livin' in exile on an estate surrounded by guards."

"That's a shit life for our son." She sniffled and dabbed at her eyes. "I think about them all the time."

I blinked. "Them?"

She closed her eyes and exhaled. "I haven't thought about Archie, Isla, and Jack in a long—"

"What did ye say?"

"What?"

"Ye said, Archie, Isla, and Jack... what dost ye mean?"

She shrugged. "I don't know. Do you know?"

"Nae."

"Then it's just one of my 'hallucinations'. My doctor says it's a sign of my disease. I don't know half of what I'm talking about and I talk about people who don't exist... He thinks it's memory loss, but I think it's despair."

I kissed the back of her hand again. "He sounds like a shite physician, does he ken ye are a time traveler? That ye hae been jumpin' from one time tae another? Dost he ken ye hae met

Mary Stuart's mother? Or the Earl of Breadalbane? Or that ye were once the Queen of Riaghalbane?"

"I did those things?"

"Aye, tis all comin' back tae me."

She chuckled. "I think if I told him I was a queen he would have me put away in a home."

"Well, then I am glad ye dinna tell him, but I doubt he kens what he is talkin' about. Ye just said, Archie, Jack, and Isla; Archie exists, so Isla and Jack must exist, I am sure of it, mo reul-iuil. When ye said those names I had a moment of sharp recognition and Archie mentioned tae me that ye and I had more children."

She nodded, looking out over the lake. "I grow weary thinking on it."

"I do as well."

She patted the back of my hand. "Let's go take a nap, we need to lay down beside each other." She stood, shakily.

I groaned as I stood up and then we held hands, a grip tae steady each other as she led me from the porch through the living room, telling Jenny we were going to lay down, then goin' tae the big bedroom and across tae the bed.

She lay down and pulled me down with a moan of content-ment beside her. "I haena been on a mattress for three decades, my old bones are grateful."

She lay on her side and I lay behind her, my arms around. She was smaller than she used tae be, but so was I. I nestled my face against her hair, carryin' the familiar scent of fruit that I had always loved. I said, "I must hae a terrible stench."

"The smell of you brings back so many memories, I can't ask you to bathe, it's your scent, it reminds me of living with you in the past." She pressed her lips against our entwined hands. "Remember when we lived alone for all that time, in the sixteenth century, but we were together?"

"Aye, mo reul-iuil, I am beginning tae remember it all."

We fell intae an afternoon sleep.

CHAPTER 57 - MAGNUS

M'DREAM

J had a short fitful dream, the same one that I had been havin' verra often m'whole life.

There was Kaitlyn. I could see her clearly, as if she had always been there, though she hadna been in the dream for years. There was a fog, the army barreling from the trees — *was this Ranulph?* They were on horses, bearing down on us, I always yelled, Run! But, this time twas different.

This time Kaitlyn and I were on horses. Before us lay the scene, men unconscious in the clearing of an ancient Scottish forest. There are vessels there and other devices and there were people searching around, stealing riches, searching for machines — we needed tae get there first, we needed what was there.

I glanced at Kaitlyn — we were armed, the army was thundering.

Ranulph yelled, "Run!"

And I boomed in return, "Nae!"

CHAPTER 58 - MAGNUS

FRAOCH WILL SEE TAE IT

*W*e woke the way we always used tae wake when we were young, with her head upon m'chest, a heavy weight on m'heart, a reminder tae get up, tae guard, tae provide, tae comfort. She raised her head and kissed my lips, a softness, and then tucked her head back tae my chest.

She asked, "What are you thinking about?"

"How I winna leave ye."

She was quiet and then she sobbed.

I pushed the hair back from her face. "Ye are cryin'? Ye daena want me tae stay?"

"No, I want you to stay, I'm so lost and alone and I know you have things to do, but please don't go, I don't think I could bear to have you go."

"Good, we are in agreement, I winna."

"What about all the things we have forgotten? What about your kingdom and all the people we need to save, the lives we need to restore and the timeline and history we have to fix?"

I stroked my hand down her shoulder. "I ken, mo reul-iuil, there is much tae do, but tis a young man's battle. I canna be the one tae solve it. It gives me pain tae stand, how am I tae fight? Ye and I are past the battle, we are soul weary. I see it, and so we are goin' tae live here, as we promised we would when we grew auld, and we will live out our days here in Maine while we still can."

"Really, you would do that with me?"

"Aye." My stomach growled. "Is yer nurse a good cook?"

"No, she's terrible."

"We will need tae ask for a cook tae come in then, that is not goin' tae work for m'needs. But beyond that I will never leave ye again, mo reul-iuil. Never again."

She raised up to grab a tissue from the box and wiped her eyes. "We will live out all our years just like this. I am so glad I stayed here, that I lived to see you again. I didn't really know, but I felt like I needed to wait for you, that you would come home eventually. Even long after I gave up, and stopped thinking about you, I was here, in case you came, and now you're here."

"Aye, now I am here. Ye can stop waiting, mo reul-iuil. We can go back tae livin'."

"We didn't solve anything though, I think we were supposed to do that."

"Nae, this is enough, bein' back here I am reminded, this is where I was meant tae end up anyway."

"Without our memories?"

I stroked the grayed hair back from her face, and nodded. "We are without our memories, but with each other. We canna change the past, and we ought not try. We canna put off another moment, it has been too many long years without each other."

She nodded.

I said, "But I should probably tell Fraoch that he is leavin' without me. Would ye like tae walk with me?"

∽

We walked up the slope tae Fraoch.

Kaitlyn said, "Hello, I'm Katie, I mean... I know we know

each other, but just in case you've forgotten, we all keep forgetting things..." Her voice trailed off.

Fraoch said, "I canna forget ye, Kaitlyn, ye are one of
m'oldest friends."

She sighed. "'Oldest' is right."

I said, "Fraoch, Kaitlyn tells me ye hae a wife, Hayley, and
she is waitin' for ye."

"Hayley... och nae, *Hayley*, m'bean ghlan, is she waitin' for
me? Imagine that." He shook his head looking out on the loch.
"I was just thinkin' on her, she dawned on me slowly — I was
sittin' here, lookin' out over the lake, thinkin' about time and the
passage of our lives, when something she used tae say came tae
me verra surely, as if it had been right in m'mind all along."

I said, "What was it?"

"She used tae say, 'Fraoch, nae matter what time of the day
tis, ye ought tae make the time tae wash yer balls if ye hae
forgotten, ye never ken when ye will hae company." He grinned.
"And I remember now she was always the company."

Kaitlyn laughed. "I wish she was here, she would love that
joke."

He said, "But I smell of fish, she wouldna like it one bit. She
always did want me tae be the better of m'self."

I said, "Speakin' of which, Fraoch, I remembered, ye hae a
boat."

"Do I? Where is it?"

"In Florida."

"A boat and a wife, that would be a good life."

Kaitlyn then said, "We have a bathroom, you can shower
before you go see her."

Fraoch nodded, slowly, as if thinking it through. "I will take
ye up on the shower, Madame Kaitlyn, but I canna go see her
yet, Magnus and I ought nae tarry — there is much tae do, we
need tae..."

His voice trailed off when he saw me shakin' my head. "I am
staying here, with Kaitlyn."

"Are ye sure, Og Maggy?"

I gripped Kaitlyn's hand. "I am sure." Then I said, "But somethin' came tae me as I napped—"

"Ye took a nap? Was it on a mattress?" He huffed. "While I was sleepin' out here under a tree."

"The mattress daena matter, Fraoch, we hae much tae do as ye just said."

He chuckled. "But ye slept *on* the soft mattress. It might matter a great deal tae the man who slept in the dirt."

"This is not the story, Fraoch, the point of the story is I hae clarity. I was in the year 1452. I remember speakin' with a man. I feel sure twas Ranulph. Then he deserted me there. The time of year was Lughnasadh, I ken because there were the sounds of a festival and the smell of baking bread filled the air, and I was despondent and confused about how I had come tae be livin' in Inchadney village. I believe this was my earliest true memory."

"Were ye young?"

"Aye, and in good health though I had a few injuries. I had been beaten, and couldna remember where or how."

"Ye think I ought tae go talk tae ye then?"

"If ye want the help of a younger man, then, aye."

"Dost ye think that if I pull ye away from then, that I will ruin yer timeline? Ye just found each other, will ye mind if yer timeline shifts?"

Kaitlyn and I met each other's eyes. I said, "We found each other, and I am meant tae be here, I ken it. Kaitlyn and I will keep each other company. I daena ken if our memories will come back or if this is how we go but I ken I winna leave her."

Fraoch nodded.

I continued, "If ye need m'younger self tae help ye, Fraoch, I will, or the young Kaitlyn will, and ye must help their young lives fix their young problems. Tell them tis not for the young tae worry about us, we will be good, winna we, Kaitlyn?"

She nodded. "We will be good."

Fraoch said, "Alright then, I will take ye up on the shower, and the big meal I was promised—"

I chuckled. "Not one morsel of food has yet been presented tae—"

I glanced at Kaitlyn, her eyes had grown misty as she stared down at the dock. "Do you see them, swimming?"

"Nae, I daena see them, mo reul-iuil."

"There is splashing, and laughter, the squeal of joy, I can, it's right there…" She tugged at her ear, then turned her back on the lake, blinking back tears.

I said, "Fraoch, Kaitlyn tells me Jenny is not a verra good cook—"

Kaitlyn said, vaguely, "We will call in for food." She began walking down the slope tae the house with us following.

Then I stopped still. "Speaking of food, Kaitlyn, where is Chef Zach?"

"He lives in Florida near his kids, but I think if I call him and tell him you're back he will be on a plane by nightfall. Quentin too."

I took a deep breath. "Och, I had nearly forgotten m'men."

Fraoch was showered. Kaitlyn had sent Jenny home, and we had a meal of burgers and fries delivered from a restaurant in town.

Fraoch had a burger in one hand, a fistful of french fries in the other. "This is all comin' back tae me, Og Maggy — why was I living by the loch all those years? By myself, just the fish for company, without m'wife tae keep me warm?"

"I daena ken, Fraoch, ye dinna hae a vessel for one. We hae learned the hard way that a vessel is necessary for traveling time."

He chuckled. "That tis, if they are taken from ye, ye hae tae hope and pray ye are left in a place with a good mattress and a warm lap."

"I was livin' in a hovel in a village that was verra near

Balloch, though Balloch hadna been built yet. Naething was as it should be, the time of everything was shifting around."

"Yet here ye are. I got ye home, and now ye hae a burger in yer hand." Fraoch grinned. "I am the hero."

"Aye, and Lochinvar, and m'son Archie."

Fraoch waved his hands at me. "Ye always give everyone else the credit."

"Or ye will grow too proud. Tis dangerous tae be proud. Ye must be humble about yer heroics."

Fraoch glanced down at Kaitlyn who was staring at her uneaten burger. "Ye are well, Kaitlyn?"

"I can see their hands. I'm passing out burgers and there are all these soft wee plump hands reaching for their meals and," She put her hand out in front of her. "If I'm lucky I can feel the soft velvety skin as it passes my fingers, the shifts in the air, the gleam at the edge of their... their breaths from their excitement, they're right there. Can you see them, Fraoch? Right in front of you?"

"Nae, Madame Kaitlyn, I daena see them."

She folded her hands in her lap and settled her eyes on the refrigerator. "I don't really see them either, not enough, I can't know if they're real. My heart breaks from the not knowing."

Fraoch quietly nodded.

Then he put the napkin on the table. "I think I ought tae head off," just as there was a knock on the door.

I said, "Who could that be, ye expectin' anyone, Kaitlyn?"

She shook her head.

"I will get it." Fraoch pulled his dirk and went tae the front door.

A moment later we heard Lochinvar's voice. "Auld man did ye forget I was comin'?"

"Aye, I did, Lochie, I dinna remember at all."

Lochinvar followed Fraoch tae the dining room, and said, "Well I see ye hae found Queen Kaitlyn and feasted without me."

Kaitlyn shook her head. "I'm not sure we have met, um..."

"Queen Kaitlyn, nae! Ye hae forgotten me?" He winced. "M'apologies, I am an auld friend, and…" He looked around as if he was confused about the whole situation.

Kaitlyn huffed. "Shit. I hate losing my memory, this is so unfair."

I said, "Ye daena remember Lochinvar?"

"No."

Lochinvar dug a few French fries from the bag. "Nae worries, my apologies again, Queen Kaitlyn."

She said, "I have a mind like a sieve, but that doesn't mean you have to be formal. If you're my friend, then call me Katie, and nice to meet you again."

I changed the subject. "So, Fraoch and Lochinvar, where are ye going first?"

Lochinvar took a seat. "Ye arna coming, Magnus?"

"Nae, I am needed here."

Lochinvar said, "Oh," with a glance at Kaitlyn.

Fraoch returned tae his seat, tilted his head back and looked me directly in the eyes. "Ye want tae ken where we are goin', but I daena think I ought tae tell ye, Og Maggy. Ye need tae leave it tae me tae solve the problem, and ye need tae spend some time with yer wife."

"Ye are worried ye might shift things?"

"Aye, and I daena ken if ye will be here while it's shifting, or ye will wake up and things have shifted and ye are aware of it, or perhaps ye arna aware of it. Either way, ye will get tae wake up in a warm bed, with a full stomach. And ye will be a comfort tae yer wife."

"Somethin' else ye need tae ken, Fraoch, I had a dream, twas about goin' tae the original encounter with the vessels—"

"Back in 1557? We went there before."

"Aye, in my dream we hae gone again, and it seemed important tae take the battle there."

He looked amused. "Do we win?"

"I daena ken."

"Then wheesht on it. This is nae help tae ken we are going tae fight, in a battle of such depravity — I am sure we can come up with a better plan."

"Alright, I winna speak on it, but remember it might be an option, and might be necessary." I nodded. "Ye will see tae m'horse?"

"Aye."

"Good, it has been a time since he had a proper ridin'. I was unable tae climb up anymore, and he had grown reproachful."

"He is probably grateful. Ye are liable tae list as ye ride, watchin' ye walk is a dreadful sight."

"I walk fine, wheesht, or I will shoot at ye again."

"Ye can shoot all ye want — ye missed. I daena believe ye *could* shoot me."

"I meant tae miss." I took a drink from m'Coke.

We smiled at each other. "Thank ye Fraoch for bringin' me home."

"Ye would hae done the same for me, Og Maggy, I ken it."

Fraoch and Lochinvar bade us farewell and took their leave and Kaitlyn and I went out tae sit on the porch. We held hands watching out over the lake as the storm grew behind the house. The sound of thunder and flashes of lightning were a distant reminder that we had been left without a vessel. We would travel nae more. We wrapped our hands together on the arms of the chair between us. She put her head on m'shoulder.

"Are we going to be alright?"

"Aye, Fraoch will see tae it."

"Or die trying."

"But either way we are going tae be alright, mo reul-iuil, daena worry."

CHAPTER 59 - MAGNUS

1452 - I MEET RANULPH IN INCHADNEY

I woke with a thud on the ground, a kick in m'stomach, I groaned. "Och nae."

The voice of Ranulph above me, assumed a falsetto tae mock me. "'Och nae, oh och nae' poor wee Magnus, son of Donnan, king of Riaghalbane, whinin' in the mud."

I spit mud from my mouth. "What do ye want?"

He kicked me in the stomach again.

I groaned.

"I want nothing, Magnus, nothing at all, nothing that you can give me."

I said, "Ye ken ye want an arse whippin'. I will gladly administer it."

He laughed, heartily. "With yer hands tied behind yer back?"

"Untie me, make it fair, we can fight it out like men."

"Nae, I am a man, or better yet, I am a god of men, a time traveler — ye are a once king, now a pig in the dirt, ye hae lost yer time, yer kingdom, and though I dinna ken it at the time, ye hae lost the memory of what ye once had — I am even better at this than I once thought."

"Yer hubris will be yer downfall."

"Will it, Magsy? Will it? I kind of think the same could be

said of ye. Ye thought ye were verra fine with yer arena battles, slayin' my father and brother."

He kicked me a third time. I groaned and spit blood on the ground. "Are ye tryin' tae kill me? Ye ought tae get it over with or cease kickin' me."

"I would like tae kill ye."

"Would ye? Then who would ye be braggin' tae?"

He exhaled.

I said, "And I wasna 'verra fine' with m'arena battles, I was forced tae fight. Donnan made me a killer, and then yer father and brother challenged me, usurped my throne, tried tae kill me, and—"

"Samuel was king."

"Tis a load of horse shite tae say it. Both of them were usurpers."

"I am not goin' tae argue with a dead man. Ye are challenging me tae a fight, but ye are lying in the dirt, tis like ye are beggin' me tae kick ye."

I rolled tae m'side and with a great deal of effort and a groan got m'self up tae standing.

He scoffed.

I said, "Did I make it look easy?"

"Nae, ye look weak."

"Said the man who has beaten m'arse while my hands are tied behind m'back." I spit to the ground, a flash of red — I worried that he might hae damaged m'insides with the pummeling. I wasna goin' tae lay there anymore, he couldna continue seeing me as a place tae kick his boot.

"The year is 1452 I am goin' tae leave ye here, tis a fine village, more than ye deserve, actually."

I looked around at the space, my eyes falling on m'horse, Dràgon. This was good. I looked down. I had m'dirk on m'hip, but nae way tae retrieve it from the belt.

"Nae vessel?"

"Nae vessel, Magnus, but," he shrugged, "with some ingenuity ye might survive. Ye hae tae live until 1557, then all the vessels—"

"Will be in one place."

Ranulph said, "That is the one thing I have learned, if ye want tae win ye hae tae hae all the vessels, ye lost them all, so ye lost yer life."

He took a few steps back.

I was weaving on m'feet, injured, worn. "Dost ye hae them all?"

He grinned. "Och aye, Magsy, I hae all of them. All through your life ye're feeling the times shift under your feet. Ye are the beach, I am the wave, and I hae crashed upon ye, now I am erodin' the verra ground ye stand on."

"I am bored of yer braggin'." I lowered a shoulder and rushed him, fast, aimed at his middle. I knocked him flat, but stumbled, then fell on him, and without my arms he wrestled me over, and in a quick moment had my head locked between his arms.

He held me tight, squeezin' the breath from me. I gasped and struggled and clawed with m'hands at his coat, ripping a pocket in m'desperation. His breath was hot and full of stench by my ear. "Ye want free, Magsy? Ye want me tae spare yer life?"

I managed a last nod afore I passed out.

I came conscious a while later, wet in the mud from a storm. I was on the edge of a forest, a rock beside me, not a sound, an eerie nothingness of sunset. My horse, standing near a tree, pluckin' green grass from the earth with his lips. "Ye are goin' tae eat in front of me? This is a fine thing, ye dinna help in any way."

I was cold and wet and hungry. And och, my stomach ached from the bruisin'. M'face was wet, possibly from the beatin' but twas difficult tae feel anythin' because I was beginnin' tae shiver from the cold or the shock. I raised my head tae twist and look at m'wrists. There was a rope bindin' them. I crawled up, leaned back against the rock, and usin' my knees tae push m'self up and down, began sawing my wrists against the sharp edge of the granite. Twas hard tae keep the position, as I was weary and everything ached. I lay for a moment, resting, but then my stomach grumbled and I knew I had tae get up or grow weaker.

I knelt with m'back tae the stone, leaning back on the edge, and began sawing once more, usin' m'shoulders, up and down, until with the full weight of my body as force, the rope ripped apart, and I fell back hard on the rock's edge. "Och, nae." I lay there for a while, on the rock, starin' up at the sky, my arms free, but without the strength tae push m'self off.

Och, I was in a terrible mess. Nae one kent where I was, nae one could come and I couldna escape. I was lost tae the world and—

A voice nearby whispered, "Wheesht, Og Maggy, what ye doin'?"

I sat up quickly. "What… who?"

Fraoch strolled from the trees with Lochinvar behind him.

I collapsed back intae the mud. "I hae never been happier tae see anyone in m'life, Fraoch, Lochinvar — what are ye doin' here?"

"I thought I was comin' tae see m'brother, Magnus, kick some arse in the fifteenth century, but instead he is layin' in the mud, like mucag — did ye kick some arse, Og Maggy, or are ye tellin' me yer arse has been kicked?"

"My arse has been fully kicked. I canna deny it."

Fraoch knelt down beside me. "Ye look like hell."

I lifted m'shirt.

He winced. "Yer middle inna supposed tae be that color, do ye think ye can walk?"

"I need water and food, first."

"We will hae a meal here then, because we will need tae be strong enough tae fight this arse-dangle."

"If ye had come a minute earlier, ye could hae done it already while I was in the dirt beggin' for m'life."

"What would hae been the fun in that?" He gave me a slice of cheese and a hunk of bread that I ate with dirty hands, famished, swallowin' down water from a canteen that Lochie passed me. Lochie gave me a slice of salami and a drink of whisky, and then another hunk of cheese. Finished, I held my stomach. "Och, that was needed, I wonder how long I was without?" Then I asked, "Fraoch, did ye just say that kickin' Ranulph's arse would not hae been fun?"

He said, "I was wonderin' if ye noticed. We dinna hae the chance, the woods were crawlin' with his men — we wanted tae make sure he dinna spook and take ye somewhere else."

"How did ye find me?"

He offered me another piece of bread.

"Nae." I shook m'head.

He folded the paper around it and stuffed it intae his bag. "Lochinvar and Archie found me on the shore of Loch Lomond, and then we all went and met ye, years later—"

"Where was I?"

"Here in this village." He gestured toward the valley where I could see a few small crofts laid out beside a river.

"For years, ye said, 'years later'?"

"Aye, ye were the age of seventy-five at least."

"Och nae."

"Och nae is right, yer knees were stiff, ye walked all hunched over."

Lochinvar said, "Yer balls hung down below the hem of yer kilt…"

"Did not." Then I asked, "Did they?"

Lochinvar laughed.

Fraoch said, "The point is, ye were auld. Ye told us tae come back and find ye young, here in the year 1452."

"And ye just left me there? With m'balls draggin' in the dirt — och, ye are nae friend."

Fraoch laughed. "Nae, I took ye tae Kaitlyn. Ye are there taegether now, on the banks of Holden Pond, drivin' each other crazy — yer welcome."

I nodded. "Ye are a good friend and the best of men."

"Yer emotions hae ye all over the place, Og Maggy, make up yer mind, am I a terrible person or the best of men?"

"I canna think straight because of m'ache all around here. Ye ought tae hae pity upon me, I almost died."

"Ye dinna, ye will live tae see another day."

I took another draft of whisky and passed it tae Lochinvar. The act of it caused me tae lose m'breath, I had tae press a hand tae my stomach. "How do we find that arse and make him pay?"

Fraoch said, "I hoped ye had an idea."

"Nae, my brain is caught up with tryin' tae survive the injuries. I want tae go home."

"We canna go home until we hae defeated this bawbag. He is defeatin' us, we canna let it go."

I nodded. "I ken, I ken." Then I asked, "When ye said ye took m'auld self tae Kaitlyn, what did ye mean? I daena want her tae see me auld when she is young, twould be… and then I would be loopin' if I ever went and—"

Fraoch said, "Daena worry on it, Og Maggy, she was auld as well, and she thought ye were just fine—"

"Even with the draggin' balls." Lochinvar grinned.

Fraoch said, "But I daena want tae talk about it anymore, tis close tae tellin' ye yer future and I daena think tis wise for a man tae ken what his life holds."

I said, "Besides, if we fix this, we will change the future and twill be immaterial."

"There is that."

"Ranulph has all the vessels."

Fraoch said, "Except the two Og Lochie and I hae."

"He has stolen them, gathered them, and hidden them somewhere — and all our activities on our timeline hae shifted."

"How did he do that?"

I lay back in the mud and stared up at the sky.

Fraoch said, "Ye daena even care anymore? Ye are a defeated man, Og Maggy, ye are just wallowin' now."

"The world has shifted, Fraoch, what are we goin' tae do?"

Lochinvar tapped his hand on his knee. "The world is rollin' Magnus, and ye are on the downside of a roll, but ye ken what happens on the downside?"

Fraoch said, "The wheel rolls over ye."

I chuckled. "Like a speed bump in the road, bu-dump, I am flattened."

Lochinvar tapped some more, a small rectangular piece of paper, up and down on his knee. "But after the wheel rolls over ye ye are goin' tae roll back up the other side, twill come around, ye ken? Ye are on the ascendency."

"I like the sound of that."

Fraoch said, "This is a fancy metaphor, Og Lochie, but it daena make it real. What we need is tae figure out where in time is Ranulph hidin' all the vessels?"

I said, "All *my* vessels. I want them back, and he was wearin' modern boots."

Fraoch said, "Exactly! So he is a man who likes modern comforts, that helps."

I said, "He had an antique gold watch on his wrist."

Fraoch sighed. "He is a man who likes comforts, this inna helpin'."

I said, "What I daena understand is this — we hae gathered the vessels afore, put all or most of them intae a vault in m'kingdom and it dinna mess up the whole world. I canna trust m'memories, it seems like, there are holes, ye ken?"

Fraoch said, "Og Lochie, if ye daena stop tappin', I am goin' tae kick yer arse and leave ye here in the dark ages."

"Fine." He stopped tapping.

Fraoch said, "What is it anyway, ye are holdin'?"

"Tis a scrap of paper I found."

I raised my head. "Where, here?"

"Aye, there in the mud."

I sat up and grabbed it from his hand. "Tis a ticket, what is it?" It was soggy and one of the numbers was rubbed off. There was an image of a car at the top, and the word Bugatti on it. "I am not sure, tis a ticket that says Bugatti, what does it mean?"

Lochinvar's eyes went dreamy. "Tis the greatest car in the history of the world, a *Bugatti*."

Fraoch said, "How does ye ken it, ye ken about cars?"

"Aye, I hae been living in the future, I ken about cars."

"Tis a ticket for one?"

"They are far more expensive than havin' a ticket, what else does it say?"

"There is a name of a restaurant, it looks like."

Lochie put his hand out and looked it over. "Maybe it's a ticket for dropping off your car to go intae the restaurant, a valet, ye ken, there is a date, 2026, and an address in London. Now we ken where he is."

"Where he *was*." I lumbered tae my feet.

Lochie said, "We could go there."

Fraoch said, "Aye, we could go, we could wait for him tae arrive, jump him in the street, torture him tae tell us where the vessels are kept. Sounds like we would get a good meal."

Lochie said, "If I am lucky I would get tae drive a Bugatti, twould be a win."

I ignored their idea of restaurants and a meal and a fast car, my eyes sweeping over the village in the valley before us. "So this is the jail he put me in, tae live out m'life, alone?"

Lochie said, "Aye, ye had been there, alone for a long time, except yer horse."

"The same horse, Dràgon, years later?"

"Aye, forty years on, the same horse, still young. Time travel is unnervin'."

I sighed. "What else happened?"

"Ye pulled a gun on Fraoch, tried tae shoot him—"

Fraoch finished with, "Ye were verra lost, and ye dinna remember much of anythin', Kaitlyn was worse."

"This is what I am getting at, we hae never had such a profound problem afore, the loss of memory, the rewriting over our time, the shifting — we are unraveled."

"That is why we are in need of decisive action, we should go now, beat the hell out of him in front of a fine restaurant."

I stood staring at the Tay river, snaking through the valley, just south of us. And I shook m'head. "Nae, tis nae enough, we will only make him stronger."

"How so?"

"He is full of hubris, he has taken my world, a woven tapestry of my life and has plucked apart the threads of it. He has un-entangled me from my wife and our bairns... I think. I think we hae bairns..." I shook my head. "He has pulled the threads apart and left me frayed. In the meantime he has collected the vessels and woven another tapestry, his own life and he is verra proud of having done it. He is crowing about it like a cock in the henhouse, livin' a life of grandiose ideas of himself, ownin' a Bugatti when a Mustang or a truck would do. Nae, if we confront him at the restaurant, it winna be enough. I could kill him and then we are still in this place, the worn out tapestry of this, what even is this, the dark ages, a world of fog? Nae, a restaurant in London inna the end of it. He will see us comin', or he will jump for a do-over."

Fraoch said, "I love a do-over, och, I miss m'wife."

"We need tae get ye home tae her, we canna let him win. We might gain one vessel, but we need all of them. We need tae win back every moment of time he has stolen."

"How do we do it? These shifts are verra profound."

I said, "I ken, tis bleak, I hae been beaten on the shore of the Tay and it inna even the right shore, the right shore is the southern shore. He has left me on the north shore without a bridge." I huffed.

Lochinvar snapped his fingers. "That's right! You need the Bridge!"

Fraoch and I looked at him blankly.

"What does… ? I feel like I heard of that before."

Lochinvar said, "You have, it's called the *Bridge* — it's a device and it stopped a time shift once before. I was there. I watched ye do it."

My brow drew down. "I hae a vague memory."

"Yer mother kent of it, she had a book." He snapped his fingers. "Ye got it and we used it and then I carried it for ye and we put it in the vault at the kingdom." He grinned and added, "Tis a chest about this big." He held out his hands tae shew me.

I said, "A small chest that we put in the vault in a kingdom. Aye, this is verra helpful, Lochie. I will get all the vessels and then I will use the Bridge."

Fraoch said, "Nae, I daena think so. Lady Mairead would hae a fit."

Lochinvar snapped his finger. "Och aye, I kent I had misgivings, Fraoch is right, ye canna use it, Lady Mairead said nae."

I scowled. "It stitches up time? Then I will gather the vessels, then use the Bridge. Lady Mairead daena tell me what tae do with the devices, they are mine."

Fraoch and Lochie looked at each other.

I said, "Daena ye think they are mine?"

Fraoch said, "Lady Mairead kens a great deal about how tae use them."

"Och, she daena ken everything, and ye are wrong, they are mine, I am the one who has spilled blood tae gather them, that has fought in the arena for the kingdom, I am the one who has collected and guarded them—"

Fraoch said, "And I."

Lochinvar said, "Also I."

I said, "Aye, we hae wagered our lives for the vessels, they belong tae the King of Riaghalbane and Lady Mairead is m'advisor, but nae more. She says she daena want me tae use the Bridge, I disagree."

Fraoch winced. "It is verra dangerous."

Lochinvar said, "I usually agree with ye, Magnus, but I daena ken."

"Well, it sounds like we might need tae go tae the first moment, when the devices all arrived, the first of November in the year 1557. The Bridge must hae come at the same time as the vessels, daena ye think? We could gather them all at once."

In Fraoch's eyes there was a moment of recognition. "Yer auld self told me something similar, he made it sound as if he had had a dream about going tae that moment."

"Then this is what we will do."

"I daena ken, tis incautious, inna it, Og Maggy? I told him not tae talk of it in front of me, as I—" He shivered. "I dinna like that night, that scene, twas a nasty battle for the vessels amongst desperate men, most of them depraved and willin' tae kill for the riches."

I nodded. "I ken, none of us want tae go, but we must. We hae both been there, but we must go again, perhaps tae loop, but I daena care. Call me incautious, I canna bear another moment of Ranulph winnin'. We can send Lochie intae the middle of the pile of unconscious men and—"

Fraoch shivered again.

"—and he can collect the devices for us, as many as he can grab."

Lochie grinned. "Och aye, ye always need me!"

Fraoch scowled and shook his head. "Ye canna crow about it, boy, or I will change m'mind. Ye canna come unless ye are properly agreeable. We are only invitin' ye because tae not invite ye would be rude."

I went tae Dràgon and petted his withers. "First though... I need tae see Kaitlyn, this is a dangerous thing we are about tae do. Time has shifted, perhaps past what we can alter. Some memories might be gone forever, we ought tae say goodbye afore we go."

Fraoch said, "Maine?"

"Nae, we will go tae Florida right after I was taken."

Fraoch said, "Och, ye are bein' reckless, Og Maggy!"

I shrugged. "Ye ken, Lochie said I was in ascendency, I am goin' tae ascend, and I am goin' tae win."

Fraoch said, "Twas a metaphor, ye canna stake yer life on it."

"If Ranulph wins I am a dead man, or worse, he will hunt me down and put me in a wee village where I live out m'days alone, I will stake m'life, I hae naething left tae lose."

I watched my arm as I stroked Dràgon, and an idea came tae my mind, God's Arm. I kent there had been a history of the world and I had been a man within that history. I had at one time been a king. It had been settled. I had tae hae the courage tae fight for that kingdom, tae fight for history and that settled time. I had tae be the man who fought for what was good and right and true. "I daena feel like usin' caution, Fraoch, I feel a murderous rage that Ranulph has managed tae shift our time, and beaten us afore we even kent we were at war with him. I need tae go home briefly, we ought tae see our wives while we still can, and then we need tae storm intae battle while we still remember what we are fightin' for."

I took ahold of Dràgon's reins.

Fraoch said, "Tis a fine speech, Og Maggy — what are we fightin' for?"

"For our family, Fraoch, we are goin' tae hae tae fight for our family."

CHAPTER 60 - KAITLYN

2024 - FLORIDA, A MATTER OF PERSPECTIVE

Quentin wandered into the living room from his bedroom.

"I just saw the weirdest shit."

Hayley, on the couch, said, "What was it, you scrolling through Twitter while on the toilet again?"

"Absolutely, those two things are exactly what you do together — I follow this handle @weirdshitinthewoods and they have this video." He scrolled for a bit then turned it on and held his phone up for us all to see.

Hayley said, "What are we looking at exactly?"

Zach came in the room with a dish towel and stood there. "It's a dude walking through the woods."

"Keep watching… it's coming."

The man on the video pushed back a branch and revealed a weird vehicle covered in overgrowth like an old plane crash site. He said, "…a mystery hidden deep within the forest, a vehicle of unknown origin, that looks like tae hae been hidden here fer hundreds of years."

Hayley said, "What has this to do with us?"

"He's got a Scottish accent! Hear it? The forest is in Scotland. It's a *mystery*."

She shrugged.

Zach returned to the kitchen.

Quentin looked down on the video on his phone. "I don't know, it seemed to be important." He wandered out of the room.

A few moments later, Emma entered chasing Zoe who was naked and zooming away. She yelled over her shoulder. "Tomorrow is shopping day, put things on the list!"

I was on the stuffed chair in the living room, staring out at the streaming rain. "I don't have anything — wait, no, I do, I'll put it on the list."

She stopped, hands on hips. "What's going on with your mood? I don't know if I've ever seen you so sluggish."

"I don't know, I'm bored."

Hayley yelled, "I need dessert!"

Zach called from the kitchen. "Dessert? Jeez Louise, what's up with you two? I literally just fed you!"

Hayley sighed. "Is a cookie too much to ask, not because you have to, but because we asked nicely, pretty please? I need sustenance before I drive home in this rain."

"Fine," he arranged Oreos on a silver platter.

I asked, "Why am I in a pantsuit?"

Emma said, "You've been in it all day."

Hayley teased, "Why do you do anything?"

Instead of laughing, I honestly answered, "I think I used to have reasons, a purpose, but now... you know, my brain used to be full, but now it feels like Swiss cheese, the thoughts I have don't go anywhere. I don't see places, or faces — my memories are just vague and useless."

I added, "I am not a fan."

"Maybe you need to go to the doctor."

I nodded. "Yeah, maybe, but I don't know if he would be able to explain why I'm wearing a long pantsuit while I just hang around the house in Florida — where did I think I was going?" I flicked the fabric on the legs. "Why does it look like it was wet and in sand?"

Ben from the other end of the couch said, "If you're covered in sand you aren't allowed on the furniture." His hand dove down in the cushions and pulled up a piece of cloth. "What's this?"

Hayley took it and looked it over. "A t-shirt that says 'Pig's Life' on it. Who the hell wears this?"

She held it out for Ben.

He scoffed. "That is not mine."

She said, "Zoe's?" Then said, "It's too stretched out around the middle. She called out, "Emma! Whose Pig's Life shirt is this?"

Emma, looking frazzled, said, "I don't know, probably came with the house."

I narrowed my eyes. "Came with the house, you said that a few times today — How long have we lived here?"

Emma said, "I don't know, years? But yeah, it's a big house, lots of stuff came with it." She plopped down in a chair. "Ugh, this toddler is exhausting."

I said, to Hayley, "You buying this business that weird stuff came with the house and—"

Hayley looked skeptical. "What's the alternative, some fairy bullshit? Are they stuffing things in the sofa cushions to play tricks?"

She sniffed the shirt. "Ugh, it even smells like pig."

Zach brought Emma a beer and sat down on the arm of the chair. "I like to think one of us has vacuumed between the cushions since we moved in."

"What are you saying, that it's fairies?"

He sipped from a beer. "Those are my only two choices, fairies or Emma never vacuumed the couch? In years? Then yeah, I think fairies."

Emma laughed, "Thank you for the support, I think."

Quentin walked in. "Whatcha talking about?"

I said, "Weird shit going on, like the sticks by the front door—"

He said, "Or the fact that we have a book of bagpipe music in my—" His eyes went to the shirt laying on the floor. "What the hell is that?"

He picked it up, looked it over, and sniffed it. "You recognize it?"

Zach said, "Nope. That's what we're all talking about. How fairies brought us a shirt."

Quentin stood looking down on it.

"But *why?*"

I sighed and watched the rain, it was pouring out there, a stream rolling down the glass door. Obscuring the view of the beach except for streaks of color, the rain was like a stained glass prism, a swath of deep weathered gray, a sandy beige stripe on the middle, a stormy charcoal sky, and then the deep blue-gray of the ocean — it roiled, powerfully, but up here in the house, the view of it was just a small sliver of the waves as they rolled. Something as powerful and majestic as a stormy ocean and yet it was way over there, distant, powerless.

It was all a matter of perspective.

I was lulled into a bit of a daze, sipping from a wine glass as Zoe squealed zooming around, Emma chasing, Hayley eating Oreos with Ben at the other end of the couch reading Harry Potter and then, I noticed a dark moving shape at the end of the decking.

First thought: *Who is out there in this rain?*

Second thought, that shape moved like Magnus.

Magnus?

Magnus.

.   .   .

I tossed the blanket off my legs and leapt from the chair, almost tripped over the ottoman and flung open the door as Magnus stood in the doorway. He was dripping wet, breathing heavy.

I said, "You came home," as my sopping wet husband wrapped his arms around me and held me in a really tight bear hug, lifting me from the ground. His face pressed to my neck. "Och, I missed ye."

"How long have you been gone?"

"I daena ken, but it feels like years hae gone by."

"Me too."

We kissed and he said, "Och, ye taste like Oreos," then he added, "Wrap yer legs."

I laughed in relief. "I missed you saying that." I started to climb him and then he groaned, miserably.

"What happened?"

"Och nae, m'whole middle is injured from an arse-kickin' I received while I was away."

"Well that is fine, no worries, you don't need a hospital?"

He shook his head.

Behind him, I saw Fraoch coming in the door and Hayley looking surprised. "Fraoch? Fraoch is that... what is, what are you...?"He swept her into his arms.

I took Magnus by the hand and led him up the stairs to our room.

CHAPTER 61 - KAITLYN

2024 - DO YE BELIEVE I LIVE HERE?

*H*e walked me straight down our hallway to the bathroom and he was kissing me as he got me into the shower, still fully clothed. I turned on the shower, drenching my back. He let the water roll down his head, his face, and pressed me up against the wall, his lips and mouth on mine, kissing and kissing, his tongue searching and his hands rubbing up and down on me. He pulled up my shirt. I pulled the sopping wet fabric off and tossed it with a damp thwap onto the tile shower floor. I giggled, breathlessly, "You're still in your shoes."

"Aye, tis a travesty, but I canna help myself, sometimes a man has tae do what he needs tae do without considerin' the civilized aspects of removin' his shoes first."

"True." I dropped my head back as his mouth settled on my neck. My feet on the ground, I squirmed my underwear down and he lifted his kilt in the front and with the warm water pouring down, we embraced. I wrapped my legs and he held me up, and we made hot steamy love in the shower full of desperate hot kisses, breathing hot breaths into his skin. My hands clutching his back, my fingers pressed into his flesh, holding on — exertion and longing, until finally released. We exhaled, my back held up against the wall by the pressing of his chest. His forehead against the tile. "Och, I needed it."

"Me too."

Wet sticky lips finding each other, fulfilled kisses, gentled hands, and then gingerly he lowered me down. I pushed his shirt off his shoulders.

"Oh no, look at your bruises!"

"Aye, I told ye, twas terrible, I got m'arse kicked by a dungbungus named Ranulph."

I leaned down and kissed his stomach and then pushed his kilt down into a soggy heap on the tile.

"Would ye take off m'boots?"

I knelt in front of him and untied his boots while he washed his hair. I grinned up at his majestic nakedness. "This is all terribly out of order."

"My whole life is out of order, mo reul-iuil, but it stops now. We are goin' tae solve this problem." He stepped out of his boots and I tossed them from the stall. I peeled off his disgusting socks. Then I stood and got a proper thank you of rubs and washes, cuddles and fondles, washing away the grime and muck of the past and cleaning us off, rubbing our hands all over each other's peaks and valleys, exploring each other, lathering up, and then rinsing off.

I squirted shampoo in my hair and he inhaled. "Tis a good scent, it gives me strength." I turned the bottle over and read: "'Fudge Brownie scent.' Holy cannoli, Master Magnus, you like me smelling like a fudge brownie?"

"Aye, I am a simple man with simple needs. Yer warm lap, a full stomach, and a big family."

I stopped in mid-lather. "A big family?"

"Aye."

"What do you mean...?"

"Nothing, we will speak on it in a moment, I need the full stomach I was telling ye about."

He stepped from the shower, and wrapped himself in a towel.

He went into the bedroom and then his voice called into the bathroom where I was drying off. "Where are m'clothes?"

I paused mid-dry. "I don't know… um, they aren't there?"

"Nae, there inna…" I heard a drawer open and close with a bang.

I said, "I think you've been gone for a long time."

He came down the hallway. "Does it seem that way tae ye?"

I nodded. "But it also, weirdly, seems like only yesterday."

He yanked open the closet door and began pushing hangers back and forth. "There is so much room, none of it is mine." Then his eyes settled on something in the back and he dragged out a box. It had 'MAGNUS'S THINGS' written on the top flap.

He opened it up and pulled out a pair of sweatpants and a pair of Nikes. He dug through it for a t-shirt. He looked pensive and upset the entire time, as if he was mulling everything over. He pulled a shirt on and ran his fingers through his hair.

He said, "Did ye ken I haena been gone for a full day?"

I blinked, "Wait… really?"

"Aye, we jumped here from m'kingdom, then I was taken by Ranulph, and then I hae returned, tis the night of the same day."

"I feel sure that it's not…"

"What hae ye been doing?"

I looked around the bathroom. "I couldn't say. Lying around, feeling sorry for myself."

He said, "Ye haena spent the five hours I was gone packin' my stuff intae boxes?"

I stood looking down on the box, blinking, confused. "No, I… kind of remember doing that but it was years ago."

He nodded. "Get dressed. We are goin' tae talk downstairs."

He picked up the box and began walking from the room.

"Why are you taking the box?"

"This is the surest sign I hae seen that we hae shifted. I hae forgotten many things, I hae wavered in how tae handle it, but this box is m'proof and m'fortitude. This inna goin' tae stand."

He stormed out of the room.

I watched him go, thinking that I didn't have the clearest sense of the thing, couldn't remember much, felt a little lost about some, but my husband had clarity, and it had come from the outrage that his stuff had been boxed up as if he didn't live here anymore.

I dressed and met him downstairs.

～

Lochinvar, someone I hadn't thought about in — how long had it been? — was standing in the middle of the living room. He waved, nervously. "Good evenin', Queen Kaitlyn."

I rushed up to him and hugged him. "Lochie! Where were you, where did you come from?"

He shrugged. "I couldna tell ye, I was livin' in the future and twas nae thinkin' on anythin' much, until I realized I kent where a vessel was. I went tae go find it and then I went and found Fraoch and then Magnus and—"

Fraoch said, "We hae Lochie tae thank for us all being back home and taegether."

We all looked around.

Quentin furrowed his brow. "Yet, somehow, there are only eight of us in this room, is that all of us? Doesn't it feel like there used to be more?"

Emma said, "The kids are in bed, it always feels like that when the kids are in bed."

He shook his head and looked out the window, as if he were mulling over something unexplainable.

It was late, ten p.m., but James was headed over.

We all felt it was important to talk and our time was all upside down. I couldn't remember the last time I slept. Had it been days ago? Was Magnus right, had I been twisted in time all day?

I kissed his forehead and sank into a chair.

Hayley and Fraoch were there.

Emma and Zach were there. Ben and Zoe were in bed.

Quentin was doing what he always did these days, sitting in the chair, a gun strapped to his chest, staring into space, looking confused. He always seemed like he was having an internal discussion with himself, or perhaps more like a dispute.

These days.

What the heck did I mean by that?

Lochie sat at one end of the table. Magnus sat at the other. Zach passed out drinks to everyone. We kind of all watched Magnus's box, but he sat behind it, the box right in front of him, his arms on the side of it.

Finally, James arrived.

"What's up? Hey Mags, hey Frookie. Lochie." He sat down.

Magnus said, "Master Cook, when was the last time ye saw me?"

He screwed up his face. "I don't know, not sure...?"

Magnus nodded, then stood. "Here's the thing — we are shifting. All of us. Our whole timeline is going..." He pulled a belt from the box and laid it out on the table and then wiggled it side to side, like a slithering snake. "It is shakin' us off."

"Hell yeah, *now* we're talking," Quentin nodded. "I *knew* something big was happening."

Emma leaned forward, "How do you know, nothing seems messed up, right?"

Quentin waved his arms around, "*Everything* is messed up!"

She said, "Well, I'm just not seeing it."

Magnus said, "I hae proof, this box, from m'closet upstairs. Do ye believe I live here?"

Everyone nodded.

"I hae been away but none of ye were surprised that I came home, correct? Ye dinna believe I was dead — did I shock ye, James?"

James said, "No, you just were there, I said, 'oh, Magnus is back.'"

He said, "Would ye believe me if I said I was here this morn?"

Everyone shook their head.

"I was here this morn. But whether ye believe me or not, ye dinna believe me gone forever, ye werna surprised tae see me, ye ken? So help me understand this." He pulled up the flap on the box.

Fraoch said, "Ye sound upset, Og Maggy."

Magnus ran his hand through his hair. "I am nae angry at anyone here, but aye, I am enraged and tryin' tae keep it in check. My apologies tae all in this room, I am not blamin' ye, but still, help me understand, *how* did this happen?"

He showed us the flap, MAGNUS'S THINGS, then tipped the box and showed us inside. There were his clothes, some toiletries, and a pair of boots.

Emma said, "I have a vague memory of helping Katie pack it, years ago."

"This is yer handwriting? I kent it wasna Kaitlyn's."

She nodded.

He said, "I was back here, just this morn. I lived here, everyone spoke tae me. Twas not a surprise that I was here."

James said, "Your point?"

"Time has shifted on all of us in verra profound ways and we need tae—"

Quentin said, "Beat the shit out of whoever did it."

I said, "Aye."

Fraoch looked around at the table. "And while we are talking on this, when was the last time ye saw me?"

Everyone looked blank.

"I hae been livin' by myself on the shore of a loch, and then Lochinvar and Archie came and—"

James said, "Who's Archie?"

Magnus pushed back his chair with a screech and stood up. "Archie is m'son. He daena live here anymore?" He looked around at our faces then said, "We must prepare in haste. We are goin' tae the year 1557 tae get the vessels. We need guns, armor, we need some campin' gear in case it takes a while tae accomplish. Do we hae enough horses? I hae m'horse Dràgon, we want more, what about vehicles? We need tae start a pile in the back of one of the trucks." He said, "Who wants tae go?"

Everyone raised their hand except Emma.

"Good, I think we need everyone. Emma will remain here with the bairns, Zoe and Ben. Those are the bairns?"

"Yes, I can take them to my parents' house."

Magnus nodded, quietly. "Aye, two bairns, they will go tae yer parents' house."

Then he said, "Everyone else will go with me. We need as many fighters as possible."

I said, "Are we worried about looping?"

Magnus said, "Nae, we arna worried. I am done thinking on time as a line, we hae tae stop leavin' history behind us — tis makin' us forgetful of our history. We need tae think on it as a wheel, a series of revolutions, we can learn from history and grow stronger, and do it over."

Zach said, "I agree, Fuck that, we aren't worried about it. Not anymore. This dude has messed up our whole fucking board game. We were playing chutes and ladders, right? Then this asshole came along and moved all our pieces around, he took some off the board, he offed with the dice. He's fucked it all up, so what do we do?"

Fraoch said, "I feel like we put our finger under the board and we flip it right over."

Zach raised his beer. "Fuck yeah, we're going to flip the whole damn game board."

We all raised our drinks and said, "Hear hear!"

And we packed for our mission. Most of us packed clothing that was a combination of good for the time and good for camping, plus would work militarily. Hayley and I wore cargo pants with pockets, because I was not going to war in a skirt and no one who mattered would see me.

As Magnus said, "If a sixteenth century man sees ye in yer pants, then ye hae been captured; kill him, and ken I am coming tae get ye."

I grinned. "Sounds good, you always do."

He had found a second box of clothes in the spare closet and dressed in his boots, his kilt and one of his royal coats, with all the appropriate leather straps for scabbard and holster. He looked like a king, headed to war.

Quentin said, "Don't want to tone it down, Boss?"

"Nae, I want them tae ken who they are dealing with."

CHAPTER 62 - AULD MAGNUS

1690 - SCOTLAND

I sat upon the side of m'bed, lost in thought —I had had another dream.

A fog rollin' in, an army advancin'—

I hadna known who I was with, but then I looked tae my side, and there was Kaitlyn. I haena seen her in a long time, not since she had left me on the side of Ben Cruachan, years afore.

She was older, and had bairns with her — I had a flash of recognition, the lad was Archie, but there was a bairn in her arms, a young lass beside her, the sight of them all caused me a sharp pain of regret — this is what I had lost.

But the army was coming. I had tae protect her.

I yelled, "Run!" And turned my horse tae charge against the advancing horde.

I shook my head. This dream was comin' regularly, causin' me tae lose sleep. It had an odd feel, as if twas real and not a dream, as if it had happened, or would happen. I couldna understand if it was a memory or a premonition and neither of those choices would make me come tae a reasonable feeling about it. I had Kaitlyn beside me, her bairns with her, an army bearing down, my heart raced — I had tae protect her.

I clutched my chest and thought about it. The scene had never been this clear before, except... this time I had noticed somethin' as I had turned m'horse, a carnage of dead men on the field. A carnage before the army had arrived.

It hit me with a certainty that this was the moment that the vessels entered our world. I had nae doubt.

I stood, my heart racing and left m'croft.

It was a market day. I walked tae the village center, drawn by hunger, the pangs nearly endless, though the memories of Chef Zach's food had faded through the years — here, the odor of animals and dirt wafted and mixed with the scent of bread. I bought a loaf, drank an ale, and was lost in thought when a cloaked woman bumped m'shoulder. "Sorry, Master, I dinna see ye there."

She was unfamiliar.

"I dinna... m'apologies, Madame, I was thinkin' on something else."

She paused. "Ye are Auld Magnus?"

"Aye, I am he."

"I hae a message for ye." She pulled a piece of creased white paper from the pocket of her cloak. She passed it tae me.

"From who?"

"A friend who will be needin' your help."

"What sort of help would I—"

"Ye are a warrior."

I looked down on the pale white paper, somethin' I hadna seen in a long time. It seemed tae be the portent of danger, comin' so soon after m'dream.

I mumbled, "I daena do that anymore," and looked up as the stranger hustled away. She blended in with the crowds of the market and was soon out of sight.

I unfolded the paper and saw there the image of the crown of the Kingdom of Riaghalbane, and under it, 'From the desk of Lady Mairead,' with the words:

November 1, 1557
You will find a vessel hidden under the oak tree at the tunnel door.

Twas written in m'mother's hand.

I dinna need tae know anything more, the tunnel, the Oak tree. The message meant Balloch. The location of the vessel meant I would time-travel once more. I dinna want tae, but I was bidden.

I gathered m'weapons and dressed for battle, and saddled my horse. It would be a three day ride.

When I arrived it was a fine morning. I noted the strong walls, the guards above as I passed through the gates. I had missed this fine old castle, my shelter and protection while growin' up. I had known these grounds for centuries, had lived within the walls when I was young, and had time traveled in and out of the region through those early years of m'marriage, seeing it in different stages as rooms and walls were added and strengthened.

Now I had been grounded from time travel, left by Kaitlyn when she had gone tae live with me when I was young... and now I was nothin' but a loop of m'self. I lived far away — I dinna come tae Balloch unless I was needed.

I gave m'reins tae the stable lad, and crossed through the busy courtyard. Then I entered the old chapel.

Twas dark inside, lit by a few candles, chilled for lack of a glass window, quiet and solemn, full of shadows except for a bit of dancin' dust seen in the crack of light from the door. I approached the altar, knelt on the cold stone, and spent a long time prayin' for guidance, and forgiveness. I had sworn I wouldna time-travel again, that I would live here, that I wouldna search for Kaitlyn or interfere in her life, and I had lived this vow without much struggle. Some despair, but in truth, there was nothin' I could do — she was lost tae me. I couldna go tae her, twas not a part of God's plan, until the message had come.

Now I kent there was a vessel. Twas within reach — and without a doubt m'vow tae not fight, tae live without struggle, tae not go tae Kaitlyn, twas all undone.

I dinna understand *why*, so I prayed, until the stiffness in m'knees caused me tae rise.

Then I left for the crowded courtyard. I retrieved m'horse from the stable and rode from the castle walls tae the banks of the river. The recent rain caused the water tae rush, the sun flashed on the surface, a startling brightness. I dismounted my horse and looked up at the branches of an old oak tree.

Twas a fine, strong tree, a perfect example of the kind — my eyes settled upon the base, where I noticed the earth had been formed intae a mound.

I pushed at it with my boot, scraping away the top layers, until I caught a glint of the edge of a chest. I dug deeper, until I couldna do it fast enough, I crouched and used a sharp stone tae dig. Finally I could make out the size and shape of the chest and at the top an ornate letter M.

I dug faster until I had it clear enough tae tug it free. Then I shoved dirt intae the hole tae hide m'doings.

I sat on a low boulder and lifted the lid.

Inside was a vessel, looking just as I remembered, from so long ago, when I had been a king of time.

CHAPTER 63 - KAITLYN

OCTOBER 31, 1557 - A CAMP NEAR BALLOCH CASTLE

*W*e built a camp to the south, up a hill from the clearing. We gave ourselves a couple of days to move equipment and set it all up. We wanted to make sure that our time travel happened well away from the first of November, in case there was tracking going on. There was bound to be tracking. Most of us had been to this scene at one time or another. Except Lochie and Zach, that's why they were our front guard.

We worked all day preparing, some making camp, some making food, some scouting, some guarding, all of us strategizing.

We had guns, we had helmets and armor and we had off-road e-bikes and horses, we had walkie-talkies, night-vision binoculars, and we had a plan.

On the last night we sat up, talking over the plan and making last minute adjustments, but mostly just talking about things — memories, or loss of them, little conversations of the kind you have with friends when you're on the cusp of something big and dangerous. We slept in stages, making sure everyone got at least a couple of hours before moving into position.

We surrounded the clearing by about one am.

There we waited for the storm. I was on an e-bike, beside and a little behind Magnus. He had his eyes on the clearing, mentally prepared for the battle to come. His horse, Dràgon, was still, power contained within. He was the perfect horse for Magnus, they were well-bonded to each other already. James was riding Osna, Fraoch on Thor, Lochie and Zach would be riding down the slope on a three-wheeled ATV. It was loud, but we had used that to our advantage before, loud might be good. Quentin had installed trip-lines around the area, and there was a speaker to play really loud music, to our advantage.

But stealth was also good, Hayley and I were on almost silent electric bikes. Our job was to circle, to watch, to engage only if necessary. Quentin was on a rock above the scene, he had a grenade launcher for mayhem and his rifle on a tripod aimed on the clearing. He was our sharpshooter, his job was to kill the bad guys.

All of us had one goal: collect the vessels. Find the Bridge. Kick some ass.

I was nervous, but wore armor, and a helmet, and had a rifle slung across my back. A handgun in a holster. Hayley and I were side by side, we were to stick together.

A fog rolled in.

I sat on the bike seat with my hands on the handlebars, staring at the clearing as we lost visibility. I said, "It looks a lot like my dream."

Without turning his head, Magnus said, "Is it too much for ye tae handle, Kaitlyn?"

I took a deep breath. "Nope."

"Good."

Quentin used the binoculars to look around at the ridges. Lochinvar looked through them at the woods. Magnus asked, "Dost ye see any other groups? Anyone else here?"

Quentin said, "No, just us."

Lochinvar said, "The woods are clear."

Quentin looked down at an iPad, watching his security video. "No triplines have been hit, we have no movement to the east or west. To the north, Balloch castle, clear."

I looked up at Magnus, a slight nod to his head on hearing the update, but that was all, his focus was on the field. His horse stamped and then stilled.

A few minutes later, the storm began. There was the headache inducing internal feeling, almost like a shriek, that signaled the use of the Trailblazer, something I hadn't remembered until now it came back to me — the Trailblazer was used to go back in time, to make the path the time-travelers could travel down.

It came clear — it was painful, that's why the original travelers had so many men, so many vessels, this was their strategy for going so far back.

I said, into the radio, "Hayley and I are headed north to watch the path." I turned and steered my bike along a trail that was less path and more a careening, winding, bouncing route through the trees. There were times when it felt like free falling. Hayley behind me muttered, "Shit!" as she fell, got back on her bike and caught up to me. "Skidded out there for a moment."

"Don't do that!" I flew down the last slope and landed on level ground and bounced over roots, fallen branches, and stones, before skidding to a stop within a shadow. I tapped the button on my radio, "We're in sight of the gates."

Magnus's voice said, "Good."

I looked at the sky behind us, thunder clouds were building. Quentin said into the radio, "Here comes the storm."

I turned to the castle and watched a group of twelve men rode thundering from the gates, heading toward the storm.

I watched them approach — There was a mist. The sound of rumbling. There were horses with warriors on them. But these weren't the warriors of my dream, filling me with dread, these were just men, sent from the castle to go check into the odd storm up the hill.

They were laughing and talking with each other as they passed.

"Twelve guardsmen, horses, headed your way." I added into the radio, "Carrying swords."

They left behind a cloud of dust as they rode down through the ravine, headed toward the clearing. I looked at Hayley. "Now what?"

She shrugged. "All the action is back that way."

"Wouldn't hurt to go up the ravine a bit closer, right?"

We followed the men up the ravine a safe distance behind.

CHAPTER 64 - MAGNUS

NOVEMBER 1, 1557 - THE BATTLE OF CHAOS

I dug my finger in my ear tae try tae get the ringin' tae cease — the Trailblazer had been at work, creating the time-travel path.

Then the storm, and now it was dissipatin' and leavin' behind a pile of unconscious men.

James's voice on the radio, "Lot of issues could have been solved if these dudes had just traveled in a proper vehicle instead of a wee handheld machine called a vessel."

I grunted, lookin' down on the men who were creating a great deal of 'issues' by their arrival here — this was at the beginning of time travel.

They were grand inventors and brave adventurers, yet they hadna invented a vehicle, they hadna learned yet about traveling ahead and havin' someone guard over them as they awakened, they dinna foresee the issues — perhaps they dinna think there would be danger, or maybe they had grown used tae the course and had become complacent. However far in the future they had begun, they had mapped a verra long route at great danger tae themselves.

Twas here they would lose their lives at the hands of Johnne Cambell and his men.

I had been here once before and had killed a man or two.

Kaitlyn had killed at least one man — we were not blameless, but we had done what we needed tae do.

The men from the castle entered the clearing, They either became frightened by seein' something they dinna understand, or were too brutal tae think twice on their actions. The lead guard gave the order tae kill and they indiscriminately stabbed intae the pile of unconscious men.

Twas a horrible sight.

Zach's voice on the radio said, "Fuck, this is awful."

"Aye, but hold back, we canna interfere."

I used a night vision binocular tae watch. The guardsmen were off their horses, killin', but now they were also collectin' their spoils of war — one of the men put a vessel intae his sporran, then another. I made out that the head guardsmen ordered them tae put what they were collecting intae his sack.

I said, "Lochie, ye see it?"

He looked through his own binoculars. "Aye, I see a bunch of murderers and a bag, tis mine, as soon as ye give the order."

"Ye see the chests near the boulder?"

"I see them."

"Get those as well."

I put down the monocular and put m'finger on the trigger. I wanted tae race down, but held m'horse back. "Fraoch, what about Lady Mairead, dost ye see her?"

"Nae." Fraoch swept his monocular back and forth around the edges of the clearing.

Quentin said, "Launcher ready."

James said, "I don't see the younger versions of ourselves."

I said, "This is good, it means time has shifted. This whole scene has changed."

Zach said intae the radio. "We're goin to flip the fucking game board, y'all, let's goooooooo!"

Fraoch chuckled. "Patience, Chef Zach, we canna interrupt their murderous rampage. They are collectin' the vessels for us, puttin' them in a sack, then we will hae our comfortable win."

I waited for a few more moments, watching as they collected more and more vessels, then most of them gathered tae look over their spoils.

I tapped the button on m'radio, "Colonel Quentin, *now*."

He fired a grenade directly at the men, with a loud explosion that shook the earth — men screamed, horses fled, there were few men left, but they were in chaos.

Quentin turned on a speaker on the other side of the clearing, and from the woods blasted a song that Zach had chosen: Sabotage, by the Beastie Boys. Twas deafeningly loud.

The leader mounted his horse, and yelled for his remaining men tae mount and follow him tae investigate.

Dràgon was excited, stamping, ready tae go, I held him back, my heart racing, and then one of our faraway trip lines was activated in the dark woods, a bomb exploded.

I gave the signal tae charge.

Zach, with Lochie ridin' on the back, drove the ATV, barrelling down intae the center of the clearin'. We followed tae guard them, James breakin' tae the left, Fraoch headed right. I rode down the middle — then urged Dràgon tae gallop around the pile, watchin' the woods, as Lochie and Zach pulled tae a skiddin' stop right where the bag had been dropped. Lochie jumped down, plucked it up, and tossed it ontae the ATV between Zach's feet. Zach revved the motor, turned the ATV and followed Lochie as he began pickin' up loose vessels and shovin' them intae the sack he had slung across his back. He shoved dead men aside, searching for the chests in the carnage. I felt sure he had picked up at least three more vessels.

Then the Balloch guards returned at once.

I fired my gun, shooting at one, as another man attacked me from behind, with his sword swingin', m'gun was dropped in the melee. I drew m'sword and horse tae horse we battled, until I saw a man gaining on Lochie, I broke away and charged in his direction. I asked, "Quentin, ye hae a shot?"

"No!"

The man brought his sword butt-end down hard on Lochie's head Lochie stumbled, then fell.

The man I had been sword fighting chased me, I turned and swung, meeting his sword just as he brought his down. Dràgon reared, nearly throwin' me in the action. Guns fired all around. I scanned the field, there was another guardsman swinging his sword at Zach, who ducked, then fired, killing the man, but my attention had been drawn and I had missed seein' a huge man leap from his horse, grab an unconscious Lochie, and swing him up over his saddle.

I was too far away. I radioed Quentin, "Got a shot?"

"No, he's..."

The rifle fired but missed, again and again, as the horse carrying Lochie raced from the clearing with two other men on horseback following, a cloud of dust in their wake.

"Och nae! They hae Lochie!"

I radioed, "Zach, dost ye still hae the vessels?"

"I have the sack, I have two chests!"

There were two men left circling the space, Quentin fired, one of them fell. Another barreled intae the woods headin' toward the source of the bullets.

I tapped my radio, "Quentin, enemy headed tae ye."

Zach was driving the ATV around the clearing, searching for vessels, spooking the last men.

I yelled, "Move in haste, more guards will be comin'! I will follow Lochie!" I turned Dràgon tae make chase, passing Kaitlyn and Hayley on the path tae Balloch, but behind me I could hear a rumbling, a violent shaking of the earth, an army of men were coming.

I whipped Dràgon around and returned tae Kaitlyn's side.

A fog rolled into the clearing. There was a hush except for the horses coming, the roar of the quaking earth.

Kaitlyn was wide eyed, frozen in fear, her mouth moving, then, "Do we run?! Magnus, are we supposed to run?"

I yelled, "Nae, mount yer bike, head tae the south, find a shot, stay clear of the battle."

Hayley grabbed her hand, yanked her, moving her from where she remained, frozen.

"Yes, yes... find a shot." She and Hayley drove their bikes through the woods to the south end of the clearing, and Kaitlyn's voice emitted from my radio, "Be safe, Highlander."

CHAPTER 65 - MAGNUS

NOVEMBER 1, 1557 - RANULPH

I said, intae the radio, "Quentin, ye see?"

"Yes… I…" His voice broke up with static.

Fraoch and James fell in behind me and we roared intae the middle of the clearing as Ranulph and his army broke from the trees. We were gravely outnumbered.

Zach spun the ATV around, shootin' from the south end of our line, James was fighting hand tae hand, Fraoch had his sword swingin' on a group of men, I headed straight for Ranulph.

The smell of mud and thick dense fog and dirt filled the air, the clash of steel, the sight of blood, the pulse of fear and fury, the hooves on the ground were thunderous. I had fought along-side Fraoch many times afore on a field much like this one.

I noted he glanced at his left flank, found m'location, a quick nod passed between us, he turned his horse tae charge a man.

I held up m'sword as I rode, my senses heightened, pleased with Dràgon's steady gait, one two three, I gained on Ranulph, swung m'sord, but his horse's tail flicked, I saw he was turnin' — m'blow missed, and I was off-balance for a moment. The movement in m'middle caused a sharp pain through m'abdomen.

He charged me, forcin' Dràgon tae rear back.

From my radio, I heard Quentin, "I've got him!"

Then the blast of the sniper rifle, Quentin's shot from the trees, missed. "Missed him!"

He said it again, "Now!" And shot again.

Then, "Make him hold still!"

James said, "We don't need the rundown, just shoot him!" A man hit James hard on the arm, knocking him from his horse.

Quentin's voice, "You okay, James? James!"

Fraoch headed toward James to check on him, when there was another shot.

Quentin said, "Damn, that guy is — shit!" The sounds of a scuffle emitted from the radio.

Hayley's voice through the radio, "I'm going to check on Quentin!" She sped up the hill on her e-bike.

With heightened senses, I could see m'men downed, yells and horse screams, the sounds of a battle being lost. Ranulph swung his sword, I spun Dràgon, and his blow missed, causing Ranulph for a moment tae be off-balance.

I sliced m'sword. It hit armor, left a dent, but slid off — the abrupt change in movement knocked the air from me.

I gasped for air.

I tried tae regain calm, m'sword hangin' heavy at m'side. *Ye must fight.*

Sweat poured down m'brow, obscurin' m'vision, but in m'blurred periphery I saw Kaitlyn on her bike descend intae the clearing, her gun blazing, she shot at Ranulph, missing twice, then hittin' his arm, but then one of the other men flung a war hammer toward her, "Kaitlyn!" I yelled as her bike slammed short, and she was thrown to the side.

Kaitlyn was down. I raced in that direction, but with Ranulph tight behind me, his sword raised. I had tae make a decision, get Kaitlyn up or turn tae fight Ranulph — I chose tae fight, turning Dràgon tae face him, the ache in my middle causin' me tae lose m'breath as I raised m'sword on a shakin' arm.

Ranulph was bearin' down on me, hard, I felt weakened and it seemed the battle was lost — when there was another low rumble, another horse ridin' intae battle behind me.

CHAPTER 66 - KAITLYN

NOVEMBER 1, 1557 - AULD MAGNUS

I was lying on the ground, a sharp pain on my shoulder, when a shadow fell over me. I cowered for a moment, the battle raging around me, but then the man above me said, "Kaitlyn!"

I looked up, and there was Auld Magnus. I hadn't seen him in years, but he was unmistakable — the look of my husband, but with the years and battles weighing heavy, his eyes full of sadness instead of the joy m'husband kept, but hot all the same. I instantly remembered lying beside him as he recounted all of his scars, and how my heart had wanted tae break when I left him on the side of the ben — now he had his sword drawn, his horse rearing and stamping, he said, "Kaitlyn, get up! I need ye tae run!"

I scrambled to my feet and raced away from the center of the battle, headed toward the woods, hearing the clash of steel behind me, the battle to the death of the men I loved.

I climbed the slope on all fours, grasping tree limbs, scrambling through the bracken and emerged where Quentin had his rifle set up, Hayley was beside him, using a scope, being his spotter.

There was a dead man beside her. She said, "Killed this guy, don't ask." Then, she said, "Who's that? Looks familiar."

I collapsed down beside them. "That's Auld Magnus, we are in a mega-loop-di-loop."

Quentin said, "Perfect, this is a nightmare... Focus up, Hayley! Where am I shooting?"

CHAPTER 67 - MAGNUS

THE AULD WARRIOR

Quentin's voice in my ear. "I can't get him, you're in the way."

I drew m'sword up, tae block Ranulph's swing, exhausted from the effort — Ranulph was injured, but he was swingin' hard, forcin' Dràgon and me tae the hill, *nae, I was goin' tae be cornered —*

When suddenly a man, charged his horse intae the battle. He was older, a full beard, wearin' furs and lookin' barbaric, he grunted my direction in greetin' then entered the fight, swingin' on Ranulph, drawing his attention away.

There was a shot from the woods. One of the last men was downed.

Quentin said, "Got him. Next Ranulph. Tell New Dude to draw him to the middle. I don't have a shot."

Ranulph and the auld warrior fought, their swords clashing, I bellowed, "Get him tae the center!"

I skirted their battle, watchin' over the rest of the field, tryin' tae regain m'strength, readyin' myself tae join in, as the auld warrior fought Ranulph with skill.

Ranulph lunged, the auld warrior pulled away, then brought his sword down on him, almost knockin' him from his horse.

Then he plowed forward, his sword swinging right and left, forcing Ranulph back until he was in the center of the clearing.

Quentin's voice emitted from my radio, "Tell him, left!"

I yelled, "Move left!"

The auld warrior turned his horse and leaned left, as Ranulph's sword came down, Ranulph's horse reared, and he tried tae control his horse, after losing his balance in the swing.

Quentin yelled, "Got him!" A shot rang out, direct tae Ranulph's head, blood sprayed, he listed and slid from his horse.

I jumped from Dràgon and grabbed Ranulph by his chest armor and looked down on him. "Ye see, Ranulph? Ye hae lost the war."

He was silent, dying in a pool of blood.

A moment later Quentin's voice, "Everyone out of the way."

James and Fraoch fled the battle in one direction, I met the eyes of the auld warrior and yelled, "South!" I mounted Dràgon and followed him.

Behind us, before Ranulph's army could react, Quentin launched a grenade tae end the battle, directly intae their ranks. The enemy exploded intae destruction and disarray.

The last remaining men turned and fled. Zach stood on the ATV, yelling, "Yee-motherfucking-Haw!" firing his rifle after them as they escaped.

I glanced at the auld warrior who was listing, holding his side, as his horse slowed he slid from his saddle tae a heap on the ground.

"Och nae!"

I dismounted my horse. And knelt beside him. "Ye are injured?"

He peeled his bloodied palm up from his side, there was a verra deep gash there.

Kaitlyn raced intae the clearing and dropped tae her knees beside us. "Oh no, oh no, oh no!"

He met her eyes. "Aye, Kaitlyn, things are not so well with me, but I am glad ye are safe."

She nodded. "I'm so sorry. We could..." She pressed her hand to the wound. "If we..."

He shook his head, "Nae, tis my endin', Kaitlyn, tis time."

I watched from her face tae his, a discomfort settling in my heart, one I couldna bear, like a glimpse of m'future endin', within someone else's form.

He weakly patted his sporran, "I hae a vessel, tis from under the oak tree..."

I asked, "What year?"

He coughed. "...the year 1690."

Kaitlyn nodded, she opened his sporran and pulled out a vessel, then a shark tooth fell from it. She sobbed and pressed it intae his hand. She said again, "I'm sorry."

"I ken, but this has been what ye needed tae do." He took a deep staggerin' breath and choked out. "I wish ye well, Madame Campbell."

Kaitlyn said, "Me too."

But he dinna speak again, his eyes closed, headed tae eternal sleep.

She patted the back of his hand and placed it on his chest, and then she put her hand on m'shoulder, leavin' there the mark of the Auld Warrior's blood, tae steady herself as she stood.

She said, "That was—"

"I ken who it was, mo reul-iuil, we ought not speak on it." I tried tae avert m'eyes, but she met them and held them.

"Are you afraid it might be looping?"

"Aye, something like that." I pulled her intae m'arms and we held on for a moment.

She said, "I'm so sorry. That was all so complicated..."

"Aye, mo reul-iuil, I ken."

· · ·

Then Zach drove the ATV toward us, his voice verra loud, "Chaos, absolute chaos! Where do you want me now?"

I said, "Next we storm the castle — spreadin' more chaos, we need tae get our man out."

Quentin's voice through the radio, "I'm coming! Hold on."

Tae Kaitlyn I said, "Ye good, mo reul-iuil?"

She looked up at me. "Yeah, I am. Where do you need me?"

He pushed the hair back from my face and said, "Grab yer bike, get Hayley and head back tae camp, ye understand? Ye hae that vessel, keep it safe."

"Where are you going?"

"Tae get Lochie."

Quentin was careening down the hill, carrying the grenade launcher and a big bag of weapons. Hayley was beside him, crashing through the bracken on her bike.

Quentin climbed on the back of Zach's ATV. "Do we have all the vessels?"

Zach said, "Most of them, a lot, we also have three chests." He patted the sack down between his feet.

I said, "Give us each a vessel."

Zach pulled vessels out and tossed one to each of us, I put mine in m'sporran and asked Kaitlyn, "Ye ken where ye are goin'?"

"I remember." She mounted her bike.

I said, "Ye haena grown confused?"

She looked up in my eyes. "No, never. It's all coming back to me, I know these lands like the back of my hand. I know this world, this life, and I know you, and I have a clarity. I love you, Master Magnus."

I patted my chest. "I love ye as well, mo reul-iuil." I groaned as I mounted Dràgon again.

"Your stomach?"

"Aye, but tis okay, I will see ye soon."

She turned her bike away.

Hayley blew Fraoch a kiss and followed Kaitlyn, speeding up the path, guns slung across their backs.

I told Zach, "Guard the vessels with yer life."

"Will do."

Zach said, "Anyone going to talk about the fact that an older version of—"

Fraoch shook his head. "Nae, we daena need tae talk on him, tis nae necessary. He was just a brave auld warrior who fought alongside us, and gave his life for our cause."

I nodded. "Aye. Twas all he was."

James pointed up the path to the castle with a whistle, "All righty then, round her up!" and we rode from the clearing.

We galloped down the ravine toward the castle, coming out on the moors around the southwest side. We hid within the early morning shadows of the forest and listened. Faintly we could hear the chaos of guards who were shocked by explosions in the woods near their walls.

The gates opened and guardsmen on horses galloped past us headed toward the clearing.

I said, "Let them pass."

Fraoch said, "What is our goal?"

"Create chaos, free Lochie."

Quentin pulled the grenade launcher tae his shoulder. "Perfect, to that end, I'm going to send them in another direction."

He fired a grenade toward the west. The explosion was loud, trees went up in flames. The men who had passed us headed that way.

Another group of men left the castle headed that direction.

"How many men hae left the castle now?"

"I would say about thirty, maybe more."

Quentin passed the grenade launcher to Zach, dug through his pack and pulled out another speaker. He turned it on as he raced over to a tree, tied a rope to the handle on it, tossed the end of the rope over a branch, and hoisted the speaker up into the branches. "What song ye want, Zach?"

Zach said, "We did the Beastie Boys, how about—"

James said, "Black Sabbath."

Quentin worked the remote control. "Sold — *Iron Man*, coming up!"

The song blared, filling the woods.

Quentin climbed back on the ATV and put the launcher tae his shoulder. "Which wall you want me to hit, Boss?"

I said, "Ye goin' tae bust up m'castle?"

"Hell yeah, we're gonna bust up that wall, then we're going to draw them away. It's a shitty wall anyway, by the time you live here it will be rebuilt, no worries."

"Aye, I warned Auld Graybeard, I told him tae build better walls but he dinna listen, make it the east wall. We will go in from the north tae the kitchen."

Quentin said, "Sure boss, see ya on the other side!" Zach roared the ATV and drove in that direction.

We turned our horses and headed around the castle grounds tae the north, hearing explosions and gunshots behind us. James left another blaring speaker behind a rock. We continued on, and left our horses tied tae a tree near the river bank. We approached the castle, hidin' in the shadows, up tae a side door with guns drawn.

James pulled his radio up to his mouth, pushed a button and loudly projected, "Testing, one, two…"

Fraoch said, "Wheesht!"

"Sorry, but I have an idea, gonna project my voice on a loud-speaker, sounds good?"

Fraoch said, "Sounds as if twill bring on a terrible headache, so ye ought tae do it."

James joked, "I'm going to tell them to put down their arms and go tae their rooms, I'll be persuasive — don't listen to me."

Fraoch said, "Och, I never listen tae ye anyway."

Using my gun I fired at the door handle. The lock splintered away.

CHAPTER 68 - MAGNUS

AN ANCESTOR

I had a light, but I dinna need it, I had been livin' in this castle m'whole life. Even a hundred years earlier I knew the layout.

From outside we could hear explosions, amplified, which meant Quentin and Zach were busy.

We raced down a passageway, through the store rooms tae the doors that led down tae the dungeons. We needed a cover so James took a place beside the door, gun drawn, projecting his voice, "Drop your weapons! Hands on your head!"

We switched on our headlamps, swung open the door, and crept down the stairs. Near the bottom I found an auld man, cowering in the corner, the last man guarding the cells.

Behind us, James's continuing command, "Put down your weapons!! Down on your knees!! Hands on your head!!"

There were three cells, I pressed my ear tae the first door and heard a moan within. I shoved up the wooden plank across the door, and found a man inside, he raised his arms tae block my light in his eyes. He moaned again.

I yelled, "I found a man, nae Lochie!"

There was a weak voice, a croak, comin' from the next cell. "Here!"

Fraoch opened that door, his voice from the cell, "Ye are well enough tae walk, Lochie?"

"Aye."

Fraoch heaved him up.

From up the steps, James fired his gun, then continued booming, "Down, get down on the ground! Hands up!"

Fraoch put his shoulder under Lochie's arm tae help him down the passage.

Lochie said, "Help the other man out!"

I said, "Who, the guard?"

"Nae the other prisoner!"

"We daena hae time! I will leave the door open."

James was repeatin' his commands and m'head ached from all the noise.

Lochie said, "Ye need tae help him, Og Maggy! His name is Nor!"

I stood still, watchin' Fraoch heft him up the steps. "Nor as in *Normond*?"

"Aye! Ye ken — ye hae tae get him free."

"Och nae." I returned tae the cell. "Ye are Normond? What are ye in here for?"

I hefted him up and put my shoulder under his arm and began draggin' him from the cell.

"I was... nabbed by a... Johnne Cambell... m'name is Nor...Duke of Awe."

"Och nae," I said, again, as I heaved him up the steps following Fraoch. "Where were ye when ye were kidnapped?"

"Florida... with m'wife."

At the top of the stair Lochie was well enough tae walk, so he led the way out. Fraoch helped me carry Nor, and James followed us guardin' our rear.

We slipped through the outer door to the grounds of the castle and dragged Nor tae our horses.

He dropped weakly tae the dirt and asked, "Who are ye?"

"M'name is Magnus, the rest is nae important, the less we ken of each other the better. Dost ye ken where ye need tae go?"

He said, "Amelia Island... the month of May, I daena remember the day, 2012."

I groaned. "Give me yer vessel, Fraoch."

He passed it tae me.

"Ye ought tae ken the date, Nor." I set the numbers and dial tae take him tae Florida, but not Amelia Island, instead I sent him tae the land near the spring in central Florida. Then I slammed the vessel intae his hand. "Daena come back here tae this time, this is too dangerous. Dost ye understand?"

"Aye."

"And daena mess with me. I live on Amelia Island, ye leave me and m'family alone, nae contact, nae incursions intae my lands or m'times, or I winna be as friendly. Dost ye understand?"

"Aye, I understand, thank ye."

"Twist it once we hae gone."

I mounted Dràgon, and gestured for James and Fraoch tae follow me away.

Quentin's voice through the radio. "Where are we meeting?"

"Head tae the camp we will meet on the way."

I called intae my radio, "Kaitlyn... Kaitlyn...?"

Then her voice, "We're good, near camp, ready to go when you get here."

We rode through the woods, being watchful for guardsmen, but most had returned tae the castle or were investigatin' the weird carnage of the clearing. We steered well away, skirting the area. Behind us a storm rose from near the castle walls.

Fraoch said, "Who was that man, Og Maggy?"

"An ancestor, tis not important."

Fraoch chuckled, "If he is an ancestor, seems he is *verra* important."

I chuckled as well. "I suppose ye are right."

As we neared the camp, we heard the ATV comin', then Zach skidded it tae a stop beside us. "Holy shit, you got Lochie! That worked! And Ranulph is dead!"

"Aye, we hae won the day against Ranulph."

Quentin said, "The Auld Warrior was awesome, but Ranulph did *not* have a good plan. I think we tricked him, he wasn't expecting us to be this much chaotic energy."

Zach said, "I bet his time travel trickery fucked him up in the end, hard to fight an army when you can't tell what's real and what's not — we were all chaos, people looping, fighting, attacking from the past and the present."

Lochie said, "Speakin' on past and present, Magnus saved an ancestor from the dungeons. As soon as I heard his name, I kent ye needed tae save him."

I said, "Well, Lochie, there are likely many Normonds in the world."

"How many men have the name of Normond, the name of the first king of Riaghalbane, same as ye, are also Dukes of Awe, same as ye, and also have wives who live in Florida, same as—?"

Zach said, "Holy shit, Magnus, you saved your ancestor?"

"Aye, I also saw a version of m'self die."

Fraoch clapped his hand on my shoulder. "Would ye like me tae see tae his body?"

"Would ye?"

"Aye, where and when?"

"I think he ought tae be buried in the graveyard at the village near Balloch but when...?"

Zach said, "Do you know where he was living?"

"He told me he got a vessel from the year 1690, but I was alive then, nine years auld, would it affect me, change m'life?"

Chef Zach, "I don't think so, you were both in the same place here, in the same battle, he's not you technically—"

I said, "I could take him intae the future a long time from now so I daena hae tae think on him and what he means..."

Chef Zach said, "But then he has disappeared from his life. It might hae been a long brutal lonely life, but what if he has a family? What if someone wants to visit his grave?"

Fraoch said, "I agree with Zach, graves are meant tae be in the past, tis the best way tae honor him."

"Aye, I suppose ye are right. Does the early spring of 1692 seem good tae ye?"

Fraoch nodded.

I passed him some gold. "Tae pay for his stone."

Fraoch nodded. "Consider it done."

Zach shook his head. "Wow, this is a fucking turducken of time travel."

We all nodded.

I said, "Aye, tis, and ye are going tae make me hungry, Chef Zach, with all this talk of turduckens."

"Have you ever had a turducken-style pie-cake? Oooh, do I have a plan for you."

We continued on tae the camp and found Hayley and Kaitlyn goin' through the pockets of a dead man.

I dismounted m'horses. "What happened?"

Kaitlyn said, "He was coming up the hill from the clearing, I think he ran and sort of crossed paths with our camp by accident."

Hayley said, "I shot his ass."

I asked, "How dost ye ken that he is from the clearing?"

Kaitlyn held up a vessel. "From his pocket."

I exhaled. "He likely found us by accident, but we ought tae make haste packing up all the same."

I said tae Hayley, "Ye heard why Fraoch inna here? He offered tae take the body of the Auld Warrior tae the village tae hae him properly buried. "

She answered, "Yeah, he said goodbye over the radio."

"Good, He took Lochinvar with him, they will meet us in Florida when they are done."

She squeezed Kaitlyn's shoulder. "You good?"

Kaitlyn said, "Yeah, no one needs to worry about me, yes, I'm good." She looked at me, "The only thought I give to him is a small branch of how I feel about you, you know that, right? He was just you when I met him long ago."

"I ken, Kaitlyn. He was an auld warrior, he laid down his life for our cause. He will be buried in the village near Balloch with a nice stone."

Hayley said, "Fraoch will see to it."

We started takin' down tents and James asked, "What I can't get out of my mind is why the *hell* did Normond have a wife in Florida?"

"Aye, seems an uncanny coincidence."

Zach waved his hands. "Don't be thinking it would be fun to ask him, you need to not cross his path, this is way too close, this is part of the time-shift — leave him alone."

Everyone nodded.

Kaitlyn said, "I agree, no reason for our paths to cross again."

I said, "I told him as such. We hae more than enough tae deal with."

Hayley had her hands on her hips. "This is too much, our camp is a mess, and I'm tired, can we just jumble it into a pile and jump it to Florida? Throw it in a truck and we will sort it later?"

We all looked at Quentin, because he was our armaments

and gear guy and he was usually verra organized. But this time he shrugged. "Good with me, we won, we winners can be as messy as we want. I would like to note though, you just used 'we'. Yes, 'we' can clean it up later."

"Fine. I'll help as long as it's after a shower."

We pushed crates together, dumped a couple of tents over, piled bags on top, and built a pile of gear and equipment in the middle of the camp. As I was carrying a load, I passed Kaitlyn and she asked, "Do you think, now that we did this, the timeline will be right again?"

I tossed my load on the pile. "I daena ken, Kaitlyn, it daena feel different, does it?"

She shook her head. "It's pretty disappointing."

I said, "Aye, but there is more for us tae do, we hae the Bridge, we will use it."

Quentin groaned. "That seems dangerous."

Hayley said, "Look around, look at our pile of weapons, we're in the sixteenth century, we have a grenade launcher, this is all dangerous."

The final load down, we gathered around it.

James said, "This is not a job well done."

Kaitlyn said, "What if...?"

Hayley said, "What do you mean by 'what if?'"

"These vessels were here in this time, this is the moment that they branched out into our story, now we have them all collected and we're taking them with us, what if...?"

I said, "We are tipping over the board game."

Zach said, "Making some mother-fucking chaos."

Kaitlyn said, "I know, but what if we take these vessels home and the whole timeline shifts? What if we lose people, like... you know, *you*, Magnus? Or Fraoch? What if by removing the vessels we never meet?"

James said, "I think, Katie, that it would be really hard to screw this timeline up any worse than it already is, it's *all* shifted, right? It's unlikely we'll make it worse."

She screwed up her face in disbelief.

James said, "We've been here before — Magnus took a bunch of the vessels, some chests, none of it made us not exist. We were all still the same after and it was like that never happened."

Zach said, "This is a great point."

Kaitlyn said, "You think?"

Zach said, "Sure, but you know, just in case, hold hands."

I put out the sack of vessels, crouched down, and counted. "We hae twenty vessels here, a few in our pockets, I think. Guess how many vessels we stole when we came the last time?"

Kaitlyn asked, "More than twenty?"

"Aye," I sifted through the large sack, "And I see we hae a few other things too, it looks like a Trailblazer, aye... and something... I think this is the Bridge... and this chest has..." I lifted a lid. "Some of the gold threads, and a band. We hae all we took the last time."

Hayley said, "As Fraoch would say, this is a do-over!"

I nodded. "We are in a good position here, Kaitlyn, I am nae worried on this point."

"Okay, that's good, usually you have concerns."

I stood up, cinched the top of the bag, and put out my hand tae hold hers. I said, "Ranulph caused a monumentally large time shift, it caused a massive malfunction, and yet... I am here now, we know where Fraoch is, we are meant tae be."

Zach said, "To paraphrase Jurassic Park, time-travel-life finds a way."

"So I'm not scared?"

I shook my head. "Ye arna scared, but ye can hold ontae me when we jump anyway."

"Good." She put her arms around me and held on. The rest of us made a circle holding hands, touching everything we could, Quentin twisted a vessel and took us all home.

CHAPTER 69 - FRAOCH

1692 - A BURIAL

Og Lochie and I sat hidden behind bushes deep in the woods, lookin' over the clearin' with binoculars. He said, "How long are we goin' tae wait?"

I said, "Wheesht." Then I whispered, "We either will hae tae fight them or we can wait until—"

"Och!" He jumped up and rushed away through the woods, rustlin' bushes as he went.

I whispered, "Ye are goin' tae get us..." He couldna hear me so I dinna finish. *Where did he go?* I looked through the binoculars, searching the edges of the clearing.

He returned a few minutes later leading a horse. "It belongs tae the Auld Warrior, I noticed him on the far side."

"Good, that was good, Og Lochie."

He grinned. "'Tis the first time ye ever said I did somethin' good."

"Aye, I ken, now wheesht."

We continued watchin' until dusk, and all the men finally left, then we brought our horses intae the middle of the clearin'. I held the reins of our horses, and Lochie placed his hand on the body of the Auld Warrior.

He kept his eyes averted. "I daena like the look of him."

"Me either, he has the face of our brother, at least tis older, maybe it will help if we think on him as an uncle."

"Maybe." Lochie glanced at the Auld Warrior's face. "Nae, it daena help." He pulled an end of his plaid across the auld warrior's face.

I twisted the vessel tae take us forward a century.

We arrived in the clearing and once we were up we did a better job of wrappin' the auld warrior's body in his plaid, and loaded him up and over the back of his horse tae carry him tae the church. We were about tae mount our own horses when the rumble of horse hooves rose through the woods as men approached.

I said, "Och, I am thankful they dinna surround us when we arrived, but ye ken, they might be trouble, wheesht and let me speak."

Lochinvar said, "Aye, auld man, I will let ye speak as long as ye let me draw first."

Six men rode intae the clearing.

I put out my hands, placatingly, "We arna causin' trouble, just carryin' our man tae the church for a burial."

The largest man said, "He has died from a wound? Ye hae murdered a man here?"

"Nae, his name is Auld Magnus he—"

A young warrior from the back rode his horse forward, "Auld Magnus ye say?"

Lochinvar burst forth, "Sean Campbell! Och, ye are young and wee!"

Sean put his hands on his sword handle. "I am nae wee, how dost ye ken m'name?"

I put my hand on Lochie's shoulder, "Mind yerself." Then said tae the leader, "What is yer name?"

"I am Baldie."

I said, before I could think better on it, "Och aye, I hae heard of ye! Og Maggy speaks verra highly on ye."

"Og Maggy?"

"Aye, Young Magnus, ye ken... he daena live here any...?" I couldna get the time straight or remember where Magnus would hae been.

Baldie's brow drew down, his horse stamped side to side. "Ye ken Young Magnus, though he has left for London?"

He was eyeing us dangerously.

"I ken Young Magnus, aye, and his mother, Lady Mairead. M'name is Fraoch and this is Lochinvar, we are here tae bring Auld Magnus home tae be buried in the village — he was killed in a battle far away. We hae traveled a long distance tae deliver him here."

Baldie turned tae Sean, "Hae ye met these men?"

Sean said, "Nae, how does this bawbag ken m'name?"

Og Lochie said with a smirk, "My apologies, Sean, ye reminded me of an older wiser warrior, I see I was mistaken."

Sean's scowl deepened and was almost comical on his verra young body, he dinna look sixteen years auld yet.

Baldie and Sean dismounted and neared the body, Baldie uncovered Auld Magnus's face, said, "Aye, this is he." He returned the fabric tae cover him. "Och, may he Rest In Peace, I haena seen him in years, but I would ken him anywhere." He pulled his dirk and cut Auld Magnus's sporran free from his waist.

I asked, "What are ye doing?"

"Checkin' his sporran tae see if ye hae robbed him."

I said, "We arna robbers, I told ye, we are bringing a warrior home."

He opened the sporran, crouched down, and dumped the contents ontae the ground. There were a few gold pieces, a shark tooth, and a folded piece of white paper. He unfolded it and looked it over.

I said, "See, we dinna steal from him, we are deliverin' him tae the church."

Baldie looked up at Sean, "This note is from yer mother."

Sean turned tae me, "How did ye say ye ken m'mother?"

I said, "We are family, think on me as a distant cousin."

Sean's brow drew down, he put his hand on his sword hilt. "Ye are bein' overly familiar."

I glanced at Og Lochie's fingers, itchin' beside his own sword hilt, ready tae draw.

Baldie stood and put out his hands. "Now, Sean, ye are young and impetuous, ye daena need tae draw on every man we come across. Get back on yer horse and wheesht."

Sean scowled as he mounted his horse.

Baldie put the contents of the sporran away in one of the leather sacks on the side of Auld Magnus's horse. "My apologies, men, family of Lady Mairead is family of mine, we will accompany ye tae the church."

Along the way, Baldie and I spoke tae each other and grew familiar. I had heard many stories about him and felt as if I knew him. We shared some bread and whisky and then continued ridin'.

He said, "Tis a difficult journey tae carry the deceased tae church."

I said, "Aye, it is a heavy burden, upon the horses and upon our souls."

"Aye, tis heavy, tis always heavy — I am recently widowed."

"I am verra sorry for yer loss."

Our path was an oft-traveled route, and we occasionally passed a horse drawn cart or a pedestrian traveling the other way. Twas a fine day for a journey, the sky overhead a high blue, with puffs of clouds, rushin' with the breeze. Then Baldie asked, "Ye say Auld Magnus passed in battle?"

"Aye, bravely and with honor."

He nodded, then said, "He always did hae a great deal of honor, he kept tae himself, but he once called out m'brother, Lowden, tae fight and beat him soundly."

I chuckled. "Most men daena think honorably on the men who beat their brothers."

He said, "Ye dinna ken m'brother, he deserved all the beatin' he received." He jerked his head tae Sean, ridin' behind us. "Sean there was Lowden's son — m'brother was a ragin' arse, as likely tae kill his own son than tae see him grow up tae be a man. Do ye hae a son, Fraoch?"

"Nae, I daena hae a livin' son, instead I look after the bairns of m'brothers. Do ye hae a son?"

Baldie shook his head. "Nae, tis why young and auld call me 'Uncle—"

"Because they ken they can count on ye."

"Aye, I suppose they do."

"I ken it, I ken they all think highly on ye, ye are their Uncle Baldie, ye are the man that Magnus and Sean will aspire tae become."

He narrowed his eyes.

I finished, "I meant, ye ken... because ye are an uncle, ye are bound tae be—"

Lochie chuckled and said, "Och nae, Uncle Frookie, what are ye talking on?"

I chuckled as I shook my head. "I daena ken."

Lochie joked, "Well, Uncle Frookie, maybe *ye* ought tae wheesht for once."

"And perhaps Baldie can continue tellin' me of the battle between the warrior, Auld Magnus, and his brother Lowden."

Baldie said, "Auld Magnus called him out tae the courtyard and beat him, mercilessly—"

Lochie said, "Swords or fists?"

"Twas swords."

Lochie said, "Seems unlikely that Lowden would survive it, Magnus is verra good with the sword."

Baldie said, "He wasna tryin' tae kill him, though, he was just frightenin' him. He held a sword tae his throat and made Lady Mairead beg for his life."

Lochie's eyes went verra big. "Was there a crowd gathered?"

"Aye, the courtyard was full, even the Earl was a witness tae it. I tell ye, twas a mercy upon the family for m'brother tae get the retribution, and then a short time later, Lowden passed away, widowin' Lady Mairead and leavin' Sean and Lizbeth orphaned, och, twas a dark time, but I did m'best tae be their uncle and m'late wife, Abigall and I devoted ourselves tae guidin' the bairns through."

My eyes drew tae Sean. "He is a fine young man."

"Aye, he is impetuous and quick tae draw his sword, but we all were at that age."

Sean *was* verra young, but carried himself proudly and watched all around, as if he were keepin' track of all that was said and done, holdin' the promise of the leader he would become with his straight back and wide shoulders.

Our road took us along the valley, then climbed a small rise that gave us a view of the village ahead. Baldie said, "I hadna thought of that fight in the courtyard in a long time, the sight of Auld Magnus's face has brought back memories."

"The death of a warrior brings out the battle stories."

He nodded. "Aye, twill do that."

Then he said, "Ye mentioned, Fraoch, that ye had met Young Magnus in London — how did ye find him, was he well?"

Sean put his horse intae a quicker pace tae draw near, and said, "Ye saw Young Magnus? I wondered if we ought tae ride tae London and bring him home — I told ye, Uncle Baldie, we ought tae go get him, he canna survive in London, tis nae fittin' for a Campbell. I bet he inna even learnin' tae use the sword."

I said, "If ye daena mind me advisin' ye, Baldie, ye ought tae leave the lad there, in London — tis true he inna learnin' tae battle, but he is learning tae be a leader and he will need those lessons, twill be good for him, but ye could bring him home when he is about yer age, Sean."

Baldie said, "Aye, that seems right, *then* we can train him tae battle."

Sean scowled. "He will be weak! He is already a bastard, he needs tae learn tae defend himself or the other men will think he is vulnerable and will be ruthless towards him."

Lochie broke his silence tae say, "Magnus is plenty strong enough — ye canna call him weak, I winna stand for it."

I said, "Og Lochie, wheesht!"

I said tae Baldie, "Disregard Lochinvar, he has strong feelings about Young Magnus who is..." I directed at Lochie, "*verra* young still."

Lochie huffed and muttered, "I forget."

Baldie said, "Aye, Young Magnus is ten years auld, he has time afore he needs tae concern himself with battlin', Sean, this is nae yer concern." He nodded tae me, "Thank ye for yer advice, Fraoch, I will take it intae consideration."

Our procession pulled up in front of the church and Baldie and I made the arrangements for a stone. Baldie assured me he would see tae the work being done.

I told them I wanted it tae say:

Auld Magnus
warrior
1692

CHAPTER 70 - KAITLYN

2024 - FLORIDA OUGHT TO BE

*W*e woke up in the sand of the beach in Florida, a brightly lit day. Magnus wasn't right beside me. I raised my head and saw that he was crouching, armed. Quentin mumbled, "Everything good?"

"Aye, I just wanted tae guard, worried… as always."

I looked around me on the sand. "Is there… is there anyone else?"

Magnus shook his head. "Nae, but we dinna expect it, mo reul-iuil, we are still on the same timeline."

My throat grew tight. "I know, I didn't expect it, not really, but…" I shook my head, sat up, and tried to brush off sand.

Slowly we all got up.

Quentin and Zach offered to run for the truck. They took off and we sat around looking at the detritus in the sand.

I said, "Where *is* everyone?"

Hayley said, "They went to get the truck, you heard them, did you bump your head?"

I huffed.

Magnus raised his shirt. "Dost ye ken where I got these bruises?"

My eyes went wide. "Magnus, that happened... it was days ago."

"Tis quite sore, I dinna remember how it happened." He lowered his shirt.

Hayley griped, "Can't believe Quentin tricked me into offering to help clean this all up."

I looked around at all the stuff.

James said, "Did you really kill a man, Hayley?"

"Yeah, yeah I did. That was—"

I interrupted, "But look at all the things we brought, a horse, two bikes, an ATV, all these tents—"

Hayley counted on her fingers. "A vehicle for each person, too much gear, if we have to pack we always have too much gear, your point?"

"I don't know, it seems like in the chaos there were more people there."

James said, "Fog of war."

Hayley said, "How many did you kill, James?"

James said, "About three."

Magnus grunted.

James said, "How many men would you say you've killed, Mags, overall?"

"Enough tae make a man's soul threadbare."

James said, "Good point, I guess I shouldn't brag, it's just... that was a peak experience you know? Murderous rampage, sure, but life and death — my heart is still racing." He added, "And Hayley, I think you would be the kind of person to say 'if you made a mess with all your death and destruction, you have to pack up the tents after.'"

She shook her head, flinging sand everywhere. "Is that what I would say?"

My brow drew down. I vaguely said, "But *why* so much gear?"

No one answered.

·   ·   ·

We loaded stuff up into the back of trucks and delivered it to the house, then I went to go stand on the back deck while Magnus and James took the horses to the stable and then they helped Quentin bring the ATV and bikes to the garage.

I felt bad that I didn't help, but the terrible thing was that my head echoed. The house echoed — the whole world.

I had grown accustomed to the changes in sight and sound, the accentuation or dampening of our senses, but this was maddening.

I ached from the echo.

My body ached from the jump, but it also felt hollow, my skin was sensitive to the touch, my breasts hurt, a dull ache, the whole thing felt like loss.

I stood on the back deck looking up and down the beach not seeing at all what I was looking for, just a pretty day, a windswept beach, white sand, a blue sea.

Why the hell was it all so empty?

I wondered if I was depressed and if I should see someone.

And then I thought about how I felt after I miscarried, that feeling — that loss of hope, of expectancy. Oh it had nearly destroyed me, and this felt so similar.

Then I thought more about the house and how it ought to be filled with children.

And the word *ought* carried a lot of weight with that idea.

Ought

Ought to be full.

And then my grandmother's voice... *Three lives.* Three. Lives.

I sighed. My chin trembled.

I heard the familiar thud thud thud of my husband's feet coming up the plank walkway behind me. "I was lookin' for ye."

"Did you get everything done?"

He pulled up close, and after a quick glance at my face, followed my eyes to the ocean. "Aye, tis all put away. Ye are weeping, mo reul-iuil?"

"I'm emotional, I don't know why. The house is emptier than I expected, than I wanted."

"I told ye not tae get yer hopes up."

I nodded. "But you know it's my way." I turned around to lean on the rail and look up at the house.

Quentin was up on the roof. "He's guarding already, didn't we kill the hell out of that bad guy?"

"Aye, we did, but he and James got intae a quarrel and so he is 'taking a fuckin' break' from all Master Cook's 'bullshit'."

I chuckled. "Ah, I see."

I turned back to the ocean. "How long were we gone since we were here last?"

"A day."

I nodded. "And at dinner we will talk about using the Bridge, first thing?"

"Aye, we will discuss the possibility."

"We need to use it, we need to. It's urgent."

He nodded, his brow drawn.

I put down my hand and took his, looking down at it I said, overcome with sadness, "I think we're losing people, what if you were gone right now, I just…"

"Ye are overcome, mo reul-iuil, we are here. I am here. I hae been here now for years, hae we ever forgotten each other?"

"No."

"We winna now, I promise, we hae won a battle, tis time tae live. We daena need tae be afraid."

I nodded.

He said, "What if we tried tae hae a bairn?"

My eyes went wide. "Magnus, I… we need to use the *Bridge*."

His brow drew down even more. "I said we would."

"Yes, but without the urgency! We *need* to use it!"

"We will."

"Promise?"

"I promise. And I am here, Kaitlyn, ye daena hae tae worry."

I shook my head looking out on the empty shore. "I am really glad you're still here. I don't know what I would do without you."

He joked, "Likely ye would hae had a great deal less sufferin'."

"But at what cost?"

"I am glad ye feel that way, mo reul-iuil, I feel the same way. I daena ken what my life would be without ye and our family."

My brow furrowed and a tear rolled down my cheek, I was crying for a loss I didn't understand.

CHAPTER 71 - KAITLYN

CRUACHAN, MY LOVE

*C*hef Zach pulled frozen soups from the freezer, talking to himself while he danced around the kitchen to some really loud music. "I am so relieved I have these, deciding to freeze soups — smartest thing I ever did, don't know why… smarty smart-smart."

He had dinner rolls in the oven, sliced, melting a little cheese and leftover roast beef in between them.

He called us all to dinner, "Ready!"

We were washed up, wearing sweats or pajamas, casually sitting around the table, after helping ourselves in the kitchen.

We had a choice to drink wine or beer for, as Zach said, with his glass raised, "…the celebration of kicking arse and creating chaos in the sixteenth century."

We all raised our glasses. "Slaintè!"

James said, "We should call it that, the Battle of Chaos."

We all agreed.

Except Quentin who was distracted, he drank a sip of Coke then said, "Seriously, I know I'm being repetitive, but look at this giant table, we are all down at one end!"

The table seated twelve with two extra chairs against the walls, plus a highchair.

I said, "Why are there only six of us?"

James said, "Six is *plenty.*"

Quentin squinted his eyes and nodded. "Sure sure. Lot of adults, but it doesn't fully explain this." He swept his arm out at all the empty chairs.

James jokingly got up, carried his plate to the end of the table, sat, and spread out his elbows and knees. "Does this help, Quennie?"

Quentin blinked. "Quennie...?" He shook his head. "That's weird, have you always called me that?"

James shrugged. "Likely."

"And I suppose it helps a little, it feels like ghosts are there when it's empty. It feels like someone is saying, 'Where am I? Don't you know where I am?' Creeps me out."

I watched their exchange and Quentin's confusion and the name 'Quennie' echoed for a moment. *Where had I heard that before?* I said, "So we use the Bridge right after dinner?"

Magnus put down his spoon and ripped one of his dinner roll sandwiches in half. "We need tae discuss it. We canna use it until we ken *when* tae do it, tis too powerful."

I said, "It's not *too* powerful, it's the right kind of powerful. It's the power we need, right?"

Magnus said, "Aye, of course, Kaitlyn, but we must be sensible. We need a plan."

I pushed my soup away. "A *plan?* We just barreled into the sixteenth century with barely a plan — using the Bridge is urgent. It sounds to me as if you're being too cautious. I think you're forgetting something."

"I am nae being cautious, or I am but not *too* cautious we—"

"See? We need to use it. You're losing your memories, we need to be brave and—"

"Kaitlyn, are ye callin' me not brave?"

"No, but I think you're losing your sense of urgency."

He exhaled.

James said, "But why so much urgency? We just had a battle, we almost died. Let's have dinner, discuss."

Magnus said, "Nae harm comes from discussion, right?"

"Sure… but I think you have forgotten the stakes. You all, except maybe *Quennie*, have forgotten the stakes."

Quentin's eyes went wide. "Where have I heard that before? Did you use to call me that, Katie, like in school?"

"I don't know, it sounds familiar to me too, and I think this is *all* something we need to focus on. We are forgetting something, something big. Yes, we can have a discussion, but it must be urgent. A plan must be an urgent plan, *that's* what I mean. Urgency."

Magnus said, "Alright, we will discuss this urgently. The Bridge — we are supposed tae use it where the timeline split, but when was that exactly?"

Hayley dipped a sandwich in her soup, and said, "We could go back to 1557, use it there, kinda the origination moment."

Zach slurped some soup. "I think that's too damn far back. It's just going to adjust the original moment and what if it puts it all back the way we found it two days ago, before that battle? That would suck. No, that's too far back."

James cupped his hand around his ear. "What did you say? Can barely hear you from way down here."

Hayley stood and slid her plate down closer to James at the end. "Fine, we'll spread out." She pretended to yell down to him, "Zach said, '1557 was too far back'!"

James said, "So, what about the future? We could go to your kingdom, Mags, use the Bridge there. Then the whole timeline would get stitched up."

Magnus screwed up his face. "Tis too many years in the future. What if it fixed the timeline for m'grandfather and great-grandfather in the wrong way?" He shook his head. "Och, I daena like the idea of changin' the line of kings or causin' other issues."

Hayley said, "Like what kind of issues?"

Magnus said, "People might disappear, timelines might get shifted. What if Normond never becomes a king and I wake up and I am not the successor tae a throne, and canna even remember any of it?"

Everyone gulped, except me. I looked around at their faces, "…But… but people have *already* disappeared. Timelines have shifted, past tense. We are *forgetting…* right?"

Hayley said, "Yes, that's what we're saying."

"No, you're not, you're kind of casual about it, acting like that *might* happen, like we want to *keep* it from happening. I'm saying it's already happened. We are past being cautious. Long past."

Hayley said, "It's just a turn of phrase, yeah, I get it, stuff is weird."

I muttered, "It's beyond weird."

Zach said, "So we use the Bridge in the present day, man, right this minute, the here and now, the moment — that's what we gotta do."

Hayley said, "Are you high?"

He grinned. "Wife and kids away, just fought a battle in the sixteenth century, what do you think?"

Magnus said, "So you think the branch is here, in the present year? This is where the river of time branches out?"

"Sure, yeah, sort of, but think of it, time branches out behind us, like roots, ahead of us like branches, we are the trunk—"

James said, "Are we talking about a river or a tree?"

"Literally both." Zach gestured that his head was exploding.

James said, "Damn, boy, you high." Then he asked, "But, what you're saying is that we are the middle where the river separates and so we should activate the Bridge here?"

"Exactly, because where else? We don't know where the timeline shifted."

Magnus said, "Everywhere."

Zach was rocking back on a chair leg, he dropped the legs of his chair down and said, "Yes! We've fractaled it!"

Magnus said, "We hae fractured the time and so that is why we use the Bridge in present day — are ye certain?"

"Naw dawg, forgot what I was talking about." Zach jumped up and asked Magnus. "Ready for dessert?"

Magnus laughed "Ye callin' me Dawg now? Tis verra funny."

Zach bowed and gestured his hand like a flourish. "My apologies, I meant King Dawg."

"Always, Chef Zach, King Dawg is *always* ready for dessert, but ye ken m'favorite."

Zach wandered into the kitchen. "We need a dog you know, I need to be able to toss food scraps into a waiting mouth — why no pets?" Cupboard doors opened and closed.

Quentin said, "Exactly!"

I looked around. "Doesn't it seem like there should be kids here to cheer? Zach is bringing dessert, Quentin said 'Exactly!' to pets, doesn't it seem too quiet?"

Zach called from the kitchen. "The kids'll be back tomorrow!"

My chin trembled. "But that's not it. Yes, Ben and Zoe, but where is all the cheering…? Right now, doesn't it seem really quiet… like silent? Like the opposite of 'they are out for the night,' but they ought to be here… it is not easy to name the pain of absence, but it's there all the same."

Hayley said, "Katie, your face is so splotchy-sad, how long have you been crying?"

I shook my head. "Kind of the whole time since we got back. I just feel desperate. This is a crisis."

"We just beat the heck out of the bad guy. We won the battle. We didn't even get hurt! You shouldn't be sad, we ought to be celebrating!"

"It just feels like we are still at a disadvantage, like the battle didn't *fix* anything."

She looked around the room. "What's broken — is what I don't get. Nothing is broken."

I shrugged. "It seems like it is."

Quentin said, "I'm with Katie on this, something's up."

I said, "So we're *really* worried that someone might disappear? Didn't we use the Bridge already, once before, and it worked, right? It was safe, no one disappeared. And people *have* disappeared, without us knowing, except we kind of do know, right?"

I looked around the table. "Right Quentin?"

He nodded.

I said, "Come on guys, think, why else are we working so hard to try to fix the timeline? We think there is something or someone missing—"

Hayley said, "Do we?"

Quentin said, "Hell yeah, I do."

"A week ago we were worried about it. We went to the past to get the vessels and the Bridge so we could solve a problem. We risked our *lives*. Now I'm worried we're becoming complacent. There's something wrong, but we're forgetting it's wrong."

I looked around the room. "Don't you see it?"

James said, "Probably, I mean, yeah, it seems like it. We did want that Bridge really badly."

Magnus said, "This is a good point, I was willin' tae lay down m'life for it."

I continued, "I think my biggest worry is that if we use the Bridge the wrong way, in the wrong time, we might write over the timeline and fix it so that those people, whoever they are, are gone completely and forever with no hope."

Hayley said, "Would that be so wrong, if you had no memory of them?"

"Yes, I feel it in my soul, it would."

Zach said, "When we used the Bridge last time, *you* came back."

I opened and closed my mouth. "Oh, yeah, I did, I was sending you a message, right? From the other timeline."

Magnus said, "Aye, I was able tae sense ye."

"Has anyone sensed anything odd lately, like a sign from another timeline? Maybe that would help us figure it out…"

They were all blank, except Quentin who said, "I haven't sensed someone, not really, but just this feeling of dread, like, that chair is empty, the rooms are empty, not just empty, but *empty*-empty. I can't shake the feeling that there's something missing."

I said, "That's something. I have a feeling like that, like there's been something carved out of my life. Not just gone, but absent."

James said, "Remind me, exactly what it is this Bridge supposed to do…?"

Magnus said, "It bridges timelines that hae been shifted, last time what it did was imperceptible beyond Kaitlyn bein' relocated."

I said, "We've had this conversation before."

James shrugged. "Sure, I don't doubt that, things are screwy, but yeah, maybe using the Bridge is easy. We just do it wherever. If anyone is lost," he snapped his fingers, "then they'll be found. Easy."

Magnus said, "Nothing is ever easy with time travel."

I said, "But regardless, we need to use the Bridge and—"

Zach placed a tray full of cookies and two pints of ice cream with scoops in the middle of the table. "And in the meantime!"

James said, "See Quennie, this is why we hae such a large table, for heaps of Zach's food."

Everyone was digging into the ice cream, sprinkling and pouring toppings on ice cream bowls and crumbling cookies on top.

I looked away toward the doors that opened onto the deck. The wind was picking up, and there was a noise that sounded

like a cry. It felt like I was being called, and the voices were high
— the voices of babies. My chest felt tight, my breasts full, my
heart raced, my breath caught, and I rose from my seat.

Magnus said, "Ye want ice cream, mo reul-iuil?"

I shook my head and left the table.

"Where ye goin'?"

"To the bathroom."

I left the dining room. I went slowly up the stairs into the
office, not even sure, consciously, why I was there.

There, my eye caught something on the bookshelf, a wee
baby hat, the stocking kind for right after they're born, in the
color blue.

How did I know that?

I picked it up.

Whose was this?

Probably Ben's, *right?*

I raised it to my nose and inhaled.

The scent filled me — it was the smell of my baby.

Oh.

My baby.

Beside the desk was the sack full of the spoils of war.

I dug through it until I found the chest holding the Bridge.

What was I doing?

I had literally no idea, but it felt like I needed to do it fast.

I rushed down the hall to my bedroom and straight into the
big closet. I shoved aside the hanging clothes, all mine, none of
them Magnus's, and shoved shoes away and sat on the floor all
the way down to the deepest far corner with my knees drawn up.

The lights were out, just the dim light from the bathroom
down the hall.

With the chest on my lap, I tried to open the lid.

It wouldn't open.

Damn it.

I burst into tears.

· · ·

There was a small knock on the wall outside.

Magnus said, "How ye doin', mo reul-iuil?"

"Well, not good, but I don't really want to talk about it." I dropped my head to the wall.

"Can I come in?"

"Sure but don't turn on the light."

He pushed open the door and stuck his head in. "What is happenin'?"

"Bit of a mental breakdown, I suspect. I'm completely convinced I have a missing baby, at least one — but also… can't get this stupid box open."

He crouched down, crawled in, and placed his hand on the lid, a moment later the box clicked open.

"Figures."

"Ye are goin' tae activate the Bridge from here in the closet?"

"Yeah, no more talking. Screw it. Cruachan!"

"Och, Kaitlyn," he shook his head, "Dost ye want me tae do it?"

I said, "No, it's for me to do."

"Why?"

"Because I think I am missing my babies, because I think we're missing so many people, and I think you are beginning to lose your memory and it's freaking me out, and no one sees how urgent this is, so yeah. My babies. They came from me, and I can feel it, that they're gone, and so therefore, *I* will be the one to push the Bridge. And if it all goes to hell, *I* will be the one to be responsible."

"Shouldna we discuss…?"

"You aren't talking me out of it."

"Ye seem verra determined."

"I am."

He sat there for a moment while I stared down in the box.

He asked in a whisper, "Dost ye ken how tae work it?"

"No." I wiped my eyes on my sleeve. "Can you show me how to work it?"

"Aye." He turned the chest facing him. " I haena ever done it, but I was told ye put yer finger, possibly yer thumb, there on the black stone."

"Okay." I nodded and turned the chest back to me.

He said, "Dost ye think if we use it I will still be here?"

"I don't know. That would break my heart, but I can't bear this, Magnus. It's maddening and tearing my heart to pieces. I'm between a rock and a hard place."

"Aye, I understand. Ye canna think of yerself as ye ride intae battle, nor of me. Ye must fight tae save yer bairns, I understand." He settled down, his back against the wall, in the shoes on the other side of the closet. "Ye're between a rock and a closet that daena hold any of m'clothes."

"I don't understand it, it's the worst thing in the world. Why aren't your clothes hanging in here?"

"This is a good reminder why we need tae ride intae battle. Because things are not the way they ought tae be."

"True." I got my thumb ready. "Cruachan, my love."

"Cruachan, mo reul-iuil."

I pressed my finger to the stone.

Nothing happened. I pressed again and again.

"Damn it."

Magnus leaned over wordlessly and pressed his thumb to the stone.

CHAPTER 72 - KAITLYN

LOVE TAKES TIME

"So now what?"

He said, "I daena ken."

"It didn't feel like anything happened or changed at all, you know? Maybe it didn't work."

He exhaled. "Maybe nae."

He lumbered up and put out a hand. Before I took it though I clicked the lid closed on the box. I put the box on the ground and dragged a sweater over the top of it, and for some reason decided that a box that we fought for but that didn't actually work should be hidden at the bottom of a closet.

It didn't make sense, but not much did.

I put out a hand and Magnus hefted me up. "We can think it through and try again, mo reul-iuil."

I nodded and we left the closet.

In our bedroom I stopped and listened. "It's really quiet, too quiet."

He said, "Och nae." The lights were out in our room except for a dim lamp by the bed. The lights in the hall were out too. Magnus opened the door and looked out. "Hello?"

He crept down the hall to the top of the stairs.

I followed right behind. "Everyone went to bed?" But in the

kitchen the lights were on, the table looked like we had just been there, this was all... my heart sank, but then the front door opened.

Quentin opened the door, carrying a suitcase with Mookie on a leash. "Hey, you guys were upstairs for a long time."

Beaty came in carrying her baby.

In my brain I thought: Beaty! Mookie! Noah!

As if I were counting them off.

Haggis rushed in and jumped up and down ecstatically in front of Magnus. Magnus dropped to a knee. "Och, ye are a cù math."

Emma came in carrying Zoe on her hip, explaining, "We decided to come back early, the beds are more comfortable here, that was a nightmare, what a drive." She snapped her finger, as Zach came in with another suitcase. "Zachary, help Sophie get the rest of the kids."

I was about to collapse, clutching nervously at my shirt, freaking all the way the hell out, but then there was a baby crying from out on the driveway. A cry I would know anywhere. "Jack!"

I pushed through the crowd to the door and out to the front porch as Sophie was coming up the steps with a wailing Jack in his baby car seat. She placed him in front of me. I dropped down on my knees, frantically undoing his seatbelt, and pulled him into my arms.

Oh my god oh my god oh my god, it was Jack, there was Jack, sweet wee Jack.

Isla, in her pajamas, sleepy, climbed to my lap, pushing me down onto my back and climbing all the way onto me. "Mammy, long drive."

I hugged her hard. "I missed you so much!" I kissed her head. I kissed Jack's head and pulled up my shirt so he could nurse, holding him to my chest. *How could I have forgotten this?*

Archie walked past me and leaned a carved walking stick in the corner of the porch with the others. *Oh.*

"Hi Mammy!"

I said, "New stick?"

He nodded, then yawned, and scratched his tummy. "Why are you on the ground?"

I said, "Because I'm a crumbling mess of missing you, please come here and hug me, I really really need a hug."

He lay down beside me on my arm on the porch and we lay there, hugging, all three of my children in my arms, with tears streaming down my face.

Tears of joy and relief, completely overcome.

Magnus came out and smiled. "First, I haena gotten any of the hugs yet."

Isla got up and put up her arms so he would lift her. Her arms draped around his neck, her face against his shoulder.

Archie said, "Hi Da, what were you doing?"

Magnus said, "Well, Archie, we had tae go save the world once more. We won."

Archie cheered and hugged his da.

Magnus said, "Mo reul-iuil, are ye going tae get up?"

"No, I need a moment, you go on ahead."

They went into the house with the last of the things.

It was quiet out here, a place I rarely spent time in, it was an in-between — the space between the house and the world. The porch we were only passing through. It felt fitting to stop here for a moment, to nurse the baby, to breathe — in and out.

We had fallen apart, but then had come back together, because life was just a passing of time, a morning to night, a birth to death, and the wheel was ongoing but sometimes in our lives, the jolt of time was enough to freeze us in our tracks.

What did we lose?

Who can we remember?

I thought of my grandmother, losing her memories as her life rolled on and I held onto Jack, nursing him, the power of connection wiping the fear from my mind — there was only this, the present, time rolling…

Hold onto them.

Hold on.

Magnus came back out a bit later, put out his hand to help me stand, and got us all onto the couch, with a new fresh diaper on Jack, and a blanket over us all. Jack fell asleep in my arms and I asked Isla and Archie, "When was the last time you saw me?"

And Isla said, "Yesterday, Mammy, don't be silly."

I smiled. "I won't be silly, I am never silly. I am very serious when I say I missed you, I missed you desperately."

Archie said, "For one day? That doesn't seem possible."

"It is possible, because we are time-travelers, you know. Our time moves faster and sometimes slower than others, and when you love someone sometimes they can go away and you don't see them for a while and they come back and it's like they were never gone, but sometimes it feels like you've been without them forever. It feels desperate. I felt that way, the desperate kind. Love can be like that, it takes time."

I knew they understood, because though they said they were only without me for mere hours, they clung to me, sitting right beside me, cuddling, most of the night. Magnus helped move suitcases into different rooms, and then there was a storm.

Zach looked at the monitor. "Not sure who that is…" he cocked his head to the side. "It might be Fraoch's vessel?"

Hayley yelled, "Fraoch!" She grabbed her keys and bolted for the front door.

Magnus and Quentin followed her out.

Later they returned with Fraoch and Lochie, who were sopping wet. Fraoch greeted us with a loud bellowing, "Hello!" They hung their wet coats on the pegs on the wall.

Magnus kissed me on the cheek. "Sorry we took so long, we had tae put the horses away. They brought home another one. Archie and Ben, ye will get tae name him, he will be yer horse tae ride."

Archie and Ben jumped up and down, "A horse! A horse!"

Fraoch said, "I think ye bairns are more excited about the horses than the Uncles!" They danced around and hugged Fraoch and Lochie.

Fraoch said, "So tis true, none of ye remembered where Lochie and I were?"

Hayley said, "No, I love you desperately, but we all completely forgot."

Fraoch blustered theatrically, "We took the Auld Warrior to be buried. We offered, at great expense tae ourselves, tae do it — we all talked about it. Ye kent we were going! How could ye forget me? I am easily the most important man here!"

Magnus loudly cleared his throat. We all laughed.

Hayley said, "I'm sorry, my love, we didn't mean to forget you, we just had a *moment*."

Lochie chuckled. "Frookie is teasin', Madame Hayley, we had 'a moment' as well. After we made the burial arrangements, I said, 'Now what are we goin' tae do, Fraoch?' And he said, 'I daena ken, maybe we ought tae go fishin'?' Twas as if we had forgotten what we were doin'."

Fraoch said, "But then Og Lochie said, 'We canna go fishin', I am hungry and fishin' winna be fast enough, we ought tae go tae Florida.' And I said, "Och aye, we ought tae,' and here we are. *Now* I remember this was the plan all along."

He put an old leather sack on the counter, and placed a sword beside it. "This is the last of the um... Auld Warrior's belongings, his dirk and sword, a few little things, a trinket or...

and um... I think tis for ye tae see, Magnus and Kaitlyn." He ran his hand through his hair awkwardly.

I met Magnus's eyes, Magnus shook his head, he looked uncomfortable about looking in the sack.

I said, "Fraoch can you bring it here? Jack's asleep and I don't want to let him go."

The leather sack was placed on the blanket spread across my lap. I peeked in. There was Auld Magnus's sporran. Inside it was a letter from Lady Mairead. I held it up to show Magnus. "Your mother sent him to the battle."

He nodded. "Aye, I suspected, she is generally behind the mysteries."

There were some shark teeth. A few coins. And a round metal locket, not the dainty jewelry kind, this one was about three inches in diameter, like a powder compact. There was a latch on the side that I clicked to pull up the top.

Inside were two photos, one of me, on the deck of our house, looking over my shoulder at the camera with a smile on my face. The other was a photo of an older Magnus, wearing his King of Riaghalbane uniform, standing beside an older Archie. Archie must have been a young man, perhaps nineteen years old. He was also wearing a uniform. They looked handsome, royal — a father and son portrait for an alternative timeline in a future kingdom.

Archie was sitting beside me on the couch, he said, "Who's that a picture of?"

"It's um..." I sighed. "It's hard to explain, not someone you know. Not really."

The photos were very aged and faded. The locket was antiqued. The edges of the photos looked like they had been cut with a knife, by a man who had been left in a time where scissors were rare, and as if they had been pressed into the locket by the thick thumbs of a man who had grown too used to battles, but had people he loved and he wanted to remember all the same.

It hurt my heart to see it. My throat tightened. I closed the locket, then pressed it to my heart for a moment. Then I put it back in the sporran, and returned it all to the sack. "This is all too... we need... I don't know where to put it..."

Magnus said, "It daena seem fair for it tae be here — tis like witnessin' the future."

Emma swooped it up along with the sword. "I have a chest in my room where I've been storing keepsakes and treasures, I can put it away. That way it's here if we need it, but out of sight out of mind. Anyone disagree with that?"

I said, "That would be good, thank you Emma."

Magnus said, "Aye, thank you Madame Emma. Twould be a relief tae hae it away."

Hayley had her arms around Fraoch, hugging him hard, then she said, "Honey, I love you, but you are ripe, you need to wash up."

He grinned. "I missed ye so much, m'bean ghlan. How long hae I been gone?"

She said, "It feels like forever," as they went down the hall.

Archie grinned at me and said, "Love takes time."

Beaty dropped into the comfy chair across from us, her feet up on Mookie, nursing Noah. "I am *exhausted*, what a drive through the night. Jack was unsettled, he is quiet now, thankfully."

I hugged him and kissed his wee soft brow.

She continued, "…I wanted tae get home, I missed Quennie so much."

I thought, *Oh, right.*

. . .

Magnus spread a blanket over us, sat down at the other end of the couch, and patted the space between us, calling Haggis up to lay across his and Archie's laps. Isla said, "We all on the couch."

Lochie collapsed into one of the stuffed chairs. "Where you want me, Boss?"

Emma teased, "Not all over the furniture in your state."

"Och, Madame Emma, my apologies. I hae forgotten tae be civilized." He stood.

Magnus said, "Lochie, are ye rested enough, can ye take a guard duty?"

"If there are cookies, aye."

Zach passed him a whole box. "Take it on up with you."

Lochie grinned. "There is nothing better, right, bairns?"

The kids didn't answer because they were all mostly asleep. Archie smiled with his eyes closed.

Lochie chuckled and tiptoed from the room.

Quentin and Beaty left for their bedroom. Zach remained in the kitchen, cleaning up. Emma left for their room.

I said, "Do you want to go up to our room? We could carry everyone up?"

"Nae, I feel the need tae be here in the center of the home, watchful, ye ken?"

"I do, I feel the same way, I don't want anyone out of my sight."

"This is true."

I said, "I just want you to know that the sporran, those things, they don't mean anything to me, you know, except that it's *you* — and I know you aren't him, that you are a different person, but I just want you to know, any feelings I hold are about... *you*."

"I ken it, Kaitlyn, I do... I understand it, but in m'heart tis difficult tae witness."

"It's far more complicated than most mere mortals must deal with."

"We arna mere mortals, mo reul-iuil. I am a king of time and ye are m'queen. Mere mortals are revolving on the wheel of time, we are conquering it."

I said, "We conquered the hell out of that wheel of time."

"Aye, twas nae always in our favor, but aye, at the end twas fully conquered. The wheel is ours."

We nodded, staring into each other's eyes, and clasped hands, and sat there in companionable silence in the quiet of the middle of the night. Jack in my lap, nursing and sleeping. Isla crashing out fast, a lovely heaviness on my arm. Archie put his head back and slept with his mouth open, a bit of a snore, until his da pulled him to his shoulder. Haggis circled to get more comfortable and plopped down on Magnus's thigh. And Magnus stayed mostly awake, watchful through the night, sleeping lightly, as always, ever being our guard.

We were a family again, rescued, remembered. I knew we were this… I had known it deep down, in my bones, my deep marrow within my bones, because we were entangled. That was the thing about being a mom, I had the DNA of my husband and my bairns, combined inside of me, even Archie, not born of me, but Magnus's son. It was enough, we were fully entwined too, and we had our entanglements, our memories, jumbled sometimes, but entangled all the same. A glorious knot of a family.

Riding together on a wheel of time, morning to night, beginning to end, together, a family.

I just had to bring them all home.

CHAPTER 73 - KAITLYN

THE DAWNING OF A NEW AGE

*T*here was a cupboard door closing in the kitchen, the sound of rustling, Zach humming. I opened my eyes. Magnus said, "Good morn."

"Good morning." I rolled my neck. "Ouch, stiff."

"Aye, seemed a good idea at the time, but ended up causing a pain in m'neck."

I grinned. "Everyone is here."

"Aye, they are mo reul-iuil, we did it."

Archie stretched and hugged us both and left to go to the bathroom. I heard him ask Zach in the kitchen. "What's for breakfast, Uncle Zach?"

"Oh you know, a simple fare of pancakes, bacon, eggs, all the things."

Isla yelled from her warm spot on my arm. "Da's favorite!"

Zach said, "Yep, Isla, the rest of us will just have to suffer eating your Da's favorite breakfast, blech, pancakes."

She giggled. "Blech."

Magnus pulled her into his arms. "'Blech'? How can ye be 'blech' on pancakes? The pancakes are delicious and they are just big golden delicious slabs of *cake,* Isla, and ye hae permission tae eat it for breakfast! Cake for breakfast is proof of the glory of God, especially when ye cover it with the syrup and then the whipped creme tae sit upon it, och nae ye canna say 'Blech'—"

Zach was stirring batter and looked over at the screen for the front gate. "Uh oh, a visitor."

Magnus put Isla to the side and stood with a stretch. Quentin entered the room. "Who you think, Boss? A town car?"

Magnus said, peering at the screen, "Och nae, tis m'mother."

Zach put down the bowl and went to his phone. "This calls for some Metallica, I think."

I changed Jack's diaper, then went to sit at the table with a cup of coffee, Jack in my arms, as Lady Mairead breezed in. Fraoch and Hayley, Beaty and Noah, Quentin and Lochinvar, James and Sophie were all there, sitting around the big table, or standing near the counter. "Hello everyone, I hope I dinna wake ye."

She looked me up and down.

I looked her up and down also, she looked fresh and smiling, radiant actually, a bit younger, possibly, and self-assured.

I said, "You did wake me, kind of, but good morning, Lady Mairead, welcome."

"Why thank ye, Kaitlyn." She went up to the counter where the coffee pot stood, and said, "Zachary, I daena ken how tae work this infernal machine."

"Of course, Lady Mairead, why don't you sit down and I will—"

"Nae, I will get my own coffee, then I will sit without someone makin' a fuss. I see ye are all casual and I will join ye, talking around the cups of coffee, as if we are barbarians — Kaitlyn, are ye nursin' the bairn at the table?"

I grinned.

"Dear God."

Zach said, "Ye put yer mug here, push this button, careful, hot, then here is the cream and sugar."

"Nae cream, I am put right off it."

She filled her mug with coffee and stirred in some sugar.

Magnus laughed, put his mug in and filled it half way, filled the rest of the cup with cream, two spoonfuls of sugar and then whipped cream on top just to make his mother roll her eyes. He drank, and left the whipped cream on his upper lip and met my eyes with a playful grin.

The kids all came into the room and Lady Mairead said, "Archie and Isla please come near, I would like tae give ye a proper greeting."

They drew near and first she looked at Archie. "Ye are growin' very tall and ye look as if ye will hae the strength of yer father, verra good. I am pleased tae see ye again." She hugged him. He mumbled, "Good to see you too, Grandmother."

Then to Isla she said, "It is always a pleasure, Isla, ye are growin' tae be a beauty."

Isla lifted her chin, looking a bit like her grandmother. "Have you been away, Gwandmother?"

"I feel as if I hae been, Isla, sometimes time passes slowly and I feel as if I hae missed the people I hold dear."

"I missed you too." Isla hugged her grandmother and then she marched into the kitchen and pushed the step-stool over to the dishes cabinet and climbed it.

Zach said, "Do you need me to get you something?"

"No, I'm getting a bowl for cereal."

He made his eyes wide. "Cereal? Ugh, you are a monster, Isla. I want no part of it."

She giggled again, pulling down a bowl.

Magnus said, "So what can we do for ye, Mother?"

She said, sipping her coffee, "Nothing really, Magnus. I woke with a feeling, as if time had shifted, and I hae taken stock — things are verra well in the kingdom. I brought some contracts for ye tae sign, there are duties of course, but nothing major, and I checked the vault. All the vessels are there, that seemed as if twas important, and our affairs are verra calm and orderly. I think I was a bit lonely tae be truthful..."

Magnus dropped in the seat across from her.

She finished, "I wanted tae see my family. I checked in on Sean and Lizbeth and their bairns, they are all thriving. Sean hopes ye will return soon. Twas a lovely visit, but then I wanted tae see ye."

Magnus asked, "Ye are lonely?"

"Well, ye ken, without Hammond, the kingdom is a bit..."

Magnus slid a notebook over and began to write. "I hae someone I want ye tae meet with, he is a—"

Lady Mairead's eyes went wide. "Magnus, are ye setting me up with someone?"

Magnus grinned and wrote as he spoke. "Aye, I am, he is a man named, JB Bettelmen—"

Lady Mairead's eyes went wide. "From the Bettelmen cider family? Our families are connected, but not for decades, how would ye...?"

"I met him once on this wheel of time we call our life. Ye invited him tae dinner. He was a verra fine fellow, and ye were smitten with him."

She blinked.

Lochinvar said, "He was helpful tae our cause as well."

"Ye met him, Lochinvar, who else was there?"

Quentin said, "I was, we had dinner with him."

Magnus slid the paper towards her. "Ye danced with him in front of us."

"Ye must certainly hae me confused with someone else."

Fraoch grinned. "Ye said at the time that he made ye laugh."

She stared down at the paper. "We do hae a ball coming up, I could use a partner. I could invite him."

Magnus nodded. "That is a verra good idea."

"Is he much younger? I wouldna want tae look..."

"Nae, he is close tae yer age, and ye ought not worry on it, ye look regal and assured."

She tucked the paper into her pocket. "I feel verra 'regal and assured', I feel energetic and hopeful for the coming period, the dawning of a new age — peace over Riaghalbane. I am thinking it might be time tae widen our boundaries, there is a neighbor tae our west with some resources—"

Magnus groaned.

She smiled. "Daena worry, I am simply dreaming on building and strengthening our empire, but there is time enough."

She added, "Ultimately, this is why I am here, I wanted tae come and express m'gratitude, because there is a peace. I am well, I see all my grandchildren are well, and somehow... I daena ken what ye hae done, Magnus, but it seems as if ye hae settled something, put us straight, and I appreciate the risk involved tae ye tae accomplish it. Ye hae put yer house in order and I thank ye."

"We all accomplished it, but aye, tis ordered, finally." Magnus met my eyes and I put my head to his shoulder and he kissed my forehead, leaving a bit of sweetness there.

I inhaled it all, the compliments from the bitch-mother, the accomplishment of having won, something, but beginning to lose the memory of the hardness of it, keeping the memory of the glory, and reveling in a feeling of calm, surrounded by the wealth of a big breakfast, of the warmth and health of a large family, the hopeful scent of a new bairn, of strength in my husband's shoulder,

the love in his gaze,

the taste of his lips,

and the comfort of his voice,

I love ye—

Yes.

Aye.

The end.

THANK YOU

*T*his might seem like a 'the end' to Magnus and Kaitlyn's story, everything is tied up*, there is peace in the kingdom, it's all good.

But it's not 'the end', not really, because I'm not quite ready to say goodbye to Mr and Mrs Magnus Campbell. There must be more to tell.

This *is* an excellent place to pause though, to reflect. To rest.

And while we do that, what will I be writing?

Book 2, then Book 3 of the Scottish Duke... coming fast, promise — preorder here:

The Second Rule of Time Travel

If you miss Magnus and Kaitlyn already, there is a Facebook group here: Kaitlyn and the Highlander

I would love it if you would join my Substack, here: Diana Knightley's Stories

Thank you for taking the time to read this book. The world is full of entertainment and I appreciate that you chose to spend some time with Magnus and Kaitlyn. I fell in love with Magnus when I was writing him, and I hope you fell in love a little bit, too.

As you all know, reviews are the best social proof a book can have, and I would greatly appreciate your review on this book.

There is one loose end, Archie and Ben need to name a horse.

SOME THOUGHTS AND RESEARCH...

Characters:

Kaitlyn Maude Sheffield - born December 5, 1993

Magnus Archibald Caelhin Campbell - born August 11, 1681

Archibald (Archie) Caelhin Campbell - born August 12, 2382

Isla Peace Barbara Campbell - born October 4, 2020

Jack Duncan Campbell - born July 31, 1709

Lady Mairead (Campbell) Delapointe - Magnus's mother, born 1660

Hayley Sherman - Kaitlyn's best friend, now married to Fraoch MacDonald

Fraoch MacDonald - Married to Hayley. Born in 1714, meets Magnus in 1740, and pretends to be a MacLeod after his mother, Agnie MacLeod. His father is also Donnan, which makes him Magnus's brother.

Quentin Peters - Magnus's security guard/colonel in his future army

Beaty Peters - Quentin's wife, born in the late 1680s

Noah Peters - Born June 1, 2024

Zach Greene- The chef, married to Emma

Emma Garcia - Household manager, married to Zach

Ben Greene - born May 15, 2018

Zoe Greene - born September 7, 2021

James Cook - former boyfriend of Kaitlyn. Now friend and frequent traveler. He's a contractor, so it's handy to have him around.

Sophie - wife of James Cook. She is the great-great-granddaughter of Lady Mairead, her mother is Rebecca.

Lochinvar - A son of Donnan

Auld Magnus - rescued by Kaitlyn at the end of book 5, he was scarred and battle weary from living alone, and fighting for his kingdom for many long years. He and Kaitlyn decided she would leave him there, in the year 1679, and she would rescue Young Magnus instead.

She left him on the side of Ben Cruachan.

We saw Auld Magnus when he fought for Lady Mairead and her bairns in book 13.

Sean Campbell - Magnus's older half-brother

Lizbeth Campbell - Magnus's older half-sister

Sean and Lizbeth are the children of Lady Mairead and her first husband, the Earl of Lowden.

Grandma Barb - Kaitlyn's grandmother

Grandpa Jack - Kaitlyn's grandfather

Ancestral charts for our Campbell family (ordered by Angelique and Jackie, created and designed by Ky and Cindy White for ancestralcharts.com)

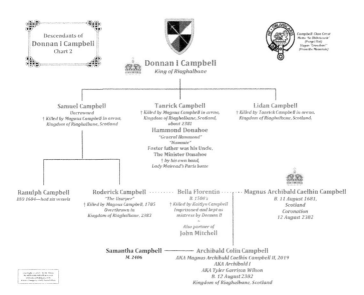

Descendants of Donnan I Campbell Chart 2

Donnan I Campbell
King of Riaghalbane

Campbell Clan Crest
Motto: "Ne Obliviscaris"
(Forget Not)
Slogan: "Cruachan"
(From the Mountain)

Samuel Campbell
Uncrowned
† *Killed by Magnus Campbell in arena,*
Kingdom of Riaghalbane, Scotland

Tanrick Campbell
† *Killed by Magnus Campbell in arena,*
Kingdom of Riaghalbane, Scotland,
about 2381

Lidan Campbell
† *Killed by Tanrick Campbell in arena,*
Kingdom of Riaghalbane, Scotland,

Hammond Donahoe
"General Hammond"
"Hammie"
Foster father was his Uncle,
The Minister Donahoe
† *by his own hand,*
Lady Mairead's Paris home

Ranulph Campbell
B10 1604 — had six vessels

Roderick Campbell ········· **Bella Florentin** ········· **Magnus Archibald Caelhin Campbell**
"The Usurper" *B. 1500's* *B. 11 August 1681,*
† *Killed by Magnus Campbell, 1705* † *Killed by Kaitlyn Campbell* *Scotland*
Overthrown in *Imprisoned and kept as* *Coronation*
Kingdom of Riaghalbane, 2383 *mistress by Donnan II* *12 August 2382*

Also partner of
John Mitchell

Samantha Campbell ——————— **Archibald Colin Campbell**
M. 2406 *AKA Magnus Archibald Caelhin Campbell II, 2019*
AKA Archibald I
AKA Tyler Garrison Wilson
B. 12 August 2382
Kingdom of Riaghalbane, Scotland

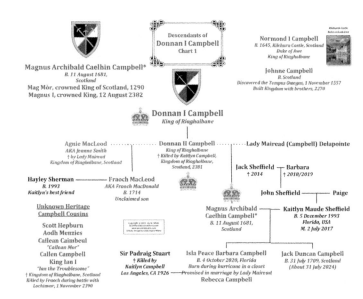

Descendants of
Donnan I Campbell
Chart 1

Normond I Campbell
B. 1645, Kilchurn Castle, Scotland
Duke of Awe
King of Riaghalbane

Johnne Campbell
B. Scotland
Discovered the Tempus Omegas, 1 November 1557
Built Kingdom with brothers, 2270

Magnus Archibald Caelhin Campbell*
B. 11 August 1681,
Scotland
Mag Mòr, crowned King of Scotland, 1290
Magnus I, crowned King, 12 August 2382

Donnan I Campbell
King of Riaghalbane

Agnie MacLeod
AKA Jeanne Smith
by Lady Mairead
Kingdom of Riaghalbane, Scotland

Donnan II Campbell
King of Riaghalbane
† Killed by Kaitlyn Campbell,
Kingdom of Riaghalbane,
Scotland, 2381

Lady Mairead (Campbell) Delapointe

Jack Sheffield — **Barbara**
† 2014   *† 2018/2019*

Hayley Sherman — **Fraoch MacLeod**
B. 1993   *AKA Fraoch MacDonald*
Kaitlyn's best friend   *B. 1714*
Unclaimed son

John Sheffield — **Paige**

Unknown Heritage
Campbell Cousins

Scott Hepburn
Aodh Menzies
Cailean Caimbeul
"Cailean Mor"
Callen Campbell
King Ian I
"Ian the Troublesome"
† Kingdom of Riaghalbane, Scotland
Killed by Fraoch during battle with
Lochinvar, 1 November 2390

Magnus Archibald — **Kaitlyn Maude Sheffield**
Caelhin Campbell*   *B. 5 December 1993*
B. 11 August 1681,   *Florida, USA*
Scotland   *M. 2 July 2017*

Sir Padraig Stuart   **Isla Peace Barbara Campbell**   **Jack Duncan Campbell**
† Killed by   *B. 4 October 2020, Florida*   *B. 31 July 1709, Scotland*
Kaitlyn Campbell   *Born during hurricane in a closet*   *(About 31 July 2024)*
Los Angeles, CA 1926 — *Promised in marriage by Lady Mairead*
                          Rebecca Campbell

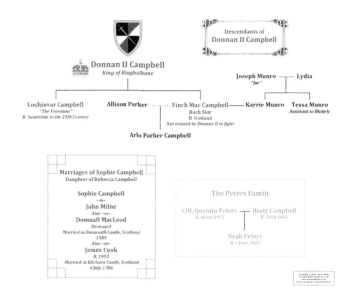

Descendants of Donnan II Campbell

Donnan II Campbell
King of Riaghalbane

Joseph Munro — **Lydia**
"Joe"

Lochinvar Campbell
"The Fearsome"
B. Sometime in the 25th Century

Allison Parker · · · · · · · · **Finch Mac Campbell** —— **Karrie Munro**
Rock Star
B. Scotland
Not trained by Donnan II to fight

Tessa Munro
Assistant to Blakely

Arlo Parker Campbell

Marriages of Sophie Campbell
Daughter of Rebecca Campbell

Sophie Campbell
~m~
John Milne
Also ~m~
Domnall MacLeod
Deceased
Married in Dunaraith Castle, Scotland
1589
Also ~m~
James Cook
B. 1993
Married in Kilchurn Castle, Scotland
4 July 1706

The Peters Family

COL Quentin Peters —— **Beaty Campbell**
B. about 1993 — *B. 1604-1685*

Noah Peters
B. 1 June 2024

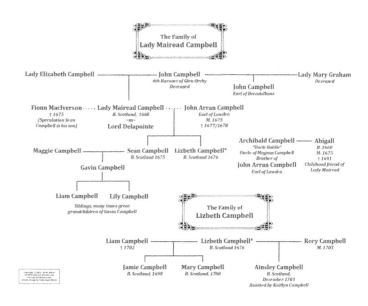

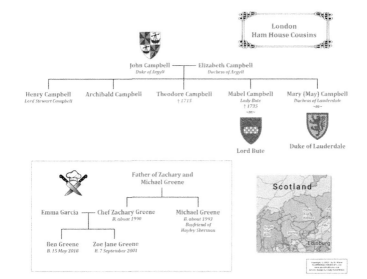

The horses:

Sunny - belongs to Magnus

Osna - belongs to Kaitlyn

When Magnus and Kaitlyn were in the 16th century they rode Cynric and Hurley.

Hayley and Fraoch have the horses Gatorbelle and Thor

Lochinvar has a horse now named Cookie

Magnus now has Dràgon

～

The line of kings in Riaghalbane

Normond I - the first king

Donnan I -

Donnan II - Magnus's father, murdered by Kaitlyn Campbell in the year 2381

Magnus I - crowned August 11, 2382 the day before the birth of his son, Archibald Campbell, next in line for the throne.

～

Some **Scottish and Gaelic words** that appear within the book series:

dreich - dull and miserable weather

mo reul-iuil - my North Star (nickname)

osna - a sigh

dinna ken - didn't know

tae - to

winna - won't or will not

daena - don't

tis - it is or there is. This is most often a contraction 'tis, but it looked messy and hard to read on the page so I removed the apostrophe. For Magnus it's not a contraction, it's a word.

och nae - Oh no.

ken, kent, kens - know, knew, knows

mucag - is Gaelic for piglet

m'bhean - my wife

m'bhean ghlan - means clean wife, Fraoch's nickname for Hayley.

cù-sith - a mythological hound found in Scottish folklore.

cù - dog

~

Locations:

Fernandina Beach on Amelia Island, Florida, present day. Their beach house is on the south end of the island.

Magnus's homes in Scotland - **Balloch**. Built in 1552. In the early 1800s it was rebuilt as **Taymouth Castle**. It lays near Loch Tay near the River Tay

Kilchurn Castle - Magnus's childhood home, favorite castle of his uncle, Baldie. On an island at the northeastern end of Loch Awe. In the region Argyll.

The kingdom of Magnus I, **Riaghalbane**, is in Scotland. Its name comes from *Riaghladh Albainn*, and like the name Breadalbane (from *Bràghad Albainn)* it was shortened as time went on. I decided it would now be **Riaghalbane.**

Magnus' castle, called, **Caisteal Morag,** is very near where Balloch Castle once stood, near Loch Tay.

Inchadney village -

This village was on the north side of the river Tay and was known as Inchadney. In 1540 Sir Colin Campbell of Glenorchy started the construction of Balloch castle on the opposite bank of the river and the entire village was moved to the shores of Loch Tay and renamed Kenmore.

Magnus mentions passing an old well, which is called the *Holy Well of Inchadney* and was probably old when he lived there in 1499.

Holden Lake, Maine

ACKNOWLEDGMENTS

Thank you so much Cynthia Tyler, for your bountiful notes, for reading through twice as you do, your edits, thoughts, historical advisements, and the proofing. You reminded me how Magnus would dress in his great kilt, reworded a billion sentences, asked me to clear some things up, and complimented me on at least one passage, thank you! This is one of my favorite notes this round, giving such care and attention to the writing, I really appreciate it.

You are so good at noticing and advising, I'm filled with gratitude that you're so good at this, thank you.

Thank you so much David Sutton for your abundant notes. You helped with the choreography of fight scenes, and advocated for Fraoch and Hayley, remembered Auld Magnus's horse, and advised on the best way to move a dead body in the 17th century. Your notes make me laugh, like this one:

And this one:

And this one:

12:15 PM Mar 24

There has been a thousand metaphors in
this book. You gotta stop with the
metaphors.

(I took out about a thousand.)
And another:

And... ha ha ha:

And in an emergency character issue, you'll call because
there was too much to say in the notes... Thank you for caring
that much.

Thank you to Kristen Schoenmann De Haan for your notes
about what you love and what you didn't. I dove back in and
rewrote, tightened, reorganized, and added a whole 'nother character, and you were, as always, right, so much better now.

For still being here after so many books, thank you thank you thank you!

∾

Thank you to Jessica Fox, for starting your thoughts with this: "I absolutely loved the opening with the dream within the dreams and from there you took me on a wild ride where I no longer knew what was real and what was a shifted timeline...." And for recommending: "in vomiting there is no try- hilarious and funny merch potential." (I agree!)

Thank you for all your notes and for still reading after all these years, all these books.

∾

Thank you to *Jackie Malecki* and *Angelique Mahfood* (the admins) for hiring ancestralcharts.com to design wonderful, awe-inspiring, beautiful ancestral family trees.

And thank you to Ky W. White and Cindy White for the designs, they are perfect.

(The charts are in the 'Some thoughts and research' section)

∾

And thank you to Keira Stevens for narrating and bringing Kaitlyn and Magnus to life. I'm so proud that you're a part of the team.

∾

And thank you to Shane East for voicing Magnus. He sounds exactly how I dreamed he would.

∾

Thank you to Gill Gayle and Emily Stouffer for believing in this story and working so tirelessly to bring Kaitlyn and Magnus to a broader audience. Your championing of Kaitlyn means so much to me.

~

And more thanks to Jackie and Angelique for being admins of the big and growing FB group. 8K members! Your energy and positivity and humor and spirit, your calm demeanor when we need it, all the things you do and say and bring to the conversation fill me with gratitude.

You've blown me away with so many things. So many awesome things. Your enthusiasm is freaking amazing. Thank you.

~

Which brings me to a huge thank you to every single member of the FB group, Kaitlyn and the Highlander. If I could thank you individually I would, I do try. Thank you for every day, in every way, sharing your thoughts, joys, and loves with me. It's so amazing, thank you. You inspire me to try harder.

And for going beyond the ordinary and posting, commenting, contributing, and adding to discussions, thank you to:

Anna Fay, Mariposa Flatts, Lori Balise, Tina Rox, Debra Walter, Nadeen Lough, Dev Daniel, JD Figueroa Diaz, Cynthia Tyler, Dawn Underferth, Stacey Eddings, David Sutton, Kathleen Fullerton, Ellie Mae, Reney Lorditch, Shannon Campbell Haubrich, Bev Burns, Karin Coll, Lillian Llewellyn, Irene Walker, Linda Rose Lynch, April Bochantin, Crislee Anderson Moreno, Leisha Israel, Maureen Woeller, Joann Splonskowski, Christine Ann, Dorothy Chafin Hobbs, Liz MacGregor, Joleen Ramirez, Jenniffer Vasiento, Elidyr Selene Brynelis, Cheryl

Rushing, Julie Lynch-Allen, Patricia Howard Burke, Lasseter Wooten, Kelley Fouraker McCade, Debi Mahle O'Keefe, Julie Chavez, Maria Sidoli, Retha Russell Martin, Monica Logan, Angelika Barrineau Gardiner, Julie Dath, Erika Bentley, Lisa D Yasko, Tracy Zeller Eichler, Diane M Porter, Azucena Uctum, Cherylinn Nicklas, Kim Mertz Pennington, Sharon DeWitt Lindquist, Linda Epstein, Liz Leotsakos, Kathy Janette Brown Murray, Jenni Branchaw, Katie Carman, Mary Horton, Michelle Small-Davis Bey, Bobbi Stevens, Linda Colwell Mitchell-Turner, Makaylla Alexander, Margot Schellhas, Ellen McManus, Enza Ciaccia, Shari Burns Howe, Carol Wossidlo Leslie, Harley Moore, Cindy Straniero, Sherri Hartis Hudson, Jan Werner, Diane McGroarty McGowan, Nancy Josey Massengill, Gerry Pirone, Becky Epstein, Jackie Briggs, Christine Todd Champeaux, Susan Sparks Klinect, Sabariel Torsen, Lupe Skye, Joy Johns, Veronica Martinez, Sharon Crowder, Marie Smith, Jennifer Prince Reed, Rhonda Johnson, Kim Glenn, Lyndee Robb-Vierck, Michelle Lynn Cochran, Francie Meza, Anne Mitchell, Shanni Hendler, Amanda Ralph Thomas, Sylvia Guasch, Thunda Quinn, and Victoria Girard.

When I am writing and I get to a spot that needs research, or there is a detail I can't remember, I go to Facebook, ask, and my loyal readers step up to help. You find answers to my questions, fill in my memory lapses, and come up with so many new and clever ideas... I am forever ever ever grateful.

This round I needed to know:

Would you say that Kaitlyn has the Johnne Cambell book or Lady Mairead?

Are they still sharing custody through the painting?

You assured me that Lady Mairead was in possession of the book, but then I realized that Kaitlyn had photocopied it, of course.

Thank you to Anna Spain, Francie Meza, Kelley McCade,

Sherri Hudson, Retha Russell Martin, Alana K Mahler, April Bochantin, Angelique Mahfood, Sylvia Guasch, Julie Lynch-Allen, Tonja Townsend Owens, JD Figueroa Diaz, Monica Logan, Jennifer Prince Reed, Julie Richards, Patricia Howard Burke, Alison Caudle, Nadeen Lough, Candace Stuart-Findlay, Harley Moore, Maureen Woeller, Jan Werner, Joleen Ramirez, and Sharon Schroder for helping me remember.

∾

I also asked for how many vessels and other devices the gang had in their possession and Angelique answered quickly with, which seems nonsensical but was exactly what I needed to know:

Here we go
AVERT YOUR EYES -SPOILER
1. *(6)*
2. *Yes-*
3. *(26)*
4. *They have 17?*
5. *A ring and a remote retrieval device*
And yes- the same vessels are found in outer timelines and some are buried in the kingdom.

Thank you to Patricia Burke, Alison Caudle, April Bochantin, JD Figueroa Diaz, and Marie Smith for helping to clarify.

∾

And when I ask 'research questions' you give such great answers…

I asked for a name for Lochie's horse and chose from so many great answers, Cookie.

Thank you Enza Ciaccia, Alana Mahler, Marie Smith,

Crislee Moreno, Shanni Hendler, Harley Moore, Trish Spelman, and Tonja Owens for the idea!

And I asked for the name for a lair for a bad guy named Ranulph, and appreciate everyone who played, but oops, didn't need that one!

Thank you to *Kevin Dowdee* for being there for me in the real world as I submerge into this world to write these stories of Magnus and Kaitlyn. I appreciate you so much.

Thank you to my kids, *Ean, Gwynnie, Fiona,* and *Isobel,* for listening to me go on and on about these characters, advising me whenever you can, and accepting them as real parts of our lives. I love you.

THE SCOTTISH DUKE, THE RULES OF TIME TRAVEL, AND ME

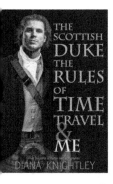

The year is 1670 and a young Duke has ridden out to explore a mysterious gale. He finds, in the center of a clearing, a strange apparatus.

He reaches for it and—

In Florida, 2012, a young storm-chaser has gone to investigate a storm — lightning arcs, the winds howl, trees whip around her, but when the storm clears she sees it: a small weird piece of tech jutting out of the sand.

She reaches out and—

The portals — active in two different times, in two different places — vibrate, grab hold, and rip them both through time.

They have just learned the first rule: Don't touch an active portal.

THE KAITLYN AND THE HIGHLANDER SERIES

Kaitlyn and the Highlander (Book 1)

Time and Space Between Us (Book 2)

Warrior of My Own (Book 3)

Begin Where We Are (Book 4)

Entangled with You (Book 5)

Magnus and a Love Beyond Words (Book 6)

Under the Same Sky (Book 7)

Nothing But Dust (Book 8)

Again My Love (Book 9)

Our Shared Horizon (Book 10)

Son and Throne (Book 11)

The Wellspring (Book 12)

Lady Mairead (Book 13)

The Guardian (Book 14)

Magnus the First (Book 15)

Only a Breath Away (Book 16)

Promises to Keep (Book 17)

Time is a Wheel (Book 18)

BOOKS IN THE CAMPBELL SONS SERIES...

Why would I, a successful woman, bring a date to a funeral like a psychopath?

Because Finch Mac, the deliciously hot, Scottish, bearded, tattooed, incredibly famous rock star, who was once the love of my life... will be there.

And it's to signal — that I have totally moved on.

But... at some point in the last six years I went from righteous fury to... something that might involve second chances and happy endings.

Because while Finch Mac is dealing with his son, a world tour, and a custody battle,

I've been learning about forgiveness and the kind of love that rises above the past.

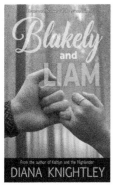

We were so lost until we found each other.

I left my husband because he's a great big cheater, but decided to go *alone* on our big, long hike in the-middle-of-nowhere anyway. Destroyed. Wrecked. I wandered into a pub and found... Liam Campbell, hot, Scottish, a former-rugby star, now turned owner of a small-town pub and hotel.

And he found me.

My dear old dad left me this failing pub, this run down motel and now m'days are spent worrying on money and how tae no'die of boredom in this wee town.

And then Blakely walked intae the pub, needing help.

The moment I lay eyes on her I knew she would be the love of m'life.

And that's where our story begins...

ABOUT ME, DIANA KNIGHTLEY

I write about heroes and tragedies and magical whisperings and always forever happily ever afters.

I love that scene where the two are desperate to be together but can't be because of war or apocalyptic-stuff or (scientifically sound!) time-jumping and he is begging the universe with a plead in his heart and she is distraught (yet still strong) and somehow — through kisses and steam and hope and heaps and piles of true love, they manage to come out on the other side.

My couples so far include Beckett and Luna, who battle their fear to search for each other during an apocalypse of rising waters.

Liam and Blakely, who find each other at the edge of a trail leading to big life changes.

Karrie and Finch Mac, who find forgiveness and a second chance at true love.

Nor and Livvy who are beginning a grand adventure.

Hayley and Fraoch, Quentin and Beaty, Zach and Emma, and James and Sophie who have all taken their relationships from side story in Kaitlyn and the Highlander to love story in their own rights.

And Magnus and Kaitlyn, who find themselves traveling through time to build a marriage and a family together.

I write under two pen names, this one here, Diana Knightley, and another one, H. D. Knightley, where I write books for Young Adults. (They are still romantic and fun and sometimes steamy though because love is grand at any age.)

DianaKnightley.com
Diana@dianaknightley.com
Substack: Diana Knightley's Stories

Printed in Great Britain
by Amazon

22323096R00249